SINS

Penny Jordan has been writing for over 25 years. In that time, she has written over 170 books and sold almost 90 million copies worldwide. She also writes under the name Annie Groves and is a mentor for new writers. *Sins* is set in the rag trade and inspired by the silk manufacturing industry in Macclesfield in Cheshire where Penny lived for 25 years with her late husband. She still lives in Cheshire today. For more information on Penny, please go to www.penny-jordan.co.uk

By the same author:

Silk

PENNY JORDAN

Sins

AVON

AVON

A division of HarperCollins*Publishers*
77–85 Fulham Palace Road,
London W6 8JB

www.harpercollins.co.uk

A Paperback Original 2009

First published in Great Britain by
HarperCollins*Publishers* 2009

A catalogue record for this book is
available from the British Library

ISBN-13: 978-1-84756-074-2

Typeset in Minion by Palimpsest Book Production Limited,
Grangemouth, Stirlingshire

Printed and bound in Great Britain by
Clays Ltd, St Ives plc

Mixed Sources

Product group from well-managed
forests and other controlled sources
www.fsc.org Cert no. SW-COC-1806
© 1996 Forest Stewardship Council

FSC

I would like to thank the following people for their invaluable and much appreciated help:

Teresa Chris, my agent.

Maxine Hitchcock and all her staff at Avon, for their patience and understanding.

Yvonne Holland, who as always, has done a wonderful job copyediting and alerting me to any factual errors.

Tony Bosson, my business partner for all his hard work in helping me to write *Sins*.

I would like to dedicate this book to all my readers, but especially to all the kind people who have written to tell me how much they enjoyed *Silk* and asking me when *Sins* would be coming out.

Part One

Chapter One

London, January 1957

Rose Pickford exhaled a small sigh of relief as she opened the door and stepped into the familiar scented warmth of her aunt Amber's Walton Street shop, with its smell of vanilla and roses – the scent blended especially for her aunt.

One day – or so her aunt had told her – Rose would not just be managing the exclusive Chelsea shop where the furnishing fabrics from her aunt's Macclesfield silk mill were sold, she would also be in charge of advising clients on the most stylish ways to redecorate their homes.

One day.

Right now, though, she was simply a raw, newly qualified art student, working as little more than a general dogsbody for Ivor Hammond, one of London's most prestigious interior designers.

'Hello, Rose, we're just about to have a cup of tea. Would you like one?'

Rose smiled gratefully. 'Yes, please, Anna.'

Anna Polaski, who currently managed the shop, had

originally come to England with her musician husband, Paul, as refugees from Poland at the beginning of the Second World War. Anna was always very kind, and Rose suspected that she felt sorry for her – because she recognised that Rose, too, was, in a way, an 'outsider'?

'I hate January. It's a horrid month, so cold and miserable,' Rose said to Anna, as she pulled off the beautifully soft Italian leather gloves that had been a Christmas present from her aunt.

'Pah, you call this cold? In Poland we have proper winters, with snow many feet deep,' Anna told her. 'We shall be having lunch soon,' she added. 'I have brought some homemade vegetable soup and you are welcome to join us.'

'I'd love to,' Rose replied, 'but I can't. I've got to be back by half-past one so that Piers can go out and measure up for a new commission.'

Piers Jeffries was Ivor's senior assistant, a good-looking young man, who affected to like Rose and want to help her, but who at the same time seemed to have the knack of somehow working things so that whenever anything went wrong, she ended up being blamed. Piers might publicly sympathise with her and even take her side with their impatient and quick-tempered employer, but Rose suspected that privately he enjoyed her falls from grace.

'I need to check the provenance of one of my great-uncle's designs,' Rose explained. 'Ivor has a client who wants to use it and he's enquired about its origins. The trouble is that he doesn't know the name, he can only describe it.'

Anna gave a derisory snort. 'And he thinks you'll be able to find it in half an hour! Didn't you remind him that we have over two hundred different designs available here from your great-uncle's drawings?'

'There's a bit of a panic on. The client is impatient to get things moving, and Ivor has promised him the information this afternoon. Ivor doesn't like it if we make things seem other than effortless. I think it's one of the Greek frieze designs, so I'll start with that book.'

'You run upstairs then, and I'll send Belinda up with a cup of tea for you.'

Whilst the ground floor of the Walton Street premises were used as a showroom, the pattern books were kept upstairs in the workroom, which was also used as an office.

Since her aunt kept meticulous record and pattern books, it didn't take Rose very long to find the fabric for which she was searching. Decorated with an imposing Greek frieze border, the fabric came in four different colourways: a warm red, royal blue, dark green and a rich golden yellow. The border pattern came from an original frieze held in a London museum, which her great-uncle had sketched, the piece of stone frieze itself having been brought back from his Continental grand tour by the Earl of Carsworth in the 1780s, according to the notes with the samples.

After writing down this information Rose swallowed her now cold tea before making for the stairs.

Outside it was even colder than it had been earlier, with an east wind that knifed through her, despite the thick warmth of her navy-blue cashmere coat – a present from her aunt when she had started her job – a coat that created 'the right impression', Amber had said.

The right impression. Sadness shadowed Rose's eyes as she flagged down a taxi. She would have to pay the fare herself, of course, but that would be better than risking being late back. What her aunt had not said, but what they both knew, was that with her physical inheritance from her mother, it would be all too easy for people to place her not as the niece of one of Cheshire's richest women, a woman whose first husband had been the Duke of Lenchester and whose second was the local gentry, but instead as the daughter of a poor Chinese immigrant.

The truth was, of course, that her mother had not been anything as respectable as that.

'Your mother was a whore, a prostitute who sold her body to men for money,' her cousin Emerald had once taunted Rose.

Rose knew that Emerald had hoped to shock and hurt her but how could she when Rose had heard her late father saying the same thing so often in his drink- and drug-induced outbursts.

She was the reason he had had to turn to drink, to drown out the despair and misery of the life her existence had forced on him, her father had often told her. Her, the child he loathed and detested, and who looked just like her Chinese whore of a mother.

After his death, Rose had been terrified that she would be sent away – back to China, where Emerald had told her that their great-grandmother wanted her to be sent, but thanks to her aunt she had been given a home beyond her wildest dreams.

Her aunt Amber and her husband, Jay, had been wonderfully kind and generous to her. She had been brought up at Denham Place, alongside her cousin Emerald, the product of Amber's first marriage, Jay's two daughters from his first marriage, Ella and Janey, and Amber and Jay's twin girls. She had been sent to the same exclusive boarding school as Ella and Janey, and, like them, had gone to St Martins, the famous art and design college in London. She was made to feel just like one of the family – a blessed relief after her wretched early childhood, when her taking one step out of place had provoked her father into a rage – by everyone, that was, except Emerald. For some reason, she loathed Rose and even now, her barbed remarks were frequent and just as poisonous as ever.

Now Rose lived with Ella and Janey in a four-storey Chelsea house, Amber's *pied-à-terre* during her bimonthly visits to London to oversee her interior design business.

Rose thought the world of her aunt. There was nothing she wouldn't have done for her. Amber had protected her and supported her and, more than that, she had loved her too. So when Rose had realised how much it pleased her aunt that she enjoyed talking about interior design, Rose had determined to learn as much about that world as she could. That in turn had led to her aunt encouraging Rose to train as an interior designer so that one day she could take over the running of the business from Amber.

The knowledge that her aunt placed so much trust and had so much belief in her had filled Rose with renewed determination to do everything she could to repay her love and kindness. And that was why she was determined not to let anyone see how much she disliked working for Ivor Hammond.

Her aunt had been so pleased when her old friend Cecil Beaton had announced that he had recommended that Ivor Hammond take Rose on as a trainee.

'You'll learn so much more than I could ever teach you, darling, working with him, and I know that one day you will be London's most sought-after interior designer.'

The taxi was coming to a halt outside the Bond Street showroom of her employer.

The window of the showroom was decorated with an impressive pair of Regency carver chairs, and a mahogany bureau on which stood a heavy Georgian silver candlestick.

Ivor specialised in the kind of furniture and décor that was already familiar to the upper classes, and which appealed to those who aspired to it. Rose's own taste ran to a look that was less fussy and more modern, but she knew that she would never say so. If her aunt believed that Ivor was the right person to teach her about interior design then Rose was going to believe it as well, and she was going to crush down those rebellious ideas of her own that had her longing for something more exciting and innovative.

'Oh, there you are, Chinky.'

Even though Piers' words made her flinch inwardly,

Rose did not voice any objection. She had been called worse, after all. Her great-grandmother had made no secret of the fact that she abhorred having 'an ugly yellow brat' for a great-granddaughter.

'Got the info the boss wants, have you? Only I wouldn't want to be in your shoes if you haven't 'cos he isn't in a very good mood. The pools winner came in whilst you were out and cancelled her order.'

'I thought he'd said that he didn't want to take her on as a client anyway,' Rose responded.

Their employer had been, Rose thought, unnecessarily cruel about the peroxide blonde, who had tripped into the shop wearing a leopardskin coat and too much scent, to announce that she and her hubby had had a win on the football pools and that they were buying a 'posh mansion flat' that they wanted redecorated for them.

'He may not have wanted *her*, but he wanted her money all right.' Piers gave a disparaging sniff. 'Personally, I'm beginning to think that I really ought to think about accepting one of the other offers I've had. As dear Oliver Messel was saying to me only the other day, I really would need to think about my reputation and my future if I were to become too associated with the kind of new-money clients Ivor seems to be attracting these days. Word gets round, after all. And, of course, the fact that he's taken you on doesn't help. Well, it wouldn't do, would it? I'm surprised we haven't been inundated with requests for quotes for redecorating Soho's Chinese restaurants.'

Rose's face burned as he sniggered at his own wit. She longed for it to be the end of the day so that she could escape from the poisonous atmosphere of the shop.

The only time she felt totally comfortable and safe and accepted was when she was with her aunt Amber, and if it hadn't been for the fact that she wanted to please her aunt so much, Rose would have begged her to help her find another job.

She got on well with Jay's daughters and they had fun together but, despite their kindness, Rose was still very much aware that she was 'different' and an outsider, whose looks meant that people – men – often felt that they had a right to behave towards her in a way that made her feel vulnerable and afraid. They looked at her as though they knew about her mother, as though they wanted her to be like her mother. But she never would be, never . . .

'Oh, for goodness' sake, Ella, do be careful. You really are so dreadfully clumsy.'

Clumsy and plain, Ella Fulshawe thought miserably, as she bent down to pick up the clothes pegs that had fallen off the desk where the fashion editor's junior had left them. They were used to hold in the backs of dresses worn by very slim models so that, photographed from the front, the clothes appeared to fit.

Ella had never really wanted to work for *Vogue* in the first place; she had wanted to be a proper reporter on a proper newspaper. Her sister Janey might have been filled with envy when she had been offered the job, but then Janey lived and breathed fashion whilst Ella wasn't the least bit interested in it. She wanted to write about important things, not silly clothes, but her father had been so pleased and proud of her when she had been offered the job that she hadn't felt able to refuse.

'I expect your father is hoping that working for *Vogue* will transform you from an ugly duckling into a swan, Ella,' had been Emerald's taunting comment.

Had her father thought that working for *Vogue* would turn her into someone pretty and confident? If so, his hopes had been bitterly disappointed. If anything working alongside pretty, glamorous models only served to emphasise her own plainness, she thought. The models, with their small bosoms and skinny legs, made her feel so clumsy and huge. She had grown to hate her own full breasts and the curves of her body.

'It's such a pity that if you had to inherit your poor mother's facial features you didn't inherit her figure as well. Frankly, Ella, there is something decidedly bucolic and almost common about so much fleshy excess. Your poor mother would be horrified if she could see you now; she was so slender herself.'

Her aunt Cassandra's unkind criticism, delivered when Ella had entered puberty, had left its mark, hurting her far more than her stepsister, Emerald's, catty comments ever could. It was, in fact, burned into Ella's heart.

The models were so slim and pretty, and she could see the admiration in the eyes of the male photographers who worked with them, whilst those same photographers dismissed her with one brief glance. Or rather, most of them did. There was one who had made his contempt of her far plainer. Oliver Charters.

Charters was an up-and-coming young photographer who had just struck out on his own. He was, according

11

to *Vogue*'s Art and Fashion Departments, amazingly talented and bound 'to go far'. He seduced models and editorial staff alike with just one look from his brilliant green eyes.

But when that green-eyed gaze had been turned in her direction, all the careless interest with which it rested on other girls had been banished, to be replaced with a look of disbelief. And if that hadn't been bad enough, the exclamation that had accompanied it had underlined his feelings, causing the assistant art director to snigger, and then later repeat the incident to what now felt like the whole of *Vogue*'s office staff.

Oliver Charters was here now in the small cramped office, where Ella's boss, the features editor, and the fashion editor were surveying the pretty model wearing the cream woollen dress that was far too big for her. More Ella's size than the model's.

Ella tried her best to disguise her unfashionable shape, wearing large baggy sweaters over pleated skirts and white shirts – rather as though she were still wearing their old school uniform, Janey had once told her disapprovingly.

At home at Denham she was the eldest, and there she felt confident enough to take her responsibility towards the younger ones, especially Janey, who was so prone to doing things without thinking and getting into trouble, sometimes very seriously indeed. All the more so when it came to her taking on lame ducks of every description – both animal and human. But here at *Vogue*, deprived of the protection of her father and her stepmother's love, Ella felt awkward and vulnerable and stupid. Now her clumsiness had her face burning and her throat closing on the threat of tears.

'I can't write about that. It looks dreadful,' Ella's boss was complaining. 'I'm supposed to be covering exciting new young fashion; that looks more like something a county farmer's wife, or a girl like Ella would wear. Where's that dress we got from Mary Quant? Go and find it, will you, Ella?' she demanded.

Oliver, who was standing in the open doorway, propping himself up as he talked to the model, was blocking her exit. The leather jacket he was wearing, combined with a pair of jeans and a black T-shirt, gave him a raffish air that matched his overlong dark hair and the cigarette dangling from his mouth. Janey would have thoroughly approved of him but Ella most certainly did not.

'Excuse me.'

He was so engrossed in the model that he hadn't even heard her apology, never mind realised that she couldn't get through the door.

Ella cleared her throat and tried again. 'Excuse me, please.'

The model tugged on his leather-clad arm. 'Ella wants to get past you, Oliver.'

'Squeeze through then, love. I don't mind if you rub up against me bum.'

He was being deliberately vulgar, Ella knew, hoping no doubt to embarrass her, so she gave his back a freezing look. The model giggled as Oliver arched his back to create a space large enough, perhaps, for her to wriggle through, but nowhere near wide enough for Ella.

'Ella can't get through there. Ollie, you'll have to move,' the model told him.

Now he was looking Ella up and down and then up again, his inspection coming to an end when his gaze rested on her now flushed face.

'Going to make the tea, are you, love?' he asked her, giving her a wicked grin. 'Two lumps in mine,' he added, before deliberately letting his gaze rest on her breasts.

As she left the office Ella could hear the model saying bitchily, 'Poor Ella, being so huge. I'd hate to be like that. She's the size of an elephant. I'm surprised she doesn't try to lose some weight.'

This was followed by Oliver Charters' laughter as he announced, 'There's no point in her trying. She'd never succeed.'

Her face on fire, Ella was rooted to the spot, forced to listen to them discussing her until she was finally able to make herself walk away. She hated them both but she hated him, Oliver Charters, the most, she thought bitterly. Horrible wicked man! She could hear their laughter following her down the corridor.

So, Oliver Charters thought that she didn't have the willpower to lose weight, did he? Well, she'd show him. She'd show them all.

The Duchess.

Dougie Smith stared hard at the faded name on the prow of the ship berthed in the dry dock.

'Laid her up because she ain't wanted any more. Bin pushed out of her place by summat new,' an old tar standing on the dockside, lighting up a Capstan Full

Strength cigarette, told Dougie, before breaking into a fit of coughing.

Dougie wondered if the vessel's silent, almost ominous presence in its enforced retirement was some kind of message for him. He nodded in acknowledgement of the sailor's comment and then turned away, careful to avoid the busy activity on the dockside, with its smell of stagnant water, cargoes from the ships, and the familiar mingling of tar, oil, rope and myriad other aromas.

Ducking under hawsers and ropes, he huddled deeper into the reefer jacket he'd been warned to buy in the balmy warmth of Jamaica, where he'd changed ships.

The cargo ship he'd worked his passage on from there to London loomed up out of the cold January fog like a grey ghost. Dougie shivered. He'd been warned about London's cold, foggy weather by the crew of merchant seamen he'd sailed with. Toughened old tars, most of them, they'd been suspicious of him at first, a young Australian wanting a cheap passage to the 'old country', but once he'd proved he could pull his weight they'd taken him under their wing.

He felt bad about the lies he'd told them and the truth he'd had to keep from them, but he doubted they would have believed him if he had told them. What would he have said? 'Oh, by the way, lads, I just thought I'd better tell you that some solicitor in London reckons that I'm a duke.' Dougie could just imagine how they would have reacted. After all, he remembered how he had reacted when he'd first heard the news.

He picked up his kitbag, turning his back on the grey hull of what had been his home for the last few months, and headed in what he hoped would be the right direction for the Seamen's Mission he'd been told about, where he could get a clean bed for the night.

At least they drove on the same side of the road here, he acknowledged, as a truck came towards him out of the fog, its driver blasting his horn as a warning to get out of the way.

The docks were busy, no one paying Dougie any attention. Seamen didn't ask questions of one another; like outback drovers they shared a common code that meant that they respected one another's right not to talk about the past.

Dougie had been grateful for that on his long voyage to England. He still wasn't sure how he felt about the fact that he might be a duke. His uncle, who had despised the British upper class for reasons he had never properly explained, would have told him in no uncertain terms to ignore the solicitor's letters.

But what about his parents – what would they have thought? Dougie didn't know. They had been drowned in a flash flood shortly after his birth, and if it hadn't been for his uncle, he would have ended up in an orphanage. His uncle had never said much to him about his parents. All Dougie had known growing up was that his uncle was his mother's brother, and that he hadn't really approved of her marrying Dougie's father.

'A softie, with an English accent and fancy ways, who couldn't shear a sheep to save his life,' had been how his uncle had described Dougie's father.

It had been a hard life growing up in the Australian

outback on a large sheep station miles from the nearest town, but no harder than the lives of plenty of other youngsters like himself. Like them, he had done his schoolwork sitting in the station kitchen, taught by teachers who educated their pupils over the airwaves, and like them too he had had to do his bit around the station.

When he had finished his schooling and passed his exams he had been sent by his uncle to work on a neighbouring station as a 'jackeroo', as the young men, the next generation who would one day inherit their own family stations, were known.

Times had been hard after the war, and had continued to be hard. When his uncle had fallen sick and had been told by the flying doctor that he had a weak heart and should give up work, he had flatly refused, dying just as he had wished, one evening at sundown on the veranda of the old dilapidated bungalow, with its tin roof on which the rain rattled like bullets in the 'wet'.

As his only relative, Dougie had inherited the station, with its debts, and his uncle's responsibilities towards the people who worked for him: Mrs Mac, the house-keeper; Tom, Hugh, Bert and Ralph, the drovers; and their wives and families.

It hadn't taken Dougie long to work out that the only thing he could do was accept the offer of partnership from a wealthy neighbour, who bought a half-share in the station.

That had been five years ago. Since then the station had prospered and Dougie had taken time out to finish his education in Sydney. He had been there when the solicitor's first letter had caught up with him and he'd been disinclined to pay it any attention.

Half a dozen letters down the line, and with a growing awareness of just how little he knew about his father or his father's family, he had decided that maybe he ought to find out just who he was – and who he wasn't.

The solicitor had offered to advance his airfare. Not that Dougie needed such an advance – he had money of his own now, thanks to the success of the station – but he had been reluctant to get involved in a situation that might not suit him without knowing more about it. And more about himself.

Working his passage to England might not have been the swiftest way to get here, but it sure as hell had been the most instructive, Dougie acknowledged as he walked out of the dock gate and into a fog-enshrouded street.

He was Dougie Smith, Smith being his late uncle's surname and the name by which he had always been known, but according to his birth certificate he was Drogo Montpelier. Maybe, just maybe, he was also the Duke of Lenchester, but right now he was a merchant seaman in need of a decent meal, a bath and a bed, in that order. The solicitor had explained in his letters the family setup that existed here in England, and how the deaths of the last duke and his son and heir had meant that he, the grandson of the late duke's great-uncle – if that was who he was – was now the next in line.

But what about the last duke's widow, who was now remarried? What about his daughter, Lady Emerald? Dougie couldn't imagine them welcoming him, muscling in on what he guessed they must think of as their territory.

He might not know much about the British upper classes, but he knew one thing and that was that like any other tight-knit group of people, they would recognise an outsider when they saw one and close ranks. That was the way of the world, and nature's way too.

A young woman with tired eyes and shabby clothes, her hair dyed bright yellow, her skin sallow, pushed herself off the wall on which she had been leaning and called out to him, 'Welcome 'ome, sailor. 'Ow about buying a pretty girl a drink, and letting 'er show you a good time?'

Shaking his head, Dougie walked past her. *Welcome home.* Would he be welcome? Did he want to be?

Hefting his heavy kitbag further up on his shoulder, Dougie straightened his back. There was only one way he was going to find out.

Chapter Two

Janey felt wonderfully happy. She should, she knew, have been feeling guilty, because she should be at St Martins right now, listening to a lecture on the history of the button. Mind you, she was in one sense concentrating on the importance of the button. She had unfastened the buttons on Dan's shirt very carefully indeed.

An excited giggle bubbled up in her throat. What she was doing was dreadfully bad, of course. Not only had she skipped a lecture, she had come back to Dan's basement flat with him and they were now cuddled up against the January icy damp in Dan's single bed with its lumpy mattress. Whilst Dan's shirt now lay on the floor, Janey was still wearing her sweater, although the bra she was wearing underneath had been unfastened and pushed out of the way so that Dan could squeeze and knead her breasts, causing delicious quivers of pleasure to run right through her.

Yes, she was *very* bad. Her sister Ella would certainly think so. Ella would never have missed a lecture, never mind let a boy fondle her naked breasts. But she, Janey, wasn't Ella, thank goodness, and Dan, an actor whose sister was also at St Martins, was such a gorgeous boy. Janey had been attracted to him the minute she had laid eyes on him. And Dan was so very happy that she was here with him. Janey adored making people feel happy. She could remember the first time she had realised that she could stop herself from feeling frightened and unhappy simply by doing things that other people had wanted her to do. It had been when her mother had been in one of her frightening, erratic moods, and Aunt Cassandra had come to visit.

'I'm glad you're here, Auntie Cass,' Janey had told her aunt, 'because you make Mummy happy.'

To Janey's relief, immediately the atmosphere had changed. Her mother had started to laugh and had actually hugged her, whilst her aunt had been so pleased by her comment that she had given her a penny. Janey had been very young when her mother had died but she could still remember very clearly how frightened and miserable she had felt when her mother had been angry. From then on she had gone out of her way to say and do things that would make people feel happy . . .

She had continued 'being thoughtful', as her teachers approvingly described her behaviour, all through school. Janey had always been eager to share her sweets and her pocket money with her schoolfriends, especially if she thought it would stop them from being cross about something. And now she somehow needed those around her to be happy before she could be happy herself. If one of her friends was unhappy then it was Janey who went out of her way to coax a smile from her. She hated quarrels and angry, raised voices. They reminded her too uncomfortably of her childhood.

She was so glad that she wasn't like Ella – poor Ella, who always took things so seriously, who could be so snippy and unfriendly at times, especially with boys, and who thought that having fun was a sin.

Janey gave a small squirm of pleasure. She would have liked to have pleased Dan even more, and been even more adventurous than she was being but she didn't dare risk it. Last term there had been two girls who had had to drop out of St Martins because they had got into trouble. She certainly didn't want to end up pregnant, and then have to leave without finishing her course. Dan had said that he perfectly understood, which made everything especially wonderful; some boys could be very difficult and unkind to girls when they said 'no'.

Janey loved London and St Martins; she adored being part of the King's Road crowd that filled the coffee bars and pubs at weekends, and went to noisy parties in dark smoky cellars where beat music played. Already she had made up her mind that there could be no better place in the world to be than the King's Road, Chelsea. It was just so exciting to be in the 'know', part of that select group of young people who were making the area their personal playground, and putting their stamp on it. It was the place to be, to see and to be seen. Everyone who knew anything knew that. Even the big fashion magazines were beginning to take notice of what was going on.

Janey's ambition, once she left St Martins, was to join the ranks of the lucky young designers who had already set up shop on the King's Road, following Mary Quant's example and selling their designs from their own boutiques. She could hardly wait.

'What's that you're reading, Ella?'

'Nothing,' Ella fibbed, trying to conceal the article she had been reading in *Woman*, about how eating Ryvita biscuits could help a person to lose weight.

She'd been so determined when she'd first decided that she would lost weight, but somehow the harder she tried not to eat, the more she wanted to do so, with the result that this morning when she had weighed herself on the scales in the entrance hall to the tube station she had discovered that she had actually put on three pounds.

'Fibber,' Libby, the art director's assistant, retorted cheerfully. 'Let me see.' She tweaked the magazine out of Ella's hold before she could stop her, Libby's eyebrows lifting queryingly. 'You're trying to lose weight?'

Ella's heart sank. Soon the elegantly slender Libby would be telling everyone and then the whole office would be laughing at her.

'Well, you don't need to waste your time eating Ryvita biscuits,' Libby told her without waiting for her to reply. 'What you need to do is go and see my doctor and get some of his special pills. I lost a stone in a month. They're amazing.'

'Diet pills?' Ella questioned uncertainly. She hadn't known such things existed. She'd seen advertisements for some kind of toffees one was supposed to eat three times a day, but nothing for diet pills.

'Yes, that's right. Everyone takes them, all the models,

only of course no one admits to it. Look, why don't I ring Dr Williamson now and make an appointment for you? But you must promise not to tell anyone that I told you.'

'I . . .'

Before she could say anything, Libby was picking up the telephone receiver and giving the operator a number she was reading from her pretty leather-covered diary.

'There, it's all fixed,' she announced triumphantly a few minutes later. 'Dr Williamson can see you at lunchtime. He's only in Harley Street.'

The man was still watching her. Not that Emerald was surprised. Of course he was. She was very beautiful, after all. Everyone said so. The visit to the Louvre, one of the cultural activities organised by the French finishing school she was attending, had threatened to be so dull that she had been tempted to find an excuse to escape from it, but now, with an admirer for her to tease and torment behind the back of the ancient art historian who was accompanying her round the museum's treasures, the afternoon was promising to be far less dull than she had expected. Very deliberately, almost provocatively, she smoothed her hand over the neat fit of her fawn cashmere sweater. She would have preferred to have worn something in a more noticeable colour, but typically her mother had insisted that the neutral shade was far more elegant. Far more correct had been what she had really meant, of course. Far more likely not to draw the admiring male attention to Emerald's figure that her face already received. How foolish of her mother to

24

imagine that she could stop men admiring her, Emerald thought contemptuously. That was impossible. Not that her mother had ever come anywhere near acknowledging that. It infuriated Emerald that her family, her step- and half-siblings, but most especially her mother, should refuse to admire and pay homage to her undeniable superiority – of birth and breeding as well as looks. Her mother behaved as though she were no different from any of the others: Ella and Janey, the daughters of Jay; the twins, Cathy and Polly, still at school, who were her half-sisters, but most of all, Emerald's half-Chinese cousin, Rose. Just thinking about Rose made Emerald feel furious. A half-Chinese bastard who, for some unimaginable and irritating reason, Emerald's own mother actually treated as though she were her own child. Her mother had fussed over Rose and given her more attention than she had ever given Emerald, her own daughter. Emerald would never forgive her mother for doing that. Never. Both Nanny and Great-grandma had always said that Rose was a mere nobody; a child who should have been left to die, whilst Emerald was the daughter of a duke, one of England's richest men; an honourable heroic man, whom everyone had admired, not like Rose's father, a wastrel and a drunk. Great-grandmother had always said that the reason Uncle Greg drank so much was because he was so bitterly ashamed of Rose. By rights Emerald's mother should have felt the same way instead of treating Rose as though she was someone special – more special than Emerald herself. That, of course, was impossible. Emerald believed that the reason her mother made such a fuss of Rose was because she was jealous of Emerald, jealous of the fact that Emerald had been born a duke's daughter and had been so much loved by her father that he had left her virtually all his money. A fortune . . .

If she could have done so, during her childhood Emerald would have demanded that she be allowed to live in one of her father's houses, as befitted her status, and not at Denham with her mother and Jay and the others.

She had flatly refused to attend the same school as the others, and where they had treated their coming-out parties and presentation at court as old-fashioned rituals to be gone through for form's sake, Emerald had deliberately held back from having her own until afterwards so that she didn't have to share with them. Now she was insisting on having the kind of season that her great-grandmother had told her about when she had been younger. Blanche Pickford might not have possessed any blue blood herself but she knew its importance and she had made sure that Emerald knew it as well.

Well, it wasn't Rose who had a title and a fortune, and it wasn't Rose who would be the débutante of the season and who would marry a man who would make her even more important. Then Emerald's mother wouldn't be able to ignore her in favour of a Hong Kong gutter brat, or insist, as she had tried to do so often, that Emerald and Rose were equals. Emerald had always been determined that she must be the winner in every contest with a member of her own sex.

Always.

The man who had been watching her was standing

up and looking as though he was about to come over to her. Emerald eyed him calculatingly. Her admirer wasn't very tall and his hair was thinning a little. Disdainfully Emerald turned her back on him. Only the very best of the best was good enough for her: the tallest, the most handsome, the richest and the most titled of men. Her step-siblings, with their ridiculous plans to work, like common little shop girls, would have no option other than to end up with dull ordinary husbands, whilst Rose, of course, would be lucky if she found any decent man willing to marry her at all. But it was different for Emerald. She could have and must have the most eligible, the most prized husband there was.

In fact Emerald had already chosen her husband. There was in reality only one man it could be: the elder son of Princess Marina, the Duke of Kent, who was not just a duke like her father had been but, even better, a *royal* duke. Emerald could see herself now, surrounded by the envious gaggle of bridesmaids, all of them green with envy because she was marrying the season's most eligible man.

They would be in huge demand, invited everywhere, and other men would look at her and envy her husband, other women would look at her and be filled with jealousy because of her beauty. Emerald intended to cut herself off from her family. She certainly intended to refuse to have anything to do with Rose. As a royal duke her husband couldn't be expected to socialise with someone like Rose, and since her mother thought so much of her then she wouldn't mind being excluded from Emerald's guest lists so that she could keep Rose company, would she? Emerald smiled at the thought.

The young Duke of Kent had celebrated his twenty-first birthday only the previous year, and had already gained a reputation for being very difficult to pin down when it came to accepting invitations, but of course she would have no trouble in attracting him, Emerald knew. He wouldn't be able to help falling in love with her. No man could.

It was a pity that the Duke of Kent didn't own a proper stately home, not one of those dreadful ugly places that even the National Trust wouldn't take on, but rather somewhere like Blenheim or Osterby. She would have to have a word with Mr Melrose, her late father's solicitor and her own trustee, Emerald decided. It was surely only right and proper that, as a royal duchess, she should have the use of her late father's property and estate; there was Lenchester House in London, where she was having her coming-out ball, and the family seat as well. Her mother had tried to prevent her from having her coming-out ball at Lenchester by saying that technically they had no right to use the house, which now had been inherited through the rule of primogeniture, along with everything else that was entailed to the dukedom, by the new 'heir': the grandson of her late father's great-uncle, the 'black sheep' of the family who had been shipped off to Australia as a young man. Initially, it had been thought that this black sheep had died without marrying, but then it had come to light that there had been a marriage and a son, who in turn had produced a son of his own. Now Mr Melrose was trying to track him down. However,

Mr Melrose had agreed with Emerald that there was really no reason why, as her late father's daughter, she shouldn't have her ball at Lenchester House. Her father would have wanted her to do so, Emerald was sure. And she was sure that he would much rather have seen *her* living at Osterby and Lenchester House than some heir he had never met. And who would now inherit Osterby and everything else, simply because he was male.

Lenchester House was magnificent. Until recently it had been let out to a Greek millionaire, and Emerald could see no reason why she and the duke shouldn't lease it from the estate once they were married.

Mademoiselle Jeanne was still droning on about the Mona Lisa. Emerald gave the portrait a dismissive look. She was far prettier. And anyway, she thought the portrait dull. She preferred the striking strokes of brilliant colour favoured by more modern artists, the kind of paintings her mother would never dream of hanging at Denham. Emerald rather thought that she might become a patroness of modern art once she was married. She could imagine the praise she would receive from the press for her excellent eye and taste, and the entries in the gossip columns that would confirm her status: 'HRH The Duchess of Kent is London's premier hostess, as well as being a well-known patroness of modern art.'

Her Royal Highness, The Duchess of Kent. Emerald preened, thinking how well the title suited her.

Ella shivered as she stepped out of the building that housed Dr Williamson's rooms and into Harley Street, not so much from the raw biting wind as from shocked disbelief and excitement that she had actually done what she had done.

She had been weighed and measured by a smartly uniformed nurse, had filled in a long form giving all her medical details, and had then been told by the serious-looking Dr Williamson that for the good of her health she really did need to take the course of medication he was going to prescribe for her in order that she could lose weight.

She was to take two pills per day, one after breakfast and one late afternoon, and then after a month she was to return to him to be weighed and measured and given another prescription.

It wasn't cheating, Ella had reassured herself. All the diet pills would do was help her to control her appetite. And when she had controlled it and lost some weight, then no one, but especially Oliver Charters, would laugh at her behind her back ever again.

Chapter Three

'Janey, I'm still not sure that we should be going to this party,' Ella protested, feeling irritated and exasperated when she saw that, instead of listening to her, Janey was concentrating on drawing a thick black line round her eyes, the tip of her tongue protruding slightly between her lips as she did so.

'We can't not go,' Janey announced, proving that she had been listening all along. 'I've promised.'

Promised Dan that she'd be there, was what she meant and she didn't want to disappoint him. Not when things were getting so exciting.

Ella made no response. She knew there was no point. She wished, though, that her sister looked more conventional. Janey considered herself to be bohemian, or at least she had done until she had started frequenting Mary Quant's shop Bazaar on the King's Road, and had fallen in love with her signature style. It was Janey's greatest ambition to have her own designs admired by Mary – designs that Ella thought quite frankly were far too daring. Take the short-skirted, A-line, striped ticking fabric dress Janey had made herself and had insisted on

31

wearing this afternoon when she had bullied and coaxed Ella and Rose into going with her to her favourite coffee bar, the Fantasy.

The Fantasy, the only 'proper' coffee bar outside Soho, was owned by Archie McNair, friend and sponsor of Mary Quant, and Janey had told Ella and Rose excitedly that she hoped that her idol might come in and spot her in her new creation. That had not happened, but Janey had attracted a good deal of attention. No wonder people, or rather men, had stared at Janey so much. Much as she loved her younger sister, there were times when Ella couldn't help wishing that Janey acted with more decorum and wore sensible proper grown-up clothes, not garments that made people stare.

Attracting attention of any kind was something that made Ella feel anxious. As they were growing up, whenever she and Janey had been the focus of their late mother's attention it had been because they had done something 'wrong' – something that had made their mother cross and for which Ella, as the elder of the two, always got the blame.

Her stepmother was nothing like her mother. Ella's father's marriage to Amber had been a blessed relief. Amber was a proper mother, who understood about things of importance, like not wearing wet socks or going upstairs in the dark without the light on.

At least one thing she would not be attracting attention for soon would be her weight, Ella acknowledged with a small spurt of pleasure. Dr Williamson's diet pills had done everything both he and Libby had promised her they would, and already she was losing weight. Not that she had told anyone else about them, or about how much the cruel words and laughter she had overheard had hurt her. She would be lost now without her small yellow pills and their magical ability to make her not want to eat.

'You can always stay here, if you want to,' Janey told her sister. 'You don't have to come.'

The last thing Ella felt like doing on a cold winter night was going out to a party in some grubby smoke-filled cellar packed with people she didn't know and with whom it was impossible to talk above the noise, but Janey's words had aroused her suspicions.

'Of course I'm going to go,' Ella insisted. 'It's up to me to make sure that you don't get into trouble, after all.'

'Don't be silly. Of course I'm not going to get into trouble,' Janey defended herself indignantly.

Ella, though, wasn't impressed. 'There's no "of course" about it,' she told Janey. 'I haven't forgotten those men you brought back with you from that jazz club the other week, the ones I found sleeping downstairs.'

'It was a freezing cold night, Ella, and they didn't have anywhere else to go.'

'We could have been murdered in our beds, or worse,' Ella retaliated, her anger growing as Janey giggled.

'Don't be silly, they were far too drunk.'

'It isn't funny, Janey,' Ella remonstrated. 'The parents wouldn't have approved at all.'

'You fuss too much, Ella.'

Janey was beginning to wish that Ella would stay behind if she was going to be so stuffy. Janey had arranged to meet Dan at the party and she didn't want Ella cramping her style.

Dan. Just thinking about him gave her a delicious squiggly feeling in her tummy.

'If this party is going to be one of those rowdy parties at some dreadful smoky dive and filled with scruffy musicians, then—' Ella began, only to be interrupted by Janey, who had finished making up her eyes and was now applying what looked like white lipstick to her mouth.

'Is that really what you're going to wear?' Janey challenged her sister, looking disapprovingly at Ella's pleated tartan skirt and navy-blue jumper. 'We're going to a party, not school . . .'

'In some cold damp cellar,' Ella retorted. 'Anyway, there's nothing wrong with what I'm wearing.'

'I bet they don't think that at *Vogue*,' Janey grimaced. 'I'll design something for you, if you like.'

Ella shuddered. 'No thank you.'

'Well, you could at least wear a dress, Ella. Look how pretty Rose is in hers.'

The sisters both looked at Rose as she walked into the room in her dark green mohair dress.

'Don't be silly,' Ella objected. 'I could never wear anything like that. I'm too big, and anyway, that colour wouldn't suit me like it does Rose.'

Whilst Ella and Janey were both tall and fair-haired, with grey eyes and good English skin, Rose was an exotic mix of East and West, fine-boned and only five foot one. Her skin was olive-toned, her face heart-shaped with high cheekbones and soft full lips, whilst her dark brown eyes were European in shape. Her long hair was silky straight and inky black, and she always wore it in a chignon.

Janey looked impatiently at Ella. If she could have done so, Janey would far rather have been sharing a dingy bedsit with one of her arty friends than living in luxury in her parents' elegant red-brick house on Cheyne Walk. Still, at least it was in Chelsea, which sort of made it all right. Janey loved her family dearly but she had always been something of a rebel, loving the unconventional, passionate about fashion and music, art and life itself.

It was a pity that Ella had insisted on dragging her back to Cheyne Walk when, if they'd have stayed in the coffee bar, there must have been a good chance of Mary Quant coming in and spotting her. Only her sister could be old-fashioned enough to think that the ritual of 'afternoon tea' actually mattered and not understand that just to mention it in the circles in which Janey moved at once rendered a person hideously unhip. A person would never have thought that Ella herself had graduated from St Martins, but then Ella had been happy to go and work in *Vogue*'s offices, whereas nothing other than creating her own fashion designs would do for Janey. She had wanted to be a dress designer for as long as she could remember. As a little girl she had always been begging scraps of silk from Amber to make clothes for her dolls.

'Well, I just hope that this party is respectable,' Ella warned, 'because Mama has enough to worry about at the moment with Emerald, without having to worry about you as well.'

Ella wished that Janey was more like Amber. She worried dreadfully about her younger sister's casual

35

attitude to life and its dangers. Where Ella frowned anxiously, Janey laughed; where Ella retreated warily, Janey stepped forward and embraced; where Ella saw danger, Janey saw only excitement. But Janey could not remember what Ella could, and she did not know what Ella knew either. Their real mother had loved excitement. She had craved it. Ella had heard her saying so in that wild manner she had sometimes had as she paced the floor like a bird beating itself against the bars of its cage. Her mother had laughed wildly with their aunt Cassandra, the two of them disappearing upstairs into Ella's parents' bedroom.

Janey had been their mother's favourite too, somehow always managing to win a smile from her, where Ella got only cross words.

Janey didn't understand how afraid Ella was of either of them possessing the traits of their mother, and Ella couldn't tell her why she feared that. Janey didn't remember their mother as well as she did – she was lucky. Even now Ella sometimes woke up in the night worrying about what their lives would have been like if their real mother had lived. She remembered vividly her mother's moods, the rages that could come out of nowhere and then the tears, the way she had screamed at them.

The truth was that their mother had been a little mad – more than a little. Her madness had been brought on by the births of Ella herself and then Janey, so Blanche, Amber's grandmother, had once let slip. Ella hated to think of her mother's illness. In fact, Ella hated to think of her mother at all. She envied Emerald having Amber as her real mother.

Whenever Ella found herself beginning to feel upset

or angry about anything she deliberately reminded herself of her mother and then she shut her feelings away. She would never marry – or have children – she didn't want to end up like her mother.

But what about Janey? Janey didn't know why she had to be afraid of what they might have inherited from their mother and Ella couldn't bring herself to tell her because, much as she worried about her young sister and her giddiness and recklessness, Ella also loved her dearly. She didn't want to take away Janey's happiness and replace it with the fear she had herself.

Chapter Four

Paris

'Well, your father might have been a duke, Emerald, but you certainly aren't a duchess.'

Emerald only just managed to stop herself from glaring at Gwendolyn.

The three of them, Emerald herself, the Hon Lydia Munroe, and Lady Gwendolyn, her godmother's niece, were all going to be coming out together.

Gwendolyn might be as plain as her dull-looking and boring mother, whose sharp gaze had already warned Emerald that she had not found favour with her, but Emerald knew how highly her godmother thought of her. Gwendolyn's father was Lady Beth's brother, the Earl of Levington, and she thought the world of him and his family. If Emerald gave in to her longing to put 'Glum Gwennie', as she had privately nicknamed her, in her place, she'd risk her going telling tales to her mother and her aunt, and that would mean that Emerald could lose a valuable ally. No, sadly Gwendolyn's comeuppance would have to wait for a more propitious occasion. So instead Emerald smiled falsely at the other girl.

Obviously thinking that she got the better of the exchange Gwendolyn seized on her moment of triumph and, determined to prolong it, continued recklessly, 'And it isn't as though your mother has any family either. No one knows how *she* managed to marry your father.'

Since it was no secret that her parents' first child had been born eight months after their hastily arranged marriage, Emerald had a pretty good idea herself. But at least her mother had been clever enough to hold out for marriage.

As much as she resented her mother, Emerald was thankful that she *had* held out for the status of marriage and not remained merely a mistress. She would have hated being illegitimate, people knowing, laughing at her behind her back, looking down on her.

Emerald, Lydia and Gwendolyn were seated on their beds, in the bedroom they shared in their finishing school, which was in fact a villa, close to the Bois de Boulogne, owned by the Comtesse de la Calle. The comtesse's finishing school had the reputation for being the smartest of such schools. Being finished in Paris had a cachet to it that was not given to those girls who were finished at one of the two 'acceptable' London schools, so naturally Emerald had insisted on coming to the Bois de Boulogne villa.

Buoyed up by her triumph Gwendolyn continued happily, 'Mummy and Auntie Beth both think that your mother was awfully lucky to marry as well as she did and neither of them thinks that you'll be able to do the same.'

Emerald tensed. Gwendolyn's words were like a match to the dry tinder of her pride. Springing up off her bed, she stood over the younger girl, her hands on her hips, the full skirts of her silk dress emphasising the narrowness of her waist,

'Well, that's all you know.'

'What? Do you mean that you think that you'll get to marry a duke like your mother did?' Lydia demanded excitedly, joining the conversation. Lydia was two years younger than Emerald and inclined to hero-worship her, something that Emerald fostered.

Gwendolyn, though, wasn't looking anything like as impressed.

'A duke, yes, but like my mother, no. I shall do better than she did,' Emerald confirmed fiercely.

There was a small sharp sound – the sucking in of air from Gwendolyn as though it tasted as sour as any lemon, followed by a thrilled gasp from Lydia.

'Oh, Emerald, you mean the Duke of Kent, don't you?'

'He has to marry someone, doesn't he, and since he can have his pick of the débutantes, he's bound to want one of the prettiest . . .' was all Emerald permitted herself to say.

She didn't finish her sentence, but then she didn't need to. Its meaning was plain to both of the girls sitting looking at her. Emerald was a beauty, and quite clearly destined to be *the* beauty of the season. Whilst Lydia had a certain fresh healthy country-girl charm about her, Gwendolyn was very close to the ugly edge of plain.

That was Gwendolyn dealt with, Emerald decided with satisfaction. Emerald wasn't in any way fond of

40

her own sex. She had had friends at school, of course –
one had to if one wished to be the most popular girl in
school – but those friends had been impressionable naïve
girls rather like Lydia, easy to manipulate. There was no
way that a plain, overweight girl like Gwendolyn could
be admitted to that circle; she was the kind of girl that
Emerald despised and treated with contempt. By rights
Gwendolyn ought to have tried to seek her approval, but
instead, to Emerald's irritation, she was forever making
unwanted, even critical comments in that toneless voice
of hers. What a joke Glum Gwennie was, daring to think
that she could criticise her, looking at her with those
small sharp eyes of hers as she asked her equally sharp
questions. But she would get her revenge once she was
married to the Duke of Kent.

Emerald threw down the copy of the *Queen* magazine she had been reading and got up, pacing the room
impatiently. She was bored with Paris now. She'd
expected being here to be far more exciting than it was.
Thank heavens they and school would soon be 'finished'
and the fun could start in earnest.

The magazine she had discarded caught her eye.
Although the season hadn't officially started yet,
already the *Queen* was carrying studio portraits of some
of the débutantes due to come out. Her own photograph had been taken by Cecil Beaton and she had
been pleased with it, but now that she had seen the
photograph of another deb, taken by Lewis Coulter,
an ex-Etonian with no title but excellent connections,
and who had recently become *the* society photographer,
Emerald had decided that she had to have a fresh

41

photograph done. Never backward in coming forward when she wanted something, she had already written to him to this effect, giving him the date of her return to London and announcing that she would call on him then. It might say in the magazine that he was in such demand that he was turning away commissions but he was a *photographer* taking people's photographs for *money*. And money was a commodity that Emerald's mother possessed in great abundance. As did Emerald herself. Or rather as she would have when she reached the age of twenty-five, and she didn't have to bother coaxing Mr Melrose into agreeing to pay for things she wanted from her trust fund.

Of course, her mother hated it that she was going to be so very rich . . .

And as for Rose . . . Emerald's mouth hardened. How could her mother even acknowledge her, never mind make such a fuss over her? Didn't her mother realise how badly having a cousin like Rose could reflect on Emerald? Emerald's great-grandmother had been right: Rose should have been sent back to Hong Kong to live in the slums where Uncle Greg had found her mother.

It was just as well that she had had the forethought to persuade her godmother to offer to present her, and have her to stay in London with her, 'so that Mummy can get on with her work, Auntie Beth,' as she'd put it to her sponsor. She'd have far more licence to arrange things how she wanted under the aegis of her godmother than she would with her own mother.

Emerald was well aware that her godmother had high hopes of a match between her and her own second son.

After all, Rupert had no money to speak of, and one day Emerald would have rather a lot. But she certainly did not intend to waste either herself or her fortune on such a nonentity. Equally, Emerald was also aware of exactly what was meant by the damp forceful squeeze Gwendolyn's father had given her hand when he had called at the villa 'to see how my little girl is'. Of course he would find her attractive, because she was.

Emerald was saving the pleasure of telling Gwendolyn exactly how revolting her father was – making up to girls his daughter's age when he was married – as something to savour when the time was right. For now, she had more important things to think about, like what she wanted to be wearing the first time the Duke of Kent saw her . . .

Chapter Five

London, February 1957

Dougie looked round the empty basement beneath the Pimlico Road photographic studio, which would soon be packed with the young and the beautiful, all intent on partying the night away.

He reckoned he'd been lucky to have met Lewis Coulter. Lew – to those he knew well – supposedly employed Dougie as a junior photographer, not a general dogsbody, but when you were an Aussie newly arrived in the old country, no longer sure of your station in life, and you had your own private reasons for being here, you didn't start protesting to the employer who had taken you on simply because he'd liked the look of you.

Besides, Dougie liked his boss and his work. He'd learned a lot from watching Lew doing his stuff – and not just with his camera. For all his outwardly lazy charm, Lew could move with the speed of lightning when he saw a girl he wanted – so fast, in fact, that the poor thing was as dazzled by him as though she had been a rabbit blinded by the headlights of his Jaguar sports car.

The fact that Lew was a member of the upper class only made the situation even better. Working for him gave Dougie an entrée into a world in which he might otherwise never have been accepted. He could study this exclusive world at first hand, something he needed to do all right, since by all accounts, if this lawyer bloke was right, then he was a member of the aristocracy himself. A duke no less. Strewth, he still hadn't got his head round that. After all, he wasn't sure he wanted to be a duke. He'd done pretty well for himself without being one, keeping his supposed title a secret from his new friends in London, along with his real reason for being here. He didn't want to be tracked down and revealed to be a duke, so he had also kept quiet about his background in Australia. He didn't want anyone putting two and two together.

He'd taken a look at the house in Eaton Square that was supposedly his, although he hadn't been to see the other place yet, the one in the country. From what he'd heard Lew saying about Britain's aristocrats, they were all so deep in debt that they couldn't wait to offload their old houses onto the National Trust, and he certainly didn't intend to part with any of his inheritance keeping an old ruin going.

Dougie reckoned he'd been lucky in meeting Lew. But then Lew wasn't your normal upper-class snob. He was a true decent bonzer bloke, who could out-drink anyone, including Dougie himself. Not that Dougie had been doing much serious drinking recently. He was too busy working for Lew.

They'd first met in a pub in Soho and, for some reason

that he couldn't remember now, Dougie had challenged Lew to a drinking contest. Dougie had fallen in with a lively group of fellow Aussies, and egged on by them, he had been sure he would win. How could he not when he was six foot two, heavily muscled and an ex-sheep shearer, and his opposition was barely five foot ten, had manicured nails, spoke with an irritating drawl and dressed like a tailor's dummy? No contest, mate, as Dougie had boasted to his new friends.

He had kept on being sure he would win right up until he had collapsed on the pub floor.

When Dougie had finally come round he had been in a strange bed in a strange room, which he had later discovered was the spare bedroom of his now employer.

When he had asked Lew what he was doing there, the other man had shrugged and responded, 'Couldn't leave you on the bar floor, old chap. It isn't the done thing to leave one's mess behind, don't y'know, and since your own friends had gone, I had no choice other than to bring you back here, unappealing though that prospect was.'

Still half drunk, Dougie had promptly come over all emotional and had thanked him profusely. 'You know what, you're a real mate.'

Lew had responded, 'I can assure you I am no such thing. I had to remove you from the pub because the landlord was threatening to make me pay for a room for you. The last thing I wanted in my spare room was a sweaty drunken Aussie stinking of beer and sheep.'

Dougie had soon realised that Lew was something of a ladies' man, bedding them faster than Dougie could count and then dropping them even faster. It was nothing for him to have three or four girls on he go at the same time. Dougie had never had any trouble attracting girls himself, but he freely admitted that Lew was in another league altogether.

Lew explained to Dougie that he was the only son of a younger son, 'which means I'm afraid that whilst my veins might be filled with blue blood, my bank account sadly is not filled with anything. D'you see, old chap, the eldest son gets the title and the estate, the second son goes into the army, and the youngest into the Church, unless they can find heiresses to marry. Such a bore having to earn one's own crust, but I'm afraid needs must.'

From what Dougie had seen, Lew's life was anything but boring. When Lew wasn't photographing, he was either out partying or, like tonight, throwing parties of his own. Tonight was to be a 'bring a bottle' get-together, to celebrate the birthday of one of Lew's many friends.

There'd be models, and the more daring society girls and their upper-class escorts, sneaking a look at Lew's bohemian and louche way of life, actors coming in from the nearby Royal Court Theatre, arty types; writers and musicians.

Pretty soon now people would start arriving. A smooth Ella Fitzgerald number was playing on the gramophone. Dougie always felt nervous on these occasions. He was proud of what he was – an Aussie from the outback – but he knew that the more sophisticated young Londoners liked to make fun of colonials and laugh at their gaucherie and inadvertent mistakes. Dougie was constantly getting things wrong, putting his size elevens in it and ending up looking like a prize fool. There'd been no call where Dougie had grown up for the fancy manners and customs that Lew's sort took for granted. His uncle had been too busy running his sheep station to have time to teach his orphaned nephew all that kind of fancy stuff, even if he had known about it himself, which Dougie doubted.

It had been Mrs Mac, his uncle's housekeeper, who had seen to it that he knew how to use a knife and fork properly and who had taught him his manners.

As a boy, Dougie had worked alongside the station rousabouts, drovers and the skilful shearers, learning the male culture that meant that questions weren't asked about a person's past, and that a man earned respect for what he was and what he did in the here and now, and not because he had some fancy title. It might have been a hard life but it had been a fair one.

Now he was having to learn to live by a different set of rules and customs. He'd caught on pretty quickly to some things – he'd had to, or risk going around with his ears permanently burning from humiliation.

Dougie checked his watch. Dressed in black trousers, and a black polo-neck jumper with the sleeves pushed back to reveal the muscular arms and the remnants of his Australian tan, his thick wavy dark brown hair faintly bleached at the ends from the sun, Dougie had quickly adopted the working 'uniform' of his boss, and mentor.

He wondered if the pretty little actress he had his eye on for the last couple of weeks would be at the party.

But even if she did bite, he could hardly invite her back to the run-down bedsit in the 'Little Australia' area of the city, which he shared with what felt like an entire colony of bedbugs, and two hairy, beer-swilling, foul-mouthed ex-sheep shearers, whom he suspected knew one end of a sheep from the other better than they did one end of a girl from the other. Sooner or later he was going to have to find a place of his own.

'Quick, there's a taxi.'

They'd had to run through the rain, Janey laughing and pulling the plastic rain hood off her new beehive hairstyle as the three of them scrambled into the taxi and squashed up together on the back seat.

'Twenty Pimlico Road, please,' Janey told the driver before turning to Ella.

'You'll have to pay out of Mama's kitty, Ella. I haven't got a bean.'

Like any protective mother, Amber wanted to keep her children safe, but wisely she and Jay had also agreed that they didn't want to spoil them, so the rule was that on shared outings, when a taxi was needed, this could be paid for from a shared 'kitty' of which Ella was in charge.

'We could have walked,' Ella pointed out.

'What, in this rain? We'd have arrived looking like drowned rats.'

Her sister was right, Ella knew. But though the Fulshawes might be rich – very rich, in fact – that did not mean they went in for vulgar ostentation or throwing their money around. Ella knew for a fact that the workers at Denby Mill, her stepmother's silk mill, were paid in excess of the workers in any of the other Macclesfield mills. But millworkers could not afford to ride to parties in taxis and Ella's social conscience grieved her that she was doing so.

On the other hand, without passengers how would the cabby be able to earn his living? Her conscience momentarily quietened she looked down at her ankles, hoping that her stockings would not be splashed when she got out.

They were halfway to their destination, stopped at a red traffic light, when suddenly the door was yanked open.

''Ere, can't you see I've already got a fare?' the cabby protested.

But the young man getting into the cab and pulling down the extra seat ignored him, shaking the rain off his black hair and grinning at the three girls as he demanded, 'You don't mind, do you, girls?' in an accent that held more than a trace of cockney, before turning to the driver: 'Trafalgar Square, mate, when you've dropped these three lovelies off.'

Ella had shrunk back into the corner of the cab the minute she had seen the intruder. Oliver Charters. She'd recognised him straight away. Her face burned. Of all the bad luck.

Ella had disliked Oliver Charters the minute she had set eyes on him, and she had disliked him even more when he had started to poke fun at her, mimicking her accent, and generally teasing her.

Her boss had noticed and had asked her why she didn't like him.

'I just don't,' was all she had been able to say. 'I don't like the way he talks, or looks, or . . . or the way he smells.'

To Ella's chagrin, her boss had burst out laughing.

'That, my dear, is the heady aphrodisiacal smell of raw male sexuality, so you had better get used to it.'

Remembering the way he had behaved towards her in the *Vogue* office, Ella could feel herself stiffening with resentment.

Janey, of course, had no reservations about the intruder. Eager to please as usual, she smiled warmly at him as she said, 'You're playing that new dare game that's all the rage, aren't you? The one where you have to jump into someone else's taxi and get the driver to take you somewhere without them complaining?'

Oliver flashed her a grin that revealed the cleft in his chin, pushing back his thick floppy ink-black hair and smiling at her with the brilliant malachite-green eyes that mesmerised cute little popsies like this one at sixty paces.

'Play games? Nah, not me. It's you posh nobs that do that. Me, I've better things to do wiv me time.'

Janey looked so entranced that Ella couldn't help but give a small snort of disgust. He was putting on that cockney accent, exaggerating the way he normally spoke, and now that he'd got Janey on the edge of her seat, all wide-eyed with excitement, he was laying it on like nobody's business.

The snort had Ollie turning his head towards the corner of the taxi. Ella, realising her mistake, shrunk deeper into the shadows and lowered her head so that he couldn't see her face.

Oliver gave a dismissive shrug – the girl in the corner had probably got spots and puppy fat – and turned back to Janey, who quite obviously did not have either, and neither did the little beauty with the Eurasian looks.

'We're going to a party – why don't you come with us?' Janey offered.

'No he can't.'

Now it wasn't only him who was looking at her, Ella realised, it was Janey and Rose as well, and just then the taxi turned a sharp corner, throwing her forward so that she had to grab the edge of the seat to steady herself, and the light from the street revealed her face to Oliver.

The posh stuck-up girl from *Vogue*, who was always looking down her nose at him; the one who didn't just have frigid virgin written all over her, it was probably written right through her as well, like the lettering on a stick of Brighton rock. Yep, that was what she was: a posh virgin, all pink-candy-coated exterior with 'virgin for marriage only' written into her pure sexless little body.

He could see the familiar cold dislike in her eyes, and for a minute he was tempted to punish her just a little, to tease her, and put the real fear of God into her and make her cling to her knickers, but he had other things to do, like talking an idiot of a younger cousin from getting involved with one of the East End's most notorious gangs, daft bugger.

Oliver had trained as a boxer until his widowed mother, who had not liked the thought of her only child ending up with his brains addled, like so many boxers did, had had a word with a chap she went cleaning for.

He'd put in a good word for Ollie, who'd been taken on by a local photographer, his mother somehow managing to find the money to pay the indenture for his apprenticeship. No one, least of all Oliver himself, had expected that he'd not only develop a talent for photography but that he'd also become so passionate about it that he'd give up the boxing ring to work for next to nothing, going out in all weathers to take pictures that he then had to hawk round gritty world-weary newspaper picture editors' offices. He'd got his first break with a photograph of a couple of East End toughs, the Kray twins, at a boxing match. They'd been in the foreground of the shot, whilst in the background there'd been a couple of society women and their partners, the women dressed up to the nines in mink and diamonds.

Now he'd built himself a reputation for photographing society where it met London's lowlife, as well as photographing fashion models for glossy magazines like *Vogue*.

'Wot, me go to a party wiv you toffs?' he teased Janey, who was wriggling with pleasure. 'Not ruddy likely. I'd be frown out.'

'Janey, do come on,' Ella demanded.

They had reached their destination and Ella was already out of the taxi and standing on the pavement, having handed over their fare to the cab driver.

As she followed Ella, Janey was conscious of the fact that Oliver was watching her or, more correctly, her breasts. She was wearing one of the circular-stitched cone-shaped brassieres that daring girls wore to give them a film star sweater-girl shape beneath their jumpers, and the effect, even beneath her oversized jumper, was making Janey feel very pleased with herself indeed. Ella didn't approve of her new brassiere one little bit. She had pursed her lips earlier and said that she thought it was vulgar. Sexy was what her elder sister had really meant, but of course, being Ella, she would never be able to bring herself to use such a word, Janey knew. She smiled at Oliver in response to his wink as he closed the door and the taxi shot off in the direction of Trafalgar Square, leaving the three girls standing on the pavement.

'Janey, you're going to get soaked,' Ella complained. 'Why haven't you got your coat on?'

Because her coat concealed her newly shaped breasts, was the truthful answer, but of course it wasn't one that Janey was going to give.

'Quick, let's get inside,' she said instead, darting across the wet pavement, leaving the other two to follow her, torn between feeling guilty and triumphant, and all sort of squishy and excited inside. Maybe tonight would be the night she'd go all the way with Dan.

Janey hadn't said anything to the others about having even met Dan, never mind that she was hoping that he would be at the party, but Ella wasn't deceived. Janey was up to something and, what was more, Ella knew instinctively that it was the very kind of something that could lead Janey into trouble.

Ella didn't like trouble of any kind. Just the thought of it was enough to bring a dreaded and familiarly unpleasant feeling into her tummy. She could remember having that feeling as a very little girl when, on one humiliating occasion in the nursery, when her mother had been in one of her moods, Ella had wet her knickers because she had been too afraid to interrupt her mother to tell her that she needed the lavatory. How cross her mother had been. Ella had been made to wear her wet knickers for the rest of the day as punishment.

Hidden away inside her memory where she kept all those shameful things she didn't really want to remember were images of the black lace underwear she had once seen her mother wearing. It had been one hot afternoon when Ella was supposed to be having a nap. She had woken up feeling thirsty and, since her nanny hadn't been there, she had got up to go downstairs to the kitchen to ask Cook for a drink. On the way she had heard laughter coming from her parents' bedroom and she had paused on the landing outside and then opened the bedroom door.

Her mother had been lying on the bed in her black lace underwear, whilst Auntie Cassandra, wearing a bathrobe, had been fanning her with a black feather fan.

The minute they had seen her the two women had gone very still, and then her mother had screeched furiously, 'How dare you come in here, you wicked girl? Get out. Get out.'

Ella had backed out of the room and run back upstairs to the nursery.

She desperately wanted to warn Janey how important it was not to emulate their mother and turn out like her, but at the same time she couldn't find the words to explain just what it was about their late mother's wildness that worried and upset her so much.

*   *   *

Dougie let the girls in, grinning appreciatively at all three of them, introducing himself and asking their names.

'Ella and Janey Fulshawe, and Rose Pickford,' Janey answered.

Fulshawe? Pickford? Dougie knew *those* names. He'd seen them often enough in the correspondence sent to him by the late duke's solicitor. The solicitor had set out all the intricate details of the widowed duchess's family connections in a lengthy letter, accompanied by a family tree, while Dougie had been in Australia. He hadn't paid much attention to it at first, but since coming to London he had studied the family tree. He hadn't expected his first meeting with young women listed there to come about like this, though. If it was them and he wasn't jumping to the wrong conclusion. It must be them, he assured himself, giving Rose a quick assessing look. He remembered now that there had been something on the family tree to show that the duchess's brother had a half-Chinese daughter, and Rose was beautifully Eurasian. Dougie cursed himself now for not having paid more attention to the finer details of the genealogy, such as the exact names of the duchess's extended family. The only name he could remember was that of the duchess's daughter, Emerald. Surely it had to be *them*, though?

'You're Australian,' Janey guessed, breaking into Dougie's thoughts.

'I reckon the accent gives me away,' Dougie agreed ruefully. He was desperate to find out more about them, to find out if it really was *them*.

'Just a bit,' Janey agreed, smiling at him.

Rose tensed. She knew exactly why the young Australian

who had let them in had looked at her the way he had when she had given him her name. He'd assumed, as so many others did, that because of the way she looked she belonged to a different stratum of society, and her upper-class accent had surprised him. He probably thought, as she was aware people who did not know her family history often did, that she had deliberately changed the way she spoke in an attempt to pass for something that she wasn't.

The year Amber had brought them out, Rose had been shocked and hurt by the number of young men who had taken it for granted that they could take liberties with her that they would never have dreamed of doing with Ella and Janey.

The white-painted sitting room was heaving with people, the pitch of the conversation such that it was almost impossible to hear the swing music playing in the background.

Janey surveyed the room as best she could, disappointed not to be able to see Dan immediately, but then plunging into the mêlée when she finally managed to pick out her St Martins friends, leaving Ella to protest and then grab hold of Rose's hand so that they could follow her.

Dougie was desperate to keep the girls with him so that he could find out a bit more about their lives. He knew that it was the deaths of both the duchess's husband and her son that had resulted in him being next in line to inherit the dukedom. The solicitor had implied in his letters that the duchess was anxious to make him welcome in England, but Dougie suspected those words were just good manners, and that in reality she was bound to resent him.

Dougie had never had what he thought of as a proper family, with aunts and uncles, and cousins of his own age, and the obvious warmth and attachment between Ella, Janey and Rose drew him to them. OK, they might not strictly be cousins, but they were 'family'. Weren't they?

It would be easy enough to find out – but not by declaring himself. He wasn't ready for that yet.

He was still clutching the coats the girls had given him and he could see that they were turning away from him and looking into the room. This might be his only chance to find out for sure.

Clearing his throat, he said as nonchalantly as he could, 'So where's Emerald, then?'

The effect on all three of them was electric. They turned almost as one to look at him. Well, at least they knew who *she* was. Dougie had been half afraid that they would look blankly at him and that he'd be forced to accept that he had got it all wrong.

'She's still in Paris,' Ella informed Dougie.

'Do you know Emerald then?' That was Janey.

'Er, no,' Dougie admitted, 'but I've heard about her. That is, I've heard her name.'

They knew Emerald all right, but for some reason the mention of her name had changed the atmosphere from easy warmth to quite definitely very cool.

'Emerald isn't like us,' Janey explained, taking pity on the young Australian, who was now looking self-conscious. 'You see, Emerald isn't just Emerald, she's *Lady* Emerald.' As she finished speaking Janey turned to scan the room.

Pleasant though the young Australian was, he wasn't Dan. 'Excuse us.' She smiled at Dougie, heading into the centre of the room, leaving Ella and Rose to follow her.

Within a few minutes of joining the party the girls had become separated, Janey deliberately escaping from Ella's watchful eye so that she could find Dan, Ella ending up in the kitchen where she was asked so often for a clean glass that she had busied herself collecting empties and washing them. At least it gave her something to do and helped her to feel less self-conscious. Nearly all the other girls were wearing the same kind of clothes as Janey. None of them was dressed like her. But then none of them was as big and lumpy and plain as she was. One girl, with hair such a bright shade of red that it could only be dyed, did have large bosoms, which she was showing off proudly in a thin black jumper, but she was the sort who obviously didn't mind flaunting herself. Ella shuddered over the kitchen sink at the thought of the way the other girl had laughed when one of the men had touched her breast. Ella went hot and then cold with horror at the thought of being subjected to that kind of treatment.

''Scuse me . . . oh, sorry,' a tall dark-haired young man apologised to Rose as he tried to get past her and ended up almost spilling his drink over her. 'Blame my friends.' He indicated a group of young men congregated by the table of drinks. 'If I don't reach them soon, they'll have drunk all the beer we brought with us.'

'Hey, Jew boy, stop trying it on with the Chink and get over here.'

Just for a second before he masked it with a small

shrug of his shoulders and an easy smile, Rose saw the anger tightening his mouth.

'Sorry about that,' he apologised to her again. 'He's got a big mouth and, like they say, empty vessels make the most noise.'

Rose inclined her head and looked away. She wished she could move away as well, but that was impossible with the room packed so tightly with people.

'Over a hundred years my family have lived in London, and yet I still get identified as an outsider because of the way I look.' He was smiling – apparently more resigned than resentful – revealing strong white teeth and a dimple in the middle of his chin.

Her surprise that he should continue the conversation had Rose looking back at him before she could stop herself.

'What about you? Have your family been here long?'

'That depends which side of my family you're asking about. My mother never made it here from the slums of Hong Kong, whilst my father's family have lived here for many generations.'

'That must be hard for you.'

'What must? Looking like my mother when I'm living in my father's country?'

'Living here, but feeling like you aren't accepted,' he corrected her gently.

Rose stiffened, but either he hadn't seen how much she disliked the direction the conversation was taking or he didn't care, because he continued, 'The trouble is that when you're like us you're an outsider wherever you go. I worked on a kibbutz in Israel after I finished my national service. There were Jewish kids there from all over the world, we were made welcome, but we weren't at home. The thing is that people like you and me, we aren't the past because we don't fit in, but our children will be the future. One day we and they will be the past, just like the Romans are, and the Vikings and all those others who came here as outsiders. What's your name? Mine's Josh, by the way. Joshua.'

'Rose – Rose Pickford.'

He nodded, then demanded, 'So what do you do, Rose Pickford, when you aren't out partying?'

'I'm training to be an interior designer.'

To her surprise he gave an exultant whoop of approval. 'You know what? I think that you and me were destined to meet, because what I need right now more than anything else is an interior designer.'

Rose eyed him suspiciously. 'I really must go and find my friends,' she told him coolly, but as she made to edge past him, someone pushed by her, and would have sent her slamming into the wall if Josh hadn't reacted quickly and scooped her towards himself so that it was his forearm that connected with the wall and not her back.

She could feel his exhaled breath against her forehead. 'Are you OK?'

This close up she could smell the scent of his skin, sort of citrussy, causing her to clench her stomach muscles. Her gaze was almost on a level with his Adam's apple and her heart jerked. Rose struggled against a back-wash of unfamiliar emotions.

'Yes, thanks, I'm fine.' Her response was unsteady. It was impossible for her even to think about trying to stand independently of him, the room was so packed. He was towering over her, his shoulders broad, the prominent hook of his nose casting a shadow over the olive-toned flesh of his face, his hair thick and as dark as her own, although a very different texture with its natural wave flopped over his forehead and curled over the collar of his shirt. He was undeniably handsome and Rose suspected probably very sexy, but there was also a kindness about him that, like his natural ebullience, disarmed her and somehow drew her to him.

He was bending his head towards her ear. 'Want to guess what I do?'

Rose wanted to shake her head, but without waiting for her response he told her, 'I'm a hairdresser.'

Now he had surprised her.

'That's why I need an interior designer,' Josh continued. 'I'm setting meself up in business and I've got this salon, see, but it needs tarting up a bit, and I reckon you could be just the person to help me get it sorted.' He grinned at her.

Josh was aware that a new mood was rushing across the Atlantic from America and sweeping Britain's youth up into its very own new culture. Rock and roll had arrived, a brand-new form of music that belonged only to the young, and one that demanded that the young changed the way they looked and acted to separate themselves from their parents' generation. New hairstyles were a part of that culture, and Josh intended to ride the crest of the new wave by opening his own salon so that he could make his name and his fortune.

'I can't pay you anything,' he continued, 'but I'll give

you a free haircut and it will be the best you'll ever have.'

He had so much confidence, and so much vitality and energy, Rose couldn't help but smile.

He was looking at her hair and Rose automatically touched her chignon protectively.

'I don't want my hair cut.'

She was a one-off and no mistake, Josh decided, amused by her defensiveness. Normally he had girls pushing eagerly for his attention within minutes of meeting them, even if some of them masked their interest in him by acting all hoity-toity. This one was different, though, with her serious dark eyes and her cautious manner, as though she were afraid of saying or doing the wrong thing. Josh had a large and a very warm heart. He had grown up in the East End in a community where you looked out for your own and protected them. Rose, he recognised, aroused that protective instinct in him. She was looking as though she wanted to get away from him, but he didn't want her to.

'All right, I won't cut it then, but I still want you to sort out the salon for me.'

'But how can you say that? You don't know anything about me.'

'Well, that's soon solved, isn't it? Come on, I'll go first and tell you my life story, then you can tell me yours.'

There was no stopping him, Rose decided with resignation.

'My dad wanted me to be a tailor, like him, and even now he still doesn't think that hairdressing is a man's job, even though I've told him that it's his fault that that's what I do. He was the one who got me a Saturday job sweeping up hair from the floor of the salon close to where he works, and he's the one who taught me how to use a pair of scissors, even it was on cloth and not hair. He didn't speak to me for a week when I told him that I wanted to be apprenticed and learn to become a proper hairdresser. He told me he'd rather disown me, but my mother talked him round in the end, and once he'd met Charlie, who owned the salon where I wanted to train, and realised that he wasn't a pouf, he calmed down a bit.'

Josh wasn't going to say so to Rose, but Charlie had been as rampant as a ram and ready to get his leg over anything female that moved, including most of his staff, as well as his younger and prettier clients. But it was the fact that he drove a fancy car and swaggered through the salon, come Saturday afternoon, wearing a sharp suit, eyeing up the birds for a date for Saturday night that had helped to make Josh decide that he wouldn't mind a bit of that life.

Rose was a cut above the girls he knew, Josh could tell that, not because she talked posh – that would never have impressed Josh – but because she was . . . he hunted around for the right way to describe her and then gave a satisfied nod when he finally came up with the words . . . *delicate and refined*. That was it: Rose was refined, and needed to be treated right.

'I'd seen Charlie coming into the salon all dressed up in a fancy suit, and I'd reckoned that hairdressing must be a good way to make a bit of money. And, of course, me being a Jew boy, I fancied making a bit meself.' He grinned at his joke. 'He worked his apprentices damn near into the grave and paid us peanuts, but I learned a lot whilst I was working for Charlie.'

He certainly had. Josh had quickly learned about offering to do the prettier girls' hair for free in their own homes on his day off, and getting to have a bit of a smooch with them in payment.

'Of course, I'd got my sights on better things, even then. I'd made up my mind that as soon as I was qualified I was going to find myself a job as a stylist at some posh West End place and start saving for my own salon. That's where the money is: owning your own place. Only I had to do my national service first, of course, and then this other hairdresser, another Jewish lad, persuaded me to go out to Israel with him,'

'To work on the kibbutz?' Rose asked, remembering what he had said earlier. She was more interested in his story than she had expected.

Josh shook his head. 'Not exactly. Or at least that wasn't the original plan, although we did end up doing a spell in one.'

Rose's eyes widened. 'You went there to fight,' she guessed.

'It wasn't my idea,' Josh told her. 'It was Vidal's. And by the time I'd realised what he'd volunteered us for, and that it wasn't a few weeks in the sunshine picking fruit, it was too late. I reckon that Vidal was hoping that would be the end of me, what with us both wanting to open our own salons and me being a better hairdresser than him.'

He was laughing to show that he was only joking, so Rose smiled too.

'Me and Vidal both worked for Raymond, Mr Teasy Weasy,' he explained to Rose. 'You'll have heard of him?'

Rose nodded. Raymond was one of London's best known society hairdressers.

'Tell me all about him . . .' she said.

Ella was longing for the evening to be over. Not because of the smoke-filled air that was stinging her eyes, or because she was tired, but because for the last five minutes Janey had been sitting in a dark corner of the room with a decidedly louche-looking dishevelled type, whom she was snogging for all she was worth, and who right now had his hand on her mohair-covered breast.

Ella was filled with anxiety and misery. She wanted desperately to go over and put an end to what was going on but at the same time she didn't want to do anything that would draw attention to her sister's reckless behaviour.

Meanwhile, Janey felt bitterly disappointed. She'd waited and waited for Dan to arrive, but he hadn't done, and then she'd heard one of the girls from a theatrical school in Markham Square saying that Dan and some of the others from their crowd had gone to Soho to a new jazz club instead of coming to the party. And then Larry had pounced on her and she was trapped with him now, because she hadn't had the heart to say 'no' when he had looked so pleased to see her. She'd been so excited about the party but it was turning out to be anything but enjoyable. Larry's breath smelled of beer, and being kissed by him wasn't a bit like being kissed by Dan, and she wished she hadn't got involved with him.

*   *   *

Dougie didn't quite know what to do. He knew what he wanted to do, of course. The pretty little actress hadn't shown – not that Dougie was too disappointed; there were plenty of other equally pretty girls here, after all – and, more importantly, *they* were here: the three girls who could tell him so much that he didn't yet know about the dukedom, and the duchess's feelings about someone taking what should have been her own son's place.

Although Dougie understood all about the law of primogeniture, he still felt uncomfortable about stepping into shoes that should belong to someone else, especially when he was pretty sure that they weren't going to fit him or be his style. There was a big difference between the dusty boots worn by outback stockmen and the laced-up brogues and polished leather shoes of the British aristocrat.

The three girls could give him an insight into how things were that he could never get from anyone else. It was a golden opportunity and he'd be a fool to let it go to waste.

He looked round for Janey. She'd been the friendliest of the three, but the only member of the trio he could see was Ella. She was standing on her own.

He hesitated and then plunged through the crowd towards her before he could change his mind.

'Cigarette?' he said, quickly wiping his now damp palm against his pocket as he offered her the pack, and then apologised, red-faced with embarrassment when it nearly slipped out of his hand.

His obvious gaucheness had the effect of both disarming Ella and arousing her sympathy. He was so big that it was no wonder he was clumsy. Although normally she would have refused the offered cigarette, she accepted it instead, giving him a smile that, although she didn't know it, filled Dougie with relief. He'd been half expecting that she'd cold-shoulder him.

'I still haven't got the hang of doing this,' he admitted ruefully when he had finally managed to tap out a cigarette for her. His awkwardness helped Ella to relax and drop her guard.

'Didn't you smoke before you came to England?' she asked.

'Oh, yes, but not these. We rolled our own, on the sheep station. It's cheaper.'

Ella's sympathy for him grew. He might be good-looking but he was as out of place at the party as she was. His obvious discomfort brought out her 'big sister' protective instinct. She suspected he felt a bit out of his depth in London.

'You must miss Australia,' she guessed.

Dougie felt some of his tension ease. She was more sympathetic than he had expected.

'It's different here, and sometimes that does make me feel a bit out of things,' he admitted truthfully. Another couple of minutes and she'd have smoked her cigarette and he'd have lost the opportunity he had created. Dare he ask her what he wanted to ask her? And if he did, would she walk off in disgust? There was only one way to find out. He took a deep breath.

'You looked a bit put out earlier when I mentioned Em— Lady Emerald, but she's your sister, right? I get a bit confused with your English setup with titles.'

'Stepsister,' Ella corrected him. 'Emerald's mother is

68

married to my and Janey's father. They were each married before, our father to our mother, and Emerald's mother to the duke, which is how Emerald gets her title.'

'So that makes Emerald's mother a duchess, and in time that will mean that your stepsister will be a duchess as well?' Of course Dougie knew that was not the case, but there was something he was desperate to know.

Normally people simply did not ask that kind of question, but Ella couldn't help but take pity on the young Australian. There was something engaging about him, something friendly and, well, safe. He reminded Ella in an odd sort of way of a large, well-meaning but clumsy dog. It wasn't his fault that he didn't know any better. He was from overseas after all, and allowances had to be made.

Taking a deep breath she corrected him firmly, 'No, Emerald can never be a duchess, unless of course she married a duke. The title descends through the male line, you see.'

'I get it,' Dougie answered truthfully, fighting the superstitious temptation to cross his fingers as he asked his all-important question as casually as he could. 'So who is the duke then?'

'We don't know. You see, both Emerald's father and her brother were killed in the same accident, and Lord Robert, Emerald's father, was an only child. The family solicitor thinks that he's traced someone who might be the heir, but he's still waiting to hear back from him – that's if he is the right man, and he's still alive.'

Circumspect as always, Ella didn't want to say too much to Dougie, although of course she knew that the family solicitor was desperately trying to make contact with the new heir.

'I dare say your stepmother isn't too keen on having some stranger take what should have been her son's place,' Dougie suggested, trying not to feel too guilty about his deceit.

'No, that's not the case at all,' Ella defended her step-mother vehemently. 'Quite the opposite. Mama just isn't like that. She desperately wants there to be an heir, because otherwise the title will die out and the estate will be broken up, and she says that Lord Robert would have hated that. It was so awful what happened, Lord Robert and Luc being killed in a car accident.'

'You knew them?'

'Yes. They used to come and visit Mama's grand-mother. My father was her estate manager. I was only young, of course, but I can remember them. Mama says that only when the dukedom has been passed on to a new heir will she be able to feel that Lord Robert is finally at peace.'

'So you reckon, then, that this heir, whoever he is, would be welcomed by the duchess?'

'I'm sure of it,' Ella confirmed, adding, 'I'm not so sure that Emerald would welcome him, though. She's planning to have her coming-out ball at the house in Eaton Square, which really belongs to the duke. Mama didn't want her to but Emerald always manages to get her own way.'

'I dare say the estate is pretty run down, there not being an heir?' Dougie probed further.

'Oh, no,' Ella assured him firmly. 'Mama is a trustee,

along with Mr Melrose, the family solicitor, and although Osterby – that's the main house in the country – is shut up and not used, there's a skeleton staff there to keep everything in order and there's an estate manager to take care of the land.'

'Strewth, that must be costing someone a bob or two,' Dougie commented.

'Well, the money comes out of the estate itself. The duke was very rich, and Mama says that everything must be kept in order whilst there's the slightest hope of finding the heir so that it can be handed over to him as Robert would have wanted it to be.'

'Emerald will feel her nose has been put out of joint then, won't she, if some heir arrives and then she gets nothing?'

'Emerald couldn't have inherited the estate – it's entailed – and besides, her father set up a very generous trust fund for her.'

'So she's a rich heiress then, is she?'

'I expect she will be one day.'

'And you don't mind?'

'No. Not at all.'

Ella might understand that Australians did not know any better than to ask the kind of questions that were normally taboo but she drew the line at informing Dougie that her stepmother was independently wealthy, and that none of them had any need to feel envious of Emerald, in any way.

Ella knew that she should not have said as much as she already had, but the truth was that talking about Emerald helped to keep her mind off her anxiety over

Janey, who was still locked in an embrace in the corner. Now when Ella looked she could see that the dishevelled one's hand had disappeared up inside Janey's jumper. She opened her mouth in shock and the small anxious sound she made had Dougie looking in the same direction.

'Looks like someone is enjoying the party,' he chuckled, offering Ella another cigarette.

'I'm sorry. Please excuse me.'

Ella was obviously flustered. Her set expression and pale face indicated how alarmed she was by her sister's behaviour, and Dougie wasn't really surprised by her obvious desire to do something about it.

How awful of her to be so rude, but she had to stop what was going on, Ella comforted herself as she hurried over to her sister. She came to a halt, standing determinedly in front of Janey.

'It's time for us to go, Janey.'

Janey, who had been struggling to stop Larry's hands from roving far more intimately over her body than she welcomed, greeted her sister's arrival with relief – not that she intended to let Ella know that – and extracted herself from his embrace.

'Where's Rose?' she asked Ella.

The honest answer was that Ella didn't know, but she could hardly say that unless she wanted to risk Janey accusing her of pretending she wanted to leave. The last thing she wanted was a row with Janey, which would result in her impetuous sister going straight back to the man Ella had just prised her away from.

To her relief Janey announced, 'Oh, there she is, over there.'

'Look, I meant what I said about wanting you to come and take a look at my salon,' Josh was saying to Rose.

There was more space around them now and she had been able to step back from him. She started to shake her head, but he stopped her, reaching into his pocket and producing a business card with a theatrical flourish.

'Here's my card. Think about it.'

Rose could see Ella beckoning her urgently, Janey beside her, so she took the card and slipped it into her handbag.

'I must go,' she stammered hurriedly, before making her way to Ella's side.

'Look, leave it out, will you, Ollie? I know what I'm doing.'

The stubborn look on his cousin's face as he pulled his arm free of Oliver's restraining hand told Oliver all he needed to know about Willie's frame of mind.

They were in their local East End pub, the Royal Crown, standing at the bar with their beers.

'I thought like you meself once, Willie. In fact I was all for making meself a career in the boxing ring, but then I got to thinking—'

'You mean that your ma got to thinking for you,' Willie interrupted him. 'Well, I'm not being told what to do by you, Ollie. Harry Malcolms reckons I've got a good future ahead of me, and that there's bin talk of either the Richardsons or the Krays tekkin' an interest.'

The mention of two of the East End's most notorious gangs made Oliver frown.

'If you go down that route you'll be expected to throw matches as well as win them, Willie,' he warned.

His cousin gave a dismissive shrug. 'It's only them lads that aren't good enough that get told to lose, and that ain't going to happen to *me*. Reggie came down to watch me sparring the other night, and he wouldn't do that if he didn't fink he wanted me on board.'

Willie might think he had what it took to make the big time but Oliver had asked around and the word on the street was that he was more boxing ring fodder than a future champion, and would end up merely as a sparring partner for more skilled boxers, working for a pittance in a boxing club rather than earning big money in prize fights.

The trouble with Willie was that he was easily led and just as easily deceived.

'You're a fool, Willie,' Oliver complained, beginning to lose patience. 'Throw in your lot with them and my bet is that you'll end up with your brains turned to jelly, or working as one of their enforcers.'

'You're just jealous,' Willie accused him, his cheeks flushed. 'You know what your problem is, don't you? It's that mother of yours. My dad reckons—' He broke off suddenly, looking self-conscious and scuffing his shoe on the ground.

Oliver froze. This wasn't the first time there'd been dark hints thrown out about his mother.

'Go on, Willie. Your dad reckons what exactly?' he challenged, his voice hard.

'Oh, leave it out, will you, Ollie? I didn't mean nothing. It's just that your ma always carries on like nothing's good enough for her. Me ma reckons that it's rich, her coming on the way she does when she works as a ruddy cleaner, but me dad—'

He broke off again, his face reddening whilst Oliver's mouth compressed into a thin line of fury.

He should be used to it by now. After all, he'd pretty much grown up shrugging off the whispers and sly looks that people exchanged when they talked about his mother. The gossips whispered that the rich widower for whom she cleaned was responsible for her good figure and her smart appearance.

Oliver scowled. He was no stranger to the pleasure of sex – far from it – but the thought of his mother tarting herself up for her wealthy boss wasn't one that sat comfortably with him, and all the more so because of the benefits that had come his way over the years, courtesy of Herbert Sawyer.

He bunched his fist and then slowly and deliberately relaxed it. He hadn't come here to get involved in a fight with his younger cousin – or anyone else, for that matter. He'd left all that business behind long ago.

'Please yourself,' he told his cousin, putting down his beer glass, 'but don't come crying to me when you're standing in the dock about to be sent down because you've used them fists of yours on someone you shouldn't on Reggie Kray's orders.'

'Give over, Ollie. Come on, let's have another drink,' Willie tried to appease him.

Oliver looked round the bar. He wasn't really in the mood for the kind of drinking session that Willie no doubt had in mind.

Before he could reply, the door from the street opened

and a group of men came in, Reggie Kray in their midst. He was dressed in the dapper fashion he favoured, a cigarette dangling from his lips.

Automatically Willie stepped back – no one stood in the way of the Krays – lowering his head, almost as though in obeisance.

Reggie stopped, causing the enforcers behind him to trip over their own crepe-soled brothel creepers in their efforts not to bump into 'the boss'. It wasn't Willie Reggie stopped in front of, though, but Oliver.

'Saw that photograph you took of me and Ronnie,' he announced, drawing deeply on his cigarette and then exhaling before adding, 'Smart piece of work. Me and Ronnie liked it. Next time, though, make sure you get some bits of smart upper-crust skirt in as well, not them old dames.'

Without taking his gaze from Oliver he called out to the barman, 'Alf, give my friend here a drink.' Then he continued, 'Mind you, there's to be no photograph taking in here, mate, understand?'

Oliver certainly did. The pub was a seedy dive where the Krays came to talk business, not flash their East End smartness for public view. Like rats coming up from the sewers, those with whom the Krays did business often preferred to conduct that business under the cover of darkness.

Chapter Six

Paris

Emerald arched her foot, the better to admire the elegance of her new Italian leather shoes, and the slenderness of her legs in their Dior silk stockings. This time next week she would be back in London, and she couldn't wait. The Dior dress she had been coveting, and which she suspected her mother would not have permitted her to have, on the grounds that it was too grown up, was safely packed ready to be taken back with her. By the time her mother got the bill it would be too late for her to do anything about it. She certainly couldn't send it back as the couture gown had been made especially for her.

Emerald had known she had to have it the minute she had seen it at the autumn season's show. She would wear it for the formal official photographs that would celebrate the announcement of her engagement to the Duke of Kent. His mother, Princess Marina, was well known for being stylish and elegant. Emerald intended to make it plain that, in future, as the new Duchess of Kent, *she* would be the most stylish and elegant member of the extended Royal Family. Emerald intended to be a very popular duchess.

With her future all mapped out and waiting for her, Emerald was impatient to put her plans into action. She planned to make sure that she encouraged the duke to fall in love with her from the minute they were introduced. The official purpose of being finished might be to equip girls with good social skills, but Emerald had been using her time in Paris to hone skills that she felt would be far more use to her than conversational French.

Today she was going to polish those skills a little more, having managed to escape from under Madame la Comtesse's eagle eye. She smiled triumphantly to herself, but then frowned.

Trust nosy Gwendolyn to insist on coming with her, and dragging Lydia along as well. It served them right that they were looking so uncomfortable. Emerald was enjoying herself, though, basking in the admiration of the four young men seated at the table with them in the artistic quarter of Montmartre. But it was the solitary older man sitting close by, reading his newspaper, in whom Emerald was more interested, and for whose benefit she had just been admiring her silk-stocking-clad legs. Narrow-faced, with his dark hair just beginning to grey, there was something about him that sent a shiver of anticipation and expectation through her. Instinctively Emerald knew that he was the kind who knew a very great deal about her sex, the kind of man any woman would be proud to have as a conquest, the kind of man it would be a challenge to turn into a devoted admirer, unlike the four boys, who were making it plain that they were ready to adore her. Emerald liked older men, or rather a certain kind of older man – not ones like Gwendolyn's revolting father. It excited her when they flirted with her, hinting deliciously about improper pleasures.

Emerald hadn't had a lover yet – she couldn't risk the scandal. And she would certainly never be tempted to let boys take liberties or go too far. She was far too well aware of her value as an 'unspoiled' virgin to do that. But if she did take a lover, it would have to be one who knew what he was doing, not some silly boy. That couldn't happen until after she was married to the duke, of course. Some girls thought it was old-fashioned to hang on to their virginity but Emerald didn't agree; they were the kind of girls who would probably be happy with any kind of husband, whereas she only wanted the best.

The young men they were with were students at the Sorbonne, or so they had said when, earlier in the week, she had dropped her purse in the Bois de Boulogne and one of them had picked it up for her.

She had agreed to meet them on impulse. After all, she had no intentions of doing anything that might render her unfit to become the wife of the Duke of Kent, but it amused her to see Gwennie looking all bug-eyed and mutinous, as though the act of enjoying a cup of coffee in a café was something akin to taking up residence in a brothel. Emerald liked knowing that Gwennie felt uncomfortable. How silly she was. Did she really think that any man would look at her whilst she, Emerald, was there?

'I really don't think you should have brought us here, Emerald,' Gwendolyn was muttering.

'I didn't bring you, you insisted on coming with me,' Emerald pointed out, opening her gold cigarette case, with its inlaid semi-precious stones the exact colour of her eyes – another new purchase from a jewellers on the Faubourg St-Honoré, and removing one of the prettily coloured Sobranie cigarettes.

Immediately all four young men produced cigarette lighters. Really, it was almost like one of those advertisements one saw in *Vogue*, Emerald thought. How silly and immature Lydia and Gwendolyn looked, both of them plain and lumpen. Emerald smoothed down the hem of her black wool frock, allowing her fingertips to rest deliberately on her sheer-stocking-clad legs. She would hate to be as plain as Gwennie. She would rather be dead.

She allowed the best-looking of the four boys to light her cigarette, and laughed when he caught hold of her free hand and brought it to his lips. French boys were such flirts and so charming. Charming, but not, of course, dukes.

Emerald removed her hand, and announced with insincere regret, 'We really must go.'

'I'm going to have to tell the comtesse what you've done,' Gwendolyn announced self-righteously as they made their way back.

'I haven't done anything,' Emerald denied.

'Yes, you have. You met those boys and you let one of them kiss you. You do know, don't you, that something like that could ruin your reputation, and bring shame on your whole family?'

Emerald stopped dead in the middle of the pavement, causing the other two girls to stop as well.

80

'I wouldn't be quite so keen to talk about tale-telling, people's reputations being ruined, and shame being brought on their family, if I were you, Gwendolyn. Not in your shoes.'

The words, spoken with such a quiet, almost a deadly conviction, caused Lydia to look anxious, whilst Gwendolyn declared primly, 'What do you mean, in my shoes? I haven't done anything wrong.'

'You may not have done.' Emerald paused. 'Your father is very fond of pretty girls, isn't he, Gwendolyn?'

Gwendolyn's face began to burn a miserable bright red.

'Did I tell you that I saw him coming out of a shop in the Faubourg St-Honoré with a very pretty girl on his arm? No, I don't think I did, did I? But then you see, Gwendolyn, I am not a nasty little sneak, like some people I could name. I wonder what would happen to your reputation if people knew that your father has a common little showgirl for a mistress?'

'That's not true,' Gwendolyn shouted, panic-stricken and almost in tears. Lydia gave Emerald an anguished look that implored her to stop, but Emerald ignored it. Gwendolyn, with her holier-than-thou attitude and her determination to get Emerald into trouble, deserved to be put in her place.

'Yes it is. Your father is an adulterer, Gwendolyn. He has broken his marriage vows to your mother.'

'No.' Gwendolyn's mouth was trembling, her face screwed up like a pig's, Emerald thought unkindly, as she gulped and snivelled, 'You're lying. And I won't let you say things like that.'

Emerald smiled mockingly. 'Am I? Then I'm lying too

about your father trying to put his hand up my skirt and kiss me as well, am I?'

Lydia piped up naïvely, 'Oh, I'm sure Uncle Henry didn't mean anything by it, Emerald. He kissed me the last time I saw him.'

Gwendolyn's face went from scarlet to a blotchy red and white.

'You see, Gwendolyn,' Emerald said mock sweetly. 'Now, do you want me to tell the comtesse about your father, or—'

'All right, I won't say anything to her about those boys,' Gwendolyn gave in.

Emerald inclined her head in regal acceptance of Gwendolyn's submission. It had been truly clever of her to make up that story about seeing Gwendolyn's father with a showgirl. What a fool Gwendolyn was. Everyone knew that her family had no money, so how on earth did she think her father could afford to keep a mistress?

Chapter Seven

London

Head down and umbrella up against the driving February rain, Rose hurried up King's Road on her way home from work. The wind was icy and she couldn't wait to get inside. In her haste, Rose didn't see the two men standing on the pavement in front of her until she had virtually collided with them. In her attempt to sidestep them she almost lost her footing and a strong hand reached out to steady her. As she looked up to thank him, Rose recognised the hairdresser from the party, Josh Simons.

'Well, I never, it's the interior designer,' he joked.

'Training to be an interior designer,' Rose corrected him.

'Where am I going wrong, Vidal?' he asked his companion sadly. 'I've offered her a free haircut in exchange for some decorating advice for my new salon, but she still hasn't taken me up on my offer.'

'Wise girl,' the other man responded with a grin. 'Look, love, if you really want a decent haircut come and see me, Vidal Sassoon.'

'He gave me a job when we left Raymond, then helped me to set up on my own,' Josh put in.

'He means in the end I had to pay him to go.'

They were both laughing, and obviously such good friends that Rose found herself relaxing.

Josh smiled warmly at her, shaking his head in warning as he told Vidal, 'I know what you're up to, and no way are you getting your scissors on that hair, Vidal. I saw it first. Look,' he said to Rose, whose arm he was still holding, 'since you're here anyway why don't you come up and have a look at my salon?'

'You may as well go with him,' Vidal said. 'I can tell you that there's no point in trying to argue with him – he never gives up when he's set his mind on something. Besides, you'd be doing the rest of the world and me a favour if you did help him out. From what I've seen of his salon, no girl worthy of the name is going to want to get her hair cut there. And since I've only loaned him this money I'd like to see him earning something so that he can pay me back.'

What could she say? It would be churlish to refuse now, after such an appeal.

'Very well,' Rose agreed, 'but I'm only in training and I don't know the first thing about designing hairdressing salons.'

'You don't need to,' Josh told her promptly. 'Come on, it's up here.'

Still holding on to her arm, he started to guide her towards the door behind them, and it was only Josh's farewell to Vidal that alerted Rose to the fact that there was now only the two of them. But by then it was too late: Josh was already reaching for the shabby door and opening it for her.

The door opened straight onto a long narrow staircase, its walls painted a sludgy dark brown, the paint chipped in places to show an even more repellent shade of green underneath.

'You need something light and bright in here,' Rose announced, immediately inspired, 'something with a finish that can be wiped clean as people are bound to put their hands on the walls on their way up because the stairs are so narrow.' She eyed the wall thoughtfully. 'A sort of off-white shiny paint would be best, and then you could break up the wall with some black-and-white photographs, in plain black frames – head-and-shoulder shots showing off various hairstyles, perhaps.'

Rose was thinking aloud, her imagination taking off and quashing her reluctance to get involved. The shabbiness of her surroundings and the challenge of transforming them was affecting her like an itch she had to scratch.

'That's a terrific idea. I've got a mate who's a photographer; always photographing pretty girls, he is. I might be able to do a bit of a deal with him.'

Rose, who was already halfway up the stairs, turned back to look at him. Standing below her brought him to the same eye level. He had extraordinary long eyelashes for a man, and those deep-set dark brown eyes were even more mesmerising close up. He definitely wasn't her type, though. She liked quiet studious young men, like the young Chinese medical student she had recently got to know whose family owned a Chinese restaurant patronised by Janey's arty crowd. Lee worked in the restaurant when he wasn't studying, and one evening, when they had been the last customers to leave, he had sat down with them at Janey's insistence and told them about his dreams and plans.

Not that Rose had any romantic interest in Lee, or was likely to develop one. Her heart was already given to John, Lord Fitton Legh. John's stepmother was Ella and Janey's aunt Cassandra, who his father had married after the death of John's mother, and the girls had known John all their lives. He was quiet and kind, and Rose loved him for that and for treating her as though she were no different to the others ... She had developed a crush on him when she was twelve years old and he had saved her when Emerald had tricked her into getting up on a far too mettlesome horse, knowing that she was a nervous rider. John had come into the yard just as Rose was clinging in terror to the rearing horse's reins. Within seconds he had calmed it down and had scooped Rose up off its back. In that moment he had become for her the most wonderful person in the whole world. Not that she would ever allow either John himself, or anyone else, to know how she felt. Emerald would have had a field day taunting her if she had guessed, because it was, of course, impossible that John would return her feelings. She had heard her aunt and uncle talking about John's future, saying that he would probably marry a girl from one of the local aristocratic families, someone who would share his deep commitment to the land and his inheritance, and she had known, young as she had been, that someone in John's position would never want to marry a girl like her. The Fittons were, after all, a very old and proud Cheshire family.

But that hadn't prevented her from having her daydreams.

Later on, when she had been at college and she had seen the way that men looked at her, knowing that she loved John had made her feel safe. Because if she loved John then there was no need for her to worry about falling in love with anyone else – with someone who might pretend to love her but who would really only want to treat her as her father had treated her mother.

No other man could hurt her or reject her whilst she loved John. And she always would. Always. Even though she knew that nothing could ever come of it. Instead she hid her private love for him in her heart and concentrated on her work and on making sure that she repaid her aunt Amber's faith in her.

'When I said head-and-shoulder portraits of girls, that was exactly what I meant,' she told Josh severely now, as she focused firmly on the present, 'not poses more suitable for a certain type of magazine.'

Josh burst out laughing. 'Ollie would be mortified if he heard you say that. He photographs models for *Vogue*, not *Men Only*.'

Rose could feel her face starting to burn. Quickly she turned round and headed to the top of the stairs where the first door in front of her had an unsteady 'WC' painted on it.

'You'll have to make sure that there are proper cloakroom facilities,' she announced. 'At least you will if you want to attract girls.'

She hadn't realised that there was a *double entendre* to her words until she heard Josh laugh again.

'So that's where I've been going wrong when I've taken girls back to my place,' he joked. 'And there I've been, changing my toothpaste, thinking I might have bad breath. You reckon I'd be better getting one of those fancy crocheted covers for the toilet roll, do you?'

Rose laughed in spite of herself. She wasn't fooled for a minute; she doubted that any girl who agreed to go home with this man cared two hoots about his bathroom. She wasn't going to boost his ego by telling him so, though, not when she was pretty sure that he already knew it himself.

Instead she said loftily, 'Of course I don't know what kind of clientele you want to attract.'

'But posh girls like you wouldn't come and get their hair done in a salon run by a working-class Jewish hairdresser whose salon that hasn't got the right kind of "cloakroom", is that it?'

He sounded more curt than amused now. His obvious contempt made Rose flinch, but she stood her ground.

'That wasn't what I meant at all. It isn't a matter of being "posh". In fact, some of the grandest houses in the country have the most antiquated bathrooms you can imagine. It's just a matter of making your clientele feel that you appreciate and value them, especially when that clientele is going to be female. Making them feel comfortable, but at the same time making them feel that they deserve something that's special, and . . . and the best. That is after all why you want them to come to you, isn't it?' she challenged him. 'Not just so that you can do their hair but because you think you can do their hair better than anyone else?'

Josh was taken aback and impressed by her astuteness. He looked at her as though he hadn't really seen her before and in one sense he realised he hadn't. Previously he'd seen her as a stunning-looking girl whose Eurasian beauty would make her an excellent model for the avant-garde hairstyles he and Vidal talked about so passionately into the early hours. They were both in their different ways determined to do away with the old-established hairdressing model of rigidly arranged and lacquered 'set' styles, and to replace them with precision cutting that focused on the natural movement of a woman's hair.

Whilst he and Vidal understood one another's drive, Rose had astonished Josh with the speed at which she had tapped into his ambitions. She was, he decided ruefully, bang on the money, though, and that was exactly what he wanted.

In that moment Josh made up his mind that Rose and no one else was going to be responsible for the décor of his salon, no matter how much cajoling he had to do to get her to do it – and somehow he knew he would have to cajole her. He was no fool, though. There was no point in scaring her off by telling her what he had decided. Instead he stepped past her and pushed open the door into the long dilapidated room that he planned to turn into his salon.

'Come and have a look at this . . .'

Chapter Eight

The sound of someone knocking on the door, when Lew was out at lunch with his latest girl, distracted Dougie's attention from the small portable typewriter on which he was typing up a list of potential clients Lew had left him. There were no sittings booked for the afternoon and, knowing Lew as he now did, Dougie suspected that when he returned it would be with the young woman he had been pursuing and that he himself would be told to shoot off for the day. Cursing under his breath as the knocking continued and he hit two wrong keys in succession, Dougie pushed back his chair and stood up.

Emerald waited impatiently at the door. She hadn't been put off when the new top society photographer, lauded in *Tatler* and the *Queen*, hadn't replied to her letter to him from Paris insisting that she wanted him to take her new official débutante photograph, and nor had she changed her mind about the importance of having him do just that.

She had quickly discovered on her return to London that she was far from the only contender for the position of HRH The Duchess of Kent, and that invitations offering an opportunity for débutantes to meet the duke were very carefully monitored by those who managed to secure his presence at any event. Naturally, she was not going to be readily invited to parties the duke was attending by the mothers of other débutantes, for instance. Emerald quite understood that, and she understood too that she was going to have to use subtle, even underhand, means to ensure that she brought herself to the duke's attention. Getting herself photographed by Lewis Coulter, and then being described as the season's prettiest débutante would do her campaign no harm. His mother was bound to have copies of all the top magazines, and Emerald could easily imagine her pointing her photograph out to her son and saying what an impeccable lineage. At least on her father's side. It was a pity that her mother wasn't better born. Emerald's mouth thinned. Had she been, then Emerald wouldn't have to think about strategies for bringing herself to the duke's attention because her mother would naturally have numbered Princess Marina amongst her social circle.

Irritatingly, the young duke, instead of establishing himself in London and taking part in its social scene, seemed to spend most of his time in the country. Emerald made a small grimace of distaste. Once they were married that would have to change. She didn't like the country at all. Of course, once she had given birth to their first child – a son, of course – it would be quite permissible for her husband to go to the country if he wished, whilst she spent time with her friends in

London, but initially, as a newly engaged and then a newly married couple, they would appear together, he looking very much in love with her – which of course he would be.

She knocked again. Once Emerald had made up her mind about something she didn't like any delay in putting it into action, and she was impatient to get the duke's courtship of her started.

The cold wet February weather had brought almost the entire household down with heavy colds, with the exception of Emerald, enabling her to escape from her godmother's chaperonage to visit the photographer.

Emerald was enjoying living at Lenchester House. It was, after all, by rights more her house than anyone else's. It was all very well for her mother to point out that Mr Melrose doggedly believed that there was an heir. Mr Melrose was an old man, after all, and if there was such an heir then why hadn't he made himself known and claimed his inheritance?

Emerald raised her hand to bang on the door again, only to find that it was being opened by a tall broad-shouldered young man with thick untidy dark brown hair, which was fairer at the ends, and a cross expression.

Emerald, who had seen photographs of Lewis Coulter in the society columns, gave Dougie a haughty look and declared, 'I'm here to see Lew.' Then she swept past him, leaving him no option other than to close the door behind her.

'He won't see you without an appointment,' Dougie warned, but Emerald simply shrugged.

'I wrote to him to tell him that I'd be coming to see him and he *will* see me. My mother particularly wants him to take my coming-out photograph.' She delivered the lie without a blink.

'Lew's out at the moment and he won't be back until, well, much later, but you can leave your details, if you like, and I'll tell him that you called. What's your name?'

'Lady Emerald Devenish,' Emerald told Dougie haughtily, his Australian accent causing her to view him with open contempt.

Lady Emerald Devenish. That was the family name of the Lenchesters. This then was . . . Dougie let go of the door he was still holding open, hurrying after Emerald as she stalked into the room, and then bumped into his own desk.

Emerald gave him a withering look. She certainly wasn't going to waste her charm on a boring colonial with a dreadful Australian accent. How very odd that a photographer with Lew's reputation, who surely ought to have known better, was actually employing this uncouth Australian.

Dougie watched Emerald warily. She was everything he had assumed the upper classes would be. And she was also the nearest thing he had to 'family', someone who shared his blood – a true blood relative if this Melrose bloke had got his facts right. Perhaps he should go and see him, after all. Right now it would have given him a great deal of pleasure to tell her exactly who he was. From what he'd observed of high-society life, it wasn't so very long ago that, when the head of a titled

94

family spoke, that family jumped to attention. The thought of this arrogant little beauty being forced to kowtow to him was an appealing one, he had to admit. On the other hand, didn't this head of the family stuff also carry a lot of responsibility? There was all that business of keeping the family name unsullied – at least that was what he'd gathered from some of the tales Lew had told him. The Lenchester family name wasn't likely to remain unsullied for long once Lew got his hands on this minx.

Dougie's sudden surge of protective responsibility was an unfamiliar and unwanted feeling, and one he determinedly pushed out of the way. After all, it wasn't even proved yet that he was this ruddy duke, and so long as he didn't go and see Mr Melrose, it wasn't *ever* going to be proved. What did he want with a title, and the responsibility for a girl like this one who had already got his back up?

'Look, why don't I make you an appointment and then you can come back when Lew is here?' he offered, having decided that for now it made sense to get her out of the way, for his own sake, if nothing else. If he ran true to form, any minute now Lew was likely to return with his latest conquest.

Did this . . . this Australian nobody think she was going to fall for that, Emerald wondered. She looked round the small sitting room and then made her way to one of the sofas, seating herself carefully on it to ensure that her legs were displayed to their best advantage.

'I'll wait,' she announced, before picking up one of

the magazines on the coffee table and starting to flick through it.

She certainly was a little madam, Dougie decided. Someone should have put her across their knee years ago and paddled her backside until she learned a few manners. It was too late now, of course. She was certainly nothing like the three girls he remembered from the party; they had all been really decent sorts, not arrogant little snobs like her. Well, she'd certainly get her come-uppance when Lew did show up. His favourite mantra was that no day was worth living unless it contained both sex and work, and when he returned it would be with sex on his mind. Lew could deliver caustically cruel put-downs when he was so minded. Dougie had seen Lew reduce girls to tears with his unkindness when he was irritated or bored with them.

But so what if he did hurt this little madam's feelings? Why should he care? He returned to his typing, breathing heavily over the unwanted task made all the more difficult by the small keyboard and the size of his hands.

Really, the man was disgustingly boorish, Emerald decided contemptuously. All that heavy breathing interspersed with the odd swear word. He looked as though he'd be more at home on a farm than working here, although no doubt the nature of his work was equally menial. He wasn't even properly dressed. Instead of a business suit he was wearing a pair of those silly narrow black trousers that a certain type of bohemian young man wore teamed with a black polo-neck jumper, its sleeves pushed back to display muscular tanned forearms. A lock of his thick dark brown hair had fallen down almost over his eyes, adding to his uncouth appearance. Emerald was more used to men with the traditional short back and sides, favoured by the establishment and the services.

The sound of the front door suddenly opening had them both looking towards it, Emerald's quickly prepared smile faltering for a moment as she saw the man coming in and immediately recognised him as the society photographer. What she hadn't expected, though, was that he would be dressed in the same bohemian fashion as his dogsbody, only his polo-neck jumper was enlivened by a red and white spotted handkerchief knotted round his neck.

Lew was back and on his own. Dougie immediately recognised that his employer was not in a good mood. He had that air of suppressed tension and irritation about him that Dougie had learned to recognise. Predictably, though, the instant he saw Emerald that tension was broken, replaced by one of his deliberately caressing looks accompanied by a warm smile.

Now the fat was really in the fire, Dougie recognised. Deprived of his afternoon of sex with his girl, Lew would be like a cat on hot bricks until he had relieved his sexual tension, and who better to do so with than the snobby little madam sitting there looking at him with such confident expectation. Well, it would serve her right if he simply left her to her fate and she became yet another of the girls Lew picked up, seduced and then very publicly dropped, ruining her reputation as he did so.

Lew, predictably, was all charm, going over to Emerald to offer his hand and an apology.

'I'm sorry. I hope you haven't been waiting too long.'

'She hasn't got an appointment,' Dougie felt obliged to point out, but neither of them was listening. Instead they were gazing deeply into one another's eyes.

'I did write to you, about you taking my coming-out photograph,' Emerald was saying, her cut-glass accent suddenly accentuated and grating on Dougie's already frayed nerves. 'Once I'd seen the photograph you took of Amelia Longhurst I told Mummy that I couldn't possibly have my photographs done by anyone else.' She smoothed her hand over her skirt as she spoke. She had dressed very carefully for this meeting in the palest of pink cashmere twinsets, its plainness relieved by a string of startlingly lustrous pearls, and a deep rose-pink full mohair skirt that showed off her narrow waist, cinched in with a wide black patent belt. On her feet were a pair of high heels, and her handbag was from Hermès. Her hair, newly done that morning in a beehive, looked as delicate as spun glass, and she had outlined her lips in a soft pink lipstick. She looked, she had decided before leaving her bedroom, totally delectable and she had already visualised the photograph of her that would appear in *Tatler* and the words that would accompany it.

'Lady Emerald Devenish is tipped to be *the* débutante of the season. Her ball will be held in her late father's London house in Eaton Square, and HRH The Duke of Kent will be attending along with his mother, Princess Marina.'

The invitations had already gone out, and Emerald knew exactly what kind of speculation that wording beneath her photograph would give rise to. In the language of gossip columns it was tantamount to a pre-engagement declaration, but of course if anyone were to accuse her of exaggerating the situation she would simply pretend not to know what they meant.

The photographer was disappointingly short for a man who featured so often in the gossip columns as a man about town and a flirt, but Emerald had no more interest in him as a man than she did in the uncouth Australian. He was simply a means to an end.

'Indeed not.'

Lew had been furious when his lunch date – a pretty young wife whose husband hated town and preferred to remain on their estate in the country – had refused to play ball, pretending that she hadn't realised why he had suggested they had lunch together or what he had had in mind for the rest of the afternoon. But now the clouds that had darkened his temper had lifted. This girl was, if anything, even prettier than Louise, and unless he was wrong, far more sensual. One could always tell. They had a certain look about them that had nothing to do with experience. It shone from them like a special luminosity on the skin or like a definite scent on the air that surrounded them. This girl, a typical virginal deb on the outside, would on the inside be a positive volcano of passion. Teaching her to enjoy her sexuality would be like eating hot chocolate sauce on cold ice cream.

'You'd better come up to my studio,' he told Emerald. Without taking his gaze from her face, he added to Dougie, 'Please see to it that I'm not disturbed for the rest of the afternoon.'

Dougie's heart sank.

Well, why should he want to stop him? If she wanted to make a fool of herself and lose her reputation with a man who was known to be lethal, then why should he care?

Because if he was this duke, then she was family, that was why, and it was his duty to do what he could to keep his family and its name safe. Girls like this one married men to whom the virginity of their bride was almost as important as their lineage and their wealth, and all because of that important first-born son – and it had to be a son. Once the line was secured they didn't seem to mind who their wives slept with, or so it seemed to him. He was not saying that he agreed with such practice; he didn't really agree with hereditary titles either, if he were honest, but that didn't mean that they didn't exist. He was proof of that. One day an ordinary farmer back in Oz, the next a duke!

But perhaps he should go and see this Mr Melrose before he went round acting like some kind of saviour of the family name and reputation.

Lew loved his work every bit as much as he loved sex, and so taking photographs of Emerald before he seduced her was no hardship. In fact, photographing girls was the best part of his seduction technique, one that excited and aroused him as he watched them becoming excited and aroused at the thought of the lens of his camera capturing their beauty and freezing it for eternity. And then, of course, there were all those little touches as he showed them how he wanted them to pose for him, directing them, rearranging their limbs, caressing them with theatrical compliments and teasing little kisses. No wonder by the time he eventually took them to bed they were so eager for him.

He put on a smoochy Frank Sinatra record to help set the mood, whilst Emerald looked round the studio incuriously. She was well aware now just how Lew expected the photography session to end, but he was going to be disappointed. She was certainly not going to throw away her virginity on him, but since she wanted him to take her photograph she knew that she would have to string him along. Telling him that she had got her period should keep him at bay for today and when she called round to see the proofs she'd make sure that she had Lyddy with her. A call to *Tatler* pretending to be her mother should ensure that the magazine got on to Lew for the photographs and she could make sure that they added the wording she wanted at the same time.

A quick check through his camera lens assured Lew that Emerald was as photogenic as he had guessed she would be.

He removed his leather jacket and threw it over a chair, then pushed back the sleeves of his black jumper, telling her easily, 'The twinset will have to go. There's a screen there you can pop behind to change. There should be a robe there as well.'

Since the photograph that had brought her here had shown the bare shoulders of the deb he had photographed, Emerald wasn't too alarmed by this suggestion. Once she was behind the screen and removing her twinset, though, his casual, 'Oh, and you'd better take off your bra as well,' caused her to tense for a moment. The robe he'd mentioned was a flimsy piece of silk through which it would be perfectly easy to see her bare breasts, but Emerald suspected that if she objected he would simply refuse to take her photograph. It wasn't that she was particularly bothered about him seeing her breasts – in different circumstances she acknowledged that she might have enjoyed teasing him – but she had her reputation to consider and her planned future as HRH The Duchess of Kent. It would not do at all for her to have allowed any man, never mind a mere photographer, to have seen her naked to her waist.

'What's wrong? Do you need some help?'

Lew's sudden appearance round the back of the screen, holding a glass and a bottle of whisky just as she was about to unfasten her bra, had Emerald whisking the wrap around herself and saying coquettishly, 'No peeking.'

His response was to laugh and then say, 'I dare say you are far too young and innocent for me to offer you a glass of whisky?'

Emerald made a small *moue* of distaste. 'I'd have preferred a Martini.'

She had the most wonderful figure, Lew decided, firm pert breasts, and a tiny waist that together made her look almost voluptuous. He glanced at the pearls she had put with her twinset. Compared with the modest single or double row of pearls worn by most débutantes these were almost rococo in appearance, and glowing with colour.

'Nice pearls,' he commented,

'They belonged to my great-grandmother.'

An idea had suddenly come to him. Reaching for them he told Emerald, 'What I want you to do is to take off the wrap, put these on and then I want you to pose like so . . .' Putting down his glass, he went over to the corner of the studio and picked up a dark green length of silk from his collection of 'props', which he threw on the floor and then lay down on it on his stomach, lifting his torso and propping his chin up with his hands.

Emerald frowned. The pose was an enticing one, a very promising one, in fact, for a girl who wanted to make her mark and stand out from the crowd, and it was one that appealed to her ego. Normally she would have jumped at the chance to show off, but the pose was also a very provocative one – far too provocative for the future wife of the Duke of Kent.

'I think it would be far better if you simply photographed me sitting down and from the neck upwards,' she told Lew firmly, as he got to his feet.

He looked at her in astonishment. 'My dear girl, *I* am the photographer.'

'And I am the client, and it is my mother who will pay your bill,' Emerald pointed out sweetly.

Downstairs Dougie pushed back his chair and stood up. He'd agonised long enough. It was no good. He had to do something.

Upstairs, Lew's mood changed swiftly from amusement to angry irritation.

'Either I photograph you as I wish or not at all.'

Emerald glared at him. She was used to people giving in to her, not giving her ultimatums. She had desperately wanted him to take her photograph but not in a pose that would make it obvious that she had been half nude when he had done so.

Without bothering to answer him Emerald went back behind the screen and started to dress, only realising once she had her bra on that her twinset had fallen down the other side of the screen.

Dougie knocked loudly on the door and then pushed it open, without waiting for a response. They wouldn't be in bed yet. Lew always worked up to bed via a photographic session.

Just as Dougie walked in Emerald emerged from behind the screen in the diaphanous wrap to retrieve her clothes, and almost bumped into him. They each came to an abrupt halt and stared at one another.

Lew scowled when he saw Dougie. 'What do you want?'

'You said you wanted me to remind you that you're having dinner with Lady Pamela later to discuss the arrangements for the photographs for the christening.'

'You came up here to tell me that? It's only three o'clock in the afternoon.'

Quickly grabbing her clothes, Emerald retreated back behind the screen and hurriedly got dressed. Damn, damn, damn. Why had that wretched Australian had to come in and see her like that?

'Well, since you are here you can show Lady Emerald out, since she's had second thoughts and is leaving. So silly of you to panic like that, darling,' Lew told Emerald with spiky malice. 'You were quite safe. I never shag girls who wear pink twinsets, and even if I did, shagging virginal débutantes simply isn't my style, far too unrewarding. Oh, and a bit of advice for you: don't wear pink, it doesn't suit you. Makes you look sallow.' The acid tone in which the comments were delivered left Emerald in no doubt as to what Lew thought of her. And of course the Australian had overheard it all and would be enjoying her humiliation. Emerald's scalded pride burned her cheeks bright pink.

So Lady Emerald was leaving of her own accord and he needn't have come up here risking his employer's displeasure after all? Dougie cursed under his breath.

'It seems Lady Emerald got the wrong photographer,' Lew was telling him disdainfully.

'Next time try Cecil Beaton, sweetheart. He does a lovely soft focus pearls-and-twinset look that's just right for prudish little virgins,' he added unkindly to Emerald.

Glaring at Dougie, Emerald shot past him. She knew she had made a fool of herself and she could imagine how they would laugh about her once she'd left.

'I'll see you out,' Dougie told her, catching up with her outside the door.

'Don't bother,' Emerald snapped.

The dreadful Australian might be keeping a straight face but she just knew that inside he was laughing at her. She hated them both, but she hated the horrid Australian the most.

As for her photograph . . . She'd just have to make do with Cecil Beaton's original photograph of her now, and that had already appeared in *Tatler*. Well, she'd think of some other way of publicly linking her name with the duke's. Perhaps she could manipulate things so that they were photographed together at one of the deb balls? If only her father had still been alive she could have persuaded him to invite the duke to stay at

Osterby. There was no point in even thinking about inviting him to Denham. He was a royal duke, after all, and hardly likely to accept an invitation to a millowner's house.

Chapter Nine

April 1957

Rose hoped that she wasn't going to be late as she hurried through the Saturday crowd thronging the King's Road, on her way to the salon. She felt guilty about putting Janey off instead of having coffee with her as they'd originally planned, but thankfully Janey had understood when she'd explained that she'd had a last-minute telephone call from Josh, wanting her to meet up with him at the salon because he'd arranged a meeting with his photographer friend who was going to bring some shots he had done for *Vogue* so that Rose could look through them and pick some out for the stair wall.

Time seemed to be rushing by so fast; the days longer and the air warmer with spring flowers in bloom. Even her job wasn't making her as miserable as it had done, although she knew she would never be totally happy at Ivor Hammond's, not with the way she was treated.

At least she'd soon be getting a break from work with the Easter holiday coming up.

Easter. Easter meant going home to Denham and, if

she was very lucky and fortune smiled on her, seeing John.

She was still smiling, lost in her own private daydreams, as she opened the door to the salon using the key that Josh had insisted on giving her, and ran quickly up the stairs.

The friend Josh had found was typical of the kind of working-class young men with East End accents and wicked teasing smiles that Josh seemed to know. Despite their bold manners, they treated Rose with deference, instantly ceasing to pepper their conversation with swear words when she was in earshot. A couple of them had plastered the stair wall after Rose's attempts to remove the old paint had resulted in half the rotten plaster coming away too, and had done an excellent job. So too had the painter whom Josh had insisted on hiring, looking horrified when Rose had told him that she planned to paint the high wall herself.

'Over my dead body you are,' Josh had told her. 'I'm not having my designer breaking her neck falling off a pair of ladders, not when she hasn't come up with a design for my salon yet.'

'I've told you, I think we should stick to the black and white theme but spice it up with touches of shocking pink.'

'Shocking pink . . .' Josh had groaned. 'Take a look at me, will you, and then tell me, do I look like a bloke who does poncy shocking pink?'

Rose had giggled, despite her attempt to remain professional.

'There's nothing poncy about shocking pink,' she'd

told him firmly. 'And besides, girls like it. Your stylists could wear black and shocking-pink turbans and head-bands, and uniforms in black with shocking-pink scissors and hairdryers appliquéd onto them. What are you going to call the salon?'

'I haven't decided yet, why?'

'Well, we could appliqué the name onto the uniforms as well.'

'Fine, but what if these juniors and stylists you seem to think I'm going to be taking on aren't all girls? What if some of them are male?'

'Then they can wear black trousers and a black shirt with the appliqués on it, and perhaps a shocking-pink tie.'

She had seen that Josh was impressed but that he didn't want to say so, so she went on lightly, 'You're going to have to come up with a name soon. I really like the way Vidal has called his salon simply Vidal Sassoon.'

'Well, I suppose I could call mine Josh Simons,' Josh had suggested.

From the sound of male voices now coming from the upstairs salon, it appeared that Josh and his photographer friend had already arrived. The salon, its walls also newly plastered, was still a bare empty space, apart from a folding card table and a pair of bentwood chairs so battered that Rose was inclined to believe Josh when he'd claimed to have rescued them from a skip.

She was so much happier working here than she was in the expensive Bond Street premises of her employer, Rose acknowledged. She loved the challenges that working within such a tight budget, and more importantly, creating something useful rather than merely decorative, were giving her. The contrast between working here and in the Bond Street showroom was making her increasingly aware of where her real ambitions lay and how unhappy she was. Given free choice, Rose suspected that she would have willingly switched now from studying interior design for the home to studying interior design for commercial premises, but there were at least two good reasons why she could not do that. The first and most important was that she knew that her aunt was looking to her to take over her business, and the second was that as far as Rose knew, there was no recognised 'apprenticeship' for someone wanting to specialise in commercial premises. It was true that some interior designers took on such projects – Oliver Messel, for instance – but they did not work exclusively in that area.

Working on Josh's salon had opened her eyes to so much that she now wanted to learn more about. Commercial interior design wasn't just about wallpaper, fabrics and the placement of furniture and art; there were important practicalities to be taken into consideration, such as the supplies of electricity and water, and the fact that often premises were leased and the landlord's permission for any changes needed to be obtained, change of use approved, and so much more.

It was necessary for someone to be in charge of the various tradesmen Josh had found to work on the salon, and Rose had seen what an opportunity there was for someone to offer a service that oversaw everything from the initial design right through to its eventual completion. The thought of such a challenge made her feel dizzy with excitement, but she had a duty to her aunt, who had done so much for her and who she loved so much.

Earlier in the week Josh and Vidal had been engaged in an earnest discussion about the benefits of installing wash basins that enabled the clients to tilt their heads backwards into the basin instead of leaning forward.

'Much easier for the juniors when they shampoo, and better for the clients, who won't get their makeup smudged as well,' Vidal had insisted, and Rose had been inclined to agree. 'And don't forget to make sure that you get a decent sound system installed and some cool music playing,' Vidal had added.

Josh had already found 'a friend' who was looking around for four of these basins – at the right price, of course.

'Here she is, Ollie,' she heard Josh announcing as she walked into the salon. 'Come and meet my interior designer. Rose, this is Ollie.'

The photographer was protectively nursing a Rolleiflex camera in one large hand, a bag slung over his shoulder, no doubt containing his tripod and other equipment. He was good-looking, if you liked the unkempt bad-boy type, Rose acknowledged as he reached out to shake her hand. He was also oddly familiar.

'Haven't we met somewhere before?' he asked.

'Yes,' she agreed, 'but I can't remember where.'

'I've got it.' He snapped his fingers. 'I hitched a ride in your taxi a few weeks back. You were with two other girls.'

'Oh, yes, of course,' Rose smiled. 'Ella and Janey. We were on our way to the party where I met you, Josh.'

'London's a small world,' Josh agreed. 'Come and have a look at these photographs Ollie's brought.'

Half an hour later, kneeling back on her heels as she crouched on the floor surrounded by the excellent photographs Oliver had produced for their inspection, Rose watched as Josh threw up his hands in despair.

'No. They won't do. No offence, Ollie, the photos are great, but the hair . . .'

They all looked at the assortment of stiff regulated hairstyles – beehives and backcombed, flicked ends all heavily lacquered.

'What I want to do here in my salon is to follow Vidal's example and work with hair in a new way, one that allows the hair to move and breathe and to look natural.'

When they both looked dubiously at him he told them, 'Look, I'll show you what I mean.' He took hold of Rose's hand, hauling her to her feet. 'It's time for me to cut that hair of yours, Rose. It's been driving me mad with temptation to get to work on it.'

'No, I don't want it cut,' Rose protested, her free hand going protectively to her neat French pleat.

'Why not? What's the point in keeping it long when it's always screwed up in that pleat? I'm going to cut it, and that's that. Come and sit here.'

He meant it, Rose realised weakly. He had been threatening to cut her hair ever since they'd met.

As Josh sat her down and swiftly removed the pins from her hair, letting it fall in a silky black sheet down her back, Rose was vaguely conscious of Ollie setting up his camera, but she was more concerned about her hair. She had never worn it loose, not since Amber's great-grandmother

112

had compared it to Emerald's luxurious head of dark curls and had said how ugly it was, and now automatically she tensed as though half expecting a verbal blow, wanting to cover her hair from sight and yet unable to do so because Josh was brushing it and giving both her and Ollie a running commentary on what he was planning to do.

'Just look at it, it's like finding gold,' he crooned.

'Then why cut it off?' Ollie asked as the shutter clicked and he moved round on the periphery of Rose's vision.

'Because gold is nothing in its raw state. It needs the eye and the hand of an expert to make it into something of beauty, which is exactly what I intend to do with Rose's hair. The length of it makes it so heavy that it takes away all its natural movement and rhythm. It's like trying to play jazz with a traditional orchestra: too much weight and tradition weighing down the magic of the music.'

Rose saw the light from the window flashing on the scissors Josh always carried with him.

'No,' she protested, but it was too late. Long black snakes of hair were covering the floor as she sat at Josh's command with her head bent forward, her panic soothed in some odd way by the almost rhythmic sounds of the scissors and the camera, punctuated by the staccato bursts of questions and explanations exchanged by the two men.

'Look at this,' Josh was saying. 'Look at how I'm freeing up the hair to move and swing. See how it comes to life.'

'Are you sure you aren't cutting it too short?' was Ollie's response as he moved the tripod round the back of her.

Rose wished she was in a traditional salon with a

mirror in front of her so that she could see what was going on, instead of sitting here in this empty room, terrified about the end result of Josh's endeavours.

'*Vogue* are sending my boss to Venice to cover the high-society nightlife there, and she's told me that she's taking me with her.'

Ella didn't try to keep the pride out of her voice as she relayed this information to her stepmother, who had arrived unexpectedly at the Chelsea house. As one of such a large family, Ella rarely got opportunity to have her stepmother to herself, and as the eldest child she always felt it her duty to step back and let the others claim Amber's attention, especially the younger ones.

Now, though, with both Rose and Janey out, she didn't attempt to hide her pleasure at having Amber's undivided attention.

'So you're happy, then, at *Vogue*?' Amber asked her proudly.

'Yes, but I do wish now that I'd taken a course in proper journalism. I'd love to progress to writing articles about important things, not just new lipstick colours,' she told Amber with a rueful look. 'There's so much happening now, and things are changing so much. Women aren't just daughters or wives or mothers any more, they are real people doing real things.'

She looked and sounded so earnest that Amber was determined not to smile. She could imagine, though, what her grandmother, who had single-handedly run her own business and managed her own fortune for years, would have had to say to Ella's naïve declaration.

What Ella had said was true in one sense, though. Modern young women were certainly taking for themselves far greater personal freedoms than her generation had ever had. Most observers put that down to the war and the fact that during those terrible years women had had to become far more independent, for the sake of the country.

'Well, you certainly seem happy,' Amber told Ella. 'I've never known you be such a chatterbox. Working at *Vogue* suits you, Ella. It's bringing you out of yourself.'

Ella smiled, but the real truth was that it was her diet pills that were making her more vivacious, as well as curbing her appetite. She had noticed how, within a short time of taking one, she was more inclined to start chattering. When she'd said as much to Libby, the other girl had told her that it was yet another benefit of Dr Williamson's marvellous little pills that they gave a person so much extra energy. No one had noticed her weight loss yet, but then Ella didn't particularly want them to. She was losing weight to prove that she could to herself. The last thing she wanted was Oliver Charters noticing and thinking totally the wrong thing, like she was doing it because she wanted to impress him. Because she wasn't.

Amber's real purpose in coming to London had been to discuss the final arrangements for Emerald's ball with Beth, and to meet with Mr Melrose on Monday. The lawyer had telephoned her in an excited and agitated state late on Friday evening to tell her that he had had a telephone call from a young man who claimed to be the lost heir to the dukedom. This young man was meeting with Mr Melrose on Monday and he had asked Amber if she would be kind enough to be there.

'But I know nothing of Robert's Australian family,' she had protested.

However, the lawyer had begged her to attend, saying that he would appreciate her views on the young man and adding that he felt that if he was the duke then it would ease his passage in society if he could have some support from her as Robert's widow.

Since Jay wasn't going to be at home, having agreed to go and look at a combine harvester the estate manager wanted him to buy, Amber had decided that she might as well spend the weekend in London catching up with her family, and checking that Emerald was not abusing her friend Beth's somewhat indolent chaperonage. Beth was a wonderfully kind godmother to Emerald but Amber was sure she let her get away with murder.

Her first port of call on her arrival in London had been Eaton Square, where she had left her case and learned from the housekeeper that Beth and the girls were out, so she had then taken a cab to Chelsea, to find that only her eldest stepdaughter was at home.

'And Janey and Rose are well and happy?' Amber asked with concern.

'Yes, I think so,' Ella answered her truthfully. 'Janey is still convinced that Mary Quant is going to beg her to design for her, the minute she leaves St Martins, and Rose already has her own personal interior design commission.'

She explained to Amber what Rose was doing, and Amber was relieved that her niece was settling down so well. She always worried more about Rose than the others. All she wanted for the children was that they should be loved and love in return, and know the happiness that she knew with Jay. Young people, though, needed to spread their wings; to learn about life and to follow their dreams. Amber knew that too.

'So when do you leave for Venice?' she asked Ella.

'Early next week. We'll be travelling with the fashion editor and some models, as she'll be doing a feature on travel and fashion, and fashion and Venice, so we'll be going on the Orient-Express. I'm so excited about that.'

Amber laughed. 'But you've travelled on it before, when Daddy and I took you all to Venice several years ago.'

'Yes, I know but that was different. I didn't realise then how lucky I was. Venice was just a place with lots of canals and a funny smell, where you and Daddy were going to talk to people about silk.'

She *was* excited about the coming trip, Ella acknowledged later after her stepmother had left to do some shopping. Although officially she was travelling to Venice in her capacity as the features editor's assistant, she had managed to persuade the travel editor to let her do a 'trial' piece on the city from a potential visitor's point of view. Determined to do a good job and prove that she could write a stimulating article, Ella had been reading up on the history of the city. She knew that the travel editor would expect her to write a piece that focused on the glamorous society side of Venice life, mentioning its elegant hotels and the private palazzos, where smart exclusive parties were held, including the kind of detail that would appeal to *Vogue* readers. However, privately Ella would have liked to write something more challenging than a tame piece about rich people and expensive clothes. The city had a fascinating history, and she was hoping that whilst she was there she would come across something that would enable her to give her article a true depth. Ella's favourite newspaper was the *Manchester Guardian*, and secretly she longed to write the kind of gritty no-holds-barred articles she read in its pages, articles that spoke about hardship and oppression, and not expensive frocks and the right shade of lipstick. Ella imagined that the female reporters who worked on the paper would look and speak rather like the actress Katharine Hepburn, and in her daydreams she imagined herself working in a busy newsroom, filing copy of stories of immense social importance.

She knew that everyone at *Vogue* would laugh at her if they realised what she really longed for, but she wasn't going to give up her dreams. One day she would write deep meaningful articles that would uncover social injustice and change people's lives. One day.

Chapter Ten

The back of Rose's neck was cold and bare and she felt oddly light-headed, as well as unable not to give in to the temptation to turn her head to sneak a look at her reflection in the shop windows she was walking past. The wind caught her hair, ruffling it in much the same way that Josh had done after he had cut it.

He had told her that on Monday he intended to shampoo it and go over it again.

'I'd like to put a colour rinse on it as well, something to bring out the shine. A dark plum would look fantastic.'

Rose blenched a little now at the memory, and yet a smile was tugging at her lips as well. She felt so free and so . . . so different, tossing her hair in hesitant pride instead of ducking it down when she saw people turning their heads to look at her.

'Hey, cool chick, I dig the hair,' one of a pair of young Teddy boy rockers called out to her as they walked past her in the opposite direction.

She 'dug the hair' herself, Rose admitted, although it had been a huge shock at first to see what Josh had done.

He had cut her hair so short at the back that the whole

length of her slender neck was exposed right from the nape. He had also fashioned it somehow so that it possessed an unfamiliar volume and movement, the sides longer than the back, caressing her jaw line in delicate little flicks. He had cut her a fringe too, and yet her new hairstyle had produced unexpected high cheekbones, now delicately flushed with happy colour.

She was on her way home, having left Josh and Ollie together, Ollie so eager to get back to his studio to develop the photographs he had taken of Josh in action that he had almost been ready to ignore the commission he had for the afternoon until Josh had reminded him that he owed him 'ten quid'.

Janey would adore her new hairstyle, Rose knew, but she wasn't so sure what Ella would think.

A wolf whistle from a grocer's boy cycling past from the shop further down the road made Rose laugh at his cheek, as she enjoyed the unexpected light-heartedness her new image gave her.

Well, he had done it now, Dougie acknowledged, unable to concentrate on what he should be doing, which was checking through Lew's diary for the forthcoming week. He'd telephoned the lawyer bloke and on Monday he had an appointment to see him so that Mr Melrose could go through things with him and check him out.

He hadn't said anything about having met Emerald, though, not even when Mr Melrose had told him that he proposed to invite the late duke's wife to attend their meeting, as he felt that Dougie would need a 'sponsor' to help him adapt to society and his new role within it

120

if it did turn out to be that he was indeed the heir. He'd cross that bridge as and when he came to it.

'I'm so sorry,' Emerald gasped, feigning an embarrassed self-consciousness she wasn't feeling at all as her deliberately planned 'accidental' bumping into the Duke of Kent had him turning towards her, allowing her to continue with her plan by uttering a mortified, 'Oh, Your Royal Highness.'

'It's all right. Don't worry.' The duke's smile was polite rather than warm, and he was already turning away from her but Emerald wasn't so easily put off. Ever since she had been formally and very briefly presented to him and to his mother, Princess Marina, earlier in the evening, she had been watching him and waiting for her chance to bring herself properly to his attention. A débutante party featuring an evening of chamber music would not normally have been something she would have wanted to attend, but that had been before she had learned that the duke was going to be one of the guests.

Emerald had had to be patient to make her move, waiting until the music was over, and the duke had moved to a quieter corner of the large formal reception room by one of the balconies. She certainly wasn't going to let her prey escape her.

Speedily moving so that she was standing in front of him, she affected to breathe in the evening air coming through the open balcony doors, whilst telling him, 'I seem to be dreadfully clumsy whenever I'm at one of these events. I suppose that's because I'd rather be in the country.' She gave a theatrical sigh. 'Do you like the country, Sir?'

'Yes, I do.' The duke's voice was slightly warmer now, and he was looking properly at her. Emerald felt a fierce surge of triumph. He couldn't possibly be anything other than entranced by her. She had taken extra special care over her appearance. She was wearing her hair up in a deliberately semi-regal style (so perfect for a family tiara, she had thought happily to herself earlier). Her dress of pale lilac silk emphasised her small waist, whilst its matching bolero provided just the right note of modesty. The upturned style of its collar showed off the slender length of her neck and drew the eye down to the discreetly concealed curves of her breasts. Her nails were varnished pale pink to match her lipstick. Emerald knew that she outshone every other girl in the room.

'It's very generous of people to invite me to so many lovely parties,' Emerald continued with fake modesty. 'But I lost my father when I was very young and it makes me feel sad when I see other girls with their fathers.'

'Yes, I can understand that,' the duke agreed. Now she had touched his emotions, Emerald knew, because he too had lost his father at a young age.

'I'm dreading my ball,' Emerald confided. 'It will be held at home at Lenchester House in Eaton Square, of course, just as my father would have wanted, but I won't be able to enjoy it properly without him there.'

There, she had told him now where he could find her. There was only one more thing she needed to do.

'I've always admired Her Royal Highness Princess

Marina. She's so elegant and gracious. I remember my father saying that. I'd love to meet her properly.'

Emerald managed to make her voice sound wistful and almost childlike. How could the duke refuse her? He couldn't, of course.

'Then please do allow me to introduce you.'

Already he was crooking his arm and politely waiting for her to place her hand on it.

'Oh, would you?' Emerald was the epitome of sparkling delight. Out of the corner of her eye she registered the resentment in Gwendolyn's expression, along with the astonishment and envy on the faces of her fellow debs as the duke led her across the floor to where his mother was standing talking with some of the chaperones. But of course her attention wasn't on her rivals but on the duke. The look in her own eyes was carefully designed to show him her pleasure in his company, just as her manner was planned to reveal her as sweetly innocent and slightly helpless, whilst at the same time extremely well born; things Emerald was sure he was bound to find attractive in a prospective wife. In forcing a one-to-one conversation on him she had achieved for herself something that even the most determined of débutante mothers had failed to do, and she had every reason to feel very pleased with herself indeed, Emerald decided as they reached the duke's mother and her small entourage.

Princess Marina was elegant, Emerald admitted, elegant and regal, and quite definitely coolly distant with Emerald as she was presented to her. Without a single word being said or a look given, Emerald knew that the duke's mother was well aware that Emerald had manipulated the duke into presenting Emerald to her, and that her behaviour had not gone down well. Princess Marina would, though, be forced to change her tune once Emerald was the new duchess, she thought smugly.

Afterwards when she had rejoined Gwendolyn and Lydia and her godmother, Emerald entertained herself by mentally rehearsing her married name: Her Royal Highness, The Duchess of Kent.

Edward and Emerald. How fortunate that they shared the same initial, almost as though it had always been meant to be, she sighed happily as Gwendolyn prattled on about tennis.

The duke was in the Royal Scots Greys, and now Emerald was intent on finding out discreetly who amongst the other debs might have a male relative with the Greys so that she could make a friend of her and suggest that some of the young officers were invited to one of the deb 'teas'. It was, after all, customary for young officers from the household regiments to attend the season's social events.

Yes, Emerald decided, all in all it had been a most successful evening.

Ollie straightened up, stretching his back in the cramped confines of his small darkroom as he looked at the prints he had just developed with growing excitement. It had still been light when he had returned from the birthday party he had been summoned to attend and capture with his camera by one of the Kray twins' stalwarts, not so much an enforcer, this one, as a fixer, although he still knew how to handle himself. Ollie had remembered sparring with him in the gym when he had been in training. Heavily built, with a typical ex-boxer's broken nose, he had delivered the twins 'request' in an affable enough manner but Ollie had known better than to suggest that he had another engagement for that afternoon.

In the event the party had been a chance for him to mix with a crowd of once familiar faces, including that of his younger cousin, Willie, who had ignored his advice and who had been strutting around obviously considering himself very much a part of the twins' 'task force'.

It wasn't the Kray brothers or the photographs he had taken of their distant cousin's seventieth birthday party that had been responsible for him working in his darkroom until the early hours of the morning, though.

He looked at the images again, a wide grin of delight creasing his face. There was no doubt about it, he was good, and one day – soon – he would be the best. The photographs he had taken of Josh cutting Rose's hair, snapping frantically as he tried to catch each movement, were a bloody work of art, even though he said so himself. If he had any sense about him he'd charge Josh a fortune for them and no mistake, 'cos they would pull in the chicks wanting their own hair cut like Rose's like no one's business. There was no point in thinking of what he could charge Josh, though. His friend was as skint as he was himself, living virtually hand to mouth, hoping to keep going in the precarious world of self-employment in which they were both taking their first faltering steps.

On the other hand, if he could get *Vogue* interested . . . Not that the posh commissioning editors who worked there were likely to welcome him acting off his own bat. They had their own ideas about the images they wanted and they were quick to reject his ideas if they conflicted. Still, it was worth a try, seeing as he would be going to Venice with the art director, the fashion editor and the models who had been hired for the feature he had been commissioned to photograph on 'The Fabled Train Journey to Venice on the Orient-Express', as well as in Venice itself.

It was the largest commission he had received from *Vogue*, and it would be worth toeing the line just to get the money. The trouble was that once he got behind his camera he almost always had trouble reminding himself of the need to earn money and instead became totally lost in his own imagination.

God, but he rated what he had done with Rose and Josh. Sometimes he could hardly believe himself what a genius he actually was.

He couldn't wait for Josh to see what he had done. He looked at his watch, frowning in disbelief and shaking his wrist when he saw that the time was four o'clock, thinking that the watch must have stopped during the afternoon, and then realising that it had not and that it actually was four o'clock in the morning.

He was tired and hungry – very hungry. Stifling a yawn, he padded barefoot across to open the door.

The place he was renting was the first he had had all to himself. He had seized on it because the single large room that, along with a long narrow bathroom, comprised the flat, had access to the roof space, and he had been able to persuade the landlord to let him turn part of it into a darkroom.

126

When he could afford it he planned to move into somewhere where he could have a proper studio, but that was still just a pipe dream at the moment.

In his living quarters, he opened the food safe and removed several rashers of bacon, dropping them into the blackened frying pan, which he then put on top of his single-ring gas cooker, turning the heat up high and adding a dollop of lard. Whilst the bacon sizzled and spat noisily, depositing fat on the double row of tiles stuck haphazardly onto the bright yellow painted wall behind the cooker, Ollie removed an already started loaf from the breadbin on the tin dresser that held his meagre supply of china and kitchen utensils. The dresser was a gift from his mother, who had nearly cried when she saw what her son had given up his room in her lovely immaculate terraced house to live in, denouncing the flat as 'a hovel'.

Cutting himself a couple of thick slices, Ollie buttered them generously and then removed the rashers of bacon from the frying pan, flattening them firmly between the thick wedges of bread.

By the time he took his first bite he was practically drooling with hungry anticipation. A bacon butty, there was nothing better. Except the sweet taste of success. It was something he hoped would become a regular event for him now.

Chapter Eleven

They were travelling from the *Vogue* office to pick up the boat train to Paris, where they would transfer to the Orient-Express, and Ella had naturally been up early, checking her small case over and over again in nervous anticipation. This trip meant so much to her – the opportunity to be noticed, to be given a senior assignment. She had everything crossed it would all work out as well as she hoped.

She didn't have to be at *Vogue*'s offices until ten, but she was too anxious to sleep, sitting instead in the kitchen in her dressing gown, her feet tucked into her slippers whilst she sipped a cup of tea. The thought of eating made her feel even more nauseous.

She could hear Janey and Rose coming down the stairs. Soon it would be time for her to leave. She stood up, carrying her now empty cup over to the sink as Janey burst into the kitchen, complaining about the cold floor.

From the minute she had seen Rose's new hairstyle on Saturday, Janey had not stopped demanding that Rose tell Josh that she wanted her own hair cutting in exactly the same style, and she was still doing so now, only breaking off to say to Ella enviously, 'Lucky you, going to Venice, where the sun will be shining and it will be warm.'

'I shall be working, not sunbathing,' Ella pointed out, checking her watch. Yes, it was definitely time for her to leave, but first she must make one last check of her handbag, just to make sure that she really hadn't forgotten anything.

Seated on the opposite side of the heavy old-fashioned mahogany partners' desk in Mr Melrose's office, Dougie tried hard not to stare too obviously at Emerald's mother.

Physically she presented no surprises to him. He had not worked for Lew for several months without learning something, and it hadn't taken him much effort to source some reasonably recent newspaper photographs of Amber. If he had been asked to describe her in one word, that word would have been 'classy'. From the top of her elegantly styled chignon to the toes of her navy-blue leather shoes, Amber almost glowed with a special patina of good looks, good manners and a gentleness that spoke of the kindness that Dougie was sure he could see in her eyes.

It was that softness and the kindness allied to it that had surprised him. It hadn't been obvious from the press photographs he had seen, and it had taken him off guard. All the more so because Emerald was her daughter. How could two women so closely related be so very different?

Amber eyed the young Australian seated opposite her

sympathetically. She had warmed to him instantly, feeling rather sorry for him as he explained the chain of events that had led to him being orphaned. It had been interesting to learn about his life in Australia. He was a wealthy young man in his own right, and from one or two comments he had let drop, it had been plain that he had been brought up to look unfavourably on the British upper class, with its archaic practices.

'I'll admit that when I first got your letters I didn't altogether like the thought of me being this duke bloke,' he had told them.

So what had made him change his mind, Amber wondered. He had told them that he worked for a society photographer and the young Australian had admitted himself that he often felt ill at ease amongst the upper-class set. His admission had increased Amber's sympathy for him, reminding her of how out of place she herself had sometimes felt as a young woman growing up amid wealth but not aristocracy. Despite his rough edges, though, Dougie had a natural pride in himself that Amber admired, even whilst she acknowledged that if he did prove to be the duke he would need a lot of help getting used to his new role.

He would, she felt, bring a freshness to the dukedom, like a clean gust of air blowing into a dusty room that had been closed up for too long. Robert would have liked and approved of him, she thought, considering her late husband. Jay would like him too. They would be able to talk together about farming matters. As those thoughts formed, Amber knew that she had already accepted him as part of her extended family, and equally that she already felt a maternal sense of protectiveness towards him.

He was obviously used to standing up for himself and living his own life, but he would be vulnerable in his new role, and the sharks that would swim close to him would not always be easily recognisable. He would need support, and who better to provide that, Amber decided, than the family he already had.

'Well, there are several things that need to be confirmed before a formal announcement can be made,' Mr Melrose was saying, 'but . . .'

He looked at Amber, who smiled back at him before turning to Dougie to say warmly, 'I don't quite know whether to congratulate you or commiserate with you, Dougie. Or should I say, Your Grace?' she added, teasing him gently.

Dougie shook his head, half bemused and half embarrassed.

'You'll want to see the Eaton Square house, I expect, and Osterby, of course,' Amber continued. 'I have a confession to make with regard to the London house. I'm afraid that I've allowed my daughter to move into it for the duration of her season and that her coming-out ball is to be held there.'

'Yes, I know,' Dougie began, and then stopped as both Mr Melrose and Amber looked curiously at him. 'That is to say, I remember reading about it,' he amended, 'and of course I'm delighted. That is, I mean that I don't . . . well, there's no problem at all with your plans, so far as I'm concerned.'

'That is very generous of you,' Amber told him. 'I know

131

you'll have made your own friends here in London but I'd like to introduce you to the rest of the family soon, if you think you could bear it. My stepdaughters and my niece live here in London, in Chelsea, and I know they would love to meet you. Jay, my husband, spends most of his time at Denham, our estate in Macclesfield, and our twin daughters are still at school. They'll be home for Easter in a few days, though, and if you haven't made any other arrangements it would be so nice if you would join us at Denham.'

Amber had caught Dougie off guard. He hadn't made any plans for Easter, and in many ways he would be very happy to accept her invitation. As he was beginning to realise, there was going to be a lot more to being a duke than being called Your Grace. However, whilst Amber seemed ready to welcome him into the family, Dougie couldn't see Emerald being equally welcoming. She wasn't going to be at all pleased when she learned that they were related.

Before he could say anything Mr Melrose was announcing with evident relief, 'Amber, my dear, that is an excellent suggestion and typically generous of you.'

It was, Dougie admitted. After all, she owed him nothing, not really.

'You must give me your address and your telephone number,' Amber was saying, 'and I shall give you ours so that we can make arrangements for your visit.'

It was too late to back out now; it would be too rude, Dougie realised.

Outside in the thin April sunshine he mounted his motorbike, kick starting it. He had followed his employer's

132

example and bought himself the sturdy but sleek chrome machine, and had soon learned to weave it in and out of the busy London traffic at high speed.

'Shit!' Ollie cursed as he stared in bleary-eyed disbelief at the alarm clock, before sinking back against his pillow. How the hell had he managed to oversleep so badly?

It was almost midday. He was due at *Vogue*'s offices at noon for a briefing, before leaving for Venice with a bunch of models, *Vogue*'s fashion editor, makeup artists, staffers, and no doubt trunks full of clothes. He ran his hand over his stubbly jaw. His eyes felt as though someone had throw a handful of grit in them and his mouth felt like the bottom of a birdcage.

His brain was refusing to wake up, creaking into action like an asthmatic old car, wheezing and protesting at every demand made on its clapped-out engine. Clapped out – that was exactly how he felt. No way was he going to make *Vogue*'s office for half-past twelve, never mind twelve. He sat up in bed, dropping his head into his hands and squeezing his eyes tightly closed against the thudding pain in his head.

He really should not have drunk that suspect bottle of wine last night after his bacon sandwich. He had been thirsty, though, and in the mood to celebrate, and the wine had been there.

The thin ray of reluctant sunshine edging its way past the faded curtains made him wince, as it lanced his aching eyes and then dappled his naked torso honey gold. His olive-toned skin tanned easily, and as soon as the weather warmed up he'd be off down to Brighton to get himself a tan and check out the girls in their swimsuits.

Quarter to one, gone that now. Hell. *Vogue*'s fashion editor would have his guts for garters, and his balls off as well. No way was he going to make the appointment. But he could still make the boat train, if he went direct to the station.

His earlier malaise forgotten, he was galvanised into action, getting out of bed to reach for the jeans he had left lying on the floor, and pulling on a sweater before heading barefoot for the door and the public telephone in the hallway to the flats. He'd ring *Vogue* and tell them that due to unforeseen circumstances he'd meet up with them on the platform.

He grinned to himself before starting to whistle under his breath. It would be OK. It always was for Oliver Charters.

Chapter Twelve

Ella grimaced beneath the weight of the bags her boss had given her to carry. She had travelled from the office to the station in a taxi with the three models and the makeup artist, and had somehow or other ended up having to help the makeup artist carry her things as well as her own and her boss's.

The platform was a chaotic mix of travellers and those who had come to see them off, heads turning to stare at the models in their 'departure outfits', ready to be photographed embarking onto the train, providing the photographer ever actually turned up.

The fashion editor had given vent to her feelings about his absence with a string of profanities that had turned the air in the offices as blue as her blood, and her assistants had been dispatched to try to drum up a stand-in.

Now that they were on the platform Ella looked round anxiously for her own boss, exhaling faintly with relief when she saw her. Their brief was to source information for an article about the way the social scene in Venice was changing, as the old guard of fashionable visitors, such as Coco Chanel and her peers, gave way to the likes of

Princess Grace of Monaco and Greek shipping millionaires, as well as the perennial British upper classes, continental aristocrats and pretty society girls.

Ella was travelling in sensible clothes, wearing a tweed coat over her plain jumper and skirt, but in deference to the specialness of the occasion she had crammed a small hat with a pretty veil down on top of her now windblown curls. She was satisfyingly aware for the first time that only this week, when she lay down in bed, she could actually feel her ribs. Losing weight had become an exciting challenge now that she knew how it was done. She'd lost over a stone and she could dare herself to lose as many pounds as she wished.

To Ella's relief, at the same time as she spied the features editor, a porter finally arrived to relieve her of her case, leaving her free to hurry to her boss's side, keeping a firm grip on her handbag and the portable typewriter which she'd been told must never leave her possession.

Ollie surveyed the seething mêlée on the platform with a grimace. He hated *Vogue* shoots, but there were certain benefits, like the money and a chance to flirt with the models, and, if he was lucky and they were willing, do more than merely flirt.

He hadn't had time to shave, merely managing a quick shower from which his overlong hair was still slightly damp, like the white T-shirt he had pulled on without bothering to dry himself properly, before stepping back into his jeans.

His well-worn leather jacket would keep the spring wind at bay, and he had managed to find clean underwear, socks and a T-shirt to throw into his camera bag before gathering up all his equipment and hot-footing it to the station.

The fashion editor greeted him with a baleful look and a threat never to employ him again, but he shrugged off her anger with a mocking smile, confident that once she saw his photographs she would forget all about his lateness.

He studied the models with an experienced assessing eye – not so much as models, more as potential bed mates. He rather thought he favoured the redhead. She'd got that look about her that suggested she'd know all the right moves. As he turned away his attention was caught by the sight of Ella making her way towards her boss, and his smile widened.

They'd had a couple of run-ins at the office since the night he'd seen her in the taxi and he'd begun to enjoy tormenting her, all the more so because she never quite managed to conceal her dislike of him.

Shouldering his bag, he made his way purposefully towards her, blocking off her access to her boss by placing himself in front of her

'Afternoon, princess.'

Oh, no, the photographer was Oliver Charters! Ella's heart sank. She detested the cocky East Ender. He was arrogant and full of himself when he had no right to be, acting as though he was something special, ignoring the rules that other people – people like her – automatically obeyed, causing mayhem whenever he came into the office, flirting with the models, and generally acting as though the world revolved around him.

As for that ridiculous name he had given her . . . Her face started to burn in anger.

'I have told you before not to call me that,' she reminded him through gritted teeth.

'It suits you,' Ollie told her unrepentantly.

A gap appeared to one side of him and, seizing her chance to escape, Ella quickly sidestepped him, the sound of his mocking laughter following her as she finally managed to reach her boss.

If she'd known that he was going to be the photographer she would have refused to come, Ella told herself, following her boss onto the train.

The Fashion Department had a carriage to themselves to accommodate the models, the makeup artist and the trunk full of clothes, along with Ollie and the fashion editor herself, whilst Ella and the other junior members of staff were sharing a carriage with other travellers. Ella had ended up scrunched up in her seat, penned in by a hugely fat businessman next to her. Still, at least she was away from that obnoxious photographer.

As the English countryside flashed by, Ella tried to enjoy the scenery but couldn't help thinking about Oliver Charters. That wretched man was like a constant irritant, rubbing her nerves raw and making her feel on edge. Her head ached and she was finding it hard to sit still, even though she had barely slept, as angry thoughts about him flew round inside her head.

* * *

138

Emerald frowned irritably. The only reason she had attended this dull luncheon party was because she had heard that the duke was coming, and now he obviously wasn't.

'Well, it looks like you've made a conquest,' one of the other girls murmured in Emerald's ear, indicating who she meant. Lavinia Halstead was already as good as engaged to her second cousin in a match that had been encouraged by their parents almost from the moment of their births, and because of that she had the air of someone who was above all the anxiety of finding a suitable beau before the end of the season.

The young man in question was indeed staring at Emerald in a very admiring way. He was also, she recognised, extremely good-looking, with a head of thick black curls and intense dark eyes. She hadn't seen him before. She would certainly have remembered him if she had. He was wearing a well-cut lounge suit, and the light from the chandeliers glinted on the heavy gold ring he was wearing on his right hand. She made a small *moue* of distaste. It was very off for men to wear jewellery, unless, of course, that jewellery was a symbol of status – a ducal ring, for instance, bearing a family crest. Still, he was awfully good-looking. And he was making no attempt to conceal his interest in her, watching her with almost feverish intensity.

'Who is he, do you know?' she asked Lavinia casually.

'Oh, yes, he was at school with my brother.'

The Halsteads were a devout Catholic family, whose sons were always schooled at a Jesuit-run Catholic boarding school in Cumbria.

'He doesn't look English,' Emerald stated, giving him another assessing glance. That olive-toned skin combined with those thick dark curls could never belong to anyone English, nor could that hotly demanding and passionate look he was giving. It was rather delicious to have such a good-looking boy gazing at her with such obvious out-of-control longing, rather like being bathed in the heat of Mediterranean sunshine.

'No, Alessandro is Laurantese.'

'Laurantese? What on earth does that mean?' Emerald demanded suspiciously, half suspecting that Lavinia was deliberately teasing her.

'It means that Alessandro is from Lauranto,' Lavinia informed her in a reproving, almost schoolmistress-like voice. 'Lauranto is a small principality, like Monaco or Liechtenstein, on the coast between Italy and France, the Côte d'Azur. In fact, Alessandro isn't merely from Lauranto, his family actually rule it – Alessandro is the Crown Prince.'

Emerald looked again at her admirer. A crown prince!

Whilst Lavinia had been talking, Gwendolyn, in that typically sneaky way of hers, had managed to detach herself from the girl she had been with to come over and listen in on their conversation.

'Foreign princes aren't proper princes,' she announced disparagingly. 'Not like our own royal family.'

'Of course they are proper princes,' Emerald told her sharply. 'How can they not be? A prince is a prince, after all.'

'Now that he's seen me talking to you, he's bound to expect me to introduce him to you,' Lavinia told Emerald.

'I should warn you that he is fearfully, well, foreign, if you know what I mean, and very intense. He only joined Michael's school in their last year. He'd been educated privately at home before that. His mother is terrified that something might happen to him, he being her only child. His father was killed in a hunting accident just after he was born and, according to what Alessandro has told Michael, his mother thinks that his father's death might not have been an accident and that it could have been part of a plot by Mussolini to annex Lauranto. His mother can't wait for him to get married and start producing lots of heirs and spares to fill the royal nurseries.'

Lyddy Munroe had joined then now, and after Lavinia had excused herself to go and rejoin her mother, who was signalling to her, Lyddy turned to Emerald and said excitedly, 'Imagine marrying a prince, and having your very own country, just like Grace Kelly marrying Prince Rainier.'

'You'd never catch me marrying a foreigner,' Gwendolyn told them sniffily.

'No, I dare say you wouldn't,' Emerald agreed unkindly. 'After all, you'd have to find one willing to marry you first.'

Gwendolyn's face went beetroot red whilst Lyddy looked uncomfortable and confused.

Gwendolyn had had it coming to her, Emerald thought with satisfaction. She never lost a chance to needle her about her boast that she would marry a title better than her mother's, and she was just waiting for her to fail so that she could crow over her. But she wasn't going to fail, Emerald assured herself, darting a teasing look in the prince's direction before turning her back on him. Gwendolyn was right about one thing: marrying a foreign prince did not have the same cachet as marrying a member of one's own royal family. However, there was no harm in her holding her new admirer in reserve, and using him to make the Duke of Kent jealous.

'The Duke of Kent isn't here then?'

The gloating note in Gwendolyn's voice made Emerald wonder angrily if the other girl had somehow read her mind.

'Are you really going to marry him, Emerald?' Lyddy asked in awe.

'I never said that I was going to marry the Duke of Kent. *You* were the one who mentioned his name,' Emerald answered sharply.

'She's saying that because she's afraid now that he won't want to marry her,' Gwendolyn told Lyddy with a smirk.

'No I am not,' Emerald snapped, temper flashing in her eyes.

'But you haven't seen him since we went to that party, have you?'

'No one's seen him. He hasn't been in London,' Emerald pointed out curtly.

It was true that she had expected to have seen the duke again by now, although she would die rather than admit that to Gwendolyn and Lydia. He had her address, after all, and he knew that she was doing the season. But then he was a royal duke, and no doubt had all manner of formal appearances to make at various events, which had obviously kept him out of London. When he did return she would undoubtedly discover that he had been desperate to get in touch with her, and he would probably bombard her with invitations as well as declarations of love.

She shook her head, refusing the offer from a passing waiter of another cup of coffee. It wasn't so very long ago that Britain had still been living with food rationing and, despite her narrow waist and slender size, Emerald loved her food. She thought longingly of the rare occasions when she'd eaten at the Ritz and the Savoy, and of the delicious pastries she'd enjoyed in Paris. It provided her with a great deal of amusement that Gwendolyn, who was chubby, with thick ankles, had been forced to endure the humiliation of thin soup and no bread whilst they had been at finishing school in an unsuccessful attempt to get her weight down.

Laughing at Gwendolyn's expense lifted Emerald's spirits no end.

The Kents were bound to accept their invitation to her ball. After all, her late father had been held in high regard, and he and her mother had been very prominent socially, being invited everywhere and knowing everyone there was to know, according to Aunt Beth. And once they were there, the duke was bound to ask her to dance, and once he had . . .

People were starting to leave, mothers and chaperones anxiously shepherding débutantes towards the exit, whilst doing swift and complicated mental arithmetic as to the likelihood of their managing to fit in the day's quota of events. Lunches were followed by afternoon teas, which were followed by cocktails, and formal dinners, evening parties, shows and, if a girl was lucky enough to have a male escort, perhaps even an outing to a nightclub.

Aunt Beth had broken away from her table of fellow chaperones and was summoning her now.

Emerald finished her glass of too sweet rosé wine and stood up to leave.

'No, please, you can't go until I have made myself known to you, and told you how much I admire you. And how very beautiful you are. The most beautiful girl in the world. A vision . . . an angel of loveliness.'

Emerald thought about looking indifferent and even haughty, but the look of shocked disapproval on Gwendolyn's face caused her instead to smile graciously at her admirer knowing it would only add to Gwendolyn's disapproval.

'A man cannot introduce himself to an unattached girl. It is not correct protocol,' she teased him, but with a warning in her voice that told him that she was the kind of girl who expected his sex – even members of it who were crown princes – to treat her with full respect.

But the Crown Prince shook his head, giving her a look of burning intensity, as he told her passionately, 'Please do not send me away. I shall be desolate if you do. My heart and my life are yours to command. Between us there can be no need for protocol. We are, I think, twin souls, and destined to meet. I feel it here, deep inside me.' Alessandro thumped his chest with his fist, his gaze pleading for her to listen to him.

Emerald was amused. His behaviour was dreadfully theatrical and foreign, it was true, but it was also true that he was extraordinarily good-looking, and a crown prince. Being royal allowed a person to behave differently.

He was certainly far better-looking than the Duke of Kent: tall and broad-shouldered, with that smouldering gaze that made her want to laugh and yet, at the same time, sent a delicious little sensation of excitement tingling down her spine. Somehow it was much easier to imagine Alessandro clasping her to his chest and covering her face with passionate kisses, just like the hero out of a film, than it was to imagine the Duke of Kent doing the same thing. His passion, whilst quite ridiculous, was deliciously flattering, and all the more enjoyable because Gwendolyn so obviously disapproved of it – jealous, of course. After all, no handsome crown prince was ever going to fall at her feet declaring undying passion for her, was he?

'We are strangers. You don't even know my name.'

'I know your heart. It is pure and good and it has captured my own heart. You are so very beautiful,' he breathed ardently.

'Do come along, you two.'

Aunt Beth was hovering now, whilst Gwendolyn's thin pursed lips showed her increasing irritation.

On the point of turning away, Emerald saw a new opportunity to get at Gwendolyn.

Touching her aunt's arm, she told her with faked innocence and naïvety, 'Aunt Beth, His Highness, Crown Prince Alessandro says that he is desolate that there is no one to introduce us. I am sure you must have met his mother at some time since she is related to one of the Queen's ladies in waiting.'

As Emerald had known they would be, the magically potent words, 'His Highness' and 'the Queen' were enough to have her godmother looking approvingly at Alessandro.

'It is true,' he agreed, proving to be rather more savvy than Emerald had expected. 'I am desolate that my mama is not here to make the necessary introductions, but sadly my mother's cousin is not well and Mama wishes to keep her company, so I have to come here without her.'

'Alessandro is the Crown Prince of the Principality of Lauranto, on the Côte d'Azur,' Emerald further explained. 'I dare say that you must have visited there, Aunt Beth.'

'Well, yes. I am sure that we must.'

'I too am sure that this must be so,' Alessandro was agreeing. He was proving to be an able henchman, Emerald decided approvingly.

'So you see,' he told Emerald, turning back to her, 'we are as good as known to one another already, and I beg that you will allow me to call on you.'

'Not until my godmother has given her permission,' Emerald stopped him demurely.

Her godmother bestowed an approving smile on her and, in no time at all, Alessandro had been given permission to call at Eaton Square whilst in turn he had given Aunt Beth his temporary address at the Savoy Hotel, where he was staying with his mother.

They had, Alessandro told them, come to London not only to see his mother's cousin but so that he could attend the coming-out ball of the sister of one of his school friends.

He meant Lavinia, Emerald guessed, making a mental

note to ensure that Lavinia's was one of the balls she attended. It would do no harm for a certain Duke of Kent to see her being admired by the dashing Alessandro.

'How could you encourage that . . . that foreigner like that?' Gwendolyn hissed once they were outside. 'My mother is right about you: you might have a title but you do not have any real breeding.'

Emerald stopped dead in the street, swinging round to confront the other girl, her face tight with anger.

'Don't you ever, ever say that to me again! I am the daughter of a duke,' she reminded Gwendolyn, adding cruelly, 'and you are the one who lacks breeding. You are the daughter of a nobody, a man who can't even father an heir on his wife; just as I told you in Paris, a man who cannot keep his hands to himself or his prick in his pants – and if you don't believe me, ask your mother. Everyone knows that your father has fucked more tarts than any other man in society.'

Gwendolyn had begun to whimper in shock, trying to cover her ears to protect herself from the coarseness of Emerald's language as much as the truths she didn't want to hear.

'A girl of my rank and wealth can be neither vulgar nor common; she can only be delightfully eccentric and perhaps a little outrageous. Compared with me you are nothing. When I am married you will still be nothing. You will be nothing all your life, poor, fat, dull Gwennie, and you know it, and that is why you are so jealous of me. I will marry well and live the kind of life you can only dream of whilst you'll end up at home darning socks and being downtrodden. You're jealous because men admire me and want me, you're jealous because Alessandro has fallen in love with me. Well, you are right to envy me because no man will ever fall in love with *you*.'

Suddenly realising that her niece and her goddaughter had fallen behind, Beth turned round to urge them to catch up.

Whilst Gwendolyn struggled to control her shocked distress, Emerald pushed past her to catch up with her godmother, a triumphant smile playing on her lips.

Chapter Thirteen

The Channel had been rough, and the fashion editor's assistant, with whom Ella had shared a cramped cabin, had been up all night being sick, and was still looking green when they all boarded the train in Calais.

The models were changing into the outfits in which they would be photographed standing outside the Orient-Express before it left Paris. The stop was only a brief one and, because of the fashion editor's assistant's sickness, Ella had been pressed into service as her stand-in, and sent scrurrying on various errands at the fashion editor's behest.

Normally Ella wouldn't have minded, but it stung her pride to have to carry messages between the fashion editor and her personal *bête noire*, especially when Oliver Charters laced his messages with so many ripe expletives – deliberately, so Ella suspected. She was determined not to give him the satisfaction of seeing her look shocked.

It was so hot in the carriage that she ended up having to remove her suit jacket and her hat as she rushed round.

The hats chosen by the fashion editor were impossible

to photograph, Ollie announced disparagingly, having studied them through the lens of his precious Rolleiflex.

He had saved up for nearly six months to buy the camera second-hand from a pawnbroker, desperately hoping that its owner wouldn't suddenly find the money to reclaim it before he had saved enough to buy it. He had spent many a Saturday afternoon arguing and bargaining with the pawnbroker, trying to wheedle down the price.

'The hat brims throw too much shadow over the models' features. They'll have to wear them back off their faces,' he told the fashion editor now.

As he went to demonstrate what he meant the fashion editor stepped protectively in front of the model, warning him, 'Don't you dare touch those hats. They cost twenty guineas each and are only on loan to us.'

Frustrated in his attempt to demonstrate what he meant, Ollie wheeled round and, catching sight of Ella, marched over to her.

'Look, this is what I meant,' he said, taking hold of Ella's precious best hat, which she'd placed safely on a table, brutally turning back the brim and then ramming the crown down firmly on Ella's curls. Moving away from her, he saw her lifting her hands to examine the damage, and he ordered sharply, 'No, don't touch it!' then stepped up to her, tilting it to one side.

With him standing so close to her in the confines of the carriage, his arms lifted up whilst he destroyed her hat, Ella could see the ripple of the muscles in his arms and torso beneath the thin T-shirt he was wearing, and smell the fresh male scent of his body.

It was too much for her. She wasn't used to this kind of proximity to this kind of man. It made her feel hot and angry and somehow dangerously light-headed. She stiffened.

Instantly Ollie's concentration left the hat, his professionalism giving way to the male instinct of the hunter sensing vulnerable prey. His gaze dropped from the hat to Ella's trembling mouth. He let his attention drop further to her throat, where a pulse thudded frantically in the pale skin, and then drop lower still to her breasts, disguised as they were by her shapeless clothes. Ollie, an expert in such matters, estimated that they were just the right size to fill his hands. Now that would be a thing, bringing Miss High-and-Mighty down to earth, if he hadn't got more important things to do. No way did he really want to get entangled with a ruddy stuck-up virgin.

He looked back at the hat, frowning as he adjusted it a second time, before telling the fashion editor, 'That's how they should be wearing their titfers, so that I can get the light on their faces.'

'Celine,' the fashion editor addressed the most senior of the three models, 'you put on Ella's hat and let me have a look. I'm not letting you loose with those model hats, Oliver, until I'm convinced you're right.'

Celine, the elegant soignée society model, gave Ella a sympathetic look as Oliver removed Ella's now ruined hat to place it on the model's carefully coiffured hair.

It was, Ella thought, going to be a long journey to Venice.

*　*　*

She would never ever want to work full time in fashion, Ella decided angrily later in the day as the train approached Paris's Gare de Lyon. She was exhausted and wrung out, her head ringing with the instructions and counter-instructions the fashion editor and Oliver Charters had both flung at her.

It was a relief to be allowed to return to her own carriage, her head pounding and her heart racing. A kind-hearted cabin attendant brought her a much-needed pot of tea and a croissant. Leaving the croissant, Ella took one of her diet pills, swallowing it down with the tea. She was definitely thinner, although since she was still wearing the same clothes, no one else had noticed – as yet. Ella didn't particularly want anyone else to notice, especially not anyone like Oliver Charters. She didn't want him, or indeed anyone, thinking she had lost weight because he had made fun of her. It was enough that she had proved to herself that she could lose weight. But only because of her magic little pills. Ella pushed that knowledge away. She didn't want to think about the pills. After all, no one else needed to know about them, and as soon as she had lost enough weight she would stop taking them.

Whilst she'd been drinking her tea they'd pulled into the Paris station, and the models had disembarked, ready for Oliver to photograph them.

They did look wonderful, Ella acknowledged, watching them through the carriage window. No one would know, looking at them from the front, that one of the suits had been so much too large for the slender model that it was pulled in all down the back with clothes pegs. Ella marvelled at the patience and good nature of the models. She would hate their job. Not that she exactly loved her own, but it wouldn't always be like this. One day she would be a proper investigative journalist, and then she wouldn't have to put up with people like Oliver Charters mocking her and laughing at her.

Ella's hands were shaking slightly as she poured herself a second cup of tea. How much weight would she have lost by the time they reached Venice, another two days from now? She wasn't going to stop dieting until she had lost two stone. Then she would weigh exactly eight stone two pounds, and be a size ten. Exactly the same size and weight as the model who had laughed at her and told Oliver Charters that Ella was the size of an elephant. Normally, before the diet pills, just remembering the humiliation of that moment would have had her reaching for her favourite dark chocolate digestive biscuits, but now she didn't want one at all.

'So what do you think?'

Standing on the pavement outside the salon, Rose dutifully looked up at the sign that had just been fixed in place and which read 'Hair by Josh Simons'.

'I like it,' she told him truthfully.

The door to the salon was open, as were the windows, the sounds and the smell of painters at work carrying out into the street.

Rose had nipped over to King's Road during her lunch hour, knowing that the sign was going up.

'I'd better get back. I've got to source some trimming for a storyboard on my way back.'

'You should be running your own business, with your talent, not working for someone else,' Josh told her for the umpteenth time.

'That isn't what I want and besides, I'm not good enough for that yet. There's still loads I need to learn. You wouldn't have left Vidal's salon before he had said that you were ready to go it alone, would you? Besides, my aunt wants me to work in the London shop eventually.'

'What about what you want?'

Josh's question had caught her off guard, and she hesitated before telling him firmly, 'I want the same as my aunt.'

'If I'd done what my dad wanted me to do,' Josh reminded her, 'I'd be cutting suits somewhere off Savile Row now, and working for someone else.'

'That's different,' Rose responded immediately.

Thinking of her aunt reminded her of the fact that soon it would be Easter and that she would be going home to Denham.

Denham. She had such mixed feelings about her childhood home. She had no memory of her father taking her there, of course – she'd been too young, little more than a baby – but she did have memories of being held in caring arms there and of being loved, of a soft voice urging her to live. Then later, when she'd recovered from the malnutrition and the fever that had nearly killed her, she'd come to recognise her aunt Amber and to love her. That love had been her only safe haven in a world where everyone else was hostile: her great-grandmother, Emerald, her nanny, and most of all her own father. Rose shuddered, remembering her father's cruelty to her.

'Hey, where have you gone?' Josh demanded.

'Nowhere.'

'Liar.'

'All right then, I was thinking about Janey,' she lied. 'She keeps begging me to ask you to let her show you her designs for the salon uniforms.'

'Does she? Well, I suppose I'd better take a butcher's then,' Josh grinned. 'Tell her to bring them over tomorrow evening. Oh, wait a minute, I'd forgotten. It will have to be the night after: I'm taking this girl out tomorrow.'

Josh seemed to date a different girl every week, and was obviously in no hurry to settle down.

Rose was glad that she was in love with John and that she wasn't one of Josh's dates. She could just imagine how unhappy and insecure it would make her feel if she was dating him and perhaps falling for him, and she knew that he was seeing other girls. Rose didn't like taking risks or exposing herself to potential emotional pain. Josh was very good-looking and fun to be with but she was relieved that they were simply friends and that she wasn't in any danger of falling for him. Thanks to John.

'I thought it was Manchester where it never stopped raining, not Venice.'

Ella watched as Oliver paced the marble floor of the elegant entrance to the Hotel Danieli, glaring towards the door through which they could see the rain, which had been falling ever since their arrival nearly two days ago, dimpling the waters of the Rio del Vin.

'It's no good,' Oliver told the fashion editor, 'I'm going

to have to take the models out and get some sample location shots done, rain or no rain.'

Ella looked discreetly at her watch. She was on edge, hoping to be able to snatch some time off so that she could visit the Italian silk firm with whom her stepmother did business. Amber had told them that Ella was visiting Venice and they had passed on to her an open invitation to call and see them. It would be rude not to do so, but on the other hand Ella didn't want to put herself in a position where she was asking for special favours.

'You can't possibly take the models out in this weather, Oliver,' the fashion editor was saying. 'The last thing I want is one of them catching a cold.'

'Well, I can't just go out and photograph a few bridges and canals for possible locations without a model.' Oliver looked and sounded irritable, pushing his hand through his overlong hair.

The fashion editor tapped one immaculate fingernail on the highly polished surface of an inlaid table and pursed her lips, as she looked round the room as though seeking inspiration, her gaze suddenly focusing on Ella.

'I've got it,' she announced. 'You can take Ella with you and she can stand in for the models.'

'Ella! What the hell . . . ?'

'Oh, no, please, I couldn't possibly.'

They were both equally opposed to the fashion editor's decision, although no doubt for very different reasons, Ella recognised.

'You can spare Ella, can't you, Daphne?' the fashion editor asked Ella's boss, ignoring the outbursts.

'Yes, I don't see why not. And don't forget, Oliver, I want some photographs for the piece I'm doing on the summer haunts of high society.'

He might be nodding his head in acknowledgement but he was looking at *her*, Ella realised, assessing her, and it was plain that he didn't much care for what he could see. Well, that was all right because she didn't care for him either.

'I hope you've got a raincoat,' he told her sulkily. He pushed back the cuff of the shabby leather jacket he always wore and looked at his watch, adding, 'We've got about three hours of light left, if we're lucky, so you'd better step on it. You've got five minutes to get whatever you need and meet me by the main entrance.'

Ella didn't have a raincoat; it was the last thing she'd thought she would need in Venice, and she certainly wasn't going to risk her good coat getting soaked. She'd have to make do with an umbrella borrowed from the hotel, she decided, as she hurried up to her room to get her bag.

There wasn't time to change out of the knitted white pleated skirt she was wearing, with its navy border just above the hem and its matching knitted cardigan, which she was wearing over a red silk blouse. The outfit wasn't something she would ever have chosen for herself, and had been a surprise gift from her stepmother, who had presented her with it especially for her trip. Personally Ella felt that the light colour made her look far too conspicuous, but she had still felt obliged to bring it with her, even if it was loose on her because of all the weight she had lost – four more pounds on the journey to Venice, with only another ten pounds to go to reach her goal.

The red beret that went with it might help to keep her hair dry, and she would just have to hope that her navy court shoes wouldn't suffer too much damage from the rain.

She was out of breath, her heart racing in that disconcerting way it had developed recently, by the time she rejoined Oliver by the main door, grasping the large umbrella she had borrowed from the porter.

'Come on,' Oliver demanded, turning up the collar of his jacket as they stepped out into the rain together, and then strode out ahead of her.

'If we go that way we'll end up in St Mark's Square,' Ella warned him when she caught up with him.

'So?' he demanded, peering beneath the umbrella to glare at her.

'You said you wanted bridge and canal locations,' Ella pointed out.

He gave a dismissive shrug. 'So we'll find some bridges and canals.'

'It will be quicker if we go this way,' Ella told him, indicating one of the narrow sidestreets leading off the square.

'And you'd know, would you? I suppose you've had your nose in a guidebook ever since we arrived. Your kind always does.'

His derisory tone stung, but Ella refused to cave in.

'Actually, I've visited Venice before. My stepmother has business connections here.' She knew she sounded prim and stuffy and, indeed, almost arrogant – she certainly wouldn't have spoken to anyone else like this – but somehow Oliver Charters brought out the worst in her.

'And that puts me in my place, does it? Me being from the East End?'

'I was simply trying to save time,' Ella told him truthfully,

They were standing in St Mark's Square now, its wide expanse for once empty not just of visitors but also of the pigeons for which it was so famous. Even the cafés that lined the square had removed their outside tables and chairs, and the whole place looked grey and miserable, not somewhere to shoot high-summer fashion at all.

'OK then, so where's the famous sighing bridge everyone goes on about?' Oliver challenged her.

'It's called the Ponte dei Sospiri,' Ella answered him. 'People refer to it as the Bridge of Sighs because it's the bridge that prisoners used to have to cross. It's this way, I think.' Ella hurried him past the sign that read 'Piazza San Marco', hoping that Oliver wouldn't ask her if she could speak Italian in that sarcastic voice of his, and then along the waterfront back the way they'd come, to the Rio del Palazzo. Standing on the bridge that crossed it, she pointed down the narrow canal to the enclosed bridge further down.

'You mean that's it?' Oliver demanded. 'How the hell am I supposed to photograph models standing on that?'

'You can't,' Ella told him, but he wasn't listening.

Instead, he was looking through the lens of his camera, finally telling her in a peremptory voice, 'Right, I want you to stand here.'

'Here' was the middle of the bridge.

Thankful that there was no one else about, Ella did as he had instructed her, her self-consciousness increasing when he started to lift his camera and look through it.

'No, not like that. You look like a block of wood. Relax, and look towards that sighing bridge, or whatever it's supposed to be, and think about something sad. And get rid of the umbrella, and the beret.'

'I'll get wet,' Ella protested.

'So?'

She hated him, she decided, as he took the umbrella from her, quickly snatching off her beret herself and putting it into her bag. She really, really hated him. She looked towards the Bridge of Sighs and shivered, trying to imagine what it must have felt like to watch someone you loved being taken over that bridge to the cells, convicted to spend the rest of his life there.

'Come on, this is no time to start looking all moony. We've got work to do.'

Ella gasped in indignation but before she could point out that he had told her to look 'sad', Oliver was continuing, 'Now we want a church, but not just any church. It's got to look right.'

He wanted a church. Venice had any number of them. Ella gritted her teeth.

'Any particular kind of church you want?'

'Yeah, a photogenic one.'

In the end she found him three churches that met with his approval, along with five bridges and, most humiliating of all, as far as Ella was concerned, a stray gondolier, whom Oliver persuaded to hand Ella into his gondola where she had to recline against one of the cushions whilst Oliver snapped busily.

At last it was over, the light was fading, and Ella was wet and cold. Her knitted suit was clinging uncomfortably to her body and would be ruined, and Ella had been all too conscious of the look the gondolier had given her breasts as he had handed her into his craft.

'Right, come on, let's get back,' Oliver announced.

He'd got some excellent shots, and although he didn't really want to admit it, Ella's knowledge of Venice had given him some locations he doubted he would ever have found by himself.

Ella was hurrying, head down, along one of the city's narrow streets with Oliver in front of her, when he suddenly turned round and grabbed hold of her, pushing her back against the wall of the building behind her, just in time to prevent her from being hit by the cyclist coming the other way at speed.

The anger that had filled her when he had grabbed hold of her vanished, to be replaced by relief when she realised how close she had come to being hurt, and then a dizzy shakiness.

'Are you OK?'

Ella nodded. She had long ago abandoned the umbrella and raindrops flew from her wet hair, which was curling wildly round her face.

She really was a good-looking girl, Oliver acknow-ledged. He was still holding her, but his hands had slipped to her waist, so narrow that he suspected he might be able to span it with his hands. She was deli-ciously curvy, with the kind of body that a man just couldn't help but want to hold. A sharp stab of desire kicked through him. He moved closer to her, tight-ening his grasp on her, and his gaze fixed on her mouth. Her lips were soft and invitingly pink.

What was Oliver doing? Ella looked up at him, her eyes widening as her heart somersaulted in disbelief. Oliver Charters was going to kiss her. No, that wasn't possible; she must be imagining it. She tried to escape his grip but it was too late. His lips felt warm and firm against her own. He was cupping her face with the free hand that wasn't securing her to him.

Ella opened her mouth to object, but her objection turned into an indrawn sigh, which was silenced and then somehow transformed into a helpless appreciation of pleasure beneath the expertise of his kiss.

She could feel the heat of his body warming her own. She felt as though she might almost melt right into him; she felt . . . Abruptly Ella realised what was happening.

She closed her lips together very firmly and pushed Oliver away. Her face was burning as she sidestepped him and started to walk very fast towards the hotel.

'There's no need to make such a big deal about it,' Oliver told her after he had caught up with her. 'It was only a kiss.'

Ella ignored him. She didn't trust herself enough to speak. How could she have let him kiss her like that? She knew what kind of man he was, after all: the kind who went around making love to as many girls as he could – and even now he was probably laughing at her, comparing her with the pretty sophisticated models on the shoot. Not that she cared if he did. Not one little bit.

Chapter Fourteen

'Oh, John, I didn't see you there.' Rose hoped that she didn't sound as breathless and self-conscious as she felt, having cycled over, as she stepped into Fitton's Great Hall. She blinked against the bright shafts of sunlight coming in through the high, narrow late-medieval windows and piercing the shadows thrown by the thick stone walls.

'I'm just on my way to the stables. I've got to go and see one of my tenant farmers and I thought I'd ride over instead of driving the Land Rover. Why don't you come with me?'

He hadn't said anything about her hair, but then perhaps he hadn't noticed yet. The Great Hall was deeply shadowed, after all.

'I'd love to say yes, but you know me and horses,' she answered him ruefully. If only he would say that he wouldn't bother riding over to see his tenant farmer but would take the Land Rover instead so that she could go with him, but to her disappointment he simply agreed.

'No, you never really took to riding, did you? In fact, if I remember correctly, of the four of you, Janey was the one who rode best.'

John was looking at the door, no doubt keen to be on his way, and not, like her, cherishing every single second they could be together.

'The reason I came over,' she told him quickly, 'is because my aunt wondered if you and Lady Fitton Legh would like to come over for dinner tonight. She would have telephoned but it's such a lovely day that I said I'd walk over. You'll have heard, I expect, that we've got the new duke staying with us at Denham?'

'An Australian chap, isn't he?' John asked. 'I heard that he owns a sheep station, and I certainly wouldn't mind picking his brains about what kind of breeding programme they run out there. I've got sheep on the Fitton land in Wales, but we can't compete with the quality of the fleeces the Australians are managing to produce. Please tell your aunt that I'd be delighted to accept. I can't speak for my stepmother, though. You'll probably find her in the yellow drawing room. I'd better go . . .'

A smile and a brief nod of his head and he was striding towards the door.

Rose waited until it had closed behind him before rushing to the window that overlooked the drive and kneeling up on the window seat – its now faded covering of silk designed by her aunt's Russian father and woven at Denby Mill especially for the Fitton family – the better to watch John for as long as she could.

He hadn't noticed her hair, she acknowledged sadly as she watched his departing back with yearning devotion.

'Rose, this is a surprise. Why, I wonder, hasn't anyone announced you?'

The sharp cold sound of Lady Fitton Legh's voice had

Rose scrambling off the window seat to face her, feeling more like a wary child than a young woman. There was something about Cassandra Fitton Legh that made Rose shiver, as though somehow her presence chilled the air around her. Where Jay was handsome and kind, his cousin Cassandra, with her once red hair now streaked with grey, was plain and harsh-natured. Just because she was in her presence, Rose immediately felt guilty and uncomfortable.

'My aunt asked me to come over to pass on to you her invitation for dinner this evening.'

How long had John's stepmother been there? Had she seen her looking yearningly through the window? The thought increased Rose's discomfort. She knew that Cassandra disliked and despised her, though she had never said so. The way she looked at her told Rose as much.

Now she arched a thin eyebrow, saying coolly, 'Did she? Amber is fortunate in having the number of staff she does at Denham. If I had a young relative staying with me with time on her hands, I'm sure I'd be able to find her plenty of things to do without sending her on an errand that could quite easily have been accomplished in much less time via a telephone call. You were lucky to catch John in – but then I'm sure that somehow or other you would have found him anyway and delivered your message.'

Rose could feel her face burning. 'John has said that he is free to accept my aunt's invitation.'

'Then of course I must do so as well.'

There was no offer of a cup of tea, no suggestion that

Rose might sit down and provide Lady Fitton Legh with an update of her life in London or those of her two nieces, nothing other than that iciness that made Rose very relieved to say goodbye and escape from her chilling presence.

'Emerald, it was awfully rude of you to turn your back on Dougie like that.'

Amber and Emerald were in Emerald's bedroom at Denham. The windows were open to make the most of the late April sunshine.

Emerald glared at her mother.

'I really wish you would be more pleasant to Dougie. He's doing his best, poor boy. He arrived with the most enormous Fortnum's hamper on Friday, but it's obvious that he feels awkward and out of his depth, and that's only natural. It's up to us to do all we can to help him through what must be a very difficult time. It isn't just rude of you to treat him the way you are doing, it's downright mean and spiteful as well. He's gone out of his way to try to fit in, chatting to Jay about estate management and—'

'Of course that would make him perfect in your eyes, Mummy, but have you thought how my father would feel, knowing that an ignorant Australian is taking his place?'

'I know that your father would have treated Dougie with a good deal more kindness than you have done, Emerald. I really am shocked by your behaviour, and all the more so in view of Dougie's generosity in agreeing that you can remain at Lenchester House and have your

166

ball there. He would be perfectly within his rights to ask you to leave and cancel the ball. The least you can do is help him to find his feet a little socially. I've invited him to your coming-out ball, and naturally, given that he is now the head of the family, he will partner you for the evening.'

'No! You can't do that. I won't have it. I won't!'

Emerald had been banking on the fact that she would not have any male relatives present at her ball as a lever she could use to manoeuvre the Duke of Kent into partnering her. Now her mother was telling her that, without consulting her, she had made arrangements for the loathsome sheep farmer who claimed that he was her father's heir to partner her.

Didn't her mother realise how humiliating it would be for her to have to acknowledge that someone so gauche was the new duke, without trying to force her to have him at her ball, spoiling all her own plans? How typical it was of her mother totally to ignore her feelings in favour of those of someone else. She had never put her first, never given her the exclusive love that Emerald had always felt should have been her right. Instead she had to favour others, people so far beneath Emerald in status that her mother fussing over them had been an added insult. People like Rose, and now this detestable Australian.

'I can't possibly have him at my ball. He hasn't got the first idea of how to behave. He'll make a laughing stock of himself.' And of her as well if she wasn't careful, thought Emerald.

'Dougie may not be well versed in the way things are

done in society, but that isn't his fault. It's up to all of us, but most especially you, to help him in that regard. It's certainly what your father would have wanted and expected. If there was one thing Robert detested, it was snobbery.'

'Fancy Mama inviting Aunt Cassandra and John over for dinner tonight. Aunt Cassandra will criticise us and John will bore on about farming,' Janey complained to Rose as they stood together in the drawing room, sipping the pre-dinner G and Ts Janey's father had made for everyone. 'He actually telephoned this afternoon and asked me if I'd like to go riding with him first thing tomorrow morning.'

Rose almost spilled her drink as first shock and then jealousy spiked through her.

'I said no, of course. I'm not getting up at the crack of dawn to listen to John going on about sheep breeding.'

'It's only natural that he should be concerned about getting the best return on Fitton's lands,' Rose defended her hero stiffly.

Janey laughed, and then pleaded, 'Rose, don't be cross with me. I didn't mean to criticise John. I know you've always had a soft spot for him.'

'No I haven't,' Rose denied immediately. 'I just don't think you should run him down, when all he's trying to do is keep the estate going.'

'What do you think about Dougie turning out to be the new duke?' Janey asked her, hastily changing the subject, not wanting to upset or antagonise Rose. 'What a surprise that was.'

'What was a surprise?' Ella asked them, coming over to join them. She'd had a bit of a fright earlier when Janey had almost walked in on her just as she was about to take her diet pill. Not that it really mattered if Janey did know, of course. After all, she wasn't doing anything wrong. It was just that she didn't want Janey telling everyone what she was doing, as her sister, with her easy, open manner, was bound to do if she were to find out.

Ella gave a small surreptitious tug at the waistband of her navy-blue linen skirt. She was sure that it was just that tiny bit less tight than it had been. There were no scales here at Denham, and it had been awfully difficult at mealtimes insisting that she wasn't hungry. In the end she'd had to pretend that she'd had a stomach upset.

'Finding out that Dougie is the new duke,' Janey answered her sister's question.

Ella gave the young Australian, who was standing talking to her father and stepmother, a quick look. No wonder he had been so keen to question her at that party.

'It's really put Emerald's nose out of joint,' Janey continued unsympathetically. 'She's refused to come down for dinner, you know. I heard Mama telling Daddy that Emerald says she's got a a bad headache. A case of green jealousy ache is more like it.'

Emerald glowered moodily at her magazine. How dare her mother make such a silly fuss over that stupid Australian? Emerald was determined that she would never, ever refer to him as 'the new duke', even in the privacy of her own thoughts. Well, she wasn't going to join in the fussing. How could such an oaf possibly be her father's heir? Emerald shuddered at the thought of how humiliating it would be to be obliged to have him at her ball. People would laugh and talk about him behind his back, and that would reflect on her. Why had he had to turn up now, just when it was so important that she created the right impression on the Duke of Kent? Any other mother would have been doing everything she could to help her daughter to impress the royal duke instead of trying to humiliate her by inviting Dougie to her ball. She hated him and she hated her mother as well.

All through dinner Rose snatched brief glimpses of John, who was sitting further up the table. As the rules of precedence demanded, the highest ranking guests sat closest to the host and hostess, which meant naturally that Dougie was seated at her aunt's right hand, at one end of the table, and John to her left, whilst Jay sat at the other end.

Had she been there Emerald would have been seated next to the duke, but because she wasn't that honour went to Lady Fitton Legh.

Darling John, he was such a good, kind person, even if he hadn't noticed her new hairstyle.

Rose was still reflecting on John's virtues later in the evening as she sat alone in the library, where she had gone to check in one of her aunt's reference books on the provenance of a sofa table pair that her employer was insisting was a Regency original, but which she thought was a copy.

The door opened and John's stepmother came in. Rose's heart sank, but she gave her a polite smile, which

Lady Fitton Legh did not return. For no logical reason Rose suddenly felt very apprehensive.

'I've come to have a word with you about my stepson.'

'John?' Rose half stammered, her apprehension increasing.

Lady Fitton Legh inclined her head. 'I do hope that it isn't necessary for me to point out to you that it would be most unwise of you to indulge in any foolish romantic notions about my stepson, Rose.'

Rose's heart skipped a beat. She desperately wanted to escape from the humiliation she knew was coming but of course it was impossible for her to do anything other than remain where she was.

'John has always been kind to me,' she said shakily. 'I think of him as a good friend, not . . . not someone I might marry.'

'Marry? Someone of your sort? I should think not indeed. If that was what you were hoping for then you are truly a fool. I was aware that you were mooning over him, but it never occurred to me that you were actually so lost to the reality of your own situation and the circumstances of your birth that you would dare to think of marriage.' Her angry contempt was plain.

Rose wanted to defend herself but the awfulness of the situation was such that she couldn't gather her thoughts.

'Let me be plain with you, Rose,' Lady Fitton Legh continued coldly. 'My stepson is a young man and, like all young men, he has, shall we say, certain needs. It is my concern that given your background and your parentage you might be unwisely tempted into satisfying those needs. To follow in the footsteps of your mother, in fact, as one hears your sort does tend to do. That would not be a good idea.'

'You have no right to talk to me like this,' Rose protested, fighting back the hollow sick feeling of shocked misery that had invaded her stomach. 'I have not done anything wrong.'

'Not yet, perhaps, but you would be doing something very wrong indeed, Rose, if you encouraged John to have any kind of physically intimate relationship with you. You see, it is not just a matter of you having a woman of the very worst sort as your mother, there is every chance that you and John could share the same father.'

If Rose had been shocked before, that shock was nothing compared with what she was feeling now.

'No. That isn't possible.'

'I'm afraid that sadly it is. There must be something in the Pickford blood that drives those who possess it to behave immorally. Before she died, John's mother confessed to me that Greg Pickford could be John's father.'

'You're just saying that; it isn't true – it can't be true. If it was then someone would have said something.' Rose felt bewildered and confused, unable to accept what Lady Fitton Legh was saying and yet at the same time sharply aware that the other woman meant every word. How could it be possible, though, for her and John to have the same father and them not know?

'Would they? Your aunt certainly knows, and so too does my brother,' Lady Fitton Legh informed her coolly. 'If you don't believe me why don't you ask them? But, of course, I must warn you that if you do you will be risking John's future. Once it becomes public knowledge that he might not be my late husband's son, then of course John, being the man that he is, would feel obliged to forfeit the title and the estate as a matter of honour.'

What Lady Fitton was saying was true, Rose knew. Now she felt nauseous.

'You are no doubt wondering why I have kept silent on this matter all these years. The truth is that it suits me to do so, since John is a very good stepson. Were he to lose the estate then I would lose my own position. But what does not suit me is for you to become involved in any way with him. There will be no more Pickford bastards foisted off on the house of Fitton Legh. You do realise what it would mean if John were your half-brother, don't you, Rose? You do know what incest is, don't you, and how disgusting and sickening a sin it is to have carnal knowledge of a person who shares your own blood? To even want that knowledge is a dreadful sin, a deviation from all that is decent and normal, although of course we cannot know with your heritage, your *parentage*, if words such as decency and normality can truly apply. No wonder poor Amber has felt obliged to keep you close to her, and keep an eye on you. At least John had someone respectable and acceptable as his mother. Your mother, of course, was little more than a whore. Have you inherited her nature, Rose? Under that seemingly innocent face you show to the world are you secretly as corrupt and vile as the woman who gave you life?

'Poor Amber, I remember how horrified she was when her brother arrived home with you. No wonder she left you here at Denham rather than take you into her own home. I dare say that secretly, like her grandmother, she hoped that you wouldn't survive. And it would have been so much better for everyone else if you hadn't, Rose, especially John. Dear John, such a conservative, respectable young man. He would be horrified if he suspected that you and he might share the same father. He is kind to you now because that is his nature, but imagine how he would feel if he were to think that you could be half-brother and -sister. He would hate you for the shame that would bring him.'

'Stop it,' Rose begged her, white-faced. 'Please stop it.'

Lady Fitton Legh's smile was cruel and contemptuous.

'Poor Rose, your very existence is a source of shame and fear to those who are closest to you, the truth a secret they are forced to keep, whilst pretending to care for you. Dear Amber always was good at appearing to be charitable. So clever of her to find a way of keeping you close to her whilst gaining everyone's approval.'

What Cassandra Fitton Legh was saying wasn't true. Amber loved her, *really* loved her, Rose wanted to say, but somehow the words stuck in her throat, whilst the barbs John's stepmother had cast into her heart were fast tearing at it.

'What I have told you is for your own good, Rose, and of course for John. If you truly love him, as I believe you do, then it must remain our secret.'

Their secret and a burden she would have to carry for the rest of her life, Rose recognised, but somehow far worse than the pain of knowing she could only love John as a brother, was that of knowing that the bond, the love, the everything she had thought she and Amber shared was a fiction, a folly, a deceit deliberately created to conceal the truth.

Lady Fitton Legh had been right to say that it would have been better if she had not survived, Rose thought bitterly.

'John himself knows nothing of it, or of his mother's dreadful behaviour, of course,' Lady Fitton Legh was continuing, 'and you must never tell anyone else, do you understand? Because if you do it will be John's future you are destroying. After all, his mother, poor fool, may have been mistaken, and John could be her husband's child after all. For John's sake we must just believe that that is so, mustn't we?'

Numbly Rose nodded. She felt sick with shock and grief. Her life as she knew it was in tatters around her feet.

Chapter Fifteen

Emerald stared at the card in front of her in disbelief.

'HRH The Princess Marina and HRH The Duke of Kent regret that they are unable to accept . . .'

No! She had planned everything so carefully, right down to rehearsing the way she would deliberately lean into the duke when he danced with her so that he couldn't help but be aware of her body. She looked at the 'with regret' card again. Surely it was a mistake, an error made by some stupid social secretary. Surely even now the duke was insisting to his mother that they must attend. He *couldn't* not be there. It was impossible, unthinkable, unbearable . . .

Her coming-out ball should have been the best, the most exciting, the most triumphant night of Emerald's life. She had planned that it would be all those months ago in Paris, imagining how she would be fêted and admired, not just as the most beautiful deb of the season but as the wife-to-be of the Duke of Kent.

But now, according to the card she had just read, HRH The Duke of Kent was unable to be present at her ball 'owing to a previous engagement'.

Emerald snatched up the copy of *The Times*, which was on the table close to the desk, quickly turning to the Court Circular, and scanned down it, her throat tight with angry tension when she could not find anything referring to any official duties for the duke or his mother.

This was Princess Marina's doing, Emerald decided bitterly. It had to be. Left to his own devices the duke would have accepted the invitation.

'Emerald.'

She closed the paper quickly and hid the card beneath the desk blotter when she heard Lydia calling her name.

They were supposed to be attending a lunch party at the Savoy, accompanied by the loathsome Dougie, who her mother had forced on her and who, to Emerald's fury, her godmother seemed to be delighted to have accompanying them on their social engagements.

'Dougie's such fun, isn't he?' Lydia giggled as she came into the room. 'He's been telling me about how they shear sheep in Australia. They have to be frightfully quick, you know.'

As Dougie himself strolled into the salon behind Lydia, Emerald glowered at him and said pointedly, 'How fascinating. I hadn't realised you were such a scintillating conversationalist, Dougie. I'm sure everyone *will* be impressed.'

'Well, I'd much rather listen to Dougie than some of those boring debs' delights any day,' Lydia defended him stalwartly.

'Tell me, Dougie, what do you say when you're asked what school you went to? Plainly you can't say Eton.'

'I tell them that I attended the school of life,' Dougie

told her, deliberately exaggerating his Australian accent, knowing how much it infuriated her, and then adding fuel to the fire by asking her, 'So what's this dinner we're going out for all about?'

'You have to say "lunch", Dougie, not "dinner", Lydia told him patiently.

'He knows that, Lyddy,' Emerald informed her grimly, standing up abruptly, her hand catching the blotter as she did so and dislodging the card she had hidden, sending it tumbling to the floor.

She bent to retrieve it but Dougie beat her to it. It had fallen face down. Her heart thumped fiercely as Dougie picked it up, and started to turn it over. Imperiously she held out her hand for it, telling him sharply, 'It's not done to read other people's correspondence.'

He was looking at her, and then at the card, as though weighing up whether or not to read it. Quickly she snatched it out of his grasp.

'What is it, Emerald?' Lyddy asked curiously.

'It's nothing,' she told her. 'Nothing at all.'

Rose stared into space. She was alone in the Chelsea house, having turned down an invitation to go out with Janey and Ella. It was over a week since Lady Fitton Legh had told her that John could be her half-brother, and she was still trying to come to terms with the shock.

Now what was tormenting her more than anything else was the fact that Amber hadn't told her about John. Why hadn't she said something to her about him, at least warned her, even if she hadn't felt able to say anything outright? Whilst Rose had been growing up her aunt had been the one person she had always felt she could turn to, the only person whom she had felt had truly loved her, the person she had felt the closest to, and it hurt to think that she had kept something so important from her.

Logically Rose could understand that when she had been a child it would have been impossible for anything to be said but surely once she had grown up Amber could have said something.

Quite plainly her aunt must have felt that she couldn't trust her. Pain and betrayal, they were both so hard to bear now.

Rose had feared her father. She had wanted him to love her so desperately but he had always rejected her. Had he loved John's mother? Had he rejected her because secretly he had longed for the son he could never claim? There were so many questions she wanted to ask, but for John's sake she must never utter them.

Oddly, the pain she felt came not from knowing that she must relinquish and repudiate her love for John – she could, after all, still love him but now it must be as a sister's love for a brother – but from feeling that the person she had trusted the most had betrayed her. The sense of closeness she had always felt towards Amber had been damaged, and instead of feeling that she had someone in her life that she would always be able to turn to, Rose felt dreadfully alone.

It would have been so wonderful to have grown up with John as her brother; he was everything that a big brother should be. Was it too fanciful of her to think that perhaps instinctively a part of her had always recognised that in him, and perhaps he had even protected her because he too had sensed that there was a special bond between them?

But John wouldn't really want her as a half-sister. He believed himself to be a Fitton Legh. He was proud of his family's history and of his name. If he could choose between being Lord Fitton Legh's son or her father's, Rose knew which he would choose, and who could blame him? Lady Fitton Legh was right: for John's sake no doubt must be put on his parentage. Another betrayal; another rejection of her, even though John was unaware of it.

Learning that John could be her half-brother had changed the way she felt about him completely. Her childhood crush, the longing she had believed she had felt for him, had been destroyed by the revulsion she had felt at the thought of having such emotions for someone so closely related to her by blood. Now, instead of looking back and wishing that just once John might have held her and kissed her, she was fiercely glad that he had not. The very thought of anything like that happening between them made her shake with horror. Both of them had been saved from that awfulness, and she was grateful for that.

Rose felt like someone who had somehow escaped from the most dreadful fate, shaken, weak, horrified, but relieved, and determined to swear that they would never ever allow themselves to risk such a circumstance in future.

Chapter Sixteen

'You'll never guess what I heard last night at Lucy Carstairs' supper party, Emerald. The Duke of Kent is spending virtually every weekend in Yorkshire visiting Katharine Worsley, only it's all supposed to be very hush-hush at the moment, because no one's supposed to know officially that he's seeing her. Poor you, Emerald, and you thought that he would fall for you. No wonder he won't be at your ball tonight; he's far too busy in Yorkshire.' Gwendolyn tittered in malicious satisfaction as she dropped her bombshell.

She might be seething inside but Emerald wasn't going to give Gwendolyn the satisfaction of seeing that. Instead she forced a smile and told her lightly, 'Oh, yes, I know all about Miss Worsley. The duke mentioned her to me.'

'But, Emerald, you were going to marry him,' Lydia protested. 'How can he be seeing someone else?'

'Perhaps His Royal Highness didn't know about Emerald's plans for his future,' Gwendolyn suggested. 'What a shame, Emerald. You aren't going to be a princess now after all.'

'What makes you think that? The Duke of Kent isn't

the only prince in the world, you know,' Emerald pointed out sharply, whilst a horrid feeling of anxiety gripped her stomach. If what Gwendolyn was saying was true – and Emerald knew that it must be – then she had made a complete fool of herself and pretty soon, thanks to Gwendolyn's wagging tongue, everyone would know that. If there was one thing Emerald couldn't bear, it was being made to look a fool. All she could hope was that by some miracle Gwendolyn would not say anything about her boast that she would marry the Duke of Kent. But she certainly wasn't going to beg her not to do so; Gwendolyn would love that.

The three girls were standing together in their ball gowns of which, naturally, Emerald's was the most outstanding. It was the custom that débutantes' ball gowns were either white or the very palest colour, but whilst Lydia and Gwendolyn were both wearing white, Emerald's gown was silver gauze over a lilac silk underdress, the silver gauze sewn with sequins that caught the light from the ballroom's chandeliers.

'Mummy says that it's definitely going to be the ball of the season,' Lyddy confided excitedly to Emerald. 'Oh, look, there's Dougie.'

Before Emerald could stop her she had waved him over, greeting him with a hug and telling him, 'Oh Dougie, you do look smart in your evening clothes, doesn't he, Emerald?'

As she opened her mouth to say that, no he didn't, Emerald realised with a small jolt of shock that in fact Lydia was right: unexpectedly Dougie did look smart.

'Any fool can buy himself a decent suit,' she responded, 'but that doesn't turn him into a gentleman.'

'Oh, Emerald, that isn't fair,' Lydia objected, but Dougie laughed and shook his head.

'It's all right, Lyddy,' he told the younger girl. 'I don't want to be a gentleman.'

'That's just as well because you never will be one,' Emerald snapped. Why didn't he go away? She hated having him standing there, towering over her.

Emerald certainly looked the part tonight, Dougie acknowledged. And there was no doubt whose ball it was, even though officially the occasion was supposed to be for all three girls. Dougie felt rather sorry for Gwendolyn, who had already confided to him that Emerald wasn't always as kind to her as she might be.

'Emerald is in a dreadful strop,' Gwendolyn informed him, giving Emerald a sly look. 'She was expecting the Duke of Kent to be here. She wants to marry him because that will make her a duchess, but he's seeing someone else.'

Emerald decided that she had never hated anyone as much as she hated Gwendolyn right now, not even Rose.

'Sounds like he made a wise move not being here,' Dougie responded casually over the sound of Emerald's exhaled breath.

'Did you hear that, Emerald?' Gwendolyn demanded. 'Dougie thinks the duke is right not to want to marry you.'

Dougie groaned inwardly. He had really gone and put his foot in it now. Emerald's eyes were glittering with fury as she looked from his face to Gwendolyn's.

Lyddy, as always oblivious to the undercurrents going on around her, exclaimed sympathetically, 'It's such a shame that he didn't come, Emerald, especially when you wanted him to so much. But Dougie's here and he can dance with you instead. Oh!' She looked at them both excitedly. 'I've just thought, wouldn't it be the most romantic thing if you ended up falling in love with one another and getting married? You would be a duchess then, Emerald, and—'

'Marry *him*, an Australian farmer?' Emerald's voice was icy with contempt. 'Never.'

Dougie had had enough. He had his pride, after all. 'Too right,' he agreed, deliberately thickening his Australian accent. 'Not that there's a chance in hell of my ever asking you to marry me. No wonder the Duke of Kent isn't here. I don't blame him. A bloke would have to be desperate to marry you, Emerald.'

Emerald turned on her heel and stalked off, leaving Lyddy looking upset and flustered, whilst Gwendolyn was tittering.

'Emerald, I'd like a word with you.'

Emerald glowered at her mother, who was waiting for her at the bottom of the stairs as she came down from her bedroom where she had gone to smoke a cigarette and reapply her lipstick. Emerald could guess what was coming from the unusually stern tone of her mother's voice, as she drew her to one side of the ballroom so that they could talk privately, out of earshot of their guests.

'What's all this nonsense I've been hearing about you boasting that you are going to marry the Duke of Kent?'

Emerald knew who to blame. 'I suppose Gwendolyn's said something, has she?' She gave a dismissive shrug.

184

'It was just a joke, but Gwendolyn took it seriously. She's so silly.'

'Perhaps, but I'm afraid you could easily find that your joke has backfired on you, Emerald. Now, whilst you're here I'd like to remind you what I said about your attitude towards Dougie. Your lack of kindness towards him reflects more badly on you than it does on him, you know, and I shouldn't be surprised, should you continue to behave as you are doing, if by the end of the season you are a very unpopular girl indeed. I really am disappointed in you, Emerald. When you were growing up I tried to teach you how important it is to be kind to those who have less than you do.'

'You mean by pushing Rose in front of me all the time and fussing over her as though she was your daughter and not me? Why should I be kind to someone like her? She's just Uncle Greg's bastard by his Chinese mistress. I'm the daughter of a duke.'

Her mother was doing it again: making her feel small and insignificant, and trying to humiliate her. Well, she would show her that she was better than her, she would show them all.

Without giving her mother the chance to say anything, Emerald picked up the long skirt of her gown and stormed off, her head so full of angry thoughts that she didn't see Alessandro until she had almost bumped into him.

'You are upset. What is it? What is wrong?'

On the point of pushing past him, Emerald stopped and looked at him. Alessandro was a year younger than she, and immature in many ways, for all his good looks and royal status, thanks, Emerald suspected, to his mother's overprotective concern for him. Normally she would have dismissed him without a thought, but now an idea had come to her, a way of revenging herself on all those who thought they could humiliate her.

'Nothing is wrong,' she answered softly, giving him a deliberately sensual look as she added, 'Not now that you are here.'

She could see the effect she was having on him. His face was flushed, and he moved towards her, reaching for her hand and clasping it in his own when she allowed him to take it.

The band were tuning up for the first dance – the dance she had planned to take with the Duke of Kent, and which her mother expected her to dance with Dougie. Well, she wasn't going to.

'Would you like to dance with me?' she asked Alessandro, moving closer to him as she did so and giving him a provocative smile as she ran her fingertip down his arm. It amused her to see him tremble visibly.

'You want me to partner you for the first dance?' His voice was thick with excitement.

'Yes, I want you to partner me,' Emerald agreed with deliberate emphasis on the word 'partner', before, right on cue, the band struck up and she slid into his arms.

She was the daughter of a duke, she was the most beautiful girl here tonight, she deserved to be fêted and praised and adored, and she would be. Her mother had told her that she must start the dancing with Dougie as her partner because he was the new duke – well, she certainly wasn't going to do that now, Emerald thought triumphantly as she danced past Dougie and her mother, in Alessandro's arms.

The dance floor was filling up, allowing Emerald to press deliberately closer to Alessandro. It gave her another thrill of triumph to feel the way his body trembled against her own. She might still be a virgin but she would never have allowed a man to know that she was so vulnerable to him, no matter how much she desired him. Poor Alessandro, though, couldn't control himself or conceal what he was feeling. She could feel his hot breath against her forehead, and was glad that he was wearing gloves because she guessed that his hands would be sticky with excitement. His obvious desire for her gave her back her confidence. She leaned into him, her breasts pressed against his chest, as she lifted her hand to caress the back of his neck.

His shuddered, '*Adorata*', would have made her laugh out aloud at any other time, he was so ridiculously foreign. But he was also a prince, a proper prince with his own country to rule, a prince who could make her a princess.

'You must not say such things to me.' She pretended to chide him, adopting a soft, almost nervous voice.

'I cannot help myself,' Alessandro told her, holding her tightly. 'You are my adored one. I have loved you from the first moment I saw you, but never until tonight did I dare to dream that I might hold you like this.'

How modest his dreams were, Emerald thought cynically as she gave him a calculating look from beneath her lowered eyelashes. Her plans were far more ambitious.

Dougie stood watching Emerald. What was she up to now? The duchess had been mortified by Emerald's behaviour and the fact that she had opened her ball with someone else, Dougie knew, but for himself he wasn't particularly bothered. In fact, he was rather relieved that he hadn't had to dance with her. She'd have been bound to find something in his dancing to complain about.

Watching her now as she danced past him, held tight in Alessandro's arms, Dougie looked at the obviously besotted young man and muttered under his breath, 'Good luck to you, cobber. You're going to need it.'

Chapter Seventeen

'What's wrong? And don't tell me nothing, because it's as plain as the nose on my face that something's up.'

Rose gave Josh a wan smile. They were sitting opposite one another in the Kardomah coffee bar near the Peter Jones department store, in one of the small dark polished-wood booths that always reminded her of church pews. The scent of the freshly roasted coffee beans filled the air, mingling with the smell of cigarettes.

'I can't tell you,' Rose answered him. 'Someone else is involved and—'

'You're not up the duff, are you?' Josh interrupted her, explaining when she gave him a blank look, 'You're not pregnant?'

'No,' she told him truthfully, but the irony of his question touched a nerve, and before she could stop them, tears had filled her eyes.

Immediately Josh looked both concerned and uncomfortable. At any other time his look of acute embarrassment would have made her smile.

'Here . . .'

The handerchief he passed her under the table was

snowy white and immaculately ironed. Josh might live in his own flat but he still took his laundry home to his mother.

'I'm sorry,' Rose apologised when she had dried her eyes. 'It's just . . . Well, when you find out something really important that you didn't know, and then you find out that someone you thought you really mattered to and who you trusted had known and hadn't told you . . . it hurts.'

'Life hurts, Rosie, but you've got to be strong.'

'I hate looking like I do, being "different". If I'd looked like my father and not my mother . . .' Fresh tears filled her eyes.

'Hey, come on, that's enough of that,' Josh chided her gently. 'You're a stunning-looking girl, Rosie, a real beauty.'

'I'm different, I'm—'

'Special,' Josh told her firmly. 'That's what being different is. It's being special. You and me, we're both special, and that's important. It's more important than anything else, because when you're special, then you've got something that other people don't have. You're luckier than them. At least that's the way I look at it. It's the way you've got to look at it.' He added fiercely, 'It's either sink or swim, Rosie. You can let the so-and-sos put you down and kick you in the arse, or you can get up and smile and promise yourself that one day you'll be the one kicking them, and I know which *I* want to be. There's no law that says that the people who think they're better than we are have it all their own way.'

Rose tried to smile. Josh was only trying to cheer her

up, but it was different for him. He might be Jewish – and some people were, she knew, antagonistic towards Jews – but at least Josh was part of a community. London had a large Jewish population and he had a family, a proper family. She was a one-off, someone who didn't fit in anywhere, neither into her father's family, nor the Chinese community in London, because she was neither one thing nor the other.

Cassandra's cruel disclosures haunted her. She had tried not to give them any credence but Cassandra had been so confident, so sure, so knowing, as though aware all along she had been privy to this secret from which Rose had been excluded.

'I thought that Amber should have told you the truth,' Cassandra had said to her. 'I said so all along. After all, you had a right to know, and I believed you could be trusted with the secret, but Amber obviously didn't agree with me. But then Greg was her brother and she had her own children to think of – and herself.'

Was Cassandra right? Rose didn't know. She only knew that she felt desperately alone and confused, and that she couldn't bear to be in Amber's company right now and had taken to avoiding her to protect herself – to protect them both and, of course, John. She would have been so proud to have been publicly able to claim John as her brother. Oddly it now felt right and much more comfortable somehow to love him in that way rather than as she had done before, with a schoolgirl crush. But as his stepmother had said, John would not be proud to claim her as his half-sister. He would not want to have the possibility of a blood relationship with her forced on him. He would be horrified and ashamed because of what she was.

'I cannot bear the thought of us having to part. When I return to my own country I shall be wishing every day that I could be here with you. I would do anything to be with you.' Alessandro was close to tears.

Emerald's emotions, on the other hand, were firmly under control and focused on something far more important than Alessandro's misery.

It had been Emerald's suggestion that they met in Hyde Park; it was one of the few places they could go where they could have some degree of privacy.

There had scarcely been a day since the night of Emerald's coming-out ball when they hadn't seen one another and, thanks in the main to Emerald, had managed to find somewhere to snatch a few private minutes together, all of which, just as she had planned, had fanned the flames of Alessandro's passion for her.

The previous day, though, he had told her that his mother was talking about summoning someone from Lauranto to escort Alessandro back to the principality because she felt that he had been away for long enough; her own return would have to be delayed to allow her to remain with her dying cousin.

Right from the start Emerald had realised that Alessandro was in awe of his mother and that she controlled him. Alessandro himself had naïvely told Emerald that his mother wasn't happy about him having the amount of personal freedom he was currently enjoying.

'Poor Mama worries so about me,' he had told Emerald. 'She would prefer to be with me but of course she cannot leave her cousin.'

'What a saint she must be,' Emerald had responded mock sweetly. 'I would so love to meet her.'

Alessandro's reaction to her suggestion had told her all she needed to know about his relationship with his mother. He had positively squirmed with discomfort and had even looked over his shoulder as though he half feared that his mother might actually appear.

'She is a saint, as you say,' he had agreed, 'but she is not used to the ways of London society.'

'Oh, what do you mean?' Emerald had asked him.

Alessandro had looked uncomfortable. 'Well, she would not approve . . . That is to say that Laurantese girls do not have the same freedom that girls have here in London. Of course, we are a Catholic country.'

'Oh dear,' Emerald had responded with false concern, 'I do hope that your mother won't disapprove of me, Alessandro. I do so want her to like me.'

'She will like you, of course,' Alessandro had rushed to assure her.

Thinking of Alessandro's mother now reminded Emerald that there was something she needed to know.

'Dearest,' she asked him sweetly, taking hold of his hand, 'it is not because of me that your mother is sending you home, is it? Only I know that you did say that she might not approve of me and—'

'Oh, no, it isn't because of you. She doesn't even know that I see you,' Alessandro answered her.

Emerald squeezed his hand and hid her real feelings.

She knew perfectly well that Alessandro's mother would not approve of her. The princess had controlled so much of her son's life that it was impossible that she wouldn't also want to control his choice of friends.

'It isn't that I haven't wanted to tell her about you,' Alessandro was saying.

'Do you think she would like me, Alessandro?'

'Of course she will,' he confirmed. 'She will love you, as I do.'

Emerald moved closer to him. The May sunshine was warm enough for her to be wearing a button-through cotton dress, the fabric splashed with large cornflowers. Emerald had unfastened the top few buttons so that the upper curves of her breasts were revealed. She smiled with satisfaction when she saw the way Alessandro's ardent gaze kept returning to the unfastened buttons.

'You mustn't look at me like that, dearest, otherwise I might be tempted to do something naughty,' she told him softly.

'I love you so much. I cannot bear the thought of us parting,' Alessandro responded emotionally.

'Oh, Alessandro . . .' They had reached a remote part of the park, sheltered from the view of others by shrubs. Emerald stopped walking and turned to him, wrapping her arms around his neck.

'Please kiss me, dearest Alessandro,' she begged him, tilting her face up towards his invitingly, then, once he had started to kiss her, pressing her body into his.

'I love you. You are my life, my soul. I would do anything for you. You are my everything.' Alessandro's passionate declarations were interspersed with equally passionate kisses.

Emerald swallowed down her impatience. His mother's decision to send him home didn't leave Emerald much time to do what she had determined she must.

The loathsome Australian was now being accepted everywhere as her father's heir – accepted and courted by mothers with débutante daughters. Not only was she not now going to be HRH The Duchess of Kent, she was also going to be upstaged by the girl the Australian eventually married. And he would marry, if only to spite her, Emerald knew. She, as the unmarried daughter of the previous duke, would be pushed into the background, whilst his wife, the new duchess, flaunted her title and position. The very thought made Emerald seethe with fresh anger and resentment. She had to marry someone who would make good her boast to Gwendolyn and elevate her above her mother and the future Duchess of Lenchester.

And that someone would have to be Alessandro. It was true that he was foreign, and foreigners were not generally considered good catches, but he was also a prince, a crown prince, and just look at the fuss that had been made over Grace Kelly when she had married Prince Rainier!

As a crown prince he would be expected to marry and produce heirs, so why shouldn't he marry her? He loved her, after all; he was always saying so.

He had stopped kissing her and Emerald pulled slightly away, feeling satisfied with what she had achieved. All she had to do now was encourage him to propose to her. Which was why she had suggested this private walk in the park.

She was glad now that she had insisted that he behaved so circumspectly with her. The few – very few – rationed kisses she had allowed him only reinforced what she already knew – that he adored her.

But Emerald was no fool. Passionate kisses and a declaration of undying love were not the same thing as a proposal of marriage. Instinctively she knew that she would not be Alessandro's mother's choice of a future wife for her son, which meant that Emerald had to ensure that Alessandro committed himself – publicly – to marrying her before he told the princess.

Normally Emerald wouldn't have wanted to be bothered with such complexities. She was used to people working to gain *her* approval, not the other way round, but the truth was that she was getting desperate. Her pride was making her desperate. She had believed that her coming-out ball would be an evening of triumph, followed by the announcement of her engagement to the Duke of Kent. Now she had been forced to admit that she had miscalculated badly and must somehow backtrack from that without losing face.

She had to secure the match of the season, and that meant marrying Alessandro. There was no way she was going to let Gwendolyn and the Australian sit there laughing at her. Emerald had spent many hours tussling mentally over her situation. Getting Alessandro to propose to her should be easy enough, but then there would be his mother to contend with. Finally Emerald had had a brilliant idea. She'd read in a magazine about a society heiress who'd eloped to Gretna Green, and immediately she'd recognised what a perfect solution such an elopement would be to her own problems – and, of course, the sooner the better.

'I cannot bear to leave you,' Alessandro told her, 'but there are duties waiting for me at home.'

Emerald knew she couldn't afford to delay.

'Duties which would be much easier for you to bear if you had a wife,' she suggested firmly, moving closer to him.

Alessandro sighed. 'Mama has said as much to me herself. Because of what happened to my father she is anxious to see me do my duty to the principality and provide an heir.'

Immediately Emerald reached for his hand and said breathlessly, 'And as the girl you love, and who loves you, there is nothing I want to do more than share that duty with you as your wife.'

Alessandro squeezed her hand. 'If only that could be so,' he told her emotionally, 'I would be the happiest man in all the world.'

'Of course it can be so,' Emerald stated firmly. 'It should be so, when we love one another so much.'

'My mother—'

Emerald could guess what was going to come next and hurried to head Alessandro off. 'Your mother loves you – you have told me so often – and she will want your happiness more than anything else. I know this is so because I know that when I have children – sons – that is how I shall feel about them. And besides, why should we not marry?'

Alessandro was wavering, she could tell. Emerald focused on making herself look vulnerable, a skill she had perfected as a child. Her bottom lip trembled and tears filled her eyes.

Adopting a breathy voice she begged him, 'You do love me like you've said that you do, don't you? Only I don't think I could bear it now if you didn't, when I love you so much.'

'Of course I love you.'

Emerald exhaled in relief. One more push and it would all be over.

'And you want to marry me.'

She could feel his uncertainty.

'Well . . .'

This was no time to hesitate. Hurling herself against his chest, Emerald pressed a tearful kiss on his cheek, sobbing, 'You do, I know you do. Oh, this is so wonderful. You've made my dreams come true, Alessandro.'

Well, that, at least, was almost true.

'I promise you that I'll be the best wife you could have, I'll give you lots of lovely sons and your mother will be so pleased to see you so happy that she will love me as much as I know I am going to love her. Oh, I can't wait for us to be married. I can't wait . . .' she repeated, voice softer and sexier, now the deliberate wriggle of her body against his making her meaning plain as she offered him her lips.

How could he resist? Alessandro had been telling the truth when he'd declared his passion for her. He was besotted with her, totally blinded. Shielded from the realities of life by an overprotective and domineering mother, he knew nothing whatsoever about girls like Emerald. How could he when the princess had taken great pains to make sure that he never met any?

Now, with Emerald in his arms and behaving in such an unfamiliar way, Alessandro's heart swelled with love and sentiment whilst his body hardened with longing.

'I want to be yours so much,' Emerald whispered to him. 'But we mustn't until we're married. You must be strong for us both, darling, darling Alessandro, because I don't think that I can be.'

Should she urge him on and then use that to put extra pressure on him, or was it true that once you'd let a boy do 'it' they thought that you were easy and didn't want you as much? Emerald wasn't prepared to take the risk.

Whisking herself out of Alessandro's arms as speedily as she had flung herself into them, she demanded, 'You must call on my mother, of course, to ask for my hand.'

Alessandro was hanging his head.

'What is it? What's wrong?' Emerald demanded. She knew perfectly well what was wrong, but she wasn't going to let him know that.

'I want to marry you. My heart is given to you for all time. But I am afraid that it will not be allowed.'

'Not allowed? When we love one another so much? Who could be so cruel? Alessandro, we cannot let anyone keep us apart. I will die without you to love me. You are my life now.'

'As you are mine.' He was close to tears again.

'We must be together. We must get married without anyone knowing. Once we are married, everyone will have to accept it.'

'It is not possible that we could do that.'

'Yes it is,' Emerald told him promptly. 'There is this place in Scotland called Gretna Green, where people elope in secret to get married.'

Alessandro was starting to look apprehensive. 'We cannot . . .'

'Yes we can,' Emerald assured him. 'I will arrange everything. All you have to do is tell your mother that you are going to stay with a friend. She cannot object since she is so busy nursing her cousin.'

'She will not give me permission to go.'

He meant it, Emerald recognised, inwardly cursing her mother-in-law-to-be.

'You are a man, Alessandro, not a child, a crown prince, how can you rule a country if you allow your mother to rule you?' Emerald asked, deliberately wounding his male pride.

'She is anxious about my safety; she cannot help it. She worries about me all the time.'

'We don't want to worry her, of course,' Emerald agreed. She certainly didn't want his mother interfering, and stopping Alessandro from marrying her. It was because she suspected that the princess would seek to do just that Emerald had suggested they elope in the first place.

Alessandro looked relieved. 'I will tell her that I want to marry you. Once she has met you she will love you just as I do.'

'But what if her cousin dies? Won't your mother want to go into mourning? That will mean that we will have to wait for ever before we can get married and I can't bear that. I want us to be together now, Alessandro. Now and for ever. If we elope, then we can be married straight away. Just think how wonderful that will be. I know your mother will be disappointed and perhaps even a little bit cross – *my* mother will be too – but I know that once they see how happy we are together and that we are meant for one another, they'll be happy for us. I know that some girls would insist on a big wedding, but all I want is to be your wife, and as quickly as possible.' How true that was, and she could still have the big wedding party once they were married.

'Instead of telling your mother in person you can post a letter to her as we leave London, saying that you are visiting a school friend, so that she isn't worrying about where you are.'

He was looking uneasy so Emerald continued, 'You said the other day that you have hardly seen her since you came to London because she spends so much time with her sick cousin.'

'That is true, yes.'

'You see, it will be simple. All you have to do is tell her that you have been invited by this school friend to visit his family estate. I will help you write the letter. Oh, my darling, darling Alessandro, it will be so wonderful,' Emerald told him, changing tack. 'Imagine it, just the two of us under the same roof, waiting to get married and then coming back here to London to tell everyone. How exciting it's going to be. We shall have a huge party and I shall have to be presented at court again, because that is what happens when you get married. Princess Emerald. Oh, I can't wait.'

She didn't intend to wait either, or to give Alessandro the chance to change his mind. The sooner they were on their way to Gretna Green, the better.

Alessandro was helpless. There was no point in him pointing out potential flaws or making logical arguments; Emerald had made up her mind and he loved her far too much to deny her anything. Besides, every time he said anything that remotely suggested that he did not adore and love her, Emerald burst into tears, and he could not bear that.

He must not let her down, Emerald told him, because if he did she would besiege his suite at the Savoy and haunt him with her broken heart for the rest of her life.

He would not let her down, Alessandro promised vehemently. He loved her and he always would.

Chapter Eighteen

Ella was feeling hot and bothered. How long was Oliver Charters going to be here for? She always did everything she could to avoid him whenever she knew he was coming into *Vogue*'s offices. If he saw her he was bound to look at her in that way of his, which made her feel so . . . so self-conscious and angry, and mixed up inside in a way she didn't like.

'Ella, I've got an errand for you.'

It was only when she was outside on the street that Ella realised that in her relief to obey her boss and escape from the office and the unwanted probability of seeing Oliver Charters, she'd left her diet pills behind in her office drawer. Angry panic engulfed her. She needed those pills; she hated being separated from them. She was terrified that if she didn't have them then she might start wanting to eat and then she'd get fat again. Her head was pounding. She felt sick, on edge, her nerves somehow rubbed raw. But she *was* still losing weight.

When she had gone to see Dr Williamson earlier in the week he had praised her for her success in losing over two stone when he had renewed her prescription.

Ella was hoping that Laura Harbold, the model who had laughed about her with Oliver, would come in for a photo shoot, so that Ella could see if she had reached her goal and now weighed less than the model. She wasn't going to give up dieting until she did.

The early morning light streamed in through the high windows, forming a pool of gold just in front of the altar. Emerald could feel its warmth on her face. Alessandro had complained the whole time they had been in Gretna that it was cold and that it never stopped raining, and this morning, when the sun had broken through, Emerald had told him that it was a good omen for their marriage. The small stone church was empty of both worshippers and wedding guests, the vicar uncurious about the history of the young couple he was now uniting together in marriage.

As she listened to the vicar intoning the marriage service Emerald gave Alessandro a disparaging look. It was just as well that she had been the one to organise everything. If it had been left to Alessandro, nothing would have got done.

All the way north on the train he'd been panicking that his mother would somehow guess that he had lied to her about staying with a friend and would stop them. The last three weeks, staying at a horrid little guesthouse, in separate rooms, of course – Emerald had no intention of risking Alessandro change his mind because he'd got what he wanted – with nothing to do other than read books and go for long walks, had been the most boring of Emerald's whole life, but now at last they were over. She was the one who ought to be feeling sorry for herself, not Alessandro. She wasn't even wearing a proper wedding dress, never mind the family tiara and veil, even if the elegance of her long cream evening dress, with its lace bodice, had drawn gasps of admiration from the locals who had seen them entering the church.

Emerald had been given away by the owner of the boarding house, after she had offered him twenty pounds to fulfil that role and provide them with two witnesses.

Alessandro's hand trembled as he slid the ring onto her finger. It was Emerald's great-grandmother's wedding ring, which she had left to Emerald, along with the rest of her jewellery.

'You may kiss the bride.'

Alessandro was trembling from head to foot and his eyes were wet with tears. Emerald looked at him impatiently. He was such a baby at times. Well, that would all have to change now that they were married. She wanted a proper man for a husband, not a boy afraid of his mother.

But she was now Princess Emerald di Lauranto. Emerald smiled to herself, her irritation instantly fading.

'Darling, darling Alessandro,' she whispered to him. 'My husband.'

There was no question of them remaining in Gretna now that they were married. Emerald had booked them into a smart hotel in Edinburgh.

'We should go back to London,' Alessandro said, packing his own bags as he had, on Emerald's instructions, left his valet in London. 'My mother will be worrying. I have never been away from her for so long before.'

'Don't be silly, you're a married man now. And besides, your mother thinks you're staying with a friend. Surely you want to have me all to yourself, and a proper honeymoon?' Emerald whispered to him suggestively.

Of course, she got her own way.

It was late afternoon before they left Waverley station in the taxi that would take them to their hotel. Edinburgh certainly wasn't London, but at least it looked as though it had some shops, Emerald acknowledged, as they drove down Princes Street.

'I hope your castle in Lauranto doesn't look as grim as this one,' she told Alessandro as they both looked up at the castle brooding on the hill above them.

Now that they were actually married, the irritation and impatience Emerald had begun to feel towards Alessandro had been replaced by a much happier mood.

The staff at the large Edwardian hotel treated her with the kind of deference that improved her mood even further, so that by the time they were finally alone in their palatial suite Emerald was on top of the world.

The physical practicalities of becoming Alessandro's wife held no fear or apprehension for her. The passionate kisses they had exchanged during their 'courtship' had increased her curiosity about sex and had also reinforced her opinion that it was something she was going to very much enjoy.

Now, with the tension and the boredom of their weeks in Gretna Green behind her, and safe in the knowledge

206

that she was legally Alessandro's wife, Emerald was not just ready to explore and enjoy the intimacies marriage permitted, but eager to do so as well.

Alessandro, though, had other matters on his mind.

'I must telephone my mother now and inform her of our marriage.'

Emerald stared at him, barely concealing her annoyance. He was such a very handsome boy, far better-looking than the Duke of Kent, or indeed any of the young men in her social circle. Lyddy could giggle as much as she liked that she thought the dreadful Australian was big and strong and soooo good-looking, but there was no way she would ever find such an uncouth person attractive, Emerald decided. She had caught her prince, but now she had to secure him. Emerald gave Alessandro a calculating look. He adored her and she fully intended that he would continue to adore her. And she knew just the way to ensure that he would.

Removing her hat and then her coat, Emerald stepped out of her shoes and then lay down on the hotel suite bed. Holding out her arms, she commanded softly, 'Come here.'

Alessandro looked at her blankly at first, and then when she gave him a long meaningful look from beneath her lowered lashes, the blood rose up under his skin, turning his face pink.

'We've been married for hours now,' Emerald pouted at him, 'and you haven't even kissed me properly yet.'

His mother quite plainly forgotten, Alessandro headed for the bed, the urgency that had him fumbling with his shoelaces making Emerald laugh in triumph.

There would be no telephone call to his mother until *she* decided one should be made, she gloated as she sat up on the edge of the bed to kiss him, glorying in the feel of his body trembling violently in her arms.

'I'm sorry. I'm sorry . . .' Fifteen minutes later Alessandro was practically crying with mortification, in between his attempts to slow his breathing.

The cause of his despair – and of Emerald's own irritation – was the damp patch darkening the fabric of his trousers, evidence of his inability to control his excitement long enough to consummate their marriage.

She supposed she ought to be pleased that he was so susceptible to her. After all, all she had done was kiss him and then slip her hand inside his trousers to explore the stiff flesh pushing against the fabric. Alessandro, in turn, had played with her breasts, tearing off one of the buttons of her blouse in his eagerness to touch them. It had been when Emerald has whispered encouragingly in his ear, 'You can kiss them, if you want to,' that the excitement of doing just that had resulted in Alessandro's face contorting as he cried out and the hard flesh she had been holding exuding the horrid sticky mess that was now staining his trousers.

Really, Alessandro was making a dreadful fuss, Emerald decided. If one of them had a right to be upset then it was her. She, after all, was the one who had been disappointed and now she had a very distinct ache low down in her body.

Frustrated, she cajoled, 'Well, never mind, we'll just have to do it again, won't we?'

Immediately Alessandro's tears ceased and he reached

for her, clasping her to his chest and telling her emotionally, 'I am so lucky to have won the love of someone so perfect. I adore you, I worship you, you are my life. I will make it up to you, I swear. Your beauty and my love for you overwhelmed me and disgraced me. Tell me that you forgive me.'

'Of course I forgive you,' Emerald assured him sweetly, but there was a determined glint in her eye. 'After all,' she added pointedly, 'we've got plenty of time before we need to get dressed for dinner.'

Emerald eyed her naked body in the ornate mirror that hung over the large claw-footed bath she had just stepped out of, admiring the smooth paleness of her skin and the curves of her body. Her nipples were still stiff and a little tender. She touched them with her own forefinger and thumb, tugging experimentally, gratified by the sudden surge of pleasure that coiled through her.

She had left Alessandro asleep on the bed where he had collapsed after he had finally penetrated her. He had wept at the sight of the few spots of blood that had marked his entry into her and her own entry into womanhood, but Emerald had been dismissive of his display of emotion. His penetration of her had hardly hurt at all, although she was not going to tell him that since he was making such a fuss about it and of her, calling her his beloved, his angel, and swearing eternal devotion to her.

The mirror threw back the reflection of her breasts, perfectly teardrop shaped, but now with the larger and stiffer nipples.

An unsatisfied ache pulsed deep inside her, its presence making her feel irritable and yet somehow at the same time also languid. She reached down and ran an investigative fingertip down over her soft dark pubic hair, parting the still swollen lips of her sex. The ache intensified and sharpened. A thrill of excitement suddenly gripped her.

In the privacy of the suite's bathroom she removed her bathrobe and lay down on the floor, cupping her own breast with one hand whilst the forefinger of the other explored and stroked, its movement quickly accelerating the pulse of the ache inside her body. She was breathing fast and shallowly, her back arched and her legs open.

Yes, that was it, that was the place . . . Her fingertip moved faster. Emerald closed her eyes, the better to sink deeper into the heat of the scarlet darkness waiting for her, and then to climb out of it, swiftly, so swiftly that its speed took her breath, leaving her only enough to make a small mewling cry of agonised pleasure when the firework display of satisfaction exploded through her.

Emerald eased herself up from the floor of the suite's bathroom and pulled on her bathrobe, trembling slightly.

Alessandro was still asleep. She felt rather tired herself. Tired but exalted and fiercely proud of the fact that she had been the one to give herself pleasure and, more importantly, take control of it.

She got on the bed and lay down next to Alessandro.

Marriage was going to be fun, especially once she had taught Alessandro how he could make her very, very happy.

*　　*　　*

'Send telegrams to our mothers? Why cannot we telephone them?' Alessandro protested almost pleadingly.

They were in their hotel suite, waiting for the porter to come and collect their luggage ready for the train journey south. Whilst Emerald was glowing with energetic triumph, Alessandro looked tired and on edge. Emerald had woken him in the night to insist that she wanted him to make love to her. Poor Alessandro, she was tiring him out, but then men did not have the endurance that women possessed. At least, though, she had taught Alessandro what she most liked him to do, even if at first he had been shocked and actually embarrassed by the explicitness of her commands.

There was no point in telling him the truth, which was that telegrams sent forewarning their mothers of their marriage would deny Alessandro's mother in particular the opportunity to be dramatic that a telephone call would give.

'Telegrams are easier,' she answered. 'And besides, your mother might not be there if we did telephone, and then we'd miss the train. Why are you looking like that?' Emerald went over to him and rubbed her body against his as she held his hand and looked soulfully at him.

'My mother is going to be very upset. I am her only child, and—'

'And now you are a married man, and when your mother sees how much you love me she is bound to understand. I know that my mother will.'

The truth was that she didn't care what her mother thought, though she was secretly delighted at the prospect of confronting her mother with the reality of her marriage and her new title – a far grander marriage and a far grander title than her mother's.

'Mmm.' Emerald kissed him swiftly. 'Do cheer up, darling. I don't want to spend all day shut up in a train carriage with a miserable husband. When we get to Lenchester House—'

'Lenchester House? But I have a suite of rooms at the Savoy.'

A suite of rooms to which his mother had open and easy access – all very well whilst Alessandro had still been single, but now he had a wife to consider. As far as Emerald was concerned, the sooner Alessandro's mother recognised the way things were now going to be, the better.

'A suite of rooms?' Emerald pouted. 'But, darling, Lenchester House is my home. It is where I have all my fondest memories of my dear father, and besides,' she added more practically, 'all my things are there.'

'But Lenchester House belongs to Dougie, surely?'

Emerald controlled her impatience and gave Alessandro a sweetly sad smile. 'It does now, but it has so many happy and special memories for me, Alessandro. Please be kind and understand that I want my happiest memories of all, those of being your bride, your wife, to be made there. It is silly of me to be so sentimental, I know . . .'

Alessandro had been brought up to understand the importance of sentiment to the female psyche, as Emerald had already discovered, and now his response was every bit as satisfactory as she had planned, an expression of obedience giving his face rather a puppy-dog melancholy.

'No, it is not silly at all,' he assured her tenderly. 'My

mother herself is often vexed by her own vulnerability to her sentiments.'

'I just know that she and I will understand one another perfectly,' Emerald told him. 'Of course we shall have to look for a house of our own in London,' she continued, having satisfied herself that she had won the first skirmish. Not that Alessandro was much of an opponent.

'A house in London? But I shall have to return to my country.'

'Well, of course, but we won't be living there *all* the time.' It was so much easier to make things work out the way one wished if one behaved as though they were already an indisputable fact, Emerald had always found. 'So it makes sense for us to find a house in London first, and then you can show me your little country.'

There was a knock on the door and then the porter came in, bringing an end to any further conversation, not that Emerald minded.

There was one thing she was completely determined on and that was that she was not going to allow Alessandro's mother to take charge of events and, ultimately, them. They may not as yet have met, but Emerald already knew that she and her mother-in-law were going to be on opposing sides in the fight for Alessandro's loyalty.

Chapter Nineteen

'You and Alessandro are married?'

Emerald watched coolly as her godmother struggled with her shock.

'It was very naughty of us, I know, to elope to Gretna, but you mustn't blame Alessandro, Aunt Beth.' Emerald gave her new husband a look of adoration as she reached for his hand. 'He was just so afraid that, with his mother's cousin being virtually on her deathbed, he would have to go through a whole year of formal mourning before we could be publicly engaged, and then with my mother being away on business . . .'

Emerald could see her godmother struggling to assess which was the worse scenario: a runaway marriage or no marriage at all.

'Alessandro desperately wanted to make me his princess,' Emerald smiled softly. 'It will be so much fun now that I'm married, holding wonderful parties here in London and on the Côte d'Azur for Lydia and Gwendolyn. I dare say that we shall even have a special ball for them in Lauranto to introduce them to scores of eligible young men.'

Her shrewd move had the desired effect. Emerald could almost see her godmother assessing the benefits to her daughter and niece of having a young married princess as a friend.

'Well, it is very unorthodox and quite shocking.'

'But so very romantic, Aunt Beth, although I did feel desperately sad that you and Mummy couldn't be there. There'll have to be an announcement of the marriage sent to *The Times*, of course.' Emerald's tone became more practical. 'And there will have to be a proper reception here at Lenchester House. I shall have to rely on you to organise that though, dear Godmother. Mummy is wonderfully clever with all her business things but she doesn't have your special touch. Do you think we should make it a wedding breakfast or—'

'No. It will have to be a reception. It's fortunate that Alessandro is foreign; foreigners are always so much more impetuous about these things,' her godmother responded automatically to Emerald's careful shepherding. 'Where will you be staying?'

'Why here, of course. I've told darling Alessandro that I couldn't imagine making happy memories for when we're old anywhere other than here. I can still see Daddy in these rooms, Aunt Beth; I can still hear his voice. Do you know, I think in a way he engineered it so that Alessandro and I would be married the way we were because he knew he wouldn't be able to give me away and he knew that I couldn't bear anyone else in the family to do it.'

'Oh, my dear girl, you are so right. To think of your father watching over you from heaven in such a way.

He was a wonderful man. I knew him before your mother, you know. My mother was his godmother.'

'I knew you'd understand. Of course, we can't possibly share my room so I think it would be best if Alessandro and I moved into the suite of rooms that used to be Mummy and Daddy's.'

Beth's sentimental tears were momentarily suspended, as she said uncertainly, 'The master suite, Emerald? Do you think you should? I mean, now that Dougie . . . well, he is the duke . . .' Her voice faltered beneath the reproach in the gaze Emerald fixed on her.

'It's what Daddy would have wanted. Dougie won't mind. After all, he isn't even like a proper duke really, is he? I mean, he's *Australian*.'

Dear Emerald, such a strong-willed girl, Beth thought weakly as she allowed her doubts to be swept aside.

'We should go and see my mother, Emerald, and we can stay tonight at the hotel with her whilst we wait to see if we have permission to stay here.'

Emerald looked at her husband. No way was she going to see her mother-in-law until she was ready. A husband though, as she was quickly discovering, was really very easy to deal with.

She lifted a hand to her forehead and protested faintly, 'Oh, Alessandro, darling, I am such a silly little thing, I know, but I've got the most horrid headache coming on and I can't possibly meet your mother until I've had a chance to rest. She has such high standards, I know, and I want her to see me looking my best. In fact, I really do think that I should go and lie down for a little while. Alessandro, you'll have to come with me otherwise I will

216

think that you are cross with me. Besides, I feel so exhausted that I don't think I could climb the stairs all by myself.'

Once she had satisfied herself that Alessandro was going to do as she wished, Emerald turned her attention back to her godmother, announcing, 'You will see to it that a notice is sent to *The Times*, won't you, Aunt Beth? And don't worry about telling Mrs Wreakin that we'll be moving into the master suite. I'll tell her myself.'

'How are you feeling now, my beloved, only I do really think that we should go and see Mama.'

It was three hours since they had originally gone upstairs, and now they had moved from Emerald's old room and into the master suite, where Emerald had been persuaded by an anxious Alessandro to eat a little of the light meal that Cook had prepared for them.

'Well, yes of course, we must,' Emerald agreed immediately, adding, 'Oh, Alessandro, I am so looking forward to meeting your mother, who has known and loved you since the minute of your birth. How overjoyed she must have been to have such a beautiful son. I hope in time, darling, that I may be as lucky. You do want a son and heir, don't you, Alessandro?'

As she spoke, Emerald sat up gracefully in the large bed with its ornate hangings of Denby silk, and let the silk dressing gown she was wearing slide down to her waist, leaving the top half of her body naked.

A smile of triumph curled Emerald's mouth as she saw the way Alessandro's eager gaze went to her naked breasts.

'Mama . . .' Alessandro tried to remind her.

But Emerald simply smiled again and sighed, 'Yes, of

course. Oh, Alessandro, I can't wait for our son to call me that.'

There was no real contest, of course. It would be tomorrow now before they saw Alessandro's mother – tomorrow afternoon. Afternoon tea, perhaps, Emerald mused as she lay looking up at the ceiling whilst Alessandro stroked and squeezed her breasts with growing urgency. They could invite her to join them for afternoon tea – so civilised and ladylike – and by then her mother-in-law was bound to have heard about their marriage. It was all working out perfectly.

Emerald made a soft purr of pleasure when she felt Alessandro's body tremble against her own as he pressed passionate kisses against her breasts. He was really getting rather good at that.

When Dougie returned to Lenchester House several hours later, Emerald's appropriation of the master suite was a *fait accompli*, and Beth's hand-wringing embarrassment at having to inform him of it told its own story.

'She's married Alessandro? I thought she was supposed to be staying with friends on the Côte d'Azur?'

'Well, yes, and it was very naughty of her to fib to us all like that, but Alessandro is foreign, and everyone knows that foreign men are so very impetuous.'

Alessandro might be, but Emerald wasn't. Calculating, manipulative, selfish – she was all *those* things – and wonderfully, dangerously, intoxicatingly able to make him feel as no other girl could. What rubbish! Having a wife like Emerald would be hard work. She would be demanding, capricious, impossible to trust, everything that was the opposite of the kind of safe comfortable reliable wife he would want when he did get married. Alessandro was welcome to her, Dougie told himself firmly, pushing down those feelings about Emerald that had begun to plague him far more than he liked.

'Presumably she's told her parents?' he asked.

Dougie thought a lot of Amber and Jay, and he hated to think of them being shocked and hurt. Besides, it was safer for him to think of them than to think of Emerald.

'She said she was going to send them a telegram. They're still away in America,' Beth defended her goddaughter.

Lady Beth was no match for Emerald, Dougie acknowledged, but then who was?

Needless to say the whole house was agog with the excitement of it all, and it was naturally the sole subject of discussion over the dinner table.

'Of course, it was very naughty of them to elope.'

'It's disgraceful, and typical of Emerald. I think she enjoys shocking and upsetting people,' was Gwendolyn's disapproving contribution to the dinner-table conversation, whilst Lydia, all starry-eyed with heroine worship and excitement, breathed giddily, 'Well, I think it's just the most romantic thing ever. Gwendolyn, do you really think that Emerald will invite us to go and stay with her?'

'Well, if she does I know that my parents certainly won't allow me to go,' Gwendolyn replied virtuously. 'Nor would I want to. I'm surprised at you, Lydia. After all, we have our reputations to think of.'

Listening to her niece, Beth felt her heart sink a little. Dear Gwendolyn was right, of course, but sometimes in certain circumstances one had to . . . well, the truth was that dear Gwendolyn was rather a plain girl and her mother had three other daughters to find husbands for.

'I do wish that Emerald had come down to dinner. She must have a dreadfully bad headache to have stayed in her room all this time,' Lydia announced naïvely. 'Do you think I should go up and see her, Mummy, perhaps take her a cup of tea . . . ?'

'Er, no, dear, I don't think that would be a good idea.' The soft pendulous flesh of Lady Beth's full cheeks quivered with the agitation in her voice.

'She won't have a headache.' Gwendolyn's voice was disapproving and sharp. 'Emerald never gets headaches. She's just attention-seeking, if you ask me.'

And he knew exactly what kind of attention she would be seeking and getting, Dougie thought enviously, even if Lydia was too naïve to think in such terms. What was it about the British upper class that made them feel it was necessary for their daughters to remain so ignorant when it came to 'the facts of life'?

If he knew his own sex, Dougie thought, then it wouldn't be a headache that was keeping Emerald and Alessandro in isolation in their bedroom – his bedroom, if you wanted to be pedantic about it. Dougie scowled. Not that it mattered a single damn to him who Emerald married or what she did with him. He'd be a fool to be anything other than glad to have her out of his hair, and not constantly mocking him and taunting, nor constantly reminding him that he could never be the man or the duke that her father had been.

The trouble was that no matter how hard he tried not to let it happen, Emerald had a way of getting under a chap's skin. It didn't matter what kind of guy she had married, he would still have felt like he did right now, Dougie admitted, as though . . . as though . . . The truth was that Dougie just did not want to consider what the thought of Emerald being married to someone else made him feel.

'Mmm, that was so nice, darling. Now hold me tight and don't leave me, will you? Yes, I know I said we'd telephone your mother, but it's far too late now. She's probably in bed asleep, and I wouldn't want to wake her.'

She really hated the décor in these rooms, Emerald decided, waiting until Alessandro's deep breathing signalled that he had fallen asleep, before moving away from him. It was so much her mother's taste, all that dowdy old-fashioned embroidered silk.

When she and Alessandro got their own house she'd have it decorated in a much more modern style, perhaps get David Hicks in.

Amber and Jay were just about to go down to dinner when Emerald's telegram arrived. They had been chatting happily about the pleasure they'd had spending a week with the twins, who were both planning to spend the summer working at camps in the United States, but Amber's relaxed happiness evaporated as she read Emerald's telegram. Having read it once she read it again, her heart sinking.

'Oh no!' she said in a strained voice, passing the telegram over to Jay so that he too could read it. 'Why would she do such a thing? Why didn't she simply tell us that she and Alessandro wanted to marry, instead of running off to Gretna Green? Surely she knows that all we want is her happiness? I do worry so about her, and this . . . this absence of the kind of relationship a mother and daughter should share. It's my fault, of course,' she added miserably.

'Of course it isn't,' Jay tried to reassure her.

'It is,' Amber insisted. 'I didn't want her, after all, not when I first realised I was carrying her, and somehow I'm sure she knows that, even though afterwards, and long before she was born, I did want her.'

Jay reached for her hands and held them tightly. 'You have been and are a wonderful mother, Amber.'

'Emerald doesn't think that. She never has. It must have been so awful for her, Jay, a new-born baby whose mother wasn't there for her.'

'You weren't there for her because you were very ill, and fighting for your life. Please stop torturing yourself with this foolishness, my love. Emerald is a very selfish and strong-willed young woman.'

'She's so young, Jay, and I can't help thinking that she may have married Alessandro because . . . because she wants someone to love her, because she feels vulnerable.'

Jay shook his head. 'Emerald, vulnerable? It's natural that you should be concerned for her, but I won't let you blame yourself for Emerald's determination to do what she wants, regardless of other people's feelings.'

'I can't help worrying about her, Jay. I just wish she'd said something; talked to us about it first, confided in me. I'm really not sure how I'll be able to hide my disappointment.'

Chapter Twenty

The salon was busy, buzzing with clients and music and stylists, whilst juniors scurried round washing hair, producing cups of coffee, and sweeping up, when Rose called in just before lunch one Saturday morning in early summer.

'Business looks good,' she told Josh, as she handed him the sandwich she had brought him. 'Don't worry, it's kosher,' she scolded, as he opened it to look inside.

'Kosher I do not worry about; making sure I get my money's worth I do,' he teased her, adopting a heavy Jewish accent.

'Saw the announcement about your cousin getting hitched.'

Rose responded with a forced smile. She was never comfortable talking about Emerald, always conscious of Emerald's contempt and hostility.

'Well, it's certainly a surprise. Knowing Emerald, I'd expected her to insist on having a huge society wedding.'

'If she had to choose between the huge society prize husband and the huge society wedding, maybe she decided it was better to get the husband,' Josh suggested, showing a sharper awareness of the situation than Rose had been prepared for.

'Emerald would have wanted to marry well,' she was obliged to agree.

'I'd certainly say she'd done that, nabbing herself a prince,' Josh grinned. 'Does that mean you'll have to curtsy to her now?'

'Never!' The speed and bitterness of Rose's reply took them both off guard. Josh frowned, and Rose flushed and looked away.

'I'm sorry,' she apologised in a stilted voice. 'It's just that Emerald and I have never got on. Even when we were children she loved telling everyone that her father was a duke whilst mine . . .'

'Whilst yours?' Josh prodded when she fell silent.

'Whilst mine was a drunk and a thief – my great-grandmother's words, not mine. Look, I'd rather not talk about it, if you don't mind, Josh.'

Josh gave a small shrug. 'I don't mind. I don't want to pry.'

Had she offended him? Rose shot him a quick look. Sometimes Josh could be so open that you could see his thoughts written on his face, and then at others, it was hard to tell just what he was feeling. She didn't want to offend him. He was a good friend, he made her laugh, and being with him helped her to forget all those things she could not bear to think about. Like John and the awful unthinkable horror that could have happened. She still had nightmares about the look of almost gloating cruelty on Lady Fitton Legh's face when she had warned her of the great sin they would have been committing.

Rose hadn't been to Denham – she couldn't think of it as 'home' any more – since Easter. She was afraid of what she might say and do if she did. Not to John – John wasn't the one who had hurt and betrayed her. No, it was Amber she was afraid to see, in case all the pain and horror trapped inside her came spilling out. Better by far that nothing was said. What good could it do, after all? None. But the terrible hurt and anger would always be there in her heart. Hadn't her aunt thought of what might happen? Hadn't she sensed, guessed, that Rose might be drawn to John and, not knowing of their possible blood connection, do something that was forbidden? Or was it as Lady Fitton Legh had implied: that her aunt had simply not cared enough to protect her from that sin? The facts spoke for themselves. Amber could have told her; she could have trusted her, she could have protected her; even if she could not love her as she had pretended to do.

'Listen, do you fancy coming out with me tonight? There's this new jazz club I've heard about.'

Josh's question brought Rose back to reality. She gave him a smile, grateful to be back on their normal footing.

'What's wrong? Has your latest girl refused to play ball?'

Josh affected a look of injured innocence. 'I was thinking of you.'

'I was planning to stay in.'

'Stay in on a Saturday night? Don't be daft, that's for squares. Come on, it will do you good.'

He was right, Rose acknowledged. There was no point staying in and brooding.

'All right,' she agreed, 'but no going off and leaving me because you've seen a girl you fancy, like you did the last time I agreed to go out with you.'

'As if I would,' Josh protested. 'I'll call round for you about eight, OK?'

Two girls who had just come into the salon looked at Rose and then one of them whispered something to the other. The photographs of Josh cutting Rose's hair that Ollie had taken now adorned the stair wall and had brought in a rush of girls wanting the same haircut after they had appeared in *Vogue*. Word was still spreading.

Almost overnight, much to her astonishment and, if she were honest, her discomfort, Rose had turned into something of a minor celebrity. She'd even been offered modelling work, which she'd turned down, and had had umpteen young men asking her out, as well as Janey begging her to model the clothes she planned to design for St Martins' end-of-year fashion show.

Her employer had teased her about her new-found fame, and another unwanted result of that fame was the attention she was now getting from the husband of one of their most important clients.

Initially when Mr Russell had come into the drawing room of his and his wife's fashionable apartment whilst Rose was there carefully taking measurements for a pair of bergère chairs their client wanted recovering, she hadn't thought anything of it. But then he had come over to her, pressing up against her from behind as he made to go past her in the confined space between the chairs and the window, his hand on her shoulder to prevent her from moving. With his free hand he had stroked her hair and then her neck, commenting on the silkiness of her hair and the softness of her skin.

At first Rose had been too shocked to say or do anything, hardly able to comprehend what was happening. Their client's husband was in his late forties – it was surely impossible that he could be doing what he had done.

To her relief the telephone had rung, and she had been able to make her escape.

She hadn't intended to say anything to anyone about what had happened but somehow she had found herself telling Josh when she had bumped into him in a pub on the King's Road, where Janey had persuaded her and Ella to go for a drink.

Josh had laughed and told her that what she needed was a long sharp hatpin. Then the very next time she had seen him he had handed her a long slim box inside which she had found a dangerous-looking hatpin with a pretty pearl and diamanté head.

'I saw it in a junk shop,' he had told her, laughing. 'And now that you've got it, you make sure you use it if old man Russell tries it on again.'

Josh could always make her laugh, no matter how down she was feeling.

And she was feeling down, Rose admitted. The John and Amber situation wasn't all that was on her mind. Her desire was growing to turn away from the traditional kind of interior design she was being trained for, the kind of interior design service provided by her aunt's Walton Street shop, and to focus instead on the creative opportunities she could see so clearly in the commercial sector. Once,

Amber would have been the first person she'd want to discuss this with because Rose would have believed that her aunt understood and knew how she was feeling, and would have put Rose's own best interests first in any advice she might have given her. But now Rose felt reluctant to share her dreams with Amber. It was a horrid feeling to know that the person you loved and trusted the most had deceived you. Amber had been like a mother to her, but now Rose felt betrayed, cheated, and very alone.

Chapter Twenty-One

'Well, of course I am delighted that you are both so happy, but I must say I am disappointed that you didn't see fit to confide in me, Alessandro.'

They were 'taking afternoon tea' at the Savoy, Emerald's strategic choice of venue, which ensured that she and Alessandro were just late enough for his mother to have arrived first and have to wait for them – a small accident with the heel on Emerald's shoe coming loose and entailing a return to the house.

The princess was every bit as formidable as Emerald had known she would be, and more. Tall and elegant, with a look of Queen Mary about her, she sat stiff-backed in her chair, affecting to smile benevolently on them whilst her eyes were cold, at least whenever her glance moved to Emerald.

Not that Emerald was at all disturbed at the thought of Alessandro's mother disliking her. There could, after all, be only one woman in control of Alessandro's life from now on, and that woman was going to be Emerald.

'Alessandro didn't want to be selfish and tell you about our happiness whilst you were having to nurse your cousin, Mama-in-law, did you, Alessandro, darling?' Emerald answered sweetly for her husband, earning herself an icy look from his mother.

'Alessandro knows that for *me*, his happiness comes first, and before anything and anyone else. And besides, what mother would not want to share in her son's happiness?'

Emerald knew that a challenge accompanied the words, the message within them hidden from Alessandro himself. His mother turned away from Emerald and towards her son, managing to block Emerald's view of Alessandro and thus effectively coming between them as she did so, to ask, 'You surely do not think your mother so inhuman, do you, Alessandro?'

It was plain to Emerald what her mother-in-law was trying to do, but she wasn't going to succeed. Whilst Alessandro was still trying to formulate his response, she stepped in – literally as well as figuratively – getting up from her chair to go to stand at her husband's side, one hand resting on his shoulder.

Emerald responded for him, 'Of course he doesn't. He thinks you are the most wonderful mother in the world. I confess that already I'm feeling rather jealous and hoping that my son will love me as much as Alessandro does you. I shall certainly do everything I can to make sure that he does.'

Now the cold gaze was measuring her and the smooth forehead was marred by a small frown. Emerald smiled, enjoying her triumph.

'We mustn't take up too much of your time, Mama-in-law. I know how difficult it must have been for you to leave your cousin's side when she is so unwell.'

'You are a very thoughtful girl, Emerald. I can see already how things will be between us.'

Indeed she could, Emerald suspected. Well, so much the better; she certainly wasn't going to be intimidated.

'Now, Alessandro and I have certain matters of state that we need to discuss, which will only bore you. You stay here and finish your tea. I shall make sure to send Alessandro back to you when we are finished.'

Emerald could only applaud her mother-in-law's briskly confident tone. However, she was more than ready for her, as she smiled sweetly through every poison-tipped word.

'Oh, no, Mama-in-law, please don't say that.' She leaned across and slipped her arm through Alessandro's, looking up at him adoringly. 'You see, we just can't bear to be apart even for the shortest time, can we, Alessandro, darling? I know I don't know anything about affairs of state, but I do so want to learn. I want to be the best wife Alessandro could ever have, so that you will both be proud of me. I know you will understand what I mean, Mama-in-law. After all, you must have felt the same when you married Alessandro's father. Alessandro, darling, do tell your mother how important it is to me that we do every-thing together. Not that we shall be able to stay long, I'm afraid, because we've been invited out for dinner tonight.'

The gauntlet had well and truly been thrown down, and Emerald was feeling very pleased with herself when, ten minutes later, she and Alessandro left the Savoy.

So much for motherly love; when it came to choosing one's weapons, sex won out every time, Emerald decided happily.

Chapter Twenty-Two

'Of course, I am delighted to hear that you have found a house you like, Emerald, dear.' A pained expression crossed the princess's face. 'Personally, I would have chosen the more substantial house we looked at. That, I thought, was better suited to becoming a royal residence as it would have had room for darling Alessandro's personal staff, but then it is perhaps rather too much for me to expect a young woman, and newly married too, to be able to think of such things, especially one so very much in love.

'Tell me, my dear, are you feeling better now? These headaches you suffer from must be such a burden to you. I have always been fortunate in having the strongest constitution, as has Alessandro. Poor health can be such a dismal thing, especially when one is expected to perform so many public duties, but then as you know I shall always be on hand to step in for you should you not be up to things.'

Emerald smiled through her mother-in-law's vengeful monologue, despite the fact that her face felt as though it was cracking.

'I wish I had taken your advice with regard to the house, Mama-in-law, but as it is Mr Melrose who will be organising the lease, I felt obliged to listen to him.'

There, let the old witch choke on that! Emerald had been furious when Alessandro had told her uncomfortably that his mother did not think the Laurantian Exchequer would authorise the expense of a London house for its newly married prince, since he would hardly be spending much time in London. Emerald fully intended that they would be spending a great deal of time there indeed, but she hadn't as yet informed Alessandro of this. Instead, she had quickly turned the situation to her own advantage, insisting that she did not want to be a burden on her darling Alessandro's little state's treasury and that she would ask dear Mr Melrose to sanction the money from her inheritance from her father.

'Well, yes, my dear, I am sure that the house is perfectly suitable in its way, and as we don't maintain an embassy here in London, you will not be burdened with the worry of having to organise official receptions and dinners. At home, of course, it is different. There we do entertain the heads of other royal families, but you need not worry: naturally I shall continue to deal with all of that, whilst you enjoy yourself.'

Emerald's smile widened. 'Oh, no, Mama-in-law, we couldn't expect that of you. Alessandro was only saying the other day, how much he was looking forward to giving you the chance to retire from your official duties so that you can spend more time with your friends, and how much he worries that at your age it isn't really wise

for you to be doing so much. I'm looking forward to it.'
Now Emerald's smile was genuine.

Alessandro's mother, though, was not giving way. Instead she gave Emerald an indulgent smile.

'Well, we shall see, I'm afraid that being the consort of a royal prince isn't always as easy as it seems . . .

'Now the reason I asked you both to come and have tea here in my suite with me – so sweet of you to suggest that I come to you, Emerald, but as one ages one does tend to prefer one's own servants around – is that I have a favour to ask you.'

Emerald smiled again, benignly this time, but her eyes were hard. She and Alessandro might have been married only just over a month but it was long enough for her to have realised that her mother-in-law was not going to give up easily her right to control her son's life.

'Alessandro, you know that this is the time of year when the finance minister presents his budget to us before it goes before the council. Normally, with you being so newly married and so busy here in London ensuring that Emerald has the house she wants, I would return to Lauranto to deal with this formality myself in my official capacity as regent in your absence, but with my cousin in such very poor health still, I feel I cannot leave her, so . . .'

The old witch was trying to force them to leave London and go to Alessandro's wretchedly dull little country where Emerald would have to live under the same roof as her – because she would find an excuse to follow them back there, Emerald was convinced of it. Well, it was not going to happen. They were *not* going to leave London.

Assuming an agonised and distressed expression, Emerald turned to Alessandro, and exclaimed, 'Oh dear, I feel so dreadful, darling, but we can't possibly go.' She turned back to Alessandro's mother. 'Mama-in-law, we hate to disappoint you but it is just impossible for us to leave London right now. I have so much to do here. There are matters relating to my own affairs that have to be dealt with, what with the lease of the new house being in my name and everything, and then I have to go to Paris for fittings for my new clothes, and Mummy is coming up to London and will expect to see me and the new house.'

'Emerald, my dear, I quite understand.' The princess's voice was soothing. 'You must not worry. You see, there is no need for you both to go, no need at all. Alessandro can go by himself, can't you, darling? After all, one of us has to be there. You know I would go, but I just couldn't bear it if my poor cousin was to pass away when I wasn't there.' The dowager had produced a lace-edged hand-kerchief and was dabbing at her eyes.

Alessandro went down on his knees and took hold of his mother's free hand, imploring her, 'Mama, please do not distress yourself. Of course I shall go.'

Damn, damn, damn! Emerald was furious, but she managed to conceal her real feelings as she pleaded, 'Alessandro, you know that I can't bear the thought of us being apart.'

But for once the blandishment and the promise behind it failed to work its magic. In fact, Alessandro barely seemed to have heard her as he concentrated on his mother, who was uttering, 'I can hardly bear to think what your father would have had to say if he thought I was neglecting my duty.'

'Papa would never have thought that of you, Mama, never,' Alessandro was quick to assure her.

'You are such a good son, Alessandro. Indeed, I am blessed in having such a good son and a truly understanding daughter-in-law. You will have to leave tomorrow, I'm afraid. I should have told you earlier but I was hoping not to have to do so.'

Liar, liar, liar, Emerald wanted to scream. She had been outmanoeuvred, tricked and, like a fool, she had fallen into her mother-in-law's carefully baited trap. Emerald was furious with herself but there was nothing she could do now.

Still, at least her mother-in-law was going to have to stay in London instead of going to Lauranto with Alessandro, as Emerald was sure she really wanted to do, the old cat. What she would have to do now was make sure that Alessandro missed her so much that when he came back she would be able to flaunt his devotion in front of his mother, and Emerald knew *exactly* how to do that.

'Rose, is something wrong? You haven't been home to see us for such a long time.'

'Nothing's wrong, Aunt Amber. It's just that I've been so busy.'

They were in the sitting room of the Chelsea house, drinking the tea that Amber had insisted on making, though Rose would have preferred to have escaped to her bedroom rather than talk to her aunt.

Amber wasn't reassured. It was selfish of her, she felt, to long for the closeness she and Rose had always shared in the past. She had ached to hold her niece in her arms and breathe in the familiar scent of her, a special bond that linked them and which had always meant so much to her. In Rose she had always thought she had found the daughter in spirit that Emerald had never been.

But Amber could sense something had changed. She wanted desperately to beg Rose to confide in her, but at the same time she was determined not to pry. It was hard, though, when Rose looked pale and quite definitely thinner, but her much-loved niece was a young woman now, and was bound to have the kind of private hopes and dreams that all young women had. Such things were not easily discussed with members of an older generation, however much loved, as Amber well knew from her own youth.

Why, Amber wondered wryly, had Nature made it so hard for the young to accept that those who had gone before them had experienced what they were experiencing? In a fairer world it would be possible to pass on to one's young the benefit of the pain one had gone through to spare them going through it themselves, instead of each generation having to undergo it in turn.

'We never seem to get time just for the two of us any more.'

Amber wished she hadn't said anything when she saw Rose's almost visible withdrawal from her, as she responded, 'The shop's very busy, and so are you, what with Emerald newly married and buying a house, and needing you to help her.'

The last thing Emerald would want was her help, Amber knew, and she had thought that Rose would know that too.

Rose couldn't bring herself to look directly at her aunt. She wished desperately that Amber wasn't here. She felt so uncomfortable with her – uncomfortable and angry – as though she was in danger of exploding with all the accusations burning inside her. What was the point, though, in saying anything? Her aunt would pretend that it was all a misunderstanding – she was bound to – and Rose knew she would end up feeling even worse than ever. A part of her longed for the days of her childhood when she had been able to run to Amber and know that her aunt would make whatever pain she felt go away with the warmth of her arms and a kiss on the top of her head. How she yearned to go back to those days, before she had been told the horrible truth that now haunted her.

'Dan, what is it, what's wrong?' Janey asked anxiously as she tried to cuddle up to him for the third time, only to have him shrug away from her, his shoulders hunched.

'I'm just not in the mood.' His voice was dull and empty. 'It's not your fault,' he assured her, 'it's mine, for being such a damn fool. Oh God, Janey, I could kick myself, I really could. Not that it would do any good, and besides, I'm all too likely to be getting a good kicking off someone else if—' He broke off and turned away from her again, to stare morosely out of the dingy window of his down-at-heel flat.

'Someone's been threatening you.' Immediately Janey was alarmed.

'Oh, damn it, I didn't mean to tell you. The last thing I want is to burden you with my problems.'

'Don't be silly. Your problems are my problems,' Janey told him lovingly.

She was so proud of him and his acting talent. Everyone in their crowd said that he was bound to go far, but Dan himself wasn't so confident. He often complained that he never seemed to have the luck to get the breaks that others got.

Janey knew from little things he'd let slip that he hadn't had the easiest childhood. His mother had died when he was very young, and his father had remarried. He'd tried to get on well with his stepmother, but she'd never had much time for him, especially when her own children had come along.

'It wouldn't be so bad if I hadn't given Dad that twenty quid I'd got put to one side. I couldn't not help out when he's been laid off. He is my dad, after all.'

Janey squeezed back her tears. Dan hated seeing her cry, but he was so very good and noble, and she just couldn't help it.

'I'd no idea that the chap who had this place before me had scarpered without paying the rent, but the landlord won't believe me and he's threatening to send round his heavies unless I pay up.'

'I can lend you the money.'

'No! I'm not having my girl lending me money. It wouldn't be right.'

'Oh, Dan. That's so typical of you, but you must let me help you, darling, please. I can't bear to see you like this. When did you last have something to eat?'

'Eat? That's the last thing I feel like doing. Not that I could afford to buy any food, even if I wanted to. That advert I was promised by that ruddy agent hasn't come through.'

'But you're bound to get something better. You are so good.'

'Good, but out of work and broke, and about to be beaten up by a bunch of heavies over someone else's debts. Oh God, Janey, I don't know why you bother with me. You'd be better off without me. The damn world would be better off without me.'

The anguish in his voice had panic clutching at Janey's tender heart. She desperately wanted to make things right for him.

'No, Dan, you mustn't say that. I shall lend you the money.'

Dan gave a short, broken laugh. 'There's no point – because I can't repay it.'

'Then I shall give it to you,' she told him firmly, 'and I warn you now, Dan, I shan't take no for an answer.' She opened her handbag and removed twenty-five pounds from her purse – a fortune really, which she only happened to have with her because Amber had given it to her to pay it into her bank account.

'Here you are,' she told him, 'and I don't want to hear another word about it – ever. In fact, I think we should forget all about it.'

'Forget your kindness?' Dan's voice was thick and raw with emotion. 'Oh God, but you are so special, Janey, so good and kind and wonderful. Come here, and let me show you how much I love you.'

When he reached for her, Janey went willingly into his arms, wrapping her own around him as he kissed the side of her neck and then just behind her ear, on the spot he knew always made her shiver with delight. She moved closer to him, her heart filled with happiness.

'You're so good to me, and for me,' Dan told her, his voice muffled because he had pushed her top out of the way and was kneading her breasts, freed from the confinement of her bra.

The damp chilliness of the air in the basement flat brought out a rash of goosebumps on her skin and made her nipples pucker.

'Great tits,' Dan told her, eyeing them with admiring approval. 'In fact they're good enough for *Tit-Bits*.'

Janey pretended to look shocked at his mention of the well-known magazine, famous for its jokes and pictures of scantily dressed girls, but Dan didn't notice. He was too busy playing with her breasts, making Janey herself forget her pretend disapproval when he sucked on one of her nipples, causing her belly to cramp up in fierce delight.

Dan was an impatient lover, their sex exciting, hot and very quick, and mostly over before they had got undressed properly.

Afterwards, when Dan said how good it had been, Janey could never bring herself to tell him that it was over too fast for her in case he thought she was one of those silly frigid girls who didn't properly understand about sex. All the boys in the crowd Janey went around with said that the worst kind of girls were the ones who had sex like virgins and were obviously frigid.

Now, with Dan pushing up her skirt and sliding his hand into her knickers, Janey longed to suggest to him that they got undressed and into bed, instead of Dan pushing her back against the wall.

'Oh, babe . . .' Dan was crooning, which meant Janey knew that it wouldn't be long now before he lifted her up and thrust into her a couple of times before coming, because 'Oh, babe' was what he always said before he did that.

'Why don't we do it on the bed?' Janey suggested, slightly breathlessly.

'It's better standing up,' Dan told her, adding softly, 'There's my good little pussy, all wet and ready for me. Want me to give you a finger fuck as a treat first for being so good to me?'

Janey nodded, closing her eyes and concentrating fiercely on the sensation aroused by Dan's fingers inside her. If she could just concentrate hard enough then surely she could capture that elusive feeling that she knew was there waiting for her, if Dan would just be patient and not so . . .

She gasped in protest when Dan stopped touching her, telling her, 'There you are, I'll bet you enjoyed that, didn't you?' before thrusting himself into her.

Janey felt so disappointed that she almost wanted to cry. She could hear Dan panting and groaning as he thrust deeper and harder, but she had preferred what he had been doing before, and she would have liked it even more, she acknowledged, if only she'd felt brave enough to tell him just where she'd really like him to touch her.

Feeling guilty because she wasn't more grateful, Janey produced an appreciative moan just as Dan came.

She cleaned herself up in the cold, grubby bathroom that Dan shared with the tenants of the other flats. Her handkerchief would have to be thrown away now but she couldn't bring herself to use the grey towel Dan had offered her. Despite her efforts she still felt sticky and uncomfortable.

'Shall we go out tonight?' she asked him. 'There's that new coffee bar that's opened.'

'I'd love to but I can't. I've promised to help a friend of my sister's work on her lines. Of course, I'd much rather be with you, but I've said I would and I wouldn't like to let her down.'

'No, of course you mustn't. I wouldn't want you to.'

The approving smile Dan gave her was, after all, all the reward she needed.

'It's a very nice little piece, Ella, now that you've polished it up properly.' The travel editor's voice was patronising but Ella didn't care. At least, she did, but she wasn't going to let her disappointment over the way she had had to water down her carefully crafted article on Venice, to suit the travel editor's demands that it be 'more glamorous, darling – *Vogue* readers adore glamour; it's positively essential to them'.

'It will go in next month's issue along with some of Oliver Charters' photographs from the Comte de Livron's Masquerade Ball.'

Dismissed from the travel editor's office, Ella made her way back to the cubbyhole of an office she shared with some of the other editorial assistants. Getting her travel piece actually in print, and with her name as a byline, was a huge step forward and she mustn't let herself dwell on her wish that the editor had not cut the two paragraphs lovingly detailing the work that went into making Venice's gondolas, and the simple lives of these boatbuilders, their skill passed down the generations, contrasting them with their glamorous passengers, being ferried from one glittering occasion to another.

Ella's heart was pounding, but she was used to that now. It was one of the side effects of the pills prescribed for her by the diet doctor, like the sudden compulsion to chatter, the feeling of restless energy that had her dashing everywhere, and, of course, not wanting to eat.

Which reminded her. As she sat down at her desk Ella reached into her handbag for her bottle of pills, putting them on her desk and then going to fill the office kettle to make herself a cup of tea.

Oliver hesitated outside the assistant editors' office. He'd just left the fashion editor, who had been praising him for the photographs he had done for the Venice shoot, and that had made him reflect reluctantly on the part Ella had played in enabling him to get those shots.

He had been feeling guilty about Ella, and, in some inexplicable way, almost responsible for her. She was so ruddy naïve when it came to men, and he had had no right to kiss her the way he had done.

He pushed open the office door. The first thing he saw was the telltale bottle of diet pills, one pill placed ready on the desk itself – Ella's desk. Oliver knew immediately what they were. All the models used them, and got hooked on them.

He strode across, picked up the bottle and turned to Ella, who stiffened in outrage, trapped in the corner by the kettle as he shook the bottle at her and demanded in angry disbelief, 'Don't tell me that you are stupid enough to be taking these?'

'It's none of your business what I do,' Ella told him. He was still holding her precious bottle of pills and she desperately wanted him to put them down so that she could retrieve them.

'Do you know what these are and what they do – apart from allowing idiotic girls to half starve themselves?' Oliver challenged her. 'They're amphetamines,' he continued without allowing her to answer him. 'Speed, that's what they're called, because that is exactly what they do: speed you up. You don't eat, you don't sleep, you talk twenty to the dozen, they speed up your heart and your life, and if you're unlucky – and plenty are – they speed it up so much that it's over almost before it's begun and you die young – of a heart attack.'

'You're just making that up,' Ella defended herself, not wanting to admit how much his outburst had shocked her, all the more so because she so clearly recognised the symptoms he had described.

'No, I'm not. And dying of a heart attack is what you get if you're lucky. This stuff sends some people mental, paranoid. I thought you were supposed to be intelligent,' he told Ella with disgust as he flung the bottle into the waste-paper bin.

Immediately Ella rushed across to rescue her precious tablets but, realising what she was going to do, Oliver got there first, standing over the bin and then grabbing her to hold her off, his expression suddenly changing from impatience to grim anger.

Before Ella could stop him he had wrenched up her top to expose her pride and joy, her ribcage with all her ribs clearly on display. It was unfortunate that her breasts were still so large, but she was sure that she could get them smaller if she just kept on dieting.

Furious with Oliver, she tried to pull free of his hold, but he was manhandling her towards the mirror on the wall, holding her in front of his own body as he positioned her before the mirror so that her bare midriff was visible in the reflection.

'Have you seen what you're doing to yourself?' he asked her savagely.

Of course she had, and she was proud of what she had achieved.

'You look like a skeleton, like someone who has just come out of Belsen.'

It was an awful thing to say to her – comparing her with the poor people on whom atrocities had been committed in the German death camps, and Ella wasn't going to let him get away with it.

Shaking with temper she threw back at him, 'Well, at least I don't look like an elephant, so if you and Laura want to find someone to make fun of and joke about behind their backs, it won't be me any more, will it?' She was literally shaking with anger, her face red and her eyes bright with emotion.

Oliver released her and stared at her in disbelief. 'You've done this to yourself because some silly model made a bitchy remark about you?'

'You agreed with her.' Ella was beyond caring now about what she was revealing about herself.

'What?'

'You agreed with her when she said that I wouldn't be able to diet. You laughed with her.'

Oliver was shaking his head. 'I don't believe this. I don't care what you think you overheard, I can tell you that there is no way I would ever, ever have agreed that you needed to lose weight. Do you want to know why I know that?' When Ella didn't say anything, he continued bitingly, 'I know it because I just happen to think that you have – had – the most gorgeous, sexy, lush, damnably lustable-after body in the entire *Vogue* setup. A proper woman's body, with curves and soft flesh and fabulous tits, the kind of woman's body that makes a grown man want to fall on his knees and thank God for making it. And now look what you've done to it.'

Too angry to wait for Ella's response, Oliver strode out of the room banging the door behind him, leaving Ella shaking with a mixture of relief and shock.

It was half an hour since Oliver had left the office and Ella was still staring into space in disbelief, her tea now cold and her diet pills, she had to assume, in Oliver's pocket.

Well, that didn't matter. She could get some more. And she would get some more because she hadn't believed a word of what he'd said to her, not one single word.

Oliver stared moodily into his pint of beer. He still couldn't believe that Ella had been stupid enough to do

247

what she had done and ruin that damn near perfect body of hers, all because of some bitchy model. OK, so maybe she could have spared a couple of pounds, four or five at the most, but to lose the amount of weight she had done . . . Along with his anger, Oliver felt a renewal of his earlier sense of responsibility towards her.

Ruddy women, especially wet-behind-the-ears women like Ella. The sooner she found some posh toff to marry her and give her a few kids to keep her busy, the better, Oliver decided grimly.

Chapter Twenty-Three

'Emerald, my dear, you look so hot and bothered, do come and sit down and let me order some tea for you.'

Shaking her head angrily in refusal, Emerald stepped towards her mother-in-law and thrust the letter she had removed from her handbag at her, stating furiously, 'I received this letter from Alessandro this morning saying that he is going to have to stay in Lauranto at least another month. I want to know what all this is about.'

The princess brushed the letter aside with a gesture that said quite clearly to Emerald that she was perfectly well aware of its contents. Because no doubt she was responsible for them, Emerald seethed.

'Well, my dear, I should have thought it was perfectly obvious to an intelligent young woman like you, Alessandro has his duties—'

'Alessandro's most important duty is to me, his wife,' Emerald interrupted her sharply.

'That might apply to an ordinary man, but Alessandro is not an ordinary man, he is a prince, and as such his first duty must always be to his position and his people.'

'Very well then, if Alessandro can't come back to London to me, then I shall go to him.'

Alessandro's mother gave her a coldly appraising look. 'Ah, yes, your marriage to my son. Conducted in such great haste and secrecy. Not what I would have expected from my son. But of course, Alessandro wasn't the one who engineered the marriage, was he?'

Before Emerald could answer, she continued, 'There is a history of hasty marriage in your family, as I discovered recently when I was looking into your background. Your own mother, for example—'

'What do you mean, you've been looking into my family background?' Emerald stopped her.

'Well, when one's son – the heir to a principality and its ruler – ends up married to a young woman unknown to his family, and in the dubious fashion in which your marriage to my son was conducted, naturally one wishes to equip oneself with whatever information is available about such a person – and her family.'

'My family history is perfectly well known. My own title testifies to the position of my father,' Emerald glared.

'You refer, I assume, to the title of Lady Emerald Devenish?'

'Yes, of course,' Emerald said impatiently. Her mother-in-law was deliberately drawing out the situation and all she wanted to do was be reunited with Alessandro.

'You are very proud of your relationship with the late duke, so I am told, Emerald.'

'With Daddy . . . of course. He was my father.'

'Ah. I'm sorry, my dear. If only that were true. Sadly, I'm afraid that it isn't. You see *your* father wasn't the duke; he was a Frenchman, an artist, a painter, who died fighting in the Spanish Civil War.'

For the first time in her life Emerald was lost for words. What her mother-in-law was saying was ridiculous.

'No,' she denied vehemently, 'that's not possible.'

'Oh, but, my dear, I'm afraid it is, and not just merely possible, but actual fact. You shall see for yourself. I have all the information, all the papers here.'

She produced a large foolscap envelope, which Emerald stared at as though it were alive, so great was her shock.

'I must say that when I instituted enquiries into your background I had not dared hope that they would yield such a rich crop. To be frank, it was for evidence of your own immoral behaviour for which I was looking, not your mother's. Such a dreadful secret to have had to keep all those years, don't you think, Emerald? Not one but two children born to a nobody, a penniless artist who supported himself by seducing foolish rich old women and amused himself by seducing even more foolish young women, of which your mother was one. No wonder she married the late duke in such haste. She would have been ruined had she not done so. A silly, common little millowner's granddaughter, who had not understood the rules that governed the society in which she was attempting to move. At best, all she could have looked forward to without the late duke's name to shield her and give her respectability would have been the life of a rich man's mistress.'

'You're lying! None of this is true.'

Why was her heart pounding so fast? She knew that what Alessandro's mother was saying couldn't be true. It was preposterous – impossible for her to be the daughter of a common painter. But Emerald didn't like the way her mother-in-law was looking at her, mockery shining in the bead-sharp eyes, like a cat at a mouse hole.

'My father—'

'I take it you mean the late duke?'

'He would never have married my mother if . . . if she had done what you are trying to say.'

'My dear, it was because she had done what I said and because he hoped there would be a child – a son – as a result that he did marry her. You see, the man you refer to as your father was incapable of fathering a child on any woman.' She gave a small shrug. 'There are such men whose preference is for their own sex, and the late duke's inclinations in that regard were, I understand, well known in certain quarters. In fact, his relationship with a certain young German was considered important enough by Winston Churchill for him to have the late duke virtually put under house arrest. That was after he and your mother had been holidaying on the Côte d'Azur where you yourself were conceived.

'Since you are now acquainted with the facts, I am sure you will understand how impossible it is that you continue as my son's wife. Fortunately, since our principality is Catholic and you are not a Catholic, the matter of annulling the marriage will be simple enough.'

Emerald managed to pull her attention out of the maelstrom of shocked and angry thoughts seething inside her head for long enough to recognise the danger of the princess's words.

'There is no question of our marriage being annulled.'

'No question indeed. On that we are agreed. My son *cannot* remain married to you.'

'Alessandro loves me.'

Alessandro's mother laughed, the first time Emerald had heard her do so, the silvery iciness of the sound chilling her own hot and turbulent emotions.

'Yes, of course he does, but Alessandro has loved many things in his life, with equal passion, only to forget them as he has outgrown them: his toy soldiers, his first pony . . . He will grieve for you for a while, but naturally I shall ensure that he has plenty of pretty girls around him to distract him and eventually he will marry the daughter of a fellow ruler, someone who understands what her duty to him and to our country is.

'Now, to the practicalities . . .'

'I am not going to let you do this. We are married.'

'Are you? You gave what in effect was a false name – a name that does not by rights belong to you since you are not the daughter of the late duke. You are a harlot, not a royal bride, you are not of our religion and you are not in possession of my son. I, on the other hand, am in possession of evidence that, if I chose to make it public, would ruin you and your mother for ever. You would lose your title and no doubt with it your inheritance. There would be no proposals or offers of future marriages. Propositions would be all that you could look forward to.

'I am being charitable, Emerald. I am prepared to keep

your mother's secret and in doing so allow you to keep the title to which you have no right, and your inherited fortune, in return for your agreement to an annulment of your marriage to my son. If, however, you refuse to give your agreement, then you can look forward to what I have just outlined to you.'

'You must think me a fool. I don't believe this concoction of lies you have told me. Anyone can produce forged documents, statements . . . anyone can tell lies.'

The dowager smiled at her. 'Why don't you tell your mother what I have told you, Emerald, and ask her to tell you the truth? I will be generous to you,' she said, getting up and moving towards the door. 'I shall give you the weekend but if I have not heard from you by Monday lunchtime then I'm afraid on Tuesday morning the papers will be carrying an exposé of your mother's secret. Fascinating reading, I'd say. Then your marriage to my son will be annulled, anyway. The Prince of Lauranto does not take as his wife the bastard daughter of a millowner and a French artist.'

Emerald returned to Eaton Square to find she had the house to herself, apart from the staff. Her godmother had taken Lydia and Gwendolyn to Gwendolyn's parents for a short visit, and Emerald had no idea where the sheep shearer was and cared even less.

How unthinkable it was that they should all get to hear of Alessandro's mother's ridiculous accusations. Unthinkable and unbearable, just like the accusations themselves. They couldn't, they must not be true. And yet deep down was a doubt, a fear, an anger that maybe they were.

Emerald looked towards the telephone. She needed to speak with her mother, but not over the telephone, with heaven alone knew who listening in to their conversation.

There was no choice. She would have to go to Denham.

Chapter Twenty-Four

It was late in the evening when Emerald's train finally pulled in to Macclesfield station. Fortunately a lone taxi driver was still in place at the rank.

'Denham, and hurry,' she told him as she stepped into the car. She didn't want to arrive to find that the house was locked up and everyone had gone to bed.

'Well, Your Ladyship, I mean Your Highness,' the housekeeper greeted her when she opened the door to Emerald's impatient knock.

'I want to see my mother – where is she?' Emerald demanded, her expression hardening as the door to the sitting room opened and her mother came into the hall.

'Emerald!' Amber exclaimed. 'What on earth . . . ? Is everything all right?'

'There's something I want to know. In private,' Emerald added, looking pointedly at Mrs Clements.

'What about the cocoa? Shall I make an extra cup for Her Highness?' the housekeeper asked Amber, ignoring Emerald.

'No, that's all right, thank you, Mrs Clements,' Amber smiled. 'I'll see to that. You go on up to bed.'

'Now, Emerald,' Amber said quietly as soon as the housekeeper had gone upstairs, 'come with me to the kitchen, and you can tell me what it is you've come here for whilst I'm making the cocoa.'

'I don't want cocoa,' Emerald objected. 'I—'

'Perhaps not, but Jay and I do.'

Whatever it was that had brought her eldest daughter here at this time of night it was obviously important – at least to Emerald herself.

Jay, who had been out with his dog, looked as astonished as Amber had when he came back into the kitchen and saw Emerald there.

Her smart London clothes looked out of place in the homely warmth of the kitchen, just as Emerald herself did, but then Emerald had never thought of Denham as home, despite the fact that she had lived there for so long. No, Denham wasn't good enough for a girl whose father was a duke, or so Emerald had always claimed. Would her daughter be happy now that she had her prince and his title? For Emerald's own sake Amber hoped that she would. She suspected that to Emerald, happiness would always have a different meaning than it ever had done to her.

'I want to speak to my mother alone,' Emerald told Jay arrogantly. She didn't want her stepfather there to defend and protect her mother as he always did. She would have a far better chance of getting the truth out of her without Jay around.

She saw the look that her stepfather gave her mother

and the small nod she gave back to him. She saw too that he was not happy about leaving them together. Emerald had never been able to see or understand why people treated her mother the way they did, fussing over her and going out of their way for her.

'Emerald, what is it? What on earth has brought you here at this time of night?' Amber asked quietly as soon as they were alone.

'I need you to tell me the truth. Who was my father?'

Chapter Twenty-Five

'Not still taking those ruddy pills, are you?'

Ella shot Oliver Charters a bitter look. 'What if I am?'

'Then you're a fool,' he told her bluntly, 'and I never had you down as that.'

Guilt and chagrin fuelled Ella's antagonism towards him. She'd got a new prescription from Dr Williamson, but she'd cut down to just one of the pills a day instead of the two she had been taking. Well, at least some days she only took one.

The fashion editor's PA came into the small cramped office, bringing a halt to their conversation as she riffled through some papers on one of the desks and then made a triumphant sound, having found what she was looking for before exiting the office, leaving Ella stuck by her own desk whilst Oliver lounged against the door.

Removing a pack of cigarettes from the pocket of his jeans, he flipped it open and offered it.

'Smoke?'

Ella shook her head. Why didn't he go away and do what he was best at, ogling the models, she thought nastily, instead of standing here in her space as though he had all the time in the world? She tried desperately hard not to look at him but somehow her gaze had a will all of its own, and as he drew on his cigarette and then exhaled with a slow sound of pleasure her eyes flew to his face as though magnetised.

'There's nothing quite like that first drag,' he said, adding in a deliberately mocking tone, 'Well, almost nothing. Stop taking them, princess,' he told her in a far more abrupt voice. 'Take my advice and go and do what you were born to do.'

'Meaning what, exactly?' Ella challenged him.

'Meaning, leave this place, get married, go and live in the country and have a couple of kids.'

'That's the last thing I want to do,' Ella snapped defiantly.

'Suit yourself.' Oliver finished his cigarette and then slouched out of the office without even saying what he had come in for in the first place.

Ella fumed as she took out her feelings on her typewriter, thumping down the keys as fiercely as though against Oliver Charters' flesh.

In the corridor outside Ella's office, Oliver cursed himself under his breath. What the hell was the matter with him? Why should he care what kind of mess she made of her life? Just because he had kissed her didn't mean he had to take ruddy responsibility for her, like she was a helpless kid or something and he was the only person around to watch out for her.

Emerald and Amber looked at one another.

She hadn't meant to say it like that, Emerald admitted

to herself as she waited for her mother to answer her. But not to spare her mother's feelings; far from it. Rather she'd planned to lead more carefully into it before she sprang the trap so that her mother wouldn't have any warning and thus be able to avoid it and lie to her.

Amber had to sit down. Somehow she had known always that this would happen eventually.

She took a deep breath and simply said, 'How did you find out?'

Emerald felt as though the ground was rocking beneath her feet. This wasn't what was supposed to happen. Her mother should have protested that Emerald knew exactly who her father was; she should have denied and denied again that there was any truth in Alessandro's mother's allegations.

Blind fury and panic filled her. She stepped up to her mother and raised her hand, slapping her so hard across the face that tears of pain filled Amber's shocked eyes.

'It can't be true. It *mustn't* be true. I will not have a painter, a filthy peasant, as my father. My father was the Duke of Lenchester. Say it,' she demanded savagely. 'Say that my father was the Duke of Lenchester.'

Amber looked away from her. She had always known that Emerald had to be protected from the truth and she had promised Robert that she would be. Robert, who had loved the little girl he had claimed as his own every bit as much as he had loved the son she and Jean-Philippe had previously given him.

Amber had been only seventeen when she had first met Jean-Philippe and been seduced by him, believing that he loved her.

It had been Robert who had helped her to face the awful truth that Jean-Philippe had no intention of marrying her, as she had believed he would. Dear kind Robert, who had rescued her, saved her from the consequences of her folly that magical hot summer in the South of France when she had succumbed to Jean-Philippe and her own love for him, offering her marriage to protect her reputation. Robert, whose own desires lay not with her sex but with his own.

Amber had never thought that she and Jean-Philippe would even meet again, never mind become lovers once more, but they had, and Emerald had been the result of that second coming-together. On that occasion Jean-Philippe had repaid any debt he might have owed her when he had helped her to protect Robert from his own folly.

'Robert loved you as his daughter, Emerald; he loved you very much. He was proud of you and proud to call you his, but . . .'

'Go on,' Emerald demanded when her mother fell silent.

'It was all such a long time ago, a different life. Robert was your father in all the ways that matter. It was his choice to treat you in every single way as his child. Please let that be your measure of his fatherhood.'

'Is it true that he was a queer and that he let you fuck with a French painter?'

The ugly words burned Amber's face as painful a red as though Emerald had physically struck her again.

'That's enough! You will not speak to your mother like that.' Neither of them had heard Jay come back into the kitchen.

'What is it about you?' Emerald screamed at her mother. 'Why is everyone so determined to protect you? Don't you realise what you've done? You've ruined my life. Thanks to you, Alessandro's mother is going to have our marriage annulled, and if I don't agree then she's going to tell the world that I'm a bastard with a father—'

'Oh, Emerald . . .' Amber raised her hand to her mouth in shock. 'But if Alessandro loves you then it won't matter to him, darling.' She reached for her daughter's hand but Emerald snatched it away.

'Don't be such a fool. Of course it will matter to him, and it matters to *me*. Do you think I want people knowing . . . laughing at me behind my back . . . ?' Emerald gave a shudder. 'My father, a common painter.'

'Emerald, Jean-Philippe was respected as a painter. He was very gifted; I have some of his work.' Amber looked towards Jay, pleading silently for his help.

'It's stored up in the attic. I'll show it to you,' Jay offered.

'No!'

'He was very brave, Emerald. He saved Robert's life at one time, and through that he saved yours as well,' Amber continued.

'Did . . . did he . . . was it really an accident that they died, my father and Luc, or was it because he found out about you and couldn't bear the thought of someone else's bastard inheriting from him?'

'No!' Amber's voice was raw with pain. '*No*. Robert adored Luc; everyone said how alike they were, how very much father and son. Luc worshipped Robert. They were so close.'

So very close in life and in death. In her head Amber could still see them as she had done that dreadful morning when she had arrived at the small cottage hospital where they had been taken. The wonderful matron had ensured that they had been made to look as 'natural' as possible. Luc's unmarked face turned towards his father, Robert . . . Amber caught back her own protest as she remembered how she had reached out to touch Robert and then discovered what they had tried to protect her from knowing – that Robert had virtually been scalped when he had tried to protect the son he had loved so much, his last action, his last thought, his last love for Luc. No child could have had a better father; no woman could have wanted a better father for her children.

'Perhaps the duke was hoping he might get to take him to bed. They like that sort of thing, don't they, men like him?' Emerald taunted her mother.

Amber's face had gone white, the skin stretched tightly over her bones. Jay stepped forward, reaching for her protectively but Amber waved him away.

'That is a vile thing to suggest, but I will forgive you. You are hurt and angry, frightened, so I will tell you again. Robert loved you both as his children – Luc as his son and heir and you as his daughter. He was the one who read you your bedtime stories, who listened to your first words, who held you and loved you. Robert was your *father*.'

'But not the man who fathered me on you. Not the man who stuck his prick into you and—'

'That's enough!' Jay stopped Emerald, moving towards her.

264

'Enough? Why, because I'm upsetting her? Oh dear. Don't you think that *I'm* upset? Don't you think that I'm affected by the filth of knowing that my father was some common seducer – worse than a gigolo, according to Alessandro's mother? I hate you. I hate you for what you are and for what you've done. You've ruined my life. It's because of you and your whoring that the princess can do what she is doing. I should never have allowed her to send Alessandro away without me.'

Watching her daughter as she paced the kitchen in her fury, Amber looked at Jay, her beloved husband, her best friend, who knew all there was to know about her and always had done. To Amber, the relationship, the love she shared with Jay, was perfect and what she yearned for her children to know in their own marriages. But Emerald wanted different things and, looking at her daughter now, Amber acknowledged sadly that it was not love for her husband that was driving her daughter's fury. But that did not stop her from feeling guilty. It wasn't hard for Amber to recognise the motivation of a woman who was prepared to destroy her son's marriage to suit her own ends. After all, her grandmother had been very much in the same mould, trying to force her own parents apart because she had not liked Amber's father. 'Perhaps if Jay and Mr Melrose spoke with Alessandro's mother—'

'Don't be ridiculous,' Emerald replied. 'She wants to end our marriage. I always knew she wouldn't want Alessandro to marry me.' Her face hardened. 'But if it wasn't for you, Mother, she wouldn't be able to do a single thing about it.'

Emerald fumbled in her handbag, lit herself a cigarette and drew fiercely on it.

Even in her anger her daughter was beautiful, Amber acknowledged. Beautiful, but cold and hard, and knowing that increased Amber's guilt, for wasn't she, as Emerald had just accused her, responsible for her daughter's personality, either through the genes she had passed on to her or the trauma of the months she had carried her, and her birth?

Was it because of those early weeks and months in her womb that Emerald seemed to have been born hating her? Was it too fanciful to think that somehow her daughter knew of how fearful Amber had been, how desperately she had wished not to have conceived her? Amber didn't know, but she did know that the burden of her own guilt lay very heavily on her.

Chapter Twenty-Six

'Emerald.'

Although she was awake Emerald pretended not to hear her mother when she came into the bedroom carrying a tea tray.

'Your father, Jean-Philippe . . .' she began, sitting down on the bed.

Emerald sat upright.

'You are not to call him that. I shall *never* acknowledge him as my father.'

'I have some of his paintings, if you would like to see them. He gave them into my safekeeping. They should be seen, not shut away in an attic. They are very good. When you were little, Robert did think you might have inherited his talent; you used to love to draw, do you remember?'

'There is nothing of that . . . that peasant in me, do you hear me? Nothing. No, don't touch me,' she demanded when Amber reached out to take her hand. 'I shall never forgive you for that. No one else must ever know about this. Have you . . . did you . . . ? Thank God you aren't a Catholic, otherwise I suppose the whole world would know you'd gone snivelling to confess what you'd done. You're that kind.'

She should rebuke her, Amber knew, remind her that she was her mother, and Emerald herself not yet even twenty-one, but she couldn't. Emerald had always treated her with disdain, her strength of will magnifying everything she said and did.

'If Alessandro loves you . . .' she began hesitantly, wanting to find a way to help.

'Don't be stupid. It isn't Alessandro who matters, it's his mother. How dare she have me investigated, poking and prying? How stupid you were, Mother, not to have made sure that no one could ever find out. And now it's me who has to pay the price for your stupidity.'

Amber was too distressed to defend herself and, knowing there was no use in trying to talk to Emerald, she stood up and left the room.

Emerald sat stony-faced and silent in the first-class compartment of the train taking her back to London. Somehow, someday, she would pay back Alessandro's mother for what she was doing to her – and with interest. She looked down, a speck of something on her coat catching her eye. A tiny spot of brilliant colour, as brilliant as a St-Tropez summer sky against the cool beige of her outfit . . . She looked at it and then gave a cold hard smile as she brushed it away.

Back at Denham, Amber was sitting back on her heels in the dusty attic, her face covered with her hands as she wept.

'Oh, no, Jay. Oh, no!'

Shortly after their return to Denham, having seen a sullen Emerald off on the train to London, Amber had had a sudden impulse to go up to the attic and look at Jean-Philippe's paintings.

'Perhaps to reassure myself that neither he nor I was as dreadful as Emerald implied,' she had told Jay when she explained to him what she was going to do.

Naturally Jay had gone with her. He was anxious about his wife. She and Emerald had always had a difficult relationship but he wasn't sure they could recover from this.

She hadn't looked at the paintings for a very long time; there had been no need. To Amber they had always been something she held in trust, the physical memory of the man who had painted them with such passion and skill.

The disturbed dust had told its own tale, as had the packing case, which had been left carelessly open.

The knife marks that scored deep into the paint and the canvas had been deliberately cruel and destructive.

'Emerald . . .' Jay exhaled as he stared at the damaged canvas. 'How did she know they were here?'

'I told her. It's my fault. I thought . . . I thought she might find it comforting to know, to see how good he was . . . Oh, Jay . . .'

'It's only the two canvases,' he tried to comfort her, as he checked through the packing case. 'She obviously didn't touch the others.'

As Jay looked at the now scarred and knifed flesh of the young figure in the painting and then at the face of his wife, who still looked so remarkably like the girl she had been then, he felt an anger towards Emerald that he had rarely experienced in his life.

'Poor Jean-Philippe. I have let him down so badly. These are all that is left of him. What are we to do about Emerald, Jay?'

Understanding all that she could not say, Jay took Amber in his arms and held her whilst she wept.

Chapter Twenty-Seven

'So it's agreed then?' Emerald's mother-in-law demanded.

They were in the sitting room of Alessandro's mother's suite at the Savoy.

'With immediate effect your marriage to my son is over, and will be annulled. Poor Alessandro, I'm afraid I have already had to prepare him for your defection.'

She was dressed in her customary black, just like the horrid old crow that she was, Emerald thought bitterly.

'Alessandro was shocked, of course, to learn that you had confessed to me that your marriage to him had been a mistake, undertaken by you on the rebound from another lover,' she continued.

Fury spiked in Emerald's eyes. 'Alessandro would never believe that. He knows perfectly well that there was no one else before him.'

'Does he? I shall have to warn him that girls can be very clever about pretending to be what they are not, shan't I?' Her mother-in-law's smile was malevolent. 'I think it best if you and I don't see one another again after today, Emerald.'

Come back here, to this dreary suite with its

heavy Victorian furniture, its stuffy atmosphere, and Alessandro's mother waiting in it, like a spider at the centre of a web waiting to pounce? Emerald looked round the oppressive room, its heavy dark curtains shutting out the light and trapping her where she didn't want to be, just as the princess's Victorian values were shutting her out of Alessandro's life and trapping her in their rigid respectability.

'Oh, and a word of warning. Should there be any consequences, shall we say, of your relationship with my son then I must point out to you that any such child will naturally be considered illegitimate – rather like you, Emerald. Maybe you should follow your mother's example and look for a man willing to give you the protection of his name?'

Emerald didn't say anything. Anger burned inside her, savage and corrosive, but she couldn't allow it to escape. Not without risking further humiliation. Unceremoniously and ignominiously she had been stripped of her marital status and the title that went with it, and her humiliation was going to be made public. She was consumed with a burning hatred for Alessandro's mother. She renewed her vow to turn the tables on her and make her pay.

'It is not so very bad, Emerald,' Alessandro's mother mocked her. 'As I have already told you, publicly we shall say that the marriage was a mistake entered into by two young people who didn't realise the significance of the protocols of Alessandro's position and the laws of our country and our religion. Think how much worse it could have been for you had I had to go public about your conception and your real father. Of course, you have my word that no one will know anything of that, just so long as you continue to abide by our agreement. There, I think we have said everything that needs to be said, don't you?'

Her mother-in-law's smile was calmly triumphant as she rose from the high-backed chair she had deliberately taken as her seat, leaving Emerald obliged to take a much lower chair, or remain standing in her presence as though she were a servant.

Watching the princess walk towards the door, Emerald had never felt so much hostility towards anyone before. Her mother-in-law had outwitted her because she had been too clever for her, too Machiavellian. As Alessandro's mother waved in the direction of the door, signalling both that the 'interview' was over and that she was far too socially above Emerald to open the door for her, Emerald made herself a promise that never again would anyone be allowed to humiliate her as Alessandro's mother had done.

Emerald was still fuming as she sat in the cab taking her back to Lenchester House.

The butler, Chivers, opened the door to her, informing her, 'Mrs de la Salles telephoned, Your Highness. She wanted to remind you that you are engaged to join her supper party this evening at the Paraqueet Club.'

Emerald's heart sank and she fought off an unfamiliar feeling of panic. She had completely forgotten that she had accepted Jeannie de la Salles' invitation. The de la Salles were an extremely wealthy young couple, whose slightly louche social life had raised a few eyebrows and garnered them several inches of gossip column comment, detailing their love of nightclubs and dancing.

Emerald found them fun, especially Peter. They were on the fringe of Princess Margaret's set, some of whom were considered rather fast.

Jeannie had promised to find Emerald a partner when Emerald had told her that Alessandro would not be available. Emerald could well imagine how the de la Salles and their set would relish the gossip the end of her marriage would cause. She was tempted to have Chivers telephone Jeannie and tell her that she couldn't join them, but a voice inside her head, a strong and cool one, warned her that since the situation would inevitably become public knowledge she would be better off getting her own 'story' in first and making a bid for public sympathy and credibility. As a woman her social reputation was her most valuable asset. Lose that and she would lose everything she valued. Victorian or not, restricting or not, her mother-in-law's values were for the most part society's laws – at least where her own sex was concerned, Emerald knew.

Dougie knew that if it hadn't been for having Emerald living at Lenchester House, constantly reminding him of how unfit he was to fill her late father's shoes, he might be getting used to this new world.

So far he'd attended summer balls and country house parties, been proposed and accepted for Emerald's late father's clubs, spent enjoyable and informative weekends with Jay, both at Denham and more latterly at his own estate, using the confidence Jay had been instilling in him to arrange meetings with the estate manager Mr Melrose had appointed to run the estate after Robert's death – his own estate manager now.

He'd learned, and he felt that he'd grown too. He could acknowledge now that he was beginning to feel far more comfortable with the responsibilities of the dukedom than he had ever imagined he could do when he had first realised he had inherited it. He and it were growing together to know one another, this business of being a duke and him, and when he looked back now over the last few weeks, he recognised that he no longer felt like an imposter.

There were some down sides to his new life, though, Dougie acknowledged as he looked across the table in the thankfully relatively quiet and shadowy corner of the Paraqueet Club at his current dinner companion.

Initially it had suited him to suggest that Emerald, her godmother and the other two girls remained living in the Eaton Square house, but that had meant that he had been obliged to accept the 'friendship' of Gwendolyn's father, Henry, Lord Levington, who had become a regular visitor at the house, ostensibly calling to see his 'favourite daughter' but somehow or other always managing to attach himself to Dougie with the offer of showing him how things were done and introducing him to people 'he ought to meet'.

Dougie had gone along with this good-naturedly enough, but when Henry had insisted on taking him to a private gambling club where the stakes were eye-wateringly high, Dougie had felt suspicious enough to seek Jay's advice.

Jay's response had confirmed his own judgement – which was that Henry was a thoroughly unpleasant, and probably untrustworthy, person who Dougie would do well to avoid. However, Henry was persistent and, irritatingly, refused to be shaken off, and Dougie had been trapped into agreeing to go out with him tonight.

The evening was turning out to be every bit as bad as Dougie had feared. They had begun the evening at John Aspinall's private gaming club where Gwendolyn's father had lost several thousand pounds that Dougie suspected he didn't have. His face had looked green and sweaty in the shaded light hanging over the gaming table.

Now, despite Dougie's suggestion that they called it a night, they were here in this exclusive nightclub, where the air was thick and blue-grey with expensive cigar smoke.

Working as a teenager on the family sheep station, Dougie had never imagined that his life would bring him somewhere like this. The shearing gangs could remove a fleece at a speed that had held him spellbound. The owners of London's private clubs fleeced those who patronised them with similar speed and dexterity, Dougie thought ruefully, as he listened to the cut-crystal voices coming from the other tables.

The sound of female laughter ringing out from one of the other tables had Dougie turning discreetly, a small frown furrowing his forehead when he saw Emerald at a table right next to the dance floor with a group of people.

She was obviously the focus of attention at the table,

but especially of the men, Dougie recognised, his frown deepening as he remembered that Alessandro had returned to his own country on business.

Emerald's laughter and the manner in which she was so obviously enjoying herself certainly didn't suggest that she was missing her husband in the way that one might expect from someone so newly married. Dougie hoped that the attentive smooth-looking older man seated to Emerald's right would keep her attention so fully occupied that she didn't notice him. He could do without her giving him a hard time this evening.

Meanwhile, Emerald smiled brilliantly at Tod Newton, her dinner companion and a well-known ladies' man, a Second World War fighter pilot veteran and a gambler who had both won fortunes and lost them.

A practised flirt, Tod had been attentive to her all evening, and now, as he lit her cigarette for her, having already insisted on ordering her another White Lady, he told her provocatively, 'I must say that your husband is a braver man than I, for I certainly would not want to leave such a beautiful and, dare I say, desirable young wife on her own.'

'Oh, Alessandro is neither brave nor very much of a man,' Emerald told him, buoyed up by the cocktails and wine she had already consumed this evening. 'In fact, he's a mummy's boy, for he thinks far more of doing what his mother tells him to do than pleasing his wife.'

For once, Emerald was too full of alcohol and self-pity to notice the gleam of satisfaction that darkened her companion's assessing gaze as it swept her from head to foot.

Her dark hair was newly done in a flick-up style, her off-the-shoulder low-necked sleeveless dress showed off her figure and her pale skin, whilst the diamonds she was wearing at her throat and on her wrists proclaimed her wealth and status.

'Poor Princess,' Tod murmured sympathetically.

'Don't call me Princess,' Emerald commanded him, stopping just in time to prevent herself from blurting out that soon she would not be entitled to the name.

'No? Then what am I to call you? Enchantress, who has blinded me with her beauty and ensnared me with my own desire for her?'

'Just . . . just call me Emerald,' she told him, stumbling slightly over the words.

He'd had his eye on Emerald since she and Alessandro had first joined the de la Salles set. Tod had enjoyed many beautiful women over the years but in Emerald he could see all the things he liked the most: beauty, spirit and, best of all, a certain arrogance that would make her oh so vulnerable to him. Tod mentally calculated how much he was likely to be able to get from her to keep his silence over her 'little moment of foolishness' – tens of thousands certainly, maybe even a hundred thousand, given that she was married to royalty.

He summoned a waiter, and, as though by magic, within seconds another cocktail was being handed to Emerald.

In actual fact Emerald was beginning to feel rather light-headed, but of course it didn't do to start acting like some silly little *ingénue* when one was in such sophisticated company. Had Alessandro's mother told him yet that their marriage was over? There was a feeling inside Emerald that she didn't want to be there. It hurt her pride and something else as well to know that the hold she had believed she had over Alessandro hadn't been strong enough to make him defy his mother, that someone else had mattered more to him than she did. Just as someone else had mattered more to her mother than she had. Immediately Emerald flinched from the edge of the crevasse that opened up inside her mind, not wanting to look down into its depths for fear of what she might see there waiting to destroy her.

Alessandro was a spineless fool, she assured herself. There were other men for her to bend to her will, other men – like Tod Newton – for her to display as her trophies, and as a once-married woman she was no longer bound by the rules that tied unmarried girls to their virginity. She could be and would be the temptress, the woman of the world whom no man could resist.

These and other alcohol-induced thoughts swirled inside Emerald's head. Although she didn't want to admit it, she was missing the attention Alessandro had given her, and the satisfaction of knowing that she only had to smile at him in a certain way to get him to do anything she had wanted. Emerald had enjoyed the sense of power that had given her. She had delighted in knowing that allowing Alessandro possession of her body had meant that she had total control over him. And would still have had total control over him if it hadn't been for his mother. She wanted more of that power. She would prove to those other women – outwardly meek, good women like her own mother, and openly controlling women like

Alessandro's mother – that her own particular brand of sexual power was stronger than anything they possessed. She would be the woman that no man could resist and, because of that, all women feared.

'You see, the thing is, old chap,' Henry was saying confidingly to Dougie as he leaned across the table, 'I was rather hoping that you might be able to help me out of a bit of a hole. After all, we're almost family, what with my sister and my favourite daughter living under your roof. I can tell you that the whole family is pretty glad to see you inherit. There was always something fishy about poor old Robert's marriage to Amber Pickford – said so at the time and I wasn't the only one. Pretty little thing, of course, but hardly out of the top drawer. Never does to mix blue blood with non-blue. Glad that boy of hers didn't live to inherit, and as for the girl . . . Look at her over there now. Newton will have her in his bed before she knows what's happening to her, and then that husband of hers will have to pay him a fortune to keep her name out of the gossip columns. Either that or divorce her . . . Now, Dougie, old chap, as I was saying, the thing is that I'm in a bit of a tight spot and could do with a small loan, a couple of thousand, well, let's say five thousand.'

Dougie, who had stiffened the minute that Gwendolyn's father had started to verbally attack Amber, whom Dougie both liked and admired, now hardened his heart completely against the other man. Sitting back in his chair and shaking his head, he said firmly, 'I'm sorry but I don't have access to that kind of cash.'

It was a lie but Dougie was damned if he was going to fund the other man's gambling debts. He felt sorry for his family, very sorry, in fact, but some instinct told him that if he'd bailed Henry out now, the requests for help would never stop coming.

Dougie's refusal had caused the genial smile to slip from Henry's face, revealing the same contempt with which he had just spoken of Amber.

'Bastard,' he swore bitterly, before getting up from the table and storming out of the club, leaving Dougie sitting alone.

Getting up himself, Dougie asked for the bill and then made his way to the small front desk. He was just waiting for the coat-check girl to reappear when he saw Emerald swaying towards the desk, no doubt heading for the ladies' cloakroom, which was on the upper floor. She was very unsteady on her feet, and was plainly the worse for drink, although, of course, being Emerald, the brilliance the alcohol had brought to her eyes and the flush it gave to her cheeks only enhanced her beauty.

She had taken off her wedding ring, Dougie noticed grimly. Her poor parents would be horrified by her behaviour. He was himself.

'Oh, it's you.' She greeted him unceremoniously and with obvious dislike, the effect rather spoiled by the small hiccup she was too late to smother.

'Alessandro isn't with you?'

'No. I'm here with some friends, one very special friend, in fact, and he's going to take me somewhere that he says will be a lot more fun than this place. 'Scuse me. I must go and powder my nose.'

Every word Emerald had spoken and the manner in which she had said them, carefully spacing them out in that way that those who had had too much to drink always did, had increased Dougie's concern.

He watched Emerald walk carefully up the stairs, clinging to the banister as she did so, Henry's words reverberating inside his head. Emerald was old enough to look after herself and she certainly wouldn't thank him for interfering. On the other hand, she was a member of the ancient and proud family of which he was now the head, the daughter of someone who had shown him great kindness, and most of all she was the girl he loved. He realised that now. Hate had somehow grown into love, impossible though that should have been. By the time Emerald had come back downstairs again Dougie knew what he had to do.

He was waiting for her, out of sight of her companions and holding her coat.

'What's this?' Emerald demanded in a slurred voice. 'What are you doing with my coat?'

'I'm going to take you home so put this on because it's cold outside.'

'Go home?' Emerald stared at him, but Dougie had already taken possession of her arm and was holding her in a determined grip whilst urging her towards the exit. The last thing he wanted was for her attentive dinner partner to come over and an argument to develop.

'Don't wanna go home. Going dancing with Tod. Tod likes me. He think I'm extraor . . . he says I'm beautiful.'

They were outside on the street now and Dougie's Bentley was parked less than five yards away.

As he guided her towards it, Emerald stopped and demanded, 'Do you think I am beautiful, Dougie?'

Dougie swallowed hard. 'I think you are very beautiful, Emerald.'

How much exactly had she had to drink, Dougie wondered, as he unlocked the passenger door of his car and Emerald almost collapsed onto the seat. He had never seen her drink more than a glass of wine over dinner, and somehow he suspected that Emerald, who so prided herself on being in control, would hate it if she could see herself now.

As he got into the driving seat and made sure the doors were locked, Emerald sat up in the passenger seat and informed him, 'And desirable. Tod says I am very desirable. He wanted to kiss me, I could tell.' She paused and then asked, 'Would you like to kiss me, Dougie?'

The question shocked him, forcing him to suppress his surging desire that yes, he would like to kiss her.

Dougie wasn't sure when he had first recognised that, mixed up in the irritation that Emerald made him feel, was something very different, somehow very unwelcome. But now that he had recognised that feeling for what it was, he knew instinctively that there was no going back.

Emerald had been leaning towards him and, as he fought to remind himself that he had a duty to behave like a 'gentleman' and not take advantage of her offer, she collapsed abruptly against him, her head on his shoulder. Dougie took a deep breath and then wished that he hadn't as he inhaled her scent. His need for her ricocheted inside him like a mad steer on a death mission. Her hair was brushing against his skin and she was toying with the buttons on his jacket, whilst humming the tune the band had been playing just before they had left.

Firmly sitting her upright again, and then turning his attention to manoeuvring the car away from the kerb, Dougie reminded her hardily, 'You are a married woman, Emerald, with a husband and—'

'No I'm not.'

Had she taken leave of her senses? Was she even more drunk than he had thought?

'Emerald, this is me, Dougie,' he pointed out patiently.

'Know that. Dougie the lost heir, Duke Dougie . . .'

'I don't care what you've told that slimeball you were having dinner with, you are married to Alessandro.'

'Tod not a slimeball. He is a gentleman. And am not married to Alessandro. His mother is having our marriage annulled.'

Dougie missed his gear change and stalled the car. He turned to stare at her in stunned shock and saw that a single tear was running down her face.

'She can't do that,' he protested.

'Yes she can, because she knows that my stupid bloody mother went and had an affair with some painter and that means that I'm illegitimate.'

Emerald started to sob uncontrollably whilst Dougie wrestled with disbelief. All he could manage was an uncertain, 'I'm sure that isn't true.'

'Yes it is true,' Emerald insisted. 'I've asked her, my mother . . . It is true, and if anyone finds out it will kill me so you must promise never ever to tell anyone.'

'I promise,' Dougie assured her.

'Well, you had better mean it.'

'I do,' Dougie insisted.

They had almost reached Eaton Square and as Dougie waited to turn into it he looked again at Emerald, who had gone very quiet, only to realise that she had passed out and was fast asleep. A gentle snore shook her body as he drove into the square.

Emerald, illegitimate. She would hate him even more than she already did when she sobered up and remembered what she had told him. And if he'd been Alessandro there was no way he would have allowed anyone to blackmail Emerald into agreeing to have their marriage annulled.

They were stopping outside Lenchester House, and Emerald was still out for the count. Dougie got out and went round to the passenger door, somehow managing to get her out. Holding her in his arms, he mounted the steps to the house.

When the butler opened the door, Dougie informed him firmly, 'Her Highness has hurt her ankle, Chivers, and I'm afraid the pain has caused her to faint. I'll take her straight up to her room.'

'Do you wish me to summon a doctor, Your Grace?'

'Not at the moment, Chivers, thank you. I think it is more the shock of the pain than any injury.'

Despite Emerald's fragility, Dougie was puffing by the time he had reached her room.

Placing Emerald on the bed, Dougie then turned to leave, hesitating by the door only to go back and wrench the covers from under her body to drape them over her, whilst determinedly not looking at her lying prone.

No sense in letting her get cold, after all.

* * *

It was late morning when Emerald woke up with a pounding head and a feeling of acute nausea in her stomach. Slowly, like mere wisps of mist at first, barely there and easily ignored but steadily growing thicker and stronger, memories of the previous evening started to seep into her head.

Tod Newton, flirting so charmingly with her; her determination to prove to everyone that she was so sensual that she could make any man desire her . . . Tod had suggested they went on somewhere more intimate to dance away the rest of the night. She had agreed, she remembered, but then . . .

An image, a familiar face and an equally familiar voice slid into her thoughts. *Dougie?*

Like a high tide surge suddenly everything came back to her. What she had said, what she had told him, what she had asked.

Oh God, no! No! Not that, and to Dougie the Drover, whom she so despised. Emerald ground her teeth in fury and then had to stop because of the pain knifing into her head.

She had to see him and she had to make sure that he must never, ever breathe a word to anyone about last night . . .

Chapter Twenty-Eight

'Is the duke here, Chivers?'

Emerald had made a brave attempt at appearing groomed, but not even the aspirin she had sent her maid to get from the housekeeper, and copious cups of coffee, had been able to lift the headache that had settled round her forehead like a tight band.

'He said to tell you that he'd be in the library if you were to ask for him, Lady Emerald.'

It was only when Emerald had turned away from him that she realised that Chivers had returned to using her pre-marriage title. Her heart began to thump in time to the pain in her head. Dougie must have said something to him. It was impossible, surely, for the servants to know already otherwise. God, how the drover must be enjoying this. Why had she been such a fool and told him what she had?

She pushed open the double doors to the library. Times were changing and even in the grandest houses now the footmen who would once have sprung to attention to open the door for high-ranking members of the family and visitors were rarely seen. Unless, of course, one was royal. Alessandro had told her once how much he enjoyed the relaxed way of life in London in comparison to the strict formality upon which his mother insisted for their own court.

Alessandro . . . Unwanted angry tears burned the backs of her eyes. Blinking them away, she stepped into the room.

Dougie was waiting for her, she could tell. He might be pretending to read the papers but Emerald wasn't deceived. She could almost feel his tension. That was enough to give her back something of her spirit.

Ignoring her headache, she told him coldly, 'No doubt Tod Newton will be making enquiries today as to how and why I was practically abducted last night, and when he does call—'

'When he did call earlier this morning, he was reminded that you are a married woman, and a member of the family of which I am the head. And whose name I shall not allow to be slurred.'

If her head hadn't been aching so much she would have laughed out loud at the very idea of the drover proclaiming himself head of the family. A family that, in effect, she no longer belonged to. Her true family name was not one of proud longevity adorned with strawberry leaves and a ducal crest.

'You had no right—'

'Oh, for goodness' sake, Emerald, let's not carry on like this. Given what you told me last night, I'd have thought you'd have far more important things demanding your attention than some damned ladies' man.'

288

'Tod is not a ladies' man.'

'You're right, what he is is something far less polite. Now that we've got that out of the way let's talk about something rather more important, shall we?' Without waiting for Emerald to respond Dougie continued, 'I've spoken to Mr Melrose and your mother this morning about your marriage. Mr Melrose is to consult a barrister friend who he assures me will know the best way to ensure that Alessandro's mother keeps her word with regard to the subject of your father.

'It has been decided that the reason for the annulment of your marriage will be one of religion. Alessandro is a Catholic. You are not. You had initially felt you could convert, but on reflection you have decided that you cannot and therefore you and Alessandro have decided – with deep regret – that the marriage must be brought to an end.'

A feeling – could it actually be a grudging admission of unwanted relief to hear someone speaking in such an authoritative manner on her behalf? – briefly eased the pounding in her head.

'Alessandro's mother has been left in no doubt whatsoever that any attempt by her – or indeed anyone else – to put a different interpretation on events, will result in the full weight of the British legal system being brought to bear on her,' Dougie went on. 'There is, after all, no concrete proof confirming her allegations. My late second cousin, the previous duke, accepted you as his child, his will alone testifies to that. In the eyes of the law, therefore, you are his child.'

'You mean that as with the Emperor's lack of clothes,

whilst everyone will know that the late duke was not my father, they will pretend that he was?'

'No one will know, unless you yourself choose to tell them.'

'Why are you doing this? You don't owe me anything.'

'*Noblesse oblige*, perhaps – isn't that what they say, what's expected of a nobleman?' Dougie shook his head in amusement. 'I'm doing it for all of us, Emerald, for myself, for your mother, for the family name, but most of all for you.'

For her? He was lying, of course. Why should he do anything for her?

An odd feeling had begun to take hold of her. A mix of panic, and confusion, and an overwhelming need to run away.

She could remember feeling something similar once before, as a little girl. Inside her head the memory replayed. She had been in the nursery with Rose, and Rose had done something that had annoyed her, so she had deliberately pushed her over just as her mother walked in and witnessed the incident. Amber had gone to Rose, who was lying on the floor but not making a sound, picking her up and cuddling her, kissing her cheek as she smoothed Rose's dark hair. Emerald could feel the fury and that other feeling she refused to name building up inside her.

Then her mother had turned to her and, still holding Rose, had held out her hand to her, smiling at her as she said gently, 'Come and be friends again, Emmie.'

She had so badly wanted to go to her mother, so very badly, but something inside her, something hard and hurting and angry, refused to let her, and so instead she had stamped her feet and shouted, 'No. Not until you put her down. I hate her.'

Her mother's smile had vanished, and Rose had started to cry. Whilst her mother comforted Rose, Emerald had gone to her great-grandmother for solace, knowing that she too hated Rose.

Now that same feeling of wanting to reach out for what was being held out to her, of wanting to drop her guard and run for the comfort being offered, was there but now too that obstinacy within her would not let her respond to it.

Tossing her head Emerald ignored what Dougie had said, demanding instead, 'Did Tod Newton leave a number for me to telephone him back on?'

When Dougie bowed his head and said nothing, a feeling gripped her – not pain exactly, but something unfamiliar and soft, which somehow made her ache a little inside, as though . . . as though she had come within reach of touching something special, which had now slipped away.

All rubbish, of course.

Chapter Twenty-Nine

'Isn't it enough that I've lost Alessandro, because his mother found out about your past, without this?' Emerald berated her mother, as she stood white-faced opposite her in the newly decorated drawing room of the smart town house that was to have been her and Alessandro's marital home.

'Emerald, I am so sorry.' Amber's voice shook with emotion.

'You're sorry? It's all very well for you to say that, you aren't the one that's pregnant, are you?' Angrily Emerald paced the floor. The waist of her beautiful new Dior suit was already painfully tight and none of the other clothes she had ordered for the winter season was going to fit her now.

'Jay will write and inform Alessandro and his mother for you.'

'No! I don't want either of them to know.' Amber's response was sharp and immediate. She hadn't told her mother of the princess's warning about what would happen should she have conceived, and she wasn't going to tell her either. 'In fact I don't want anyone to know. Not yet. Not until I've decided what to do.'

It was a pity that she had fainted like that whilst her mother had been visiting and Amber had immediately insisted on her seeing a doctor.

'What do you mean, until you've decided what to do?'

Emerald could see from her mother's expression what she feared. Good. She deserved to be punished.

'What do you think I mean? Everyone knows that there are doctors who deal with this sort of thing.'

'Oh, no, Emerald, please. Promise me you won't even think of that.'

'Why?' she challenged her. 'Because you thought of it with me?'

Amber couldn't speak for her guilt.

'You did, didn't you?' Emerald guessed. 'You wanted to get rid of me? Perhaps you should have done.'

'Emerald, no. You mustn't say that. And no, I did not want . . . there was never any question of me not having you, never.'

There it was again, that weird feeling of panic and pain and longing for something almost within reach that she couldn't allow herself to stretch out for.

Alessandro's mother would, of course, want her to have her pregnancy terminated. In fact, Emerald was pretty sure she would try to insist upon it, which was enough to fill Emerald with a stubborn determination not to do so. If Alessandro's mother did not want her to have the child, then she would have it just to spite her.

'If I do have it, then it will be up to you to look after it because *I* certainly don't intend to.'

Rose looked at her watch, and then increased her pace, shielding her eyes from the brilliance of the late afternoon autumn sun. Leaves from the trees in Cadogan Place had drifted up against the railings separating the private gardens from the pavement and Rose had a momentary childish desire to kick her feet through them to enjoy the crisp sound. Inside her head she could see herself as a little girl walking down the drive at Denham in the autumn, her hand placed trustingly in her aunt Amber's hold as the two of them shuffled their feet through the crisp golden leaves that had fallen from the beech trees lining the drive. She could almost smell them now, their dry scent mingling with her aunt's rose and almond perfume, the October sky bright blue overhead, and the sun shining down through the bare branches. She'd been off school with some childhood ailment – tonsillitis, Rose suspected, as she had been prone to it at one time – and so she had had the luxury of having her aunt to herself for a few precious hours. She could still remember how happy she had felt, so much so that she thought she could almost reach out and touch that innocent childhood joy. She had felt so safe then, with her hand in her aunt's so secure, so sure that she had her love. Then! Now she would soon be seeing Amber. She had been on tenterhooks all week since she had made the decision to open her heart to her aunt and to beg her for her help and understanding.

She had known for weeks that she would have to do

something. She was missing the bond she had shared with Amber dreadfully, and now with her aunt up in London there could be no better time for Rose to put aside her pride and admit to her how desperately confused and unhappy she was and how much she needed to know why her aunt had kept from her the fact that she and John might be brother and sister. Her need for her aunt's love was, she recognised, greater than her desire to reject her.

She hurried into Sloane Square, pausing automatically to examine the window displays in Peter Jones before crossing to the King's Road and heading for home. She had deliberately taken the long way, nervous about what lay ahead and wanting to delay it, whilst at the same time walking faster to bring it closer.

When eventually she turned into Cheyne Walk she said a small prayer under her breath that all would go well, that her aunt would understand, and that they could be close once again.

Unusually, the familiarity of the Chelsea house, with its dusty, faintly musty smell of old building and Thames water, overlaid with the scent of the girls, failed to comfort Amber as she sank into one of the sitting-room sofas and tried not to let herself think about Emerald. She desperately wanted to think of something she could say or do that would ensure that her daughter had her baby, not for her own sake – never that – but because with a mother's conviction she knew that Emerald would suffer terribly if she did not.

Amber had seen what going through the termination

of a pregnancy did to a woman's body and her heart. She had seen it at first hand through a dear friend who had never quite recovered.

She heard the front door to the house being opened and sighed to herself. She loved her stepdaughters and her niece, but right now all she could think about was Emerald. If only Jay were here . . .

'Aunt Amber.'

'Rose.' Amber gave her niece a distracted smile, as they exchanged hugs.

The familiarity of her aunt's scent and the comforting warmth of her hold made Rose want to stay where she was, safe and protected, just as she had always believed she was as a child.

Was it her fault that Emerald was the way she was, Amber meanwhile worried. Had she given too much love to Rose and not tried hard enough to give just as much to the daughter who had always rejected that love? The burden of her own guilt was unbearably heavy right now.

'Aunt Amber, I'm glad it's just the two of us. You see, there's something I want to ask you, something about my future. And . . . and my past.'

But before she could say more, her aunt had stood up and was shaking her head.

'Not now, Rose, please. I've just seen Emerald and she's . . . well, I'm just so dreadfully worried about her. In fact, I think I really ought to go and telephone Jay. Excuse me.'

Rose stared after her aunt as she went into the hall and picked up the telephone, feeling as though her heart had been turned to stone. No, not stone; stone didn't feel anything and her heart felt as though it was being ripped apart.

Well, at least now she knew one part of the truth. She couldn't blame her aunt for loving Emerald more than she did her, could she? After all, Emerald was her daughter, and she was . . . she was nothing.

Chapter Thirty

It was another month before Emerald finally put her mother out of her misery by announcing that she intended to keep the baby.

Amber broke the news to Ella, Janey and Rose on a wet early November afternoon. Rose had to swallow against her own bitter feelings. No wonder her aunt no longer had any time for her.

'But Mama, won't it be really uncomfortable for Emerald to have a baby and no husband?' Ella pointed out anxiously.

'Their marriage may have been annulled for religious reasons but that doesn't alter the fact that Emerald and Alessandro were married,' Amber answered, sticking to the line that she and Jay had already agreed upon. 'Emerald will have her family to support her, and her situation won't be so very different from that of the many young widows with small children the war left behind it. Now, you'll all be coming home to Denham for Christmas, of course, and we shall have an extra special celebration this year with a new baby to welcome into the family in February.'

Rose dipped her head. The last thing she wanted to do now was spend Christmas at Denham.

Upstairs alone in her bedroom, Janey sat on the edge of her bed with her knees knocking together, feeling grateful relief. Her period had started – nearly a week late. A week during which she'd hardly eaten or slept for fear that she might be pregnant. Every night she'd prayed for her period to start, and three days ago she'd actually been contemplating hurling herself from the top of the stairs in the hope that the resultant fall would result in 'sorting things out', as she'd heard that it could.

If that had failed her next attempt would have meant sitting in as hot a bath as she could stand for as long as she could bear it whilst drinking a bottle of gin. However, thankfully it had not come to that. And now, as she sat doubled over with the wonderfully familiar pains cramping her stomach, she felt like crying with joy and thankfulness.

Never ever again would she take such a risk. Never.

It had all seemed so exciting and grown up that very first night she had given in to Dan's insistent urgings and had lost her virginity to him. At the time she had believed the experience to be the most beautiful thing, perfect in every way and a symbol of the love they shared. Only now Dan had left her for someone else, a girl who was an actress and who he had met at a casting session. Janey was heartbroken, but she hadn't said so to anyone else, particularly not her elder sister, as Ella was bound to ask her if Dan had repaid her the fifty pounds she had inadvertently let slip she had loaned him a few days before the split. The last time they had had sex. Although Janey hated admitting it even to herself, in some ways it was a relief not to have to have sex any more. The excitement of the first time had soon given way to frustration and disappointment so that she had somehow always ended up feeling thoroughly miserable and something of a failure, especially when Dan had told her that all his previous girlfriends had told him what a wonderful lover he was. She, of course, had felt obliged by her pride to do the same. Perhaps, though, he had guessed that she didn't feel as responsive and sexy as she had claimed? Perhaps that was in part why he had left her for someone else? Janey didn't know.

The money she had loaned him hadn't been repaid and Janey suspected that it never would be.

Now, of course, it was impossible for her to tell Ella or Rose about what she and Dan had done. Ella wouldn't understand and would fuss and be shocked and disapproving and go on at her, and whilst she felt that Rose would be more sympathetic she could hardly tell Rose and not her own sister. It simply wouldn't be fair.

At least she wasn't pregnant. It would have been different had she been in Emerald's shoes, of course, and married. Having a baby didn't matter once you were married. In fact, it was expected. Janey knew that she would never get married now. How could she when her heart had been broken? Her sketchbook was full of small drawings of girls with big sad eyes wearing tiny little black dresses trimmed with purple rickrack braid and felt-leaved flowers. The colours of mourning. Perhaps she would make up a dress like that for herself.

If she did, she could cut out a series of purple felt hearts that she could appliqué to the sleeves, or maybe even a broken heart. Janey reached for her sketchbook, her mind working overtime as her creative instinct took over.

She had had such plans – plans she had discussed endlessly with Dan. There was so much she wanted to do, like opening her own boutique. She and a couple of the other girls had talked about it but they had agreed that that ambition would have to wait until after they had graduated. In the meantime Janey had been hoping to get a Saturday job working at Bazaar. She'd heard on the grapevine that Mary Quant might be looking for extra sales staff over Christmas, but now that Amber had wrung a promise from them to go home for Christmas that might not be possible. Besides, what if Dan were to come into Bazaar with his new girl on his arm? Janey's tears fell onto the sketchpad, smudging the line of the drawing she had just made.

'Well, my dear, I have to say that I think you are very brave,' Jeannie de la Salles told Emerald as they sat sipping tea in Claridge's, dressed in winter furs to protect them from the cold wind whipping through the city streets. 'I shouldn't care to be in your situation myself.'

Emerald affected a heavy sigh. 'My mother says that it is no different really than if I had been widowed, but it *is* different, knowing that Alessandro is alive but knowing that neither I nor our child can ever see him. I was so foolish, thinking that love would be enough.'

Emerald paused to judge the effect of her carefully prepared admission of 'heartache' on her friend. Jeannie was such a sentimental fool that it should be easy to convince her that Emerald had a right to claim the high moral ground for herself and Alessandro's child. Emerald had no intention of allowing the fact that she was to have a child become a bar to her being accepted in society.

'I should perhaps have agreed to convert, but darling Daddy was vehemently C of E and it would have felt like a betrayal of everything he stood for to have done so.'

'Oh, no, you did right. I do so admire you, Emerald. I believe the Countess of Bexton is due to give birth around the same time as you. Her husband was at Eton with Peter. I must introduce you to her. She is the sweetest person, and frightfully well connected. Oh, and Newton was asking after you the other day.'

Emerald gave a theatrical sigh. 'I'm afraid that all I can think about at the moment is how much I miss Alessandro and how much I wish . . .' She placed her hand on her body and gave another sigh, whilst inwardly amusing herself, imagining Alessandro's mother's fury when she read in the gossip columns of Emerald's own Madonna-like bravery as she proudly carried Alessandro's child despite the pain he had caused her.

Once the brat was born, of course, she fully intended to return to the entertaining life she had been beginning to live before she had realised that she was pregnant. Her mother, who had been so keen to plead with her to have the child, could repay her by keeping it out of her way at Denham.

Well, at least she wasn't going to have to go home to Denham for Christmas now because she had the perfect

302

excuse for not doing so, Rose acknowledged. Secretly she hadn't wanted to go, dreading the difference there was bound to be between this Christmas and all the wonderful Christmases before. However, she had been unable to come up with an adequate excuse for not doing so until today, when she had been told that because of the amount of work they'd got on and Mrs Russell's insistence on having her extended revamp completed for her New Year party, they were all going to have to work late Christmas Eve and then be back at work again the day after Boxing Day.

Rose looked at her watch and started to walk a bit faster. She was supposed to be meeting Josh in the Golden Pheasant for an after work drink and if she didn't hurry she'd be late.

'Had to use the hatpin much lately?' Josh asked her after he had ordered their drinks.

Rose began to deny it, only to stop and admit, 'He just won't accept that I'm not interested. I've even threatened to tell his wife but he just laughed and said that she wouldn't believe me.'

'Bastard,' Josh castigated vehemently. 'Have you thought of telling your boss?'

'I don't think there'd be any point. The Russells are just about his best customers and they've recommended him to several of their friends. Plus, I don't know for sure but I don't think that the Russells have paid anything yet for this new work they've commissioned, so Ivor won't want to offend them. And besides . . .'

When she hesitated Josh demanded, 'And besides *what*?'

'Well, you know, Josh, people seem to think . . . that is to say, some of the other girls make certain remarks and I'm not sure that Ivor would believe that it isn't something I've done that's encouraged Mr Russell to think that I might be available. He's said as much himself.'

She felt miserable and self-conscious even telling Josh, who was so open about the most personal of things himself that he had gradually taught her to be equally open with him.

'I've never known a girl less likely to give a bloke a come-on than you,' Josh responded. 'The man's a bad hat, Rose. No one gets as rich as he's done without getting his hands dirty. He might have managed to keep himself on the right side of the law but I've heard that he does business with a hell of a lot of men who aren't.'

'Ella said that she'd heard rumours about Mrs Russell from some of the girls at *Vogue*. She was a model before they married. Her father was a South American businessman who lost all his money and then disappeared.'

Ella had told Rose that Mrs Russell had tried to persuade *Vogue* to do an article on her but that Ella's boss had said that *Vogue* didn't run articles on people who attached themselves to the fringes of society in an attempt to pretend they were something they were not.

As they drank their wine and exchanged news, Rose told Josh about having to work on Christmas Eve.

'At the Russells'?' he demanded.

Rose nodded.

'Well, you just be careful that Russell doesn't try giving you a Christmas present you don't want. But your auntie isn't going to be pleased if you don't make it home for Christmas, is she?'

'Oh, I expect she'll be so busy with Emerald that she won't even miss me, and anyway . . .'

'Anyway what?' Josh pressed. He always knew when something was bothering her or she was holding something back. Rose was so damned honest that she was incapable of dissembling about anything. Unlike him. He was a genius at it.

'Well, in some ways I'm glad that I'm not going to be able to go home.'

Why on earth had she told him that? It was the last thing she had intended to do, but somehow the admission had slipped out and now it couldn't be recalled.

'Because of this bloke you're always thinking about and then pretending to me you aren't looking like a wet weekend over?'

Rose nearly jumped out of her seat, spluttering into her glass and then looking at him in dismay before protesting, 'You can't know about John. I've never—'

'Ah, so his name's John, is it? What is he? Some posh county type you've been in love with since you and he rode your first ponies together?' Josh was just teasing her, Rose knew, but his words sliced right into the heart of her pain.

'Something like that,' she agreed. 'But I'm not in love with him. Not now.'

That was true, she recognised. She wasn't 'in love' with John any more, but she did still love him and she ached, if anything, even more because that love, a sister's love, must forever be unrecognised.

305

'Come off it, Rose, you can't fool me. I can tell by your voice that you love him. Maybe you should tell him that. You never know, he might secretly—'

'No!' Rose burst out fiercely. 'He doesn't love me. He can't. He mustn't.'

'You're not going to start all that nonsense of you not being good enough again, are you? You are every bit as good as anyone else, Rose. Repeat after me: I am—'

'No, Josh, you don't understand. It isn't like that. Please don't ask me any more. I can't tell you. I promised I wouldn't tell anyone. It would destroy John's life if he knew. I wish I didn't know myself.'

New York. She was being sent to New York for, provision-ally, six months in the new year to work for the features editor of American *Vogue*. Ella hugged the news to herself. She had known that it was on the cards, though she hadn't allowed herself to hope too much, but today her boss had confirmed it. She'd miss London, and Janey and Rose, of course, but New York! A fierce thrill went through her. She'd been told that she'd be rooming with another girl from the office who happened to have a spare bedroom, and that *Vogue* would cover all her travel expenses.

She was excited but she was worried as well. Who would keep an eye on Janey when she wasn't here? Ella didn't trust her younger sister. For one thing, she was always getting involved with such dreadful young men, lame ducks for whom she felt sorry.

And what about her diet pills? She'd need to stock up with them before she left, or find a new diet doctor in New York.

But at least she'd be away whilst Emerald was having her baby. Ella could feel herself tensing just as she always did when she thought about babies and what had happened to her mother, what she was so afraid could happen to her if she ever ended up pregnant. But that wasn't going to happen. Not ever. She wasn't like Emerald. She would never get married and she would certainly never ever have sex with a man outside of marriage. Emerald's runaway marriage and its subsequent annulment had been a *cause célèbre* for several weeks; there had been photographs of Emerald in the gossip columns and heavily veiled innuendo pieces about what had happened and her consequent 'condition', along with surely undeserved praise for Emerald's 'bravery' in remaining staunchly C of E.

The whole thing was shocking and shameful, in Ella's opinion, but somehow so very typical of Emerald, who had always loved being the centre of attention and getting away with things that no one else could.

She looked down at her desk. She'd been in the middle of writing some copy when she'd been sent for. She reached out for her notes, her wrist narrow and fine-boned. She was working so hard at the moment that she doubted she would have had time to stop and eat any lunch, even if she had wanted to do so.

Her family thought it was hard work that had melted away the schoolgirlish chubbiness she had been carrying to reveal the elegance of her bone structure, but of course Ella knew better. Oliver Charters had shocked and, yes, frightened her with what he had said about her diet pills and their dangers, but Ella had eventually convinced herself that he had exaggerated the dangers, and besides, she was still taking only one pill a day now – apart from when she was so tired and in need of an energy boost that she really felt she had to take a second tablet. It was amazing how well they worked in that regard, as well as helping to suppress her appetite. Ella didn't want to be without them – ever.

The face that looked back at her from the bathroom mirror in the morning now had cheekbones and a new oval shape that seemed to make her eyes larger and her lips fuller. She didn't dwell on these changes, though; she had far too much to do that was more interesting. And that hadn't been the point of her wanting to lose weight. The point had been to prove that she could. Somewhere inside her a small voice pointed out that since she had achieved her goal she could now stop, but Ella refused to listen to it. She was afraid that if she stopped taking her precious pills she would get fat again and that would mean that she had failed. Doing what she had promised herself she would do had made her feel so happy, so good about herself, so confident and in control of her life.

With her new confidence she had started studying journalism at night school, mixing with students who, like her, felt passionately about the really important things in life, like poverty, war, unfairness and bigotry.

Ella knew that *Vogue* was not going to give her a platform to write about these things, but New York could. America surely was far more open to modern thought and would give people like her a voice. It could be the start of something very exciting.

Chapter Thirty-One

It was six o'clock on Christmas Eve and Rose had been working all day at the Russells', helping to put up the new curtains and dress them properly. Now she was back at the shop, tired out. Ella and Janey would be at Denham by now. Their father would have met them at the station and driven them back to the house where Aunt Amber would have a huge fire burning in the drawing room with presents piled round the tree in the hall, which the twins would still be finishing decorating. The house would smell of mulled wine and mince pies and wood smoke from the fires, but it was the thought of the warmth of Amber's arms around her as she hugged her in greeting that caused the catch in Rose's throat and made her eyes sting. Things weren't like that any more, she reminded herself fiercely. They never had been, not really, and it was time she stopped being so . . . so sentimental and faced up to the truth.

She reached for her coat. Everyone else had already left and she was only still here because Ivor's secretary had called out to her as she had rushed past with her own coat on that Ivor Hammond wanted to see her before she left.

He was striding towards her from his office now, his forehead creased in a frown.

'I've just had the Russells on the phone,' he told her curtly. 'There's a problem with the curtains and you're going to have to go back and apologise. Mrs Russell has insisted.'

'But she said she loved them,' Rose protested.

'I don't care what she said then; now she's saying they aren't right, so you'd better get over there and make sure that they are. Russell is threatening to take something off the bill in lieu of good service, and if he does it will have to come out of your wages.'

Despite the fact that the shop's order book was always full, Ivor seemed to be continually anxious about money. Rose had heard a rumour that he was often pressed by suppliers for settlement of outstanding bills, and someone had told her that he was a heavy gambler playing for high stakes.

The last thing Rose felt like doing was going back to the Russells'. She'd thought they were going out for the evening, anyway, and she was supposed to be meeting up with Josh, but she knew she couldn't argue with Ivor. Not in his present mood. What a Scrooge he was.

Since it was Christmas Eve it was impossible for her to find a taxi. The streets were busy with people hurrying home, and it took her nearly twenty minutes to reach the Russells' apartment, hugging her tweed coat around herself in the cold frostiness of the evening.

The Russells' mansion flat occupied the ground and first floors of their building. The doorman recognised Rose when she walked into the handsome hallway.

She rang the bell, relieved when the door was opened straight away. She just wanted to get this over with and be on her way. She couldn't understand what it was Mrs Russell wanted her to apologise for, when less than an hour ago she had been saying how delighted she was.

As she stepped inside Rose didn't wait for Mrs Russell to start her complaint, beginning quickly instead, 'Mrs Russell—'

'Sadly my dear wife isn't here.'

The door swung closed, the lock clicking as Mr Russell turned the key in it and then looked tauntingly at Rose.

'What a good employee you are, to be sure, or did dear Ivor have to insist that you came back? I confess I did rather put the pressure on him but then you see, my dear Rose, you have been rather putting the pressure on me, and that's very naughty of you. I don't like being toyed with. No man does, and you have most definitely been toying with me.'

Rose felt as though she had become paralysed with fear. She desperately wanted to move but somehow she couldn't. She was too afraid, she recognised weakly. Arthur Russell had set a trap for her and she had fallen into it.

'Ivor said that there is a problem with the new curtains,' she croaked valiantly. 'If you could just show me what the problem is . . .'

'Oh, I'll show you that, my little lovely, and plenty more besides, and soon there won't be any problem at all because you are going to take it away. How many men have you had? Don't be afraid to tell me; it won't make any difference, I promise you.'

He was reaching for her, his breath gusting out from his loose-lipped wet mouth, hot and smelling of drink.

Rose panicked, jerking away from him, trying to evade him, but he simply laughed at her, catching hold of her wrists and holding them securely behind her back.

'Oh, yes, let's make it a bit more exciting, my dear.' His hold on her wrist tightened, but in her fear Rose struggled to break free, twisting and turning frantically.

'Defying me, eh? Well, you shall have to be punished for that.'

The flat of his hand came down hard against the side of her face with such speed and force that it jerked Rose's head to one side, compounding her shock and pain as Arthur Russell pushed her head against the wall.

Rose had never in the whole of her life experienced physical violence; even Nanny, who had never liked her, had never allowed Emerald so much as to tug her hair. Amber and Jay did not believe in chastising their children with blows, and the shock of what was happening now was almost as painful mentally for her as it was physically. She could taste blood in her mouth, she felt dizzy and slightly sick, close to tears with disbelief and fear. She had guessed that Arthur Russell was the kind that wouldn't think twice about forcing himself on a woman if he thought he could get away with it, but the physical violence that went with his sexual desire was alien to everything she had ever known. She had no defences against it, or its vileness. Arthur Russell was laughing, enjoying himself, as he watched her shudder when he drew gentle fingers down her bruised face and whispered lasciviously to her.

'Ah, poor little girl, shall I kiss it better and teach you how to enjoy a real man's passion?'

When Rose shuddered again his hand slid to her throat and gripped it. Whilst she struggled to breathe he leaned forward, pushing his body up against her, grinding its heaviness into her, his mouth at first loose and wet on hers until he started biting at her lips so that she could taste her blood.

Her arms, still held behind her back, were becoming numb. Arthur Russell slid his hand from her throat down to her breast. Rose stiffened in revulsion, unable to stop herself from crying out in horror when he ripped open the front of her blouse, and then began to toy with her breast, still thankfully covered by the brassiere and the liberty bodice which Nanny's strict rules meant that Rose was dutifully still wearing so long after leaving the nursery because of the winter cold.

This was worse than her worst nightmare, worse than anything she could ever have imagined. Rose thought of her mother, and wondered how many times she had known what she was knowing now. Shame and despair filled her. Perhaps this was what she had been born for, perhaps it was all that she was worth, a piece of flesh to be used for a man's pleasure, used and hurt, if that pleased him. Images of the mother she had never known filled her head, the most horrible kind of images in which her own face became that of the petrified young woman whose body was being abused. Panic gripped her, urging her not to fight but to give in because surely that way it would all be over much sooner and she would be free to escape from him – from him but never from what he wanted to do to her.

And then just when her panic was at its height and she was on the point of pleading with him to simply get it over with, the image inside her head changed and became instead that of her aunt Amber, smiling tenderly at her, holding out her hand to her, protecting her.

Arthur Russell gave a grunt of frustration at the barriers between him and his goal. 'What the ruddy hell are you wearing?' he demanded before starting to yank at the liberty bodice with his free hand.

Liberty bodices were, as Rose knew, anything but liberty providing, and not easily removed. He would need both hands and even then it still would not be easy. And that meant he would have to release her . . .

Josh had been waiting for Rose for over half an hour. She was never late. The pub was packed, it being Christmas Eve, heaving with bodies and a sense of cares being thrown aside in favour of celebrating the season. Outside it was freezing cold and he was knackered. One of his stylists had thrown a full-on dramatic hissy fit with one of the juniors on whom he also had a massive crush, and had ended up walking out, which had meant that Josh had had to take on his clients as well as his own. The air inside the pub surrounded him with a relaxing fug of warmth and cigarette smoke, making him reluctant to move from the table he had managed to bag when he had first come in.

But Rose was now very late. He knew she had been working at the Russells' and that was enough to have his nerves firing on all cylinders. He reached for his overcoat, a new one, bespoke, made by his father's friend

Harry Cohen in his Savile Row shop. It was black and made from pure cashmere, and he'd made poor old Harry almost weep when he'd demanded that he cut it into such a narrow fit, but Josh was well pleased with the result. He was wearing handmade shoes as well – both the coat and the shoes a Christmas present to himself. The salon was starting to make proper money for him, and it would make more. Josh grinned at the pert-looking blonde eyeing him up as he squeezed past her. He liked to change his girls as regularly as he changed his shirts; that way none of them got any silly ideas about tying him down. Josh had ambitions, big ones, and they didn't include getting married and ending up with a wife and half a dozen kids to support. He'd already started to get one or two girls coming in who hung around with the new singers and groups whose records were in the music charts, and once they'd got into the new year he intended to try to persuade Ollie to let him cut the hair of one of his many model girlfriends – one who was likely to be photographed for *Vogue*.

The air outside the pub was ball-shrinkingly cold, the sky clear and studded with stars. Josh knew the address of the Russells' mansion flat. It was a good half-hour's walk away, but there wasn't a taxi in sight. Not that that bothered Josh. He liked a challenge. The Dorchester was the nearest posh hotel, so he headed for it, using a small rear entrance and then making his way to the foyer, strolling through it and out past the uniformed doorman, who asked politely, 'Taxi, sir?'

Josh just managed to suppress his grin of triumph when the doorman hailed one of the cabs waiting for the Dorchester's wealthy clients. It was worth the tip he'd had to give the doorman just to be inside the warmth of the taxi instead of outside on the freezing cold street.

It didn't take the cabby more than a few minutes to reach the Russells' address. After telling the driver that he wanted him to wait, Josh headed for the entrance.

Initially the doorman was reluctant to answer him when Josh asked him if he'd seen Rose, but when Josh pointed out to him that if, as he suspected, she was being held in the Russells' flat against her will and Josh had to report that to the police, he gave in.

'Arrived about half an hour ago,' he told Josh. 'But no one forced her to go in. Knocked on the door, she did, and then went in herself.'

'I expect you've got a spare key for emergencies and that,' said Josh in a friendly manner.

''Ere, I can't give you no spare key. Lose me job, I would, if I was to do that.' The doorman looked and sounded anxious.

'Then I'll just have to help myself to it, won't I?' Josh told him cheerfully, adding, 'Don't worry, I did a bit of boxing when I did my national service. I'll make sure to give you a good pair of black eyes and a broken nose as well, if you like. That should convince everyone that I had to take it from you.'

The doorman's hand was trembling as he removed the key from the bunch on the heavy key ring he took out of his trouser pocket, and handed it over.

'Thanks, mate. I'd scarper for a few minutes now, if I was you.'

The doorman didn't need any urging, already disappearing in the direction of a flight of stairs.

She had escaped from him, but for how long, Rose wondered, shaking with fear as she stood trapped in a small space close to the windows, behind a sofa. Arthur Russell had picked up a ruler that had been lying on a coffee table and now he stood in front of her, bringing it down lightly on his own open palm whilst he watched her with a look that made her skin crawl.

'Now I really *am* going to have to punish you,' he warned. 'You need to learn some important lessons. I should have thought that a girl like you would have known better than to make me angry.'

Rose looked desperately towards the door.

'You can't keep me here like this,' she warned him with a bravado she was far from feeling. 'When Mrs Russell returns—'

Her words made him laugh out aloud.

'Don't bother wasting your time pinning your hopes on her. She won't be back until gone midnight and by then, my little lovely, I'll have had what I want, several times. I should warn you that my tastes are rather unconventional, and that deliciously shaped little rear end of yours has been tantalising me since the first time I saw it. Ever had it that way before? Some girls don't care for it, but I can tell that you aren't that sort. Goes with the breeding. Everyone knows that the girls in Hong Kong are the best in the business.'

Horror crawled through Rose's veins. If it hadn't been for the fact that Josh sometimes joked about the sexual practices of the homosexuals who worked in the salon, she suspected that she wouldn't really have known just what it was Arthur Russell was referring to. She certainly hadn't known that it was something that men did to women, and the thought filled her with fear and nausea. She tried frantically to dart past her aggressor but had to retreat back behind the sofa when Arthur Russell swiped out at her with the ruler, bringing it down against her hand with a stinging blow.

If the bastard had put a safety chain across the door then he was stymied, Josh acknowledged as he slid the key into the lock. But to his relief, the door opened easily, allowing him to step into the hallway with its over-ornate décor. Several doors opened off the hall and Josh approached them each in turn, listening carefully outside them, giving a grunt of satisfaction when he heard the sound of a male voice on the other side of a pair of double doors.

Rose didn't know which of them was the more surprised when the doors to the drawing room were suddenly opened by Josh.

'Josh,' was all she managed to stammer with relief as she was finally able to dart past her gaoler whilst his attention was focused on Josh.

'Thought I'd better come and get you, seeing as you didn't turn up for our date,' he mock-chided her.

'What the devil's going on?' Russell was demanding. 'How the hell did you get in here? Neither of you is going anywhere. I'm calling the police.'

'Good idea,' Josh agreed affably, whilst Rose tensed,

terrified that somehow Arthur Russell might have the power to convince the police that *they* were the wrong-doers and not he.

'I've already tipped off a mate of mine that works for the *Express* that I might have a juicy story for him all about a certain businessman,' Josh continued. 'The wife know about your little hobby, does she, 'cos if she doesn't she soon will.'

'You'll be sorry for this,' Russell warned Josh. 'I'll make bloody sure of that.'

He came at them with such speed, his fists bunched, that Rose was sure they would both end up trapped, but somehow Josh managed to push her out of the way and then sidestep Russell, turning round to raise his own fists and then deliver a blow that had Russell gasping in pain and clutching his middle as he sagged towards the floor.

Josh looked at him. He was sorely tempted to deliver a blow to the fallen man that would ensure it was a long time before he wanted to go near any woman again, but he was conscious of Rose and the need to get her away to safety, so with some reluctance he left his opponent and went to Rose, telling her firmly, 'Come on. I've got a cab running up a bloody fare that will cost me a fortune.'

Just the sound of Josh's voice somehow alleviated the horror that had gripped her. They were outside and in the taxi almost before Rose could draw breath. Once she had, she began to tremble so violently that Josh had to put his arm round her.

'I'll never be able to repay you for what you've done for me, Josh, never.'

'Course you will. You wait, some day someone will

come along and it will be your turn to help them. That's how it works, see, you pass it on.' He was only trying to help her back to normality, she knew, but for Rose the words had a resonance that burned deep inside her.

'And I will do that, Josh,' she told him passionately. 'I promise.'

His arm around her shoulders was warm and comforting, and he hugged her closer. 'I know you will, Rosie.'

Instinctively she leaned closer into him. Dear wonderful Josh, who made her feel so safe.

Then a new fear struck her. 'I'm so glad you came, Josh, and so very grateful to you, but I'm scared for you as well – after what Mr Russell said about paying you back.'

'You don't need to be. It was just talk, that's all.'

Josh sounded so confident that Rose didn't want to pursue the subject, but she couldn't help worrying and she just hoped that Josh was right.

They were in Sloane Square now and the taxi had stopped. They both got out. The cold wind made her face sting where Arthur Russell had struck her. From the old church on Sloane Street, the sound of carols reached them in disjointed wafts of sound, a few familiar words here and there. At home they had always gone to the midnight carol service at the small church nearby. Tears stung Rose's eyes.

'You OK?' Josh had reached for her hand and was squeezing it reassuringly.

'Yes, thanks to you.'

The Christmas lights twinkled and danced, the square and the King's Road beyond it both busy.

'I doubt that we'll be able to get a table in the pub now. It will be standing room only.'

'Yes.'

'Want me to take you back to your place instead?'

Rose's immediate shudder gave him his answer. 'There won't be anyone there.' She couldn't face the thought of being alone. It was, she knew, silly to be afraid that somehow Arthur Russell would track her down, but she was still too close to what had happened for logic. 'Perhaps if I were to go to Euston I might be able to find a train that will get me back to Macclesfield.'

Josh looked at her. Poor bloody girl. Thank God he'd been born male, he decided.

'OK,' he announced, having come to a decision. 'Come on.'

'Where are we going?' Rose set off down the King's Road, keeping her hand firmly within his own.

'My place,' he told her. 'You'll be safe there.'

Chapter Thirty-Two

'It's Christmas Day.'

Josh looked at his watch. It was ten minutes past midnight. 'So it is,' he agreed.

They were in his flat, warmed by the gas fire. Rose was curled up on the battered old leather chesterfield he had 'found' in a skip, and wrapped up in the eiderdown off his bed after the bath she had told him she needed to make herself feel clean again. Now she was drinking the medicinal cup of cocoa heavily laced with brandy, which he had made for her.

Since the bathroom was shared with the other tenants and did not possess a lock, Josh had gallantly stationed himself outside it whilst she had bathed.

'But what do you do? I mean, how do you stop other people coming in?' Rose had asked him.

'Whistle,' Josh had informed her. 'If you can hear someone whistling you know the bathroom's occupied. Works fine but it's tricky when you're cleaning your teeth.'

'I expect your family will be waiting for you,' Rose told him sleepily now, 'with it being Christmas.'

Josh was sitting cross-legged on the frayed Turkish rug on the floor. He got up and smiled.

'I'm Jewish – remember. We don't celebrate Christmas.'

'Oh!' Rose flushed and then laughed. She felt strangely light-headed and relaxed, and not at all as she felt she ought to feel in view of what had happened. Being here with Josh made her safe and warm and cosy, and as though she never wanted to be anywhere else.

'Sleepy?' Josh asked her.

Rose nodded.

'Come on then. I'll do the decent thing and sleep on the floor so that you can have the bed.'

Josh's bedroom was small and almost filled by the double bed, a bed that smelled familiarly of Josh himself, Rose thought tiredly as she curled up beneath the covers and closed her eyes.

The floor and the sleeping bag Josh kept for emergency guests were not exactly conducive to sleep, so he was awake several hours later when Rose cried out, her panic and fear plainly audible.

He normally slept naked but, in deference to Rose, on this occasion he had kept on his underpants. The lino was icy cold on his bare feet as he made his way to the bedroom, the light he switched on waking Rose out of her nightmare.

'I was dreaming about Mr Russell,' she told Josh. She shivered. 'I don't want to go back to sleep in case I start dreaming about him again.'

Josh looked at her. 'OK,' he decided, 'move over.'

Rose did so, too relieved at the thought of having his company to worry about any impropriety.

Josh had switched off the light and was busily making himself comfortable, thumping the thin pillow and voicing a variety of grunts as he settled down. They were comforting sounds, just as his warmth was a comforting presence.

A wave of misery flooded through Rose. 'Is it always going to be like this for me, Josh?' she asked him helplessly. 'Are men always going to think the same about me as Russell did, because of the way I look?' A single tear rolled down her face, glistening in the moonlight coming in through the gap where the curtains didn't quite meet.

Propping his head up on his hand, Josh reached over and gently wiped it away.

'No,' he told her, 'one day it will be different.'

Rose refused to be comforted. 'Different? What does that mean?'

'It means this,' Josh told her softly, leaning towards her, cupping her face with his free hand as he brushed his lips lightly against her own.

This wasn't what he had intended to happen, not at all. Seducing Rose had never even entered his head. Well, maybe there had been occasions when he had looked at her and thought about it – he was a man, after all – but certainly not tonight. It must be the unnatural situation of being in bed with a girl and not making love to her that was affecting him. And it was only a kiss.

Emerald glanced pointedly at her watch. It really was inconvenient of Dougie to have arrived at her house unannounced just as she was about to leave for the Ritz and Christmas lunch with her friends. Her mother had wanted her to spend Christmas at Denham, but Emerald had declined. She had no intention of doing something so boring and unappealing when she was having such a very pleasant time here in London being cosseted and admired for her 'bravery' in 'going it alone' after Alessandro's 'cruelty' to her. She had even warned Jeannie not to invite a spare man for her unless he was suitably elderly and very respectable. Emerald was rather enjoying her current 'Madonna' status and she wasn't about to have it spoiled by being seen in public in the company of one of society's charmers.

'So why exactly are you here, Dougie?' Emerald asked impatiently.

'There's something I want to ask you.'

'Can't it wait, only I'm on my way out,' she told him pointedly.

'I'd rather we discussed it now.'

Something in Dougie's voice – a quiet but determined force – broke through her impatience, commanding her awareness and a certain grudging respect because Dougie wasn't going to back down and let her bully him into leaving.

'Very well then,' she gave in.

'Could we go somewhere more comfortable – the library, perhaps?'

Emerald exhaled an irritable sigh. 'All right,' she agreed, leading the way into the bookshelved room, where she dropped her coat onto the desk, before sinking down into one of the leather chairs close to the fire. Emerald insisted on all the fires being kept burning whether she was in the house or not.

'Let's get it over with. What is it, Dougie? What do you want?' she demanded.

Dougie looked at her. His timing was, he realised, appalling but he was here and he was going to do what he had come here to do.

'I want to ask you to marry me,' he answered her simply. 'I want to ask you to be my duchess.'

Emerald was lost for words, lost to anything other than the shock within her that was now giving way to disbelief, confusion and – against all logic – hope.

'You want to marry me?' she asked him as soon as she could speak. 'Why?'

'Thought it would be a good thing, what with the little one coming and . . . well, everything,' Dougie told her determinedly. He might not have the expertise that Tod Newton and his ilk possessed when it came to women but Dougie knew Emerald better than to tell her that he loved her.

Emerald moved uncertainly in her chair whilst she tried to order her thoughts.

Dougie was proposing marriage to her because he thought it would be a good thing. She would be the new Duchess of Lenchester, Lenchester House and Osterby would be hers, she would have security, social position, wealth and a husband whose praises her mother never stopped singing. Something unsought and desperately fragile, so fragile that it made her hold her own breath, had started to unfurl inside her, something sweet and warm that made her want somehow to be that Emerald she had always refused to be. Fear and anger ignited inside her, uniting against their shared

326

enemy. Emerald let out her breath and welcomed her return to normality.

'Me, marry you?' She arched one beautifully curved eyebrow.

Dougie winced at the contempt in her voice.

'Certainly not.'

Marriage to anyone right now was the last thing she wanted. And as for marriage to the drover – unthinkable and impossible, of course.

From the library window, Emerald watched as Dougie crossed the square, drawing the attention of an elegantly clad young woman he passed. Emerald started to frown. Dougie was good-looking, she admitted grudgingly – good-looking and tall and broad-shouldered, and titled and rich . . . The kind of man a woman could rely on, come what may.

Her frown deepened. She wasn't actually regretting turning him down, was she?

He had known that Emerald would turn him down, Dougie tried to comfort himself as he made his way back towards Lenchester House. He was due at Osterby tomorrow morning for the Boxing Day meet and he should already have left. He had been a fool to go round to see Emerald just because Amber had happened to mention, when he had telephoned to wish them all a Happy Christmas, that Emerald had opted to remain in London. But a fool could dream, couldn't he?

Jay and the girls had gone for a walk but Amber hadn't wanted to go with them. She was worrying about Rose, who hadn't answered the telephone when she had rung her this morning to wish her a Happy Christmas. It didn't seem like a proper Christmas without her here. Ella had told her not to worry and had said that Rose would either be sleeping in because of all the work she had been doing, or alternatively might have gone to church.

She was concerned about Emerald's absence as well, but for different reasons. Amber looked out across Denham's frost-whitened gardens and the parkland beyond. She couldn't help thinking of another Christmas that had been shadowed, as this one was, by the conception of an unplanned child. Pain and guilt tightened round her heart.

Soon a new life would be born to the family, the first child of a new generation, her own first grandchild, and no matter what the circumstances of its birth the child itself would be welcome and loved. A grandchild. Hope uncurled inside her, pushing through the darkness of her guilt and despair just as, beneath the frost-hardened ground, already the spears of spring's bulbs would be uncurling themselves ready to push through their darkness and into the light.

Hope, surely one of the strongest and most enduring of all human emotions.

Chapter Thirty-Three

January 1958

Ivor called Rose into the office one morning, a week into the new year, and gave her her notice, saying that he didn't feel she was properly committed to her work. Haltingly Rose tried to explain about Mr Russell, the shock and fear she had experienced, although she did not, of course, tell him about Josh rescuing her and what had followed.

On Christmas Day, when they had eventually got up, Josh had fed her on smoked salmon and cream cheese bagels and hot strong coffee, before walking her home to the Chelsea house late in the evening.

She had felt self-conscious at first, self-conscious and uncomfortable in the light of the intimacy they had shared, but Josh had soon put her at her ease, reminding her that he was her best and closest friend, and that anything that happened between them was natural and understandable and did not need to be dwelled upon with anything other than gratitude that he had been there for her. And now at least, she told herself wryly, she had a standard against which to measure all other men's kisses, because when it came to kissing, even without any experience to help her, she knew instinctively that Josh's kisses were very good.

Her employer, though, was in no mood to listen to her account of the attack in the Russells' flat. In fact, he was so angry with her, denouncing everything she tried to say in her defence, that Rose knew that Mr Russell had already put his side of the story to Ivor.

'There's no room here for someone who disobeys orders and upsets clients,' Ivor told her.

'You mean you want me to leave?' Rose was desperately hoping she might have misunderstood.

'Yes, I want you to leave,' he agreed, 'and the sooner the better, before you cause any *more* trouble.'

It wasn't even lunchtime so there was no point in her going back to the Cheyne Walk house. Neither Ella nor Janey would be there. And besides, the person she wanted to tell first was Josh. Josh would understand.

Rose knew the minute she saw the small crowd at various stages of having their hair done, standing outside the salon on the street along with Josh's stylists and juniors, that something was wrong.

'What is it? What's happened?' she asked Irene, the receptionist, catching hold of her sleeve as the other girl stood on the pavement staring up at the windows of the salon.

'I don't know.' Irene looked frightened and upset. 'These men arrived – big and heavy and really nasty-looking, if you know what I mean – and they told us that we all had to leave. Francis said that he wasn't going anywhere because he was in charge since Josh wasn't there 'cos he'd gone to the bank, and one of them just picked up a chair and smashed it down over one of the basins and told Francis that the next time it would be his head.'

Irene was crying now, and Rose could understand why. At least Josh was safe.

'Has anyone called the police yet?' she asked Irene.

'Yes, Francis has. Oh, I do hope that Josh is all right.' Irene looked up at the salon as she spoke.

'You said that Josh had gone to the bank.'

'Yes, he had, but he came back, and when Francis told him what had happened he went running up the stairs.'

The crowd on the street was thickening with passersby stopping out of curiosity. A police car, its siren wailing, skidded to a halt outside the salon, two policemen getting out, whilst the driver stayed where he was. Francis started to tell them what had happened. Rose wondered why they were wasting time standing on the pavement when Josh could be in danger. It seemed a lifetime before they finally headed for the salon.

This was her fault, Rose knew. Mr Russell had taken his revenge on Josh because he had helped her.

Within seconds one of the policemen came back clattering down the stairs, and out into the street.

'What's happening?' Rose demanded. 'Where's Josh?'

'Now now, love,' the policeman said, then called out to the driver of the car, 'Looks like we're going to need an ambulance. Chap upstairs has been knocked about a bit.'

Josh. It had to be Josh. Rose ran into the building, ignoring the policeman's command as she raced up the stairs and into the salon.

Or rather what was left of the salon. Broken shards of the wrecked basins covered the floor, the chairs had been slashed with knives, bottles of shampoo emptied on the floor and hurled at the walls. Nothing had been left undamaged and Josh was sitting in the middle of it all, blood on his face from his obviously broken nose, his lip swollen and cut, the sleeve of his jacket slashed.

There was no sign of the men who had caused the carnage and Rose guessed that they would have left via the fire escape at the back of the building.

The policeman was now questioning Josh.

'Well, lad, this looks like a professional job to me. Got any enemies? Someone who'd do something like this?'

Josh was shaking his head, whilst giving Rose a warning glance.

The policeman sighed and looked resigned, plainly sensing that Josh wasn't being truthful.

'Well, if you suddenly remember that there is someone, you can call round at the station and tell us. In the meantime I hope that you're well insured.'

The policeman put his notebook and pencil back in his pocket and headed for the stairs, clattering down them as he went to join his colleague.

Rose dropped to her knees next to Josh, and reached for his hand. The knuckles were raw and bloody.

'At least I managed to give one of the bastards a belting,' he mumbled.

'Oh, Josh, this is all my fault, Mr Russell—'

'Nah, it's someone's idea of telling me that I need to pay them some protection money,' he told her. 'Happens all the time.'

But Rose didn't believe him – not for one moment.

'Policeman was right about me needing to be insured. Pity I didn't pay the premium when it fell due and bought myself a pair of fancy shoes instead.'

Outside another siren screeched and then stopped, indicating that the ambulance had arrived.

Rose looked at him, thinking at first that he was joking and then realising that he wasn't.

'Well, that's that, then. I reckon by the time I've paid for this little lot I'll just about be wiped out. What do you reckon? Do you think Vidal will give me a job?'

'Of course he will, but you won't need it,' Rose assured him.

There was no time to be lost. They could both hear the sound of the ambulance crew coming up the stairs. Soon Josh would be on his way to hospital and what she wanted to say had to be said now.

Knowing that it was because of her that this had happened, Rose had come to a quick decision.

'Ivor sacked me this morning,' she told him. 'Not that I'm bothered. You know how you've always said that I should set up my own business?'

Josh nodded.

'Well, that's what I'm going to do. I've got some money – a trust fund – and I'm going to use some of that to find somewhere for us both, Josh.' She was speaking faster now, desperate to get the words out whilst they were still alone. 'Somewhere that I can have my showroom on the ground floor and you can have your salon upstairs.'

It was the least she could do after what he'd done for

her. She knew how much having his own business meant to him.

'Now just a minute,' Josh said grimly, 'there's no way I'm going to be beholden to you and have you financing me.'

She'd known that would be his reaction and she was prepared for it.

'You won't be anything of the kind. I need you, Josh. You make me brave enough to do things I couldn't ever have done without you. We'll be partners, business partners, with everything done properly and legally. You'll design new hairstyles and I'll design new salons.' As she said the words Rose knew that it was what she wanted to do more than anything else, much more than draping curtains in stuffy mansion flats. She wanted to be herself, to follow her own direction, to prove to the world, and most of all to Amber, that she was more than the result – the sum – of the disgrace of her father and the poverty of her mother.

Josh looked at her. 'Partners? You and me?'

'Yes,' said Rose firmly.

The ambulance crew had arrived. Rose stood up to allow them to get to Josh.

As they set to work checking him over Josh winked at her and said, 'OK, partner.'

His face was bloody and battered, but Rose knew if the ambulance crew hadn't been there she would have flung her arms around him and hugged him right there out of sheer relief. Josh made her laugh. Josh made her feel that she could do things she'd never have believed she could do by herself. Most of all Josh made her feel safe. He was her friend and her security, and now he was her future as well.

Chapter Thirty-Four

Emerald's baby was born at three o'clock in the afternoon in an expensive private nursing home just off Harley Street, early in February.

Emerald took one look at the red-faced bawling infant and then waved the nurse away. She was pleased that he was a boy, of course, and naturally she would make sure that her ex-mother-in-law got to know that she had produced what should have been Alessandro's heir. But for now she wanted peace and quiet in a perfume-scented room, not one that smelled of blood and toil, and certainly not one filled with the roars of the red-faced 'thing' the nurse was still there holding.

Irritation brought a frown to Emerald's face. She started to wave the nurse away again but somehow the baby caught her gaze and held it with his own. Something totally unfamiliar tightened round her heart as though the baby itself had grabbed hold of it with his small fingers. A feeling, something so elemental that not even her strong will could overcome it, took possession of her. To her own astonishment she held out her arms for her son.

Silently the nurse handed him to her.

He was heavier than she had expected: eight pounds eleven ounces, the midwife had told her with approval. Emerald searched his face for some recognisable resemblance to either herself or Alessandro, but could find none. Instead he looked . . . he looked . . .

'Here, take him away,' she commanded the nurse angrily.

How was it that her son could somehow have reminded her of Dougie? That simply wasn't possible and yet Emerald could have sworn that the baby and Dougie quite definitely had the same unwavering gaze.

Emerald closed her eyes and let the nursing home staff fuss round her.

It was late evening when Amber arrived at the nursing home. Because Emerald had gone into labour a week early, Amber hadn't been with her daughter in London as she had planned. The staff welcomed her and asked if she would like to see her grandson since her daughter was still asleep.

'He's got a fine head of hair,' said the nurse who had shown her in to the nursery.

Amber agreed, but her attention was on her grandson. Her breath had caught in her lungs and her heart felt as though it was being squeezed by a giant hand. Looking at Emerald's baby was just like looking at her own son, Luc, when he had been born. Unable to stop herself, Amber reached down and lifted the baby from the cot. It was funny how certain skills and instincts never left you. A mixture of wonderment and pain filled her.

She could have been a young mother again, holding her own child for the first time, feeling that first surge of maternal love and that sense of joyful recognition as mother and child see one another for the first time and know the bond they share. The baby opened his eyes and looked at her. Amber's heart turned over.

Janey opened her eyes apprehensively and looked round the unfamiliar bedroom. She was alone in the bed, thank heavens. Unwanted images of the previous evening crowded inside her head. She couldn't remember now who out of the group of girls and boys that went out together every Saturday night had suggested going to Eel Pie Island, but she did know that they had all agreed it was a good idea.

The nightclub on Eel Pie Island had a dangerously louche and therefore a very attractive reputation. It was a place where rock and roll and jazz met and sometimes clashed. Saturday night fights were part of what it was famous for, along with the coolest music, the best musicians and the prettiest and wildest girls.

Janey had worn her newest creation, her own take on a darling little frock she had seen in Mary Quant's Bazaar the previous week – the frock she could now see lying in a heap on the dusty floor of the small cramped bedsit, which belonged to a man whose face she could barely remember, but whose smell lingered on his bedding and on her skin. Rather than think about him and what had happened, she looked instead at her dress, the cotton a dark moody plum scattered with bright pink flowers, which set off the blonde hair she was now wearing longer with the ends flicked up, just like the models in all the magazines. Just like them too she had been wearing black eyeliner and pale pink lipstick.

Janey could remember how excited she'd felt when her friends had pointed out to her that the lead guitarist with one of the groups was looking at her. She'd tried not to be impressed when he had sung from the stage and actually dedicated the song to her: 'The girl with the blonde hair right here who I'm going to take to bed just as soon as I get the chance.'

But of course she had been, and of course she had danced with him when his group had been replaced by another act. He'd had a dangerous sexy look about him, his dark hair long and sticky with sweat, his body thin and wiry, his grip on her hard and sure when they had danced together. His name, he had told her, was Jerry, and his dream was to emulate his hero, Jerry Lee Lewis, the famous American singer.

At some stage they'd drifted away from her friends to join another member of Jerry's band and the girl he was with, a striking-looking brunette called Nancy, who was older than Janey, with a slightly world-weary air about her.

At first she'd merely been slightly surprised when Jerry had started rolling his own cigarette, but that had been before Nancy had explained to her that it was a cannabis 'joint'. Janey knew people who knew people who smoked cannabis, but as far as she was aware, no one in her immediate group of friends did so, although it was talked about a great deal by some of the more daring members of the group, as something they would like to do. And now here she was with someone who was actually doing it.

Janey had been impressed but at the same time had felt slightly alarmed. Nancy had obviously guessed what she was feeling because she had dared her to try one.

Janey had wanted to refuse, but somehow, what with Nancy laughing at her and Jerry putting his arm round her and her hugging her whilst he put his own 'joint' to her lips, it had been easier to give in.

At first she had thought the roll-up was going to make her sick but then as her nausea had cleared she had started to feel pleasantly light-headed and then even more pleasantly giddy.

Before too long she had been laughing uproariously with the other three, and feeling part of some wonderful, special privileged world to which only they had the key.

She and Jerry had danced again, Jerry putting his hand up her skirt and whispering to her that he wanted her to take off her knickers. But then his friend had tapped him on the shoulder saying that they should 'swap girls' and Janey had ended up dancing with Rick, the band's drummer, who had stuck his tongue so far down her throat when he kissed her that Janey had hardly been able to breathe.

Janey couldn't remember when they had left Eel Pie Island although she could remember the four of them climbing into Rick's Morris Minor and then Rick driving them back to London and Jerry's bedsit. Which was where she was now – and thankfully alone.

Janey pushed back the bedclothes, keeping a wary eye on the door as she pulled on her clothes, relieved to discover that her coat and her handbag were on the floor under a chair.

Outside the bright light of the pale winter sunshine stung her eyes. Her head was pounding and her legs wobbly, the feeling at the top of her thighs making her glance anxiously at her reflection in a nearby shop window to see if she was actually walking like a jockey who had spent too long in the saddle. Her own mental reference set her face on fire. She really didn't want to think about what had happened when they had got back to the bedsit. How they had all smoked another joint and how then Nancy had taken off all her clothes, encouraging Rick and Jerry to help her, whilst Janey had looked on with what had then, thanks to the cannabis, been a totally unembarrassed curiosity as Rick had stroked Nancy between her legs, whilst Jerry had fondled her breasts. Janey quickened her walking pace, wishing she had been granted the blessing of a total loss of memory where the events of last night were concerned.

She didn't want to remember what had happened, she didn't want to think about it and she certainly didn't want her head to be filled with the shamefully erotic images that were now dancing around tauntingly inside her, just as she herself had danced around the bedsit last night, totally naked, in Jerry's arms, whilst Rick had pressed up behind her, joining in their dance.

'A delicious piece of super sexy filling in the men's sandwich,' was how Nancy had described her, before pulling Rick off Janey, then pushing Jerry away and starting to dance with her herself.

It made Janey want to writhe with shame and guilt

now to remember that when Nancy had started touching her breasts, instead of stopping her she had simply laughed. Just as she had gone on laughing when Jerry had joined in and slid his hand between her legs, taking her nipple into his mouth whilst Nancy cupped her breast for him. Rick had started rubbing up against Nancy's back, cupping her breasts from behind and telling Janey to lick and kiss them.

Janey shuddered.

She hadn't done so, but only because Jerry had picked her up bodily and carried her over to the bed, burying his face between her wide open legs.

The sudden tightening of her insides, as her body remembered *that* incident with embarrassing pleasure, brought Janey a fresh surge of hot shame.

Shortly after that Rick and Nancy had joined them on the bed and soon they had become a writhing mass, stroking, touching, licking, sucking, *fucking*, as Rick had said joyfully at one point, limbs, hands, lips and bodies.

It had been Nancy who had expertly rolled the condoms onto the men, insisting that that should be done – Janey admitted that she'd been too far gone at that stage to care.

What she had done was an awful terrible thing that filled her with shame, and it must never ever happen again. She must never ever even think about it again, Janey told herself firmly.

Someone was banging impatiently on the door to his flat. Oliver groaned and opened one eye to look at his watch. It wasn't even seven o'clock yet. He'd been out partying and hadn't gone to bed until gone three. Whoever it was would have to come back. He pulled the pillow over his head, but the knocking persisted and, if anything, grew even louder.

Swearing under his breath, Oliver got up, pulling on his jeans.

'All right, I can hear you,' he called out as he padded barefoot to the door. 'Christ, the whole ruddy street can hear you,' he added as he unlocked and opened it, only to step back in astonishment as he saw his mother standing outside.

'At last,' she announced before he could say anything. 'Come on, your dad's asking for you, and there isn't much time.'

'What?' Oliver scratched his head and yawned.

'I've just told you, it's your dad. He's dying and he wants to see you.' As she spoke his mother was picking up the polo-neck sweater he had dropped on the floor when he had undressed, and handing it to him, then picking up his shoes.

Automatically Oliver pulled the jumper over his head and then sat down on the bed to put on his socks and shoes, whilst his mother watched him grimly.

For as long as Oliver could remember his mother had watched him with that same look of determination, every inch of her five-foot-two frame focused on chivvying and nagging both him and his father into doing what she thought was 'right and proper'. High standards, his mother had – too high, Oliver often thought – especially when it came to cleanliness. A demon with her mop and bucket, his ma was. Never wore anything fancy but always looked spick and span, with not an ounce of extra weight on her, and the dark brown hair he had inherited from her always pulled back tightly into a bun.

Still half asleep, Oliver didn't ask her any questions, simply following her out into the street where, to his surprise, she'd got a taxi waiting with its engine running. His mother, who never wasted a farthing and who could make one shilling do the work of ten, using a taxi in the first place, never mind one with the meter ticking over, was astonishing.

'So what's happened?' Oliver demanded, once the taxi was in motion, but his mother simply shook her head and looked warningly towards the driver, indicating that she didn't want to say anything in his presence.

The taxi sped down the virtually empty road towards the East End and Bow, but then suddenly the driver changed direction, heading not for the street where Oliver had grown up and where his parents lived, but to Plaistow, the posh part of the area, coming to a halt outside the largest of a terrace of four-storey late Georgian houses.

'Come on.' His mother's hand tugged on his arm.

'What have you brought me here for?' Oliver demanded as he joined her on the pavement.

'Have you gone deaf or what? Like I told you, your dad's at his last prayers and he wants to see you before he dies.'

His dad? Oliver looked from the house to his mother. This house wasn't the one where he had grown up; it belonged to the man his mother had worked for, for as long as he could remember.

'Don't look at me like that,' his mother told him sharply. 'You've got enough brains to know that Tom Charters couldn't have fathered you. Thick as two short planks, he is, and always has been. Now get a move on. I'll never forgive meself if we're too late. Bin asking for you all night, he has.'

Was his father . . . ? Oliver swallowed the saliva that was threatening to block his throat. 'Does he know? Dad? I mean, Tom?'

'I don't know and I don't care. Now get a move on.'

They were inside the house, his mother's face shadowed with tension as a uniformed nurse came rustling down the stairs to meet them.

'Not gone yet, has he?' His mother had never been one to coat her words with honey.

'No,' the nurse confirmed, standing aside to let them go up. Oliver followed his mother, who merely nodded her head when the nurse called after her, 'I'll wait down here until you need me.'

The stairs were steep and they had to climb two flights of them. His mother reached the top without a change in her breathing, but he was out of breath, Oliver acknowledged. He was also desperate for a cigarette. If he'd ever thought of discussing with his mother the issue of exactly who his father was he hadn't imagined her doing so in such a matter-of-fact, almost impatient and nonapologetic manner. There'd been gossip when he'd been a kid, hints and that from members of his family, but somehow he'd assumed that if his mother was aware of the gossip, she would be humiliated and embarrassed by it.

As his mother opened the bedroom door, Oliver could hear the laboured rattling breathing of the man lying propped up in the bed.

'It's me, Phil,' his mother announced matter-of-factly.

A long thin hand, veined and fleshless, reached out across the bedclothes. His mother reached for it and held it.

'Have you brought him, Eileen?' The words were rasped and spaced out between what were obviously agonised breaths.

'Yes, he's here. Oliver, come over here so that your dad can see you properly.'

Reluctantly yet at the same time compelled by an urge he couldn't resist, Oliver approached the bed.

'You'll have to hold his hand,' his mother told him quietly, 'he's going fast, and he probably won't be able to see you.'

Oliver's first instinct was to refuse. The man he'd always thought of as his father had never shown him any physical affection, being more inclined to cuff him than hug him, but it still felt wrong to clasp in his own hand the hand of another 'father'. But again, though, something stronger than that instinct drove him.

One part of Oliver's brain somehow registered how similar to his own the other hand was, and similar too, the shape of the sunken eyes and the bold nose.

'Oliver.' The voice of the man in the bed, like the clasp of his hand, was stronger than Oliver had expected.

'Your dad's seen them photographs you bin taking that's bin in all them fancy magazines, *Vogue* and that lot,' his mother told him.

'He's a fine boy, Eileen. A fine son.' Tears filmed the sunken eyes. 'A son any man could be proud of, and I am proud of you, Oliver. Always have been, always, right from the minute your mother told me about you. Should have been here with me; would have been if things had been different.' His voice had started to fade, the words spaced out more slowly, and dying away with every strained-for breath. His grip on Oliver's hand slackened.

Oliver looked at his mother and then his father took a deep shuddering breath and called out, 'Eileen . . .'

'I'm here, Phil . . . I'm here.'

As she spoke Oliver could hear the breath rattling in his throat. He raised himself up off his pillows and then with a final gasp sank back on them.

His mother was still holding his hand, tears sliding down her face.

'He's left you everything,' Oliver's mother told him three hours later. They were sitting in the kitchen of the house where she had worked for so many years. The doctor had been and gone, and so had the undertaker, and now they were alone.

'Thought the world of you, he did, right from the first minute you was born.'

'Did he? Well, he had a funny way of showing it, didn't he? Getting a kid off another man's wife and—'

'That's enough of that. I'm not having you speaking ill of your dad, especially not now he's dead. Wanted to marry me, he did, but I was already married, see, and like it says in the Bible, let no man put asunder them as God has joined together. Good to me he was, though, always, and he made sure that you never wanted for anything. Remember that bike you had when you was ten?'

Oliver did. He had been the only boy in the street to have a brand-new Raleigh bike, and he'd been as proud as punch of it.

'He got that for you, your dad. I wasn't for you having it, on account of it causing gossip, but he wouldn't be argued out of it. Wanted me to take some photographs of you on it – always wanting me to take photographs of you for him, he was. He wanted to send you to a posh school as well but I wasn't having that.

'Remember that fancy camera you wanted when you first got started? It was him that got that for you.'

'I bought it second hand.'

'Brand-new it was, and it was your dad that got it and me that told you that I'd heard that old man was selling cameras.' His mother's voice was scornful and yet proud at the same time.

'He's left you everything. He told me that. Said that it was only right. Loved you, he did, and no mistake.' Her voice cracked. 'Loved you like the sun and moon shone out of you. Always talking about you. Drove me mad sometimes, asking me questions about you.'

'I never saw him, never spoke to him.'

'It was for the best. I couldn't have told you when you was a kiddy in case you said summat you shouldn't have.'

Oliver stared at the kitchen wall. It was distempered a sickly green and the distemper was flaking in places. A man he had never known but who had been his father had lived here, thinking about him, loving him, wanting him. He thought about the distance that had always existed between him and the man he had always thought of as his father, the sense of confusion and pain he had felt so often as a child, knowing that that father was irritated by him and resented him. A huge wave of loss swamped him. He looked at his mother. She had done what she had thought was right, he knew.

As her plane lifted into the steel-grey late February sky, Ella finally released her breath. There was no turning back or changing her mind now. She was on her way to New York and her new life there.

Part Two

Chapter Thirty-Five

England, June 1965

'Well, well, if it isn't *Vogue*'s much-admired Sixties Model Mother.'

Emerald, who had been trying her best to look interested as she watched her seven-year-old son running in his school's end-of-term egg and spoon race, didn't even bother to turn her head as she responded, 'Don't be tiresome, Drogo.'

Dougie had reverted to his real name on his thirtieth birthday, three years earlier, for no specific reason other than that he had wanted to reclaim a part of himself he felt that he'd somehow abandoned, and it had both amused and amazed him to be told by so many people whose opinions he valued, how comfortable they felt with the change.

Amber perhaps had said it best when she had told him affectionately, 'Drogo – it fits you so comfortably, rather like a favourite jacket that's been hanging in the wardrobe for ever because it felt a little too big, that you've suddenly rediscovered now fits you perfectly.'

Tiresome was definitely the right word for Drogo, as the family now called Dougie, Emerald decided, and it applied equally well to the way she was currently having to behave since *Vogue* published an article on the young 'with it' mother, using her as one of its examples of what modern sixties motherhood meant.

Of course, both she and Robbie were exceptionally photogenic. She felt so sorry for those women who produced ugly children; now she *did* look at Drogo. His children were going to be incredibly ugly if he did as everyone, including her own mother, thought he was going to do and proposed to Gwendolyn.

Who would have thought it, especially after the absolutely stunning models Drogo had dated over the years?

After she herself had turned down Drogo's proposal of marriage, she had assumed that he would continue to beg her to marry him. Only he hadn't. Instead he had virtually buried himself in his ducal and estate responsibilities, both in London and at Osterby, to such an extent that Emerald was glad that she had not accepted him. Who wanted to live such a dull worthy life? Certainly not her.

Naturally it had irritated her when, after Drogo had finally decided that he needed some sort of social life, he immediately became fêted and sought after by virtually every single society hostess, including those she thought of as her own particular friends. Equally naturally, that had led to them attending the same events and being in one another's company, but whilst Emerald had expected to have Drogo following her around begging to be allowed to pay court to her, instead he had made it very plain that he was grateful to her for turning him down, and had no regrets. Not that she did herself, of course. Now Drogo was very much a part of her mother's family circle, always welcome at Denham, where he was a frequent guest and, to Emerald's irritation, much loved by her own son, who practically worshipped him.

Emerald had no intentions of remarrying – ever. She liked her freedom and the right to order her own life. Having a man as an ardent lover was far, far better than having a man as a husband, and there had been plenty of men over the years who had been very ardent in their pursuit of her on their way to her bed.

Janey reckoned that if Drogo did propose to Gwen it would be out of pity because no one else wanted her. 'She's probably still a virgin,' she had added. 'Imagine!'

Emerald didn't want to, but she *could* imagine the shame of still being virginal at the age of twenty-five when the whole of swinging London had fallen on pre-marital, post-marital and outside-marital sex like the starving on a banquet. Although she hadn't said so to Janey, Emerald suspected that Gwendolyn wasn't alone in her shameful virginity, and that it was a state that Rose also shared.

Emerald thought of herself as a woman who, because she had been married, was entitled to live a very different lifestyle from someone like her cousin Rose, who, quite obviously to Emerald, knew nothing about men because she didn't have what it took to attract them.

Emerald enjoyed despising Rose almost as much as she enjoyed taunting her on the rare occasion when they met, by flaunting her own social superiority in front of her.

'Oh, no, Robbie, don't let him overtake you.' Emerald stood up on her toes to urge on her son but it was too late, Robbie had already allowed a determined red-faced little bruiser to push past him to the winning post. Emerald sighed. He had the double handicap of his own sweet nature and having been raised by Amber.

Normally Emerald did her utmost to avoid these occasions – grubby little boys and their dull parents were not her idea of fun – but on this occasion, with the *Vogue* article in mind, she had felt obliged to put in an appearance.

'Darling, over here,' she called out as Robbie looked round, searching the crowd. But either he hadn't heard her or he was ignoring her because suddenly a huge smile crossed his face and he set off at a run, heading not for her, Emerald realised, but his grandmother.

'Smart boy,' Drogo, still at her elbow, murmured.

'Well, that's something your genes will have to work overtime to produce if you go ahead and marry Glum Gwen,' Emerald told him smartly. 'Imagine having children with those awful cold squidgy fingers just like Gwennie's father's.' She shuddered. 'You'll have to be careful where they put them as well. You don't want a quiverful of little coroneted thieves, Drogo, who all take after their grandfather. Everyone knows about the money Henry's borrowed from people and never repaid. You should have married that last model you were dating, the one that went off with that pop singer.'

'Same old Emerald,' Drogo told her. 'Always ready with

the bitchy remark. But I suppose that's what happens to a woman when she's been disappointed in love and life: she becomes all sour and bitter.'

Sour and bitter. He made her sound like a dried-up old spinster, which she most certainly was not!

She was only in her mid – well, OK then, her late – twenties, for heaven's sake, and in the prime of her life. But as Max had rather unkindly reminded her last night, she was not eighteen any more and girls who were eighteen were far more forward and available than she had been at that age.

Max. The heat of last night's desire had only been damped down within her, not extinguished, and the mere sounding of his name within her thoughts was enough to have her need for him clamouring into fresh life. Emerald had never wanted any man as much as she did Max. He both aroused and infuriated her. Every time she thought she had him mastered and under her control, he proved to her that she had misjudged her power over him. He angered her and aroused her in equal measure, and Emerald knew that she would not be content until he was down on his knees admitting to her that she meant more to him than any other woman had or could. Only then would she be satisfied. Only then would she be ready to give him up.

She was seeing him later at Annabel's. She'd tried to persuade him to pick her up from her apartment so that they could arrive together and make a statement as a couple, as part of her ongoing fight to enslave him and bend him to her will, but he'd refused. Emerald wasn't used to men refusing her. She was the one who did that to them. With any other man she'd have sulked until he'd given in, but with Max she'd known that no amount of tantrums would work and that he wouldn't back down. That alone had been enough to sharpen her interest in him.

Max was different from any of the other men she'd slept with. She'd known that he would be different from the first minute she'd seen him. That had been at Annabel's too. Everyone who was anyone went there. He'd been with a crowd that had included members of the Tony Armstrong-Jones and Princess Margaret set. He'd stood out from the other men as well as slightly apart from them, in his mohair suit and well-polished Church's brogues, his suit, like his smile, sharper and skilfully tailored to enhance his maleness.

She'd wanted him even then, caught off guard by the fierce surge of her own lust. He'd been with one of an endless stream of dolly-birds with equally endless legs who filled Annabel's, and the beds of the men who went there.

One look at her had told Emerald that the girl would be no competition. She didn't have her looks and she certainly didn't look as though she had her sexuality – or her need – Emerald had recognised, watching the way the girl, thin and with a Sassoon haircut, had pouted and then pulled sulkily away from him when he had reached out for her.

Emerald had kept on watching them, deliberately so, smiling mockingly at him when he had finally felt the heat of her gaze and had looked back at her. There had been no need for her to do any more. Men, or at least the kind of men who appealed to her, always recognised her sensuality.

Annoyingly he hadn't been lured to her side to light her cigarette for her as she'd expected. Instead – and this had been something she'd definitely not experienced before – he'd returned her mocking smile, and had then produced two cigarettes, lighting them both and then holding them to cup his girl's face and kiss her slowly before handing her one.

Emerald now dived into her handbag to remove her cigarettes, remembering that incident. Her hands were shaking nearly as much now as they had been then, with the sexual excitement watching him had brought her. Max specialised in making every public act he performed with a woman resonate with a sexual intimacy.

When she had gone home she had relived his actions in the privacy of her bedroom, only this time she had been the one he had been kissing, not the stupid girl who had been with him. She could still remember how she had felt, lying naked on her bed, with the bedside lamps turned down low, her body spread across the heavy Irish linen sheet embroidered with her personal monogram, the E of Emerald entwined with the L of Lenchester, the whole surrounded by laurel leaves and surmounted with a small ducal coronet, to which, of course, she was not strictly entitled, being merely the daughter of a duke, but then she had always been prepared to break the rules to get what she wanted.

And she had wanted Max, so very badly that she had shivered with aching excitement just thinking about him as she lay there, her naked body and the bed dimly reflected in both her dressing table mirror and the full-length pier glass to one side of it, the low lighting giving the image a hazy, nebulous, almost Pre-Raphaelite sensuality.

She had taken her time stroking her body as she had wanted to imagine Max stroking it, admiring the smoothness of her own flesh, imagining his male pleasure in it, her heavy-lidded gaze observing the dark thrust of her nipples with triumphant pleasure. Emerald loved her breasts. They were the exact shape that fashion demanded, not too big and not too small, tip-tilted and firm, but it was her nipples that made them so sensually alluring. Large and dark, they looked almost as though they should belong to someone else, a woman with a fuller heavier figure, their sexuality intensified by the fact that her breasts were so prettily feminine. Men adored them. Emerald had easily been able to imagine how a man like Max would react to them; how they would arouse him to licking and sucking them with greedy pleasure, whilst she repaid the favour by reaching equally eagerly for his prick, his cock, the thick hard organ of her own pleasure. How she loved rolling those words around her mouth, tasting them with her lips, enjoying their erotic coarseness; words that were unacceptable on the lips of a well-brought-up woman, just as the desire thinking them aroused within her to treat the organ itself in the same way she was treating the words that described it, rolling her tongue around it, lapping at it with her tongue, sucking on the heavy sac of flesh below it before taking it into her mouth, was also something that no truly respectable woman should know about, never mind actually do.

What a thrill it had given her to imagine such a scene, to survey mentally, at first with warm languor and then with increasing urgency, the private images being unveiled for her enjoyment inside her head.

Of course it hadn't been long before her hand had slipped down her body, her fingers smoothing past the soft hair that masked the mound of her sex, to slide into her own wetness, stroking the receptive flesh slowly and teasingly at first, her rhythm quickly increasing, along with her heartbeat and her breathing, until her body was jerking against her expert touch, her eyes finally closing as she commanded her imagination to create for her the presence, the man she really wanted, so that it was he who touched her, who drove her, who captured her with the power he had over her to give or withhold her ultimate release from the savage ache of her pleasure.

Now, remembering that evening, Emerald gave a satisfied sigh of triumph.

Of course, merely imagining Max possessing her was nowhere near enough to satisfy her for very long.

There was no point in Emerald's book in being well connected if one did not use those connections.

By lunchtime the next day she knew virtually all there was to know about him. According to the information that was in the public domain, he was a crook turned gangland enforcer, now an entrepreneur with his fingers in some very rich pies indeed, which was how he had come to be accepted by society. According to the underground information Emerald had garnered, he was a man of incredible sexual prowess and stamina, whose charisma and charm had taken him into the beds of a long string of socially prominent women. His preferred choice was married women who wanted to stay married, and intense sexual liaisons that burned out at high speed and were *always* ended by him. Emerald had heard that he was rumoured to have a photographic collection of his conquests that would appal any censor, and that he was ruthless in getting what he wanted – both in and out of bed.

Everything she had learned about him had increased her appetite for him. It was fashionable to break the old rules and taboos, and to ignore the old social barriers. London's top nightspots were filled with swaggering young men with cockney accents and sexual machismo, unashamedly parading in front of society women whose husbands believed that sex inside marriage was simply for getting themselves an heir.

London was the place to be, and the King's Road rather like a private and exclusive club for those 'in the know'. The very air was ripe and loaded with the smell of sex and youth. Girls and rock musicians hyped up on amphetamines, the former to keep them thin and the latter to keep them awake, took to the drug-induced effect of an increase in their sexual appetites like ducks to water. And men like Max watched and smiled their crocodile smiles, waiting for the chance to feed.

He was a user, and some said an abuser, and so despite the fact that he had piqued her interest, initially Emerald had dismissed him as a potential lover, and with diffi- culty she had put him out of her mind. After all, there were plenty of other, far more worthy contenders for her favours.

She'd had an appointment that morning with the Harley Street quack who supplied her – and half of London, she suspected – with the amphetamine 'diet pills' that kept her as sleek as any eighteen-year-old, and then she'd gone for a late liquid lunch in a popular and upmarket Sloane Street pub, which was where she'd seen Max again, standing at the bar.

She'd affected not to see him, sitting down in a corner and keeping her back to him, unusually, for her, seeking out anonymity. She'd lit herself a cigarette, her hand shaking again, which she'd put down to the diet pills. She'd drunk a glass of wine and toyed with the steak she'd ordered, but for which she had no real appetite, refusing to give in to the temptation to turn round to see if he was still at the bar.

She'd just pushed the meal away virtually untouched when he'd arrived at her table, pulling out a chair and sitting opposite her.

'I hate to see good stuff wasted,' he said, and had then tucked into her discarded lunch without another word.

She should have got up and left. There hadn't been anyone forcing her to stay, after all. But she had stayed, heat coursing through her body as she watched him, unable to drag her gaze from his hands and his mouth. Somewhere along the way he had learned how to eat properly, even if his total focus on the food wasn't what she was used to or liked. But liking had nothing to do with the feelings Max aroused in her. By the time he had finished the steak, the expensive French broderie anglaise knickers she was wearing were soaked with the wetness of her arousal, thrumming through her, causing her clitoris to pulse eagerly and with increasing discomfort.

As she'd discovered with the first lover she'd taken after Robert's birth – the new husband of a smug fellow deb who'd been foolish enough to cut her and not invite her to her wedding – she was easily orgasmic, but not surely so easily orgasmic that she was actually going to come sitting watching a man eat in a pub. Enticing, exciting though the prospect of having sex with him was, *that* certainly did not fit in with her own image of herself at all. Not one little bit. She was all about control.

That had been when she had decided that it was time for her to leave.

She had got as far as the stuffy narrow corridor that led to the ladies when he had caught up with her, reaching for her and spinning her round, and then pressing her up against the wall as he kissed her, thrusting his tongue aggressively against her, and expertly sliding his hand up her skirt and into her wet knickers.

She'd come within seconds, the pressure of his mouth silencing her pleasure.

She'd still been trembling from it when he'd taken hold of her hand and hauled her into the ladies, leaning against the outer door to stop anyone else from coming in.

The ladies was a cramped airless area with a washbasin in the corner and one lavatory, a couple of feet away from the door into the corridor. He'd kicked open the lavatory door with his foot and then turned her round so that she'd had her back to him, pushing up her short skirt and pulling down her knickers, so that he could take her doggy style.

She had thought herself experienced, but being fucked by Max had been a revelation, because with Max it *was* being fucked. For one thing he was big – very big. She'd heard that but had dismissed it as exaggeration, but it was obvious that she'd been wrong. For another, he was selfish and aggressive, but somehow that had made the whole thing all the more exciting and thus her own pleasure all the more intense.

After he had come, he had washed himself in the basin, and then left.

It was only later, when she was back in her own Cadogan Place house, soaking in the bath, that she had realised that from the moment he had started to eat her discarded lunch to the moment he had left her in the ladies he had not said one single word to her.

She hadn't seen him again for nearly five weeks, despite the fact that she had virtually haunted both the pub and Annabel's ever since, hoping that she might.

Seeing a photograph of him in the *Express*, partying with a group that had included several well-known models, had filled her with a savage burst of temper that had resulted in her throwing a very expensive piece of Sèvres china – a pretty plate given to her by a previous admirer – at the marble fireplace of her drawing room.

She'd been on the point of leaving London for Denham with Robert when *Vogue* had got in touch with her, wanting to do a piece on her. She'd agreed, of course, and when the features editor had come round to the house to interview her she'd seen a photograph of Robbie and had immediately wanted to do something on them both.

Bailey had photographed her, initially with Robbie and then on her own.

It had been whilst she was at his studio that the door had opened and Max had walked in, and she had known then that somehow the *Vogue* shoot had been his idea and was his way of indicating his interest in her. The whole of society, or so it seemed, was entranced by London's underworld. Certain members of its criminal gangs were now high-profile celebrities in their own right: men like the Kray brothers, for instance, and, of course, Max, who it was rumoured had made a fortune through his involvement in boxing and, so some said, strip clubs.

They had had rough sex on the studio floor whilst Bailey had gone out to buy more cigarettes. That evening Max had taken her out to the Kray twins' club, laughing at her when she'd told him that she didn't want to go there. She'd seen and been secretly impressed by the way he fitted as easily into that world – his world – as he did into hers.

She had learned not to question him or push him, because when she did he simply disappeared. He refused to spend the night with her or take her back to his apartment. He liked his sex rough and raw, taken quickly and dangerously, in ways and places that added an exciting edge of risk. He liked sex in public places, where they could easily be caught out: Hyde Park, one morning, when he'd pulled her off the path and leaned her against a tree, pushing up her skirt and silencing her warning protest with a hard kiss as he thrust into her, leaving her weak with excitement and longing as she clung to him, urging him in deeper, even though she could hear the sound of an advancing crocodile of school children. When he had pulled out of her a split second before the children had appeared, turning his back on them whilst leaving her to cover herself as best she could, all she had cared about was having him back inside her to finish what he had started.

There had been other similar occasions, in darkened alleyways, and once in a taxi when he'd thrust his hand up her skirt and then into her knickers, bringing her so close to orgasm just as they reached their destination that she'd have given anything to have him finish what he'd started, stationary taxi and waiting cabby notwithstanding.

On that occasion he'd been escorting her home after an evening at a private gambling club where he'd won rather a lot of money, by cheating, Emerald had suspected. As soon as they were inside her house she'd headed for the stairs, but she'd only made it up the first few before Max had caught up with her, bending her over so that her hands were on a higher stair whilst he entered her from behind – his favourite position.

He had tried to persuade her to let him have anal sex with her but that was something that Emerald had resisted – so far. Such an act connected far too closely with Lord Robert, the man she had always thought of as her father, for it to have any appeal for her.

Her refusal had angered Max. He had lost his temper with her and lashed out at her, punching her hard in the stomach, the force of the blow making her sick and leaving her crawling on the floor of her bedroom in so much pain that she had neither known nor cared that he had left. Until later. Until her body had started craving him again.

She would tire of him, of course – that went without saying – and in fact she was surprised that she hadn't done so already.

She fidgeted with the hem of her mini now. It was three days since she had last seen him. She looked across the sports field to where her mother was standing with Robert. She'd better go over.

Drogo watched her walk away from him in a skirt so short she had every pair of eyes in the vicinity fixed on her. She'd got good legs and it was not surprising that *Vogue* had eulogised her, stating that with her beauty she more than matched the looks of many of the day's top models.

Bailey had done the photo shoot, Drogo had noticed, wondering cynically if the photographer had adopted what was supposed to be his favoured fashion shoot practice of closing the studio door and fucking the model.

Even he was torn between appreciation for what had to be one of the sexiest bodies he had ever seen, Drogo admitted, and his awareness of what a total bitch Emerald could be.

As he had told her, he was grateful to her for refusing his proposal – very grateful, in fact. They saw one another regularly, both socially in London, since they moved in the same circles, and more privately at Denham, for Amber had not only welcomed him as Robert's rightful successor, she had always welcomed him into her family, and Drogo appreciated that.

Emerald cared only for one person and that person was herself.

Robert was lucky he had his grandparents to give him the loving secure home they did.

Since he had a duty to the dukedom to provide it with an heir, if he could find a woman who would be as good a mother to his children and as loving a wife to him as Amber was to her children and husband, then he should, if he had any sense, marry her without hesitation, Drogo acknowledged.

The trouble was, though, that thanks to his own stupidity in not recognising the danger signs he had allowed himself to be manoeuvred into a situation where it was becoming increasingly obvious that he was expected to propose to Gwendolyn or look like a total heel. Even now he wasn't entirely sure how what he had intended merely as a kindness to Gwen, because he felt sorry for her, had come to be regarded by virtually everyone he knew, including Gwen herself, as the fore-runner to a proposal of marriage.

Chapter Thirty-Six

Robert's private London boys' school prepared most of its pupils for Eton, and it amused Emerald to see the looks of outrage on the faces of the other 'mummies' as she stalked past them in her newly fashionable miniskirt, all long legs and long straight hair.

Since she had met Max, Emerald had begun to feel as though she was two very different people: the outer Emerald and the inner Emerald. To the outer Emerald it was all-important that other people admired and envied her; that she had the best of everything, leaving other women awed and envious, and knowing that they could never match her – in anything.

The inner Emerald was different. She was wild and reckless, a hedonist and a sensualist who would go to any lengths to satisfy those desires.

The outer Emerald could only be seen in public with the right kind of man at the right kind of places, and had an image and a position to maintain.

The only position the inner Emerald wanted to maintain was one that had Max deep inside her, fucking her until she cried out as she came.

The inner Emerald was her secret and one she intended to keep. She was a temporary aberration who would disappear as quickly as she had appeared. She had to. Emerald might enjoy the *frisson* of excitement she got from living dangerously on the edge, but afterwards there was always that voice inside her head to be answered. A voice that accused her shrilly of being like her real father, the plebeian painter who had seduced her mother, a common nobody of a man, driven by his sexual desires. That voice was a voice Emerald wanted to blot out. She wasn't like that. She was what she had grown up believing herself to be, what she had been brought up to be, and that was the daughter of a duke, an aristocrat beyond the rules that bound lesser people, rather than a nobody who was quite simply beneath those rules.

Emerald despised people who gave in to fear, people who were weak and vulnerable. She would never ever allow those unbearable truths revealed to her by Alessandro's mother to instil fear in her. She would fight with every ounce of her strength and determination to continue to be accepted as Lady Emerald Devenish. No one would ever be allowed to take that from her. Nothing was more important to her than that. Not even her desire for Max.

Emerald smiled to herself. She had perfected a small depreciating shrug and a ruefully dismissive laugh as she explained to those who might not know that she was in fact not merely the daughter of a duke, but also by marriage a princess – 'although I never use the title. European titles always seem so amusingly vulgar and overdone.'

Sometimes she was tempted to use it, if only to infuriate Alessandro's mother and remind both her and the girl Alessandro had later married that whilst *their* marriage remained childless, she had Alessandro's son. Which reminded her, she must get Bailey to give her some copies of the photographs he had taken of her and Robert for the *Vogue* shoot so that she could send them to Alessandro's mother, with a thoughtful little note saying that she wouldn't want her to miss the chance to see how well Robert was growing up.

Thank goodness the school holidays were about to start and she could hand Robert over to her mother for most of the summer. Did it ever occur to her mother that, despite all the love she had lavished on others, Emerald was the only one who had provided her with a grandchild? She looked at her watch. She wanted to get home just in case Max had rung. She was supposed to be attending a dinner party tonight, but if he hadn't rung then she might cancel and go instead to the Ad Lib Club, which was so popular with everyone who was anyone, she decided, as she made her way towards where her mother was standing, only to discover that Drogo had got there before her and that Robert had attached himself to him. It really was ridiculous the way her son positively doted on the dreadful drover, and all her mother's fault for encouraging the situation.

'Robert should have won that race. I wish you wouldn't encourage him to be such a softie, Mummy,' Emerald complained to Amber. 'Mind you, Eton should put an end to that.'

'Eton? Emerald, he's only seven, still a little boy. He won't be going to Eton for years yet.'

'More's the pity.' Emerald glanced at her watch again. 'Mummy, I'm going to have to fly. I'm going out this evening.'

'With Max Preston?'

'Who told you about Max? Oh, the *drover*, I suppose.'

'Actually Beth mentioned him. She thought I ought to know. Gwendolyn had told her. I don't want to interfere, Emerald, but he does have a rather unsavoury reputation.'

The discomfort in her mother's voice made Emerald's face harden.

'Not worrying that I might follow your example, are you, Mummy? Surely I've already proved that I won't. After all, the man who fathered *my* son was a prince and *I* was married to him. Whatever I might choose to do with Max has nothing to do with anything other than the fact that at the moment I happen to find him amusing. It's the fashion you see, Mummy.'

'He's a gangster, Emerald, with a reputation for cruelty and violence, especially sexual violence towards women.'

The shock of her mother being so unexpectedly well informed and outspoken held Emerald silent for a few seconds before she came back coolly.

'Really, Mummy, you should be careful about reading the gutter press. Only a certain class of person does, you know. It's perfectly acceptable these days to have grown up in the East End. Max knows that I have standards that I expect to be met and that he has to treat me properly. I make sure of that.'

'I'm only warning you to be careful, Emerald. After all—'

'After all *what*? You don't want me to forget that you let some gutter trash of an artist father me? Don't worry, Mummy, I won't *ever* forget it.' Anger burned in Emerald's gaze. 'Max is just a small amusement, an adventure . . .'

Impatiently Emerald called Robert over to say goodbye to him, stepping back from him as he made to run into her arms.

'No, Robert, don't touch me, your hands are filthy. And besides, you are far too old now for that kind of thing.'

Ignoring the grim look Drogo was giving her, she turned on her heel. Really, her mother was so stupid. Did she honestly think that Emerald would allow anyone, man or woman, to control her or damage her in any way? She loved her freedom and her social status far too much for that. Hadn't she always promised herself that nothing could ever be more important to her than being who the world – her world – believed her to be?

She would never let anyone prejudice her status, especially not a mere man. She would never allow her reputation to be ruined for the sake of a sexual fling, as her mother had risked doing. But then she was far, far cleverer than her mother.

'Move up,' Janey demanded cheerfully as she sat down next to Rose on the sofa in the sitting room of the Cheyne Walk house, where Amber was having a family get-together prior to returning to Cheshire.

'No Emerald, I see,' Janey commented, reaching for a

chocolate digestive, 'although Mama is taking Robert back to Chesire with her in the morning. But she did look wonderful in those photographs in *Vogue*.'

Rose agreed.

'Cindy says that she should have worn one of my designs, though,' Janey complained.

After four years of working for other designers, Janey had finally fulfilled her dream of opening her own shop, Janey F, the previous autumn, using Denby silk in new modern designs to create her pretty little mini-dresses and other clothes, which had immediately proved popular.

Cindy Freeman, a girl Janey had met through her theatrical connections, had recently become Janey's official business partner, taking over the financial running of the shop, leaving Janey free to design its stock.

Janey, with her eager-to-please nature, had been allowing her hard-up friends to borrow clothes from the shop because, as she had näively told Rose in the weeks after she had first opened, 'They go everywhere and, like they say, people are bound to ask where they got their stuff from, and then come in to the shop to buy.

'Cathy McGowan off *Ready, Steady, Go!* has already asked one of the girls where she got the skirt she was wearing when she spotted her dancing on the show,' Janey had told Rose excitedly.

Sadly, though, it had turned out that Janey's friends had not always remembered to return their borrowed clothes, and Rose had been relieved when Janey had announced that she was taking on a business partner who would take a harder-headed attitude towards the running of the shop, leaving Janey free to design.

'Honestly, Rose, Cindy is just wonderful the way she gets things done and won't take no for an answer.

'Oh, and did I tell you that when Charlie and I were having dinner at the tratt the other evening Ossie Clark was there and he came over to congratulate me and tell me that he liked my work?'

Janey's face was pink with pleasure. Rose wasn't surprised. Ossie Clark and Celia Birtwell were one of the London scene's most prominent designer couples.

'Cindy has really turned things round for me. She's just the best partner I could have had. I am soooo grateful to Charlie for introducing us,' Janey enthused.

Charlie was Janey's latest lame duck. An out-of-work model-cum-would-be rock singer, who never seemed to get a job, he was stunningly good-looking and four years younger than Janey.

'Poor Charlie,' Janey continued. 'He's feeling really low at the moment because he hasn't got an advertising casting he went for. It's like he says, it's so often those who know the right person who get the best work, not the ones with the most talent. He was so sure he was going to get the ad that he'd been out and bought himself some new clothes, and now he's broke.'

And expecting you to fund him, Rose thought, but she knew better than to say anything.

'He really needs a holiday to cheer him up, but we're so busy at the shop that I just can't take any time off at the moment.'

Rose knew all about being too busy to take any time off.

Her own business had really blossomed with the advent of the swinging sixties, coupled with a chance meeting with one of the movers and shakers responsible for some of the new groups emerging on the music scene. Drew Longton adopted the manner and style of an ex-public school boy but his origins and education were middle class. He excelled at spotting – and using – talent, he specialised in funding start-up businesses – hairdressers, boutiques, clubs, that kind of thing – and Rose had received from him several commissions to decorate initially his offices, and then the shops and salons of several of his clients, and their flats. She also received frequent sexual invitations from him.

Drew was good-looking and a smooth talker, but Rose wasn't interested. She'd met too many men who wanted to take her to bed for her curiosity value. Besides, Drew already had an official fiancée, a pretty blonde-haired model who looked like Patti Boyd.

'Cindy thinks I should send some of my stuff over to Ellie in New York and ask her if she can get *Vogue* there to feature it, but you know what Ellie's like. She'd think I was being brash and pushy.'

'She is working in the Features Department, not the Fashion Department,' Rose felt bound to defend Ella. 'And I think it's to her credit that she doesn't go in for nepotism. You never know, though, Janey, with London being so cool it could be that American *Vogue* might be tempted to do a feature on a fab new London designer.'

'If they were going to do an article on a designer from swinging London, they'd be more likely to choose you,' Janey told her. 'Cindy keeps going on to me to ask you to redesign the shop for us but we aren't making enough money yet, and you've already helped me out so much, modelling for me.'

Rose had reluctantly given in to Janey's pleas to model some of her clothes in the catwalk show Janey had held at the shop when she had first opened. But it hadn't been an experience Rose had enjoyed – unlike the twins, who had revelled in the experience. They were both abroad now, training to be fabric designers with Angelli's in Venice – reputedly the most prestigious silk design and manufacturing business in the world, with offshoots on both the East and West Coasts of North America.

Amber came into the sitting room, looked at her niece and her stepdaughter talking, and wondered ruefully just where the years had gone.

In the morning she and Robbie would be leaving for Denham.

He was such a lovely and loving little boy. She'd done her best to make up for the fact that his mother seemed so emotionally detached from him, apart from those occasions when it suited her to play the doting mother.

Emerald's attitude and her way of life were alien to Amber. She had assumed that after the humiliation of her first marriage being annulled Emerald would quickly find herself a second titled husband – even if just to prove that she could. But instead Emerald had thrown herself into fast living, with a series of fleeting relation- ships with men who, though well born and wealthy, nevertheless had notorious reputations as womanisers.

Amber remembered how scornful Emerald had been on the only occasion she had tried to talk to her about her life, and the fast set of which she had become part, telling her coldly that she was in no position to talk about moral values, given her own past.

All Amber really wanted was for her family to be happy. Of course, she wasn't going to worry them with her concerns about the growing problems Denby Mill, the family's silk mill in Macclesfield, was facing.

Although she had her own considerable fortune, keeping Denby Mill going, and its workers in full-time employment, was almost a sacred duty to Amber. She had actively encouraged her family to share in her commitment to the mill and its future, but business wasn't as sound now as she had hoped. Angelli Silk, where the twins were trainee designers, had recently decreased the number of orders to Denby as their own expansion meant that they could now fill those orders themselves.

Amber and Jay were going to Venice to see Ruigi Angelli, the head of the family business, later in the summer. If, for the sake of Denby Silk, she would have to plead with Ruigi not to cut their order any further, then that was exactly what she was prepared to do.

Amber looked at Rose, a familiar pain aching inside her. It seemed impossible now that there had ever been a time when she and Rose had been so close that Amber had thought of her as her own child.

It was only natural that the young should want to be independent and make their own mark on their world, and it wasn't as though she and Rose had quarrelled or anything. No, it was just that she felt as though Rose had somehow stepped away from her and put up a barrier between them like a glass wall that could not be seen but which she felt and which would never let her in. Certainly the closeness she had once believed she would always share with her niece, and which would have allowed her to discuss her concerns for the mill's future with her, had gone.

'Are you all right, Grandma?'

The anxious question from her beloved grandson brought Amber a fresh stab of pain. How much she wished that he could be brought up surrounded by the love of a mother and a father. Was there something about their family that meant that none of its children could know that? Her own parents had died young, Emerald had been little more than a baby when she had lost the adoring father she had had in Robert, and now here was Emerald's son also growing up without his father, and without the love of his mother. She must not think that, Amber told herself, as she smiled at her grandson and reassured him, 'No, I'm just thinking how pleased Granddad will be to see you.'

'Uncle Drogo says he's going to come and see me as well.'

Drogo – there was another cause for concern. Robert adored Drogo, and Drogo had been very good to him, but if Beth was right then any day now Drogo was expected to propose to Gwendolyn. Once they were married Gwendolyn would not welcome Robert in Drogo's life, given that he was Emerald's son. Amber felt very strongly that Robert needed a younger male influence in his life than Jay could provide. She believed that the relationship, the love, that existed between Drogo and Robert echoed in some ways the love that Robert and Luc had shared, although, of course, theirs had been the closer bond of father and son.

Amber worried about Robert, and she worried about him all the more because he was Emerald's son and because Emerald would not allow her to worry about her. In worrying so much about Robert's emotional happiness, she was, Amber knew, also worrying about her daughter's. What was going to happen to Emerald when nature finally forced her to recognise that she could no longer attract a ceaseless parade of lovers? How would she cope? What, if anything, did she have within herself to sustain her once she lost the satisfaction she derived from the outward show of her female power? It grieved Amber desperately to think of her daughter as someone with nothing with which to sustain herself, and it grieved her even more to know that that was her fault.

Chapter Thirty-Seven

Rose was in a rush. She was having dinner with Josh – a regular monthly fixture – and if she wasn't careful she was going to be late.

The past few years had seen many changes in his life, but through them all his friendship with Rose and their partnership had remained a constant.

Rose had been one of the witnesses to his Caxton Hall wedding to the model he had married in 1960, and she had commiserated with him when it had ended two years later in the divorce courts. She had celebrated with him when he had opened his second and then his third salon, and she had celebrated with him again when he had been named London's top hairdresser.

She had even smiled as warmly as she could three months ago when he had introduced her to his new steady girlfriend, an American, Patsy Kleinwort, who had replaced the succession of pretty faces whose bodies had filled his bed since his divorce.

And through it all, foolishly, she knew she had cherished their friendship, their business partnership and their monthly dinner dates.

Josh was so successful now that he no longer needed a business partner, but neither of them ever referred to that fact, and Rose had taken his silence on the subject as a sign that he, like her, cherished the bond between them and the legal excuse they had for maintaining it. He must, she had decided with relief, want her in his life.

She certainly wanted him in hers. Because the truth was that on that Christmas Eve nearly a decade ago, when he had taken her to bed and banished the loathsomeness of Arthur Russell's attempted rape of her, although she hadn't known it then, nor indeed for several years afterwards, Rose suspected she had fallen in love with him. She hadn't realised what had happened to her until it was too late. She *had* known, though, standing on the steps of Caxton Hall, watching him with his new bride, and she certainly knew it now.

She had tried to get over it, busying herself with her business, even going out with other men – and going to bed with them if she had felt there was any chance at all that they could help her to stop loving Josh, at least in the early years. Now, though, she had given up hope of stopping loving him. And besides, even if he had loved her in return . . . Rose frowned. She hated herself when she started being self-pitying and allowing that sense of dark misery deep inside her that she 'wasn't good enough' to overwhelm. Things were different now. Girls from every part of the world and every nationality could be seen in London – pretty, confident, happy young women, with pride in themselves and their cultural identity; girls who were doing their own thing. The old stigmas had been trampled beneath the dancing feet of the sixties generation, and between their sheets. She knew this, so why was she still hung up on her own parentage? It was pathetic. *She* was pathetic.

She had tried. She hadn't seen Josh for virtually six months after the wedding. Too busy shagging, he'd told her happily and besottedly when he had eventually surfaced from his post-wedding bliss. She'd smiled and nodded, his happiness reinforcing her own grim determination to cling to the only thing in her life she felt she could trust, determined to prove to the world that she might be the daughter of a wastrel and a Chinese peasant, but she still had the talent and the business skills to make it on her own.

She should have broken away then, she almost had, but Josh had taken to calling round at the small office further down the King's Road that she'd found for herself, cadging cups of coffee and cigarettes and, later, pouring out his heart to her about the increasing problems within his marriage.

She had tried to look both surprised and nonjudgemental when he had told her, obviously astonished and feeling betrayed by the discovery, that Judy was a party girl who liked staying out until the small hours and then sleeping all day and that she resented the amount of time he spent working.

Rose could have told him what Judy was like right from the start.

Then there'd be the nights when Judy hadn't come home, and the rows when she did, finally ending up with her admitting that she had found someone else.

Foolishly Rose had hoped that finally Josh might turn to her for comfort.

She had hoped through three more years and ten times as many girls, during which they had shared anniversaries and Christmases and even holidays, but never ever again a bed. Hope, as Rose had discovered, was a stubbornly obstinate plant, and deeply rooted. And once it had taken root it was very difficult to remove. She had also discovered that exactly as it said in the Bible, 'Hope deferred maketh the heart sick.' And right now her heart was very sick indeed, because now Josh had met Patsy, who had taken one glance at Rose and given her a look that had said quite plainly 'hands off'.

But Patsy wouldn't be here tonight. Tonight Rose had him all to herself.

But still Rose's heart felt heavy. Was it her fault? Did she invite her own pain? Was she destined always to love those who could not or would not love her back: Greg, the father who had never wanted her; Amber, the aunt she had believed loved her but who had not really done so; John, who might be her half-brother; and most of all Josh?

They were having dinner at the Savoy – a proper grown-up dinner in a traditional hotel, served by proper waiters, not a modern sixties meal in a cramped King's Road restaurant where the air was filled with the smell of cannabis rather than the aroma of good food, and where everyone was too high to care about whether they ate anything or not; where everyone knew everyone else and belonged to a large private club with its own language in which one-to-one privacy, like celibacy, was just a joke;

where pretty girls moved from man to man and lap to lap, and peace and love were all that mattered.

At first everything went well. Josh had arrived early and was waiting for her, embracing her with an affectionate hug, and then holding her at arm's length whilst he admired her new outfit, a simple acid-yellow sheath dress ornamented with one large, beautifully detailed, multi-coloured silk flower.

'One of Janey's?' he asked knowingly.

A little guiltily Rose admitted, 'No, it's actually one of Ossie Clark's. I was at his studio the other day and whilst I was there I saw this dress and couldn't resist it.'

'Good for you,' Josh laughed. 'I'm all for not resisting temptation. Speaking of which . . .'

He had to break off from what he was saying whilst they were being shown to their table, and their conversation couldn't resume properly until they'd chosen from the menu and ordered their wine.

Josh might have grown his hair a bit longer but in essence he still looked the same as when Rose had first met him. He still favoured Savile Row suits rather than dressing in the peacock fashions now favoured by the rock group fraternity and their followers, even if his shirts had become more sharply tailored and were made of floral fabric.

When he offered her a cigarette she accepted, simply for the rush of pleasure it gave her to have him lean closer to her to light it for her.

'Don't worry, it's a straight Benson and Hedges,' he told her with a teasing grin, but Rose didn't laugh.

Her grandmother, Blanche, had been unsparing in her description of the depths to which Rose's father had descended before his death, during which he had become addicted to both drink and drugs. This had led to Rose refusing so much as a drag on a passed-round reefer, despite the contemptuous teasing this sometimes caused.

Her business came in the main from the swinging sixties fashion and pop heroes and their hangers-on; most of whom at the very least smoked dope, and a good proportion of whom were now openly boasting about being acid heads and had become converts to and advocates for LSD.

Josh was the only other person in the King's Road crowd Rose knew who didn't touch drugs.

'I believe that you can't so much as touch a door handle in some parts of Chelsea these days in case someone has rigged it with LSD,' she told him ruefully.

'I've heard the same,' Josh agreed. 'I had a young model in the other day who told me that she'd tripped for three days and that it was like going to the moon and looking down on the whole world.' He shook his head. 'When you've been brought up down the East End and you value your sanity, you don't go anywhere near any stuff that plays games inside your head. I've seen the wrecks it leaves behind dying in the gutter.'

Their first course had arrived – avocado, which they both loved – but Rose noticed that Josh was barely touching his. In fact she noticed he was looking distinctly on edge, and she wondered why.

'I've got some great news for you.'

'You're opening another salon?' Rose guessed, but he shook his head.

'Nope, it's something much better than that. I've asked Patsy to marry me and she's said yes.'

There was a horrible vacuum inside Rose's body, as though the ability to feel anything had been sucked out of her by the ferocity of her shock.

She should have guessed that this would happen, and if she hadn't then it was her own fault for being an ostrich and hiding herself away from what had been inevitable from the first time Josh had raved to her about his new girlfriend.

The vacuum was rapidly filling with the most intense, unbearable pain.

'Well. Congratulations.' Her lips felt stiff, the words unwieldy. Did her voice sound as strained as her smile felt? What did it matter if it did? Josh was hardly likely to notice in his elated state. He was beaming from ear to ear, and looking so happy that Rose badly wanted to crawl into a corner where she could give in to her own misery. Here it was again, her old enemy – self-pity.

Of course he had fallen in love with tall, blonde Patsy, who was typical of the type of girl he went for, and she was a fool for ever thinking that one day he would look at her with that besotted adoration in his eyes that she could see in them now.

'I would have told you before but, well, everything's happened so quickly. It was only when she said that she was thinking of moving back to New York that I realised that I didn't want to lose her. And guess what? I brought her here to propose.'

Fresh pain seared Rose. This was *their* place – their special place – it always had been.

'To be honest I was scared silly that she'd turn me down. I mean, why should a gorgeous girl like her take on someone like me?'

Because you are good-looking, sexy, kind, fun, and successful, the answer to every girl's prayer, Rose thought, but of course she couldn't say that. She knew him well enough to know how quickly he would pounce on even the smallest hint that she was accusing Patsy – who in Rose's opinion had a very keen eye for an opportunity that would benefit her, and who was as emotionally as cold as a fish unless it suited her to appear otherwise – of not being good enough for him.

But then again there was the possibility that she could simply be misjudging Patsy because she was so very jealous.

Josh was plainly waiting for her to say something else. Rose took a deep breath.

'Great . . . Er, have you decided when you're going to get married yet?'

How hard it was to say those words, as painful as stabbing a knife right into her own heart.

'As soon as we can. I want you to be there, naturally, although Patsy says she's a bit worried in case having you as a witness brings us bad luck. She's only joking, of course.'

'Of course,' Rose agreed, keeping to herself her belief that Patsy was not joking at all.

'Patsy is full of plans for us. She knows all about what went wrong with me and Judy and she says she's determined to get really involved with my work so that it doesn't happen to us. That's another reason why I'm glad we're seeing one another tonight. You see, there's something Patsy wants me to discuss with you.'

He was looking uncomfortable again, Rose recognised. Whatever it was Patsy wanted him to discuss with her it obviously wasn't something she was going to like.

'If she doesn't approve of us having dinner together once a month—' she began, mentally casting around for something that Patsy might want to change.

'No, it isn't that. Well, not directly, although . . . Well, the thing is, Rose, Patsy feels that there's no reason now why you and I should be business partners any more. And looking at it logically, she's right. Like she says, I don't really need . . .'

'Me?' Rose completed his sentence for him. Her voice sounded brittle, she knew, but that was exactly how she felt. Brittle and vulnerable and dangerously fragile. She was close to breaking down completely and bursting into tears. This was the last thing she had been expecting. No matter what, no matter how many girls, or indeed wives, came and went in his life she had felt secure that she would always have the closeness that their being partners afforded her. But now, thanks to the shrewdness of the woman who had taken the role in his life she had longed for, even that comfort was going to be denied her.

Was Patsy's concern really about the partnership or had she perhaps sensed Rose's true feelings for Josh?

'Don't be like that.' Josh sounded genuinely upset. 'You and I will always be friends. Nothing can change that.' He had reached for her hand before she could stop him and the familiar feel of his fingers curling round her own brought a lump to her throat. Inside her head she could hear the words of the Rolling Stones' hit record about last times, and her whole body was starting to tremble. Frantically she pulled her hand away from his in case he asked her what was wrong.

'I've so much to be grateful to you for,' he told her.

Rose couldn't allow that. 'You don't owe me anything. We've helped each other,' she reminded him.

She could see in his face his relief that she wasn't going to get emotional. Her role in his life was that of a friend, not the woman he loved.

'Patsy's right, I should have done something about repaying you before now,' he was saying. 'The salons are doing really well, and I can easily afford to buy out your share. It isn't fair of me to keep you tied up in a relationship with me when you could be using your investment somewhere else.'

Of course it's fair, she wanted to tell him, the words screaming inside her head like a toddler having a tantrum. I want to be tied to you in every way there is. What isn't fair is you marrying Patsy and what she's making you do.

'What Patsy really wants is for us to have a fresh start and for me to open a salon in New York.'

So this was it. The end of everything.

'Follow in Vidal's footsteps, you mean.'

If she was being bitchy and hurting him, then so be it. But instead of taking offence he nodded eagerly.

'He's doing really well over there and Patsy says there's no reason why I shouldn't do the same. She's got some contacts in New York and, of course, her family. You'll have to come over and see us once we're settled. And no excuses – after all, Ella's over there.'

Obediently Rose picked up the hint she suspected he was dropping. 'I'll tell her what you're planning, shall I? She's a junior features editor at *Vogue*, as you know, but I'm sure she won't mind mentioning you to the Fashion Department.'

This was the worst evening of her life, worse in its way than the night Arthur Russell had nearly raped her, because, after all, that night she had ended up in Josh's arms.

It was over, the evening and her poor silly futile dream. Josh was signalling for the bill, eager to get home to Patsy, Rose thought miserably.

Chapter Thirty-Eight

Ella sat in the window of her brownstone walk-up, trying to get some air in the stifling heat that was Manhattan in June. She was supposed to be working on the wording for an article for the Christmas issue of *Vogue* entitled 'The Giving of Art'. It was about artists' patrons. But how on earth was she supposed to be able to think about Christmas and snow when the heat was causing sweat to trickle between her breasts?

She had fallen in love with New York from the minute she had arrived in Manhattan in the winter of 'fifty-eight. In those early months she had explored it from end to end, walking most of the time, at least where it was safe to do so, learning about its past and its present, embracing the brio and the passionate attitude of its residents. Feisty, outspoken, brash but never boring, from Broadway to the Bronx, from Central Park to Staten Island, Ella loved it all for everything it was, but most of all for the way it had taken her and forced those changes on her that had turned her from the awkward, uncomfortable, plain girl she had been into the New York woman she was now, a woman who could bargain for what she wanted, who could summon a New York cab, who dressed with confidence. She had gone to parties at Studio 8, and Upper East Side apartments, she had eaten pastrami on rye at diners downtown, and gourmet meals at the Plaza, she had sunbathed in the park in summer and skated on the frozen ponds in winter. She had ridden its subways and walked its avenues. It had given her confidence in herself, and in return she had given it her heart. She'd fallen in love with it so much that she'd started forgetting about taking her diet pills, and then realising that she didn't need them. New York kept her slim, a healthy natural slimness that had set her free from her bad memories about her weight. Yes, she loved New York, but right now the city felt empty and dull. Because Brad wasn't in it?

She put aside her notebook. There was no point in trying to work any more; not now that she had let Brad into her thoughts.

She could have accepted his invitation and gone to the Hamptons with him for the weekend, she reminded herself. But then he'd have expected her to sleep with him, and she couldn't do that.

She closed her eyes. How ironic it was that the cure to her fear of pregnancy – the contraceptive pill – and the madness she believed would follow it, which had prevented her from having sex, had come too late for her. If it had been available earlier, when she had been younger, then everything would have been all right. She could have gone to bed with Brad. After all, she wanted to. She had been attracted to him from the minute they had been introduced. Handsome, debonair, rich and divorced, intelligent, with a good sense of humour, a highly acclaimed investigative journalist turned author, was it any wonder that she'd fallen for him? He confirmed everything she'd always secretly thought, which was that the men she'd mixed with in London were shallow and dull. None of them had ever made her feel as Brad did. If she had been the kind of person who said and believed such things, she could easily have thought that secretly she'd been waiting for him to come into her life.

She'd been first disbelieving and then thrilled when he had begun his subtle pursuit of her. But hard on the heels of her delight had come the harshness of reality. Brad was a liberal thinker, a man of certain strongly held views, one of which was the right of women to own their own sexuality. He had written some high-profile and acclaimed articles denouncing the kind of women who refused to join the sexual revolution and who clung to the old ethos of exchanging their virginity for a wedding ring. Traitoresses to their own sex, he had labelled them; contemptible and worthless, in the eyes of a truly liberated man.

Ella was still a virgin. Not because she had ever had any intention of using her virginity to blackmail a man into marriage – far from it. She had always sworn that she would never marry. It was her fear of having a child and then suffering the same madness that had destroyed her mother that was responsible for her virgin state.

Now, though, the contraceptive pill, which her New York gynaecologist was already prescribing for her because of the problems she'd been having with her periods, meant that she had no need to fear an unwanted pregnancy.

She could, of course, explain to Brad just why she was still a virgin, but Ella was an eldest child, driven by a need to excel at everything she did and a fear of the humiliation of revealing herself as anything less than perfect. Brad was a sophisticated man in his thirties who would, she was sure, be a superb lover and who would expect the same expertise in any woman he made love to.

How could she reveal herself to him as a gauche, totally inexperienced virgin? She couldn't! Not when her own carefully cultivated image was one of modern sophistication.

It was too late now to regret all the opportunities she had had, at those endless parties Janey had so often dragged her and Rose to back in London, to become sexually experienced.

She just couldn't bear the thought of being in bed with Brad and seeing his expression change from desire to cold contempt or, even worse, amusement when he discovered the truth. She had visualised that happening so many times inside her head. The humiliation would be unbearable. She wanted to meet Brad on his own level; to delight and surprise him, to hear him saying how totally swept away he was by her power to arouse him past the limits of his self-control. She wanted so much to please and impress him; to be better than anyone else, to be the best; to hear him say that from now on she was the only woman for him and that no other woman could compare with her. That was what she wanted. Nothing less. And since she could never have that then she must just put him out of her thoughts. If she could have waved a magic wand and transformed herself into the woman she wanted to be, she would have done so. But Ella knew from her childhood that there was no such thing as magic. For a long time after her mother had died she had gone to bed at night wishing that somehow during the night all the frightening things she knew about her mother would be magicked away and that when she woke up in the morning there would be a new Lydia, a Lydia who was normal and not mad. That had never happened. There was no magic.

Brad would soon get bored with pursuing her without the response he wanted. He would soon find someone else.

'Do you know what I like about you?' he had said to her shortly after they had first met. 'I like that you are so together, so smart-assed and clever. I like that you're a woman and not a silly girl. I can see in those eyes of yours that you know what being a woman is all about.'

She had fixed her gaze on the immaculate collar of his Brooks Brothers shirt and tried to be all the things he had just described whilst knowing that she was, in reality, none of them.

She had lived in New York for long enough now – the best part of a decade – to know that no one stayed in the city in the summer unless they had to, and even those that did hightailed it out the minute Friday afternoon came.

Everyone who worked in *Vogue*'s offices, or so it seemed, either had a place in the Hamptons, or knew someone who did, and weekends saw those members of the staff who weren't already working out of the city on an assignment heading for the fashionable summer retreat.

Ella could have gone, even though she hadn't accepted Brad's invitation to stay at the beach house he was renting for the summer, so that he could work on his new book. She wasn't short of invitations from various members of the editorial team but since she'd lied to Brad that she had some research work to do that could only be done in the city, she had had to stay put.

She loved New York but there were still times when she missed her family. Sometimes the two different sides of her head were at war with one another: the sentimental, vulnerable side longing for home and its emotional comfort, the ambitious side knowing that only New York could provide her with the opportunity to prove herself.

She was doing very well professionally. Yes, it was true that as yet she might not be writing for *Time* magazine, filing the kind of hard-hitting factual gritty exposés of the harsh realities of people's lives that appealed so much to her instinct to protect the weak and vulnerable. But Brad had complimented her on the style she brought to her articles for *Vogue*, and they'd often talked together about their shared belief in the power of television documentaries, and how much they'd both like to work as investigative journalists on them.

The article on which she was working now – about the connection between art and the rich patrons of artists – should have been demanding more of her attention than it was. On Monday morning she was interviewing a prominent socialite well known for her patronage of the arts, one of several interviews Ella had arranged. A photographer had been booked as well, but her heart had sunk when she'd realised who it was – Oliver Charters.

She'd known that he was here working in New York and contracted to *Vogue* for twelve months. The Art Department were already raving about the vibrancy and innovativeness of the first fashion shoot he'd done for them, and she'd had to admit that the photographs were good.

He had a way of making the models look sensual – so much so that, to her own irritation, Ella had not been able to look at any of the photographs without imagining that he had had sex with the models before shooting the pictures. They had that look about them somehow, that look of having been satisfied. Unlike her.

She gave a groan and threw down her notebook. She was back to Brad again. She literally ached inside for him and could not sleep at night for wanting him. Perhaps if she told him . . . But how could she? *No one* was a virgin at her age. She could visualise the look of horror on his face and the way he would back off from her. It was bad enough being a virgin, without anyone else knowing.

Brad was probably lying beside a pool now, sunbathing, a long cool drink at his side, his tanned torso rippling with male muscle. She could just imagine herself smoothing suntan lotion over his shoulders and then down his chest, over his thighs, strongly and hard, whilst his swimming shorts outlined . . . Ella gulped in air. It wasn't just pictures inside her head that her imagination was arousing. But this was neither the time nor the place for thinking the way she was thinking. She directed her thoughts into more practical channels. She and Brad had so much in common, their shared interest in investigative journalism, in particular. She wasn't a fool. She knew perfectly well that it was lust that was motivating Brad's pursuit of her; she'd seen that reaction often enough, after all, and it confirmed to her that far more men fell into lust with women first and then fell in love with them second than the other way round.

She could have lived with that had she been able to delight and enchant Brad with her sexual skill. He could fall in love with her later, once he'd realised, as she already did, just how close they were to something approaching soul mates. She'd heard, for instance, that he didn't want children. She'd read that in an article about him that she'd sourced, guiltily ashamed of the almost obsessive urge she'd felt to possess every smallest bit of information about him that she could.

She knew how passionately he felt about his writing and his mission to root out City Hall corruption and reveal the wrongdoings of 'big players' for the benefit of 'the small guy' – a mission she shared. Like her, he chose the theatre and the arts over nightclub life. He was well travelled and wanted to travel more – she too wanted to roam the globe. He was against the Vietnam War and had spoken out publicly.

Oh, yes, he was perfect. The trouble was that there

were other women, women who were far more experienced and knowing than she, who also thought that.

The reality was that for the first time in her life Ella was experiencing what it felt like to fall in love and to feel so passionately about that love that she was prepared to break what she'd previously thought of as unbreachable rules to have it. Only the rules that constrained her were rules she'd made herself, not society's, and she couldn't break them without risking destroying the desire that Brad felt for her.

He'd teased her about the ocean not being far away from his rented house and the shore being private enough for skinny-dipping. She'd had a hard time stopping her toes from curling up in her shoes, listening to him saying that. She shared an office with three other assistant editors and they all thought she was crazy for keeping Brad at a distance.

'It's that British reserve,' one of them had said, whilst one of the others had giggled and commented that she hadn't seen much British reserve in evidence the night she'd taken a visiting London rock group out to dinner.

'They were all as high as kites and fresher than a locker room full of jocks. They were just so cute and sexy.'

The heat was really getting to her, and Ella thought enviously of Denham, with its cool green gardens and large airy rooms.

Thinking about Denham was safer than thinking about Brad, in any case.

Chapter Thirty-Nine

'Got any plans for the weekend?' Janey asked Rose on Friday, the morning after Rose's dinner with Josh, as they shared the pot of tea Rose had made. The kitchen door was open to let in the fresh morning air. Like in most houses of its era, the kitchen faced northwards and was in the basement – all the better to keep food cool and fresh. Without the Aga Amber had had installed, though, it would have been freezing cold in the winter as it was always shaded in semi darkness.

Rose knew that her business was now successful enough for her to have found herself a small flat, if she had wished to do so, but even though she was the kind of person who enjoyed her privacy and her own company, she knew that she would miss the familiarity of the Cheyne Walk house if she were to move out. Janey, though, she suspected would very much like to have left and moved into a flat with her current boyfriend, if such a thing had been acceptable.

The sixties might have brought a new era, with what the establishment considered to be a disgraceful laxity of morals, but not even such young women as Patti Boyd, had lived with her Beatle boyfriend, George, before they had married. A girl might sleep with as many different young men as she chose, she might even stay over with him for days on end but, as everyone knew, it was not acceptable for her to move in with him permanently.

'I've got to go out to Sussex to look at a house for a potential commission that David Mlinaric has passed on to me,' Rose answered.

Her head was pounding from the tears she had shed silently into her pillow last night, and she was still feeling sick over Josh's news. She knew what he had told her but she still couldn't bear to accept that it was going to happen, that she was going to lose him completely. The small crumbs of his affection and friendship had nurtured her for so long, but now she was facing a brutal starvation, which somehow she would have to survive. Last night all she had wanted to do was pull the bedclothes over her head and simply stop existing, but of course she couldn't do that. She had responsibilities to her clients, after all. The years since she had learned that she and John could share the same father had taught her how to stand on her own two feet emotionally, but right now, Rose admitted sadly, she would have given anything to have someone to turn to, someone older and wiser, and most of all someone who loved her and cared about her.

Someone? Didn't she really mean her aunt Amber? That was all in the past, Rose reminded herself. She had pushed down inside herself her bitterness and feeling of betrayal when she had first realised how her aunt had let her down. In the end she had decided it was easier simply to pretend that everything was as it had always been – for everyone's sake – even if she and Amber knew that things had changed between them and even though that meant her carrying a lifelong burden of sadness and loss. Only now she had an additional loss to deal with – the loss of Josh – and Rose didn't think she was strong enough to bear that on her own.

'The Sussex house is owned by a rock singer; David didn't say which one. He just said that he's too busy to take it on and that he thought I might like the challenge,' she told Janey.

Rose hadn't been able to sleep for hours after she had come in from seeing Josh – from saying goodbye to Josh, she reminded herself – so she had to force herself to try to appear normal this morning.

'What about you, Janey, are you doing anything special?'

'No, I've got some work to get ready for the new season's fashion show in September. I'm warning you now that I'm going to want you to model for me again. Cindy thinks I should be focusing on coming up with a cheaper range for the American market, something like Mary Quant's Gingerbread range, and I've promised her that I'll try and come up with something. Charlie and I are going to Annabel's tonight. If you're back in time why don't you come with us?'

Rose nodded, although in reality the last thing she wanted to do was socialise. Josh still considered his King's Road premises to be his flagship salon and he would be there now. Rose closed her eyes and gave in to the ache of her own need.

The salon would be frenetically busy, seeing as it was a Friday, filled with King's Road dolly-birds, giggling and gossiping and flirting with the stylists as they demanded the latest cuts ready for the social whirl of the weekend.

To an outsider everything would look unbelievably chaotic, with loud music playing and the stylists working at full pace, whilst the poor terrified juniors shampooed and cleaned up, but to Josh they were all part of an orchestra that he was conducting, no part of what was going on hidden from him as he soothed, complimented, flattered and worked.

Automatically Rose touched her own perfect bob. If he did go to New York she would have to find a new hairdresser. Tears burned the backs of her eyes, forcing her to blink them back fiercely.

Rose's appointment was at three o'clock in the afternoon, later than she would have liked since she would have to drive back to London, but it couldn't be helped, she acknowledged as she set out for Sussex in her bright red Mini.

It was a sunny day and she was wearing an outfit she loved and which she'd put on in an attempt to boost her mood, a dress from Janey's summer collection in a lovely shade of antique yellow with a deep printed border in soft black rather like a Greek frieze. Janey had used the fabric so that the dress, which was short, slipped over the head in a narrow shift style, but had long, almost medieval-style sleeves. The fabric was so sheer and fine that it was virtually transparent, so underneath it Rose was wearing one of Mary Quant's new all-in-one 'bodies'

– a white one with her trademark flower emblem on it. On her feet she had a pair of yellow plastic shoes the exact same colour of her dress.

Her pattern books were in the boot, along with her portfolio containing photographs of some of her décor projects. David had been too busy to tell her much about the client or his requirements. He had simply said that he knew she wouldn't let him down.

The Sussex countryside was pretty, but its prettiness couldn't lift her spirits any more than her favourite dress could, Rose admitted later as she slowed down to look for her destination once she had driven through the village she had been told to look out for. All she could think about was losing Josh.

It seemed incredible to Rose that Josh was oblivious to her feelings, but of course she was glad that he didn't know. The last thing she wanted was for him to pity her and feel sorry for her.

She was so engrossed in her misery that she almost missed the open gates flanked by a pair of pretty gate-houses, beyond which lay an overgrown drive bordered by oak trees.

Denham had a similar drive, although Denham's, like the land that lay beyond it, was well tended and productive.

Here the grounds were neglected, rough pasture spiked with weeds, which ultimately ended with what looked like a ha-ha and then a sweep of lawn leading up to the house itself, Georgian and neat, rather than commanding, perched on top of a raised knoll so that the house had the effect of looking down over its surrounding land.

The only sound to break the drowsy heat of the day when Rose had climbed out of her Mini was distant birdsong. The house looked forlorn and abandoned, the windows grimy and curtainless, the paint on the front door chipped and blistered.

Just as she was beginning to wonder if she had come to the right place, the front door opened and a man came out.

Tall, with a tangle of light brown curls streaked with blond where the sun had touched it, and wearing jeans and an open-necked shirt, he smiled at Rose, having looked her up and down approvingly.

'Groovy.' He extended his hand and added, 'I'm Pete, by the way.'

She had recognised him, of course. It would have been impossible not to; he was the lead singer with one of the country's most successful rock groups.

Rose gave him her best professional smile and shook his hand.

'You'd better come in and have a look round,' he told her.

Rose followed him into an elegantly shaped hallway, although the shape was the only elegant thing about it. The walls were grubby, pieces of the ornamental plaster from the cornices and the ceiling lay on the floor, and the banister was missing from the staircase.

'I got it cheap because it's in a bit of a state,' Pete informed her.

Rose tried not to look as dismayed as she felt. 'I think what you really need is an architect, not an interior designer,' she told him.

'That's OK. You can find one for me, can't you? The thing is that we're off on tour in a week's time, and I've promised the rest of the band that they can come and stay here when we get back just before Christmas. Oh, that reminds me, I'm going to need a recording studio. I'll clear out my stuff before we go on tour, so that it isn't in your way.'

'You're living here?' Rose could hardly believe it.

'Yeah.'

She wanted to turn and run. The amount of work the place required was way beyond her scope.

Nearly two hours later, having been shown all over the house, Rose told Pete firmly, 'You really do need an architect.'

She was standing on the landing just outside the bedroom that Pete was using. He'd painted the purple walls himself, he'd told her, but unexpectedly the new-looking bed was covered in plain white bedlinen and looked clean and neat. He was a lot taller than Rose, broad-shouldered, with muscular arms, one hand resting on the door frame, his rolled-up sleeves and open-necked shirt revealing his tanned skin.

'Let's go down to the pub and talk about it,' was his response.

Which was how, half an hour later, Rose found herself seated opposite him in the restaurant of the village pub, with its thatched roof and quaint old-fashioned air, eating beef wellington and listening to him telling her some surely exaggerated stories about things that happened to him when he'd been on tour with his band.

He'd ordered a bottle of wine, but Rose had stopped

drinking after one glass. His stories about the disasters that had befallen them made her laugh, as he obviously intended them to do.

'There was one time in Amsterdam,' he told her with a big grin, 'our first solo tour when we were the main act. We'd finished playing at two in the morning, having only arrived in Holland in the afternoon. The last two hours of the gig, all that kept us going were the joints that Mickey, our roadie, kept passing to us between sets. Of course, once we came off stage there were the usual groupies hanging around – perk of the job,' he told her, before continuing, 'Naturally these girls expected to be taken back to some fancy hotel but thanks to our manager, who was as tight as a duck's arsehole, we were supposed to be sleeping in the van. Not that we hadn't had plenty of shags in there. But what with still being high on the joints and the gig, we ended up wandering round the red-light district 'cos Mickey had said that we'd be able to get a shag there and a bed thrown in with it for a couple of quid. Shows how much Mickey and the rest of us really knew, because the girls charged a couple of quid for a couple of minutes, not the whole evening.'

Normally Rose would have been left feeling uncomfortable by such frank disclosures from a man she was on her own with, but Pete had that way about him that somehow diffused her self-consciousness and anxiety. He even managed to make her laugh, when she felt that really she should have been disapproving. She was enjoying being with him, she realised, much to her own surprise.

It was still light when they left the pub, Pete curling himself into the passenger seat of her Mini.

Emerald looked down at the hem of her Courrèges frock, which was short enough to expose the length of her sleek tanned legs.

Max had just arrived to collect her for their dinner date at Annabel's, but there was something she wanted to discuss with him first.

'I've some exciting news,' she told him. She was feeling in a good mood, triumphant at the thought of what she had planned and how it would enable her to have Max all to herself for the summer.

'A friend of mine has offered me the use of her villa in St-Tropez for the summer. We could leave next week—'

'No.'

'What? Don't be silly, Max, of course we're going.'

His response was to grab her wrist in a painful grip and tell her curtly, 'Listen, lady, no one tells me what to do and most especially not a bird. And what's all this "we" business? There's you and there's me, but there's no "we". That's the way it is and that's the way it's going to stay.'

Emerald wasn't used to being treated so cavalierly. She pulled her wrist free and demanded, 'And what if I don't want it to stay that way?'

'Too bad,' Max told her succinctly, 'because I do. I've got business here in London so that's where I'm going to be, you can please yourself what you do and where you go. I don't give a monkey's. In fact—' he began.

Emerald stopped him, demanding, 'In fact, what?'

'Work it out for yourself.'

Was he really trying to imply that he was dropping her? For a minute she was too shocked to react. That wasn't what she had expected and it wasn't what she wanted. A feeling not quite panic, but certainly something close to it, gripped her. She wasn't ready to end things between them yet. Being with him was still too exciting. But then her confidence broke through her panic. Of course he didn't mean it. He was just doing a bit of sabre-rattling. Max knew when he was well off. He might feel that he needed to prove his machismo and his independence but the reality was that his sexual desire for her was every bit as strong as hers for him.

Feeling reassured and in control again, Emerald put her arms round his neck and pressed her body into his, grinding her hips against him as she teased him, 'Come on, you know you want me.'

'You? No, what I want is this,' he told her.

She had to take the Courrèges frock off herself; all Max had done was push it up to her waist. He probably wouldn't even have bothered to take off her knickers either, he was so impatient to have her, Emerald thought triumphantly as she watched in one of the pair of pretty gilt rococo mirrors set into the alcoves either side of the fireplace, her hands braced on the table below it as Max thrust into her.

There would be bruises on her skin in the morning from his hold on her. He was a fiercely demanding lover, but for Emerald there was a sharp sense of excitement in arousing him, pushing him to the point where he had to have her. It proved that she was the more powerful of the two of them.

His thrusts deepened and quickened, selfish just like him, not caring for her or her needs. Had it been like this for her mother and her painter? Had she felt this power and triumph at the knowledge that her bit of rough trade was sweating and gasping over his need to possess her as he drove deeper and harder into her in an act that was raw and savage? No, of course it wasn't – she could do dirty hot sex far better than her mother, and she wasn't stupid enough to get pregnant doing it either.

Max was coming, hot spurts of semen pulsing into her.

Emerald pulled a face as he withdrew from her and she turned to face him.

'I'll have to go and change,' she told him.

'No.'

Emerald's triumph deepened.

'Ah, so you want to take me out knowing that I smell of you and sex, do you?'

'What I want is my dinner,' Max corrected her, but Emerald was feeling far too pleased with herself to argue with him as she reached for a box of tissues.

'Look, just let it go, will you? It's not my fault.'

'Well, no, of course it isn't,' Janey agreed lovingly, as she padded naked round the bed, happy to be with Charlie even if, because he wasn't feeling very well, he hadn't been able to 'do it'.

She hummed to herself as she battled with the

transistor radio, finally managing to tune it in to Radio Luxembourg.

They had been supposed to be going to Annabel's, but when Janey had got to Charlie's he'd announced that he didn't feel like going out and had suggested generously that she went without him. Of course she hadn't done that.

She turned round and smiled at him. All she wanted was to make him happy. When everyone else around her was happy, then she was happy.

She was so very lucky, Janey thought; lucky to have found such a wonderful friend and source of advice and help in Cindy, and then even luckier to have met Charlie, especially after all the years when she had made so many disastrous mistakes with regard to the men in her life. Men who at first had made her so happy, only to break her heart later. Men who had sworn that they loved her, only to prove that it was her love for them and the way she showed it that they had really loved – until something or someone better had come along.

There'd been Alan, the gorgeous poet, with his dark, almost menacing monologues against wealth and status delivered in smoky cafés. Janey had sworn to him that his awkwardly arrhythmic verse was wonderful, whilst secretly finding it incomprehensible, and she'd supported him with discreet handouts of food and money, until the day he had told her that he was giving up poetry to marry a sturdy no-nonsense teacher, who was insisting that he get a proper job.

It had taken her a whole year to get over Alan, but then she had met Keith, a heavy-drinking communist with whom she had attended protest marches and for whom she had risked incurring the displeasure of Her Majesty's police and justice system.

Keith had turned out to be married to a fellow communist who 'allowed' him to have girlfriends so long as he converted them to the cause and they devoted their earnings to it as well. She had got over Keith relatively quickly, thank goodness.

After Keith had been Ray, a struggling playwright suffering under the burden of middle-class guilt. Ray had finally exorcised his guilt via the working-class girl he had made his muse. The two of them were now the darlings of the West End, and hugely bankable.

As Janey had confided to Cindy, she had resolved to give up on men and love after Ray. But then she had met Charlie and, thanks to Cindy's assurance that Charlie really did love her, Janey had for the first time in a long while felt her old love of life filling her again.

But the best thing of all, as she constantly told Cindy, was that in addition to finding someone who loved her, she had also found her first ever really close friend; someone she could look up to and admire, someone she could turn to when she needed help, someone who did not, as Ella had always done, treat every decision she made with anxious suspicion, but who at the same time did fill the empty space in her life left by her absent 'big' sister.

Oh, yes, she was lucky, Janey reflected happily, and from now on she was going to stay lucky – and happy.

*   *   *

Rose had planned to drop Pete off and then set off back for London without getting out of the car, but somehow or another she found that she had allowed Pete to persuade her to join him for a cup of coffee before she actually left.

The kitchen, though very basic, was, like the bedroom, clean, and the coffee Pete made for her surprisingly good.

It would help her stay alert whilst she was driving back, she decided, but that was the last coherent thought she was able to form because suddenly she realised that characters on the willow-pattern plates on the dresser against the wall were starting to move around. She stared at them and then tried to stand up, subsiding back into the chair when Pete reached for her arm and pulled her back down.

'Acid,' he told her, looking pleased with himself. 'Put it in your coffee . . . Come on . . .'

He was pulling her to her feet, dragging her along in his wake as they went through empty rooms in which the windows and the fireplaces seemed to take on gargoyle expressions of frighteningly leering hostility that clashed with the mind-blowing beauty of the grass and trees she could see beyond the windows.

A fierce compulsion gripped her. She pulled away from Pete, somehow finding her way outside and then throwing off her shoes so that she could walk barefoot on the grass.

She was laughing.

'Look how beautiful the grass is,' she demanded. Then, turning to Pete who had followed her: 'But I'm killing it.'

Now she was crying, huge fat tears trickling down her face.

'I love the grass,' she told Pete mournfully. 'It's so beautiful. Too beautiful.'

'Too beautiful to live,' he agreed.

A small breeze chilled over her skin, making her shiver. She was stoned, Rose recognised, high as a kite. She'd never tripped out before. Panic filled her.

'I've got to go.' She looked round for her Mini but then she noticed that even though it was still light she could see the shape of the moon in the sky. Entranced, she stared at it.

Pete came to stand beside her, looking at it as well.

'It's the moon,' he told her solemnly.

'Yes,' Rose agreed. 'I want to go there.'

'Where?'

'To see the man in the moon.'

'Come on then.'

They were back inside the house, shadows chasing and tormenting them, making them run until they were panting with relief in the safety of Pete's bedroom, the door safely closed against their pursuers.

'It's the man in the moon,' Pete announced. 'We have to draw a circle all the way round the bed to keep him away. We've got to get on the bed and stay in the middle of it.'

Laughing dizzily, Rose complied. She was filled with the most wonderful feeling, as though she had champagne inside her veins instead of blood. She felt that if she jumped high enough she would be able to fly.

'I can fly,' she told Pete, fresh tears filling her eyes as

she felt the most extraordinary sense of joy piercing her heart and elevating her to a place where she felt as though the true mystery of joy had suddenly been revealed to her.

'This is the most beautiful place in the world.' She exhaled happily. 'It isn't falling in love that's important,' she told Pete solemnly, 'it's flying and touching the stars.'

'Flying and fucking,' he agreed with equal solemnity, reaching for her.

'Oh, I can't wait for us to leave for St-Tropez, Max. Have you been there before?'

'Look, how many times do I have to tell you before it sinks into that stupid head of yours that I am not going?'

Emerald opened her mouth to insist that he must, and then closed it again when she saw that he wasn't looking at her but instead was staring at a girl sitting at another of the nightclub tables a few yards away – a brunette, who seemed more interested in Max than she was in her own dinner companion.

'Max,' Emerald persisted angrily, 'I'm trying to talk to you about St-Tropez.'

He reached across the table, and grabbed her arm. 'Now *look*.'

'Max, you're hurting me,' Emerald protested.

'Good. There'll be some more where that came from if you don't put a sock in it.'

Emerald glared at him. 'Let go of me. I'm not putting up with you talking to me like that, Max. I'm not some tarty little showgirl you've picked up in some dive.'

'Oh, aren't you? Well, let me tell you something, darlin', as far as I'm concerned you're just another pair of tits and a cunt, and you'd better remember that in future.'

He released her so forcefully that she fell back against her chair, staring at him in shocked disbelief as he stood up.

'Max . . .' Emerald faltered as she realised that he was leaving. But it was too late, he was already pushing his way past the dancers, and to go after him would only draw attention. Besides, she wasn't going to give him the satisfaction of that. She reached for her gin and tonic, and then had to put it down again when she realised that her hand was trembling. No one had ever used that kind of language to her before, or shown her so much anger. She pushed back her own chair and stood up. She certainly wasn't going to sit here and wait for him to come back. Emerald just wasn't that type of woman.

Chapter Forty

Rose knew something was wrong the minute she woke up. Initially she froze, her mind racing with fear and her heart jumping, as images and memories from the previous evening flashed through her head.

Cautiously she looked around her, her heart thudding even more frantically as the back of a man's head came into view. He was snoring slightly, obviously still asleep. On the floor beyond the bed she could see her precious yellow dress lying in a crumpled heap. She was naked beneath the bedclothes, and when she tried to move, her body reacted with a feeling she recognised from the night she had spent with Josh.

She had had sex with the man lying asleep next to her, and if her body was to be believed, not just the once.

Confusing images were jostling for space inside her head: the moon; a lawn seen close up, as though she'd been lying on it; fevered, excited hands touching bare flesh – her own hands on a male body; candles lit all around the bed shedding a soft yellow glow and smelling of incense and something darker and more sensual; her own body naked on the bed, her arms and legs spread wide in eagerness, male hands making an exploration of her flesh, mapping her body . . .

Another image, this time of him painting her skin, wetting the brush with his tongue and then scrubbing it into the paint before he transferred it to her body, slowly and carefully creating a snake curling down between her breasts and over her belly, its head her sex.

She could remember him showing her what he'd done, holding up a mirror so that she could see. She'd thought she'd never seen anything so beautiful, and when he'd told her to stroke the snake she'd complied, moved to tears by her own sense of the intensity and beauty of the moment.

They'd talked to the snake for a long time, a deeply earnest conversation, which, had she remembered, made her feel as though the true secrets of the universe had been revealed to her. The images pushing into her head showed everything in slow motion.

Hadn't there been a discussion about the snake needing to be fed? Rose shuddered, but it was too late to stop the images: Pete's face lifted to the night sky; Pete lying on the lawn, his throat arched as though in sacrifice as she crouched over him and his tongue had slid wetly between the snake's open jaws.

They had said that they had found the key to the garden of Eden, and they had marvelled joyously at the sheer clarity and enhancement of every sense they possessed, so that suddenly a mere finger touch was enough to bring them to emotional ecstasy whilst physically their bodies broke through their human capacity for pleasure. They had, they agreed, become superhuman, a god and goddess empowered and created to convey love and beauty to the rest of the human race, absorbed in the wonder of their shared images and the purity of their heightened awareness.

This was awful, dreadful, Rose thought now. How could she have been a party to this? She was shaking with shock.

Somehow she managed to get out of the bed and gather up her abandoned clothes and her bag without waking Pete.

In the bathroom she rubbed some toothpaste from the half-empty tube she'd found over her teeth, and washed the smeared paint off her body with cold water, before dressing quickly in her crumpled silk dress, and the knickers she had worn the previous day.

Her hair stank of the patchouli-scented candles; all she wanted was to get home and forget everything that had happened. It was nearly midday. The empty house smelled of dust and decay as she made her way downstairs and outside into the sunshine and her waiting Mini.

Janey smiled happily to herself as she watched the pretty girls flocking round the rails displaying the latest consignment of new clothes. They'd arrived on Monday but she'd held them back until now, knowing that she'd have far more potential customers coming in on a Saturday and knowing too how much King's Road girls liked to be the first with a new design.

The salesgirls, virtually indistinguishable from the customers in their pretty short Janey F dresses, were hurrying to and from the communal changing room, answering the pleas of their customers. The inside of the shop was faintly murky, huge yellow buttercups painted on its damson-coloured walls. Buttercups were Janey's trademark; all her clothes had one somewhere. The latest records were playing loudly, competing with the excited chatter of her customers, splashes of sunshine from the open door and the window tingeing the shop's darkness with an exotic touch of gold. The smell of incense, which was dispensed from a ceiling-hung incense burner she'd bought from a friend who'd brought it back from Marrakesh, mingled with the sharper smell of youthful perfume, warm fabric and excited anticipation.

A strikingly pretty girl, flat-chested and tall, her huge dark eyes emphasised with kohl and false eyelashes, swept into the shop. She was wearing an Ossie Clark dress of cream chiffon with a purple floral print, and she homed straight in on Janey's latest delivery, taking from the rails a dress of soft white with a print of scattered meadow flowers on it. She was a well-known model, and Janey held her breath in hope and then released it in happy pleasure when she saw her take the dress to the till, and mentally made a note to reorder plenty of it. It would be in hot demand now. Janey loved her clothes with passionate intensity; they were her creation, a part of her. She lived with them for so long when she was designing them that the end of their short lives at the change of season filled her with a melancholy that could only be banished by working on something new.

She looked at her watch, realising guiltily that it was one o'clock and she'd promised to meet Charlie for lunch at twelve thirty. She was just about to tell one of the girls that she was slipping out when the shop door was pushed open with so much force that it banged into the old-fashioned hat stand they'd decorated as a scarecrow, and on which they hung the bargain buys mixed up with the new clothes.

Janey hadn't gone as far as shops like Hung on You and Granny Takes a Trip, in making visiting her shop an experience that went beyond the mere buying of clothes, but she was proud of Dylan, the scarecrow, and she turned immediately to give the person who'd treated him with such a lack of respect a frown.

He wasn't the kind of person who normally came into her shop, being middle-aged, portly, and perspiring in a suit as shiny as his bald head, but before she could say anything to him he told her sharply, 'I want to see the boss. Where is she?'

His voice had an East End tinge to it, and he was sweating so heavily he had to remove a handkerchief from his pocket and mop his face.

'I am the boss,' Janey responded, drawing herself up to her full height and then asking pointedly in her most cut-glass accent, 'And I don't believe I know you.'

He gave a snort of derision and came closer to her, jabbing a pudgy forefinger so close to her that he was almost touching her collarbone.

'Well, you should do if you are the boss, although you certainly aren't the girl I saw the last time I came in here. American, she was.'

'You must mean my partner, Cindy,' Janey guessed.

'Partner schmartner,' he retaliated, in a way that at any other time would have made Janey smile, but any thoughts she had had of smiling were banished when he continued angrily, 'Them are my goods you've got hanging up there on them rails, my goods wot haven't been paid for.'

'You're one of our suppliers?' Janey guessed.

That would explain why she hadn't recognised him. Cindy had insisted that she take over dealing with all the orders and the manufacturers and suppliers, saying that it would leave Janey free to concentrate on being creative. Janey had been grateful to her for doing so.

'One of the many fools you owe money to,' he agreed grimly.

'There must have been some mistake,' Janey assured him confidently. She was feeling much more relaxed now that she knew why he was here. Obviously a payment to him had somehow or other been overlooked. It was easily done; she'd lived in fear of doing so herself until Cindy had taken over the accounts.

'There's no mistake,' he assured her. 'Not according to my bank. Have a look for yourself.' He removed a letter from his pocket and shoved it under her nose.

His bank was stating that their cheque had been 'referred to drawer', although Janey couldn't understand why.

Hers was a small business and she had always been careful not to overextend herself financially. Added to that, her clothes were becoming increasing popular and selling well, and the business had actually built up a rather nice surplus of cash.

'Four times I've rung here and each time I've been fobbed off with some excuse or other. Well, now I've had enough.'

He opened the door and called out into the street, 'Right, lads, come in and get it, and put it in the van.'

To Janey's horror two burly young men marched into the shop.

'It's on that rail over there,' he told them, indicating the rail that held the new delivery.

'Oh, no, please, you can't take them . . .' Janey protested. She felt mortified, conscious of the attention the men were attracting from shoppers.

'Oh yes I bloody well can.'

In desperation Janey pleaded with him, 'Look, I'm sure there's been a mistake.'

He would have to come in now, whilst Cindy was having a Saturday off and wasn't there to deal with the situation. She had told Janey that she had to go and spend the weekend with an elderly second cousin of her mother's who lived in the Home Counties somewhere.

'There certainly has, and you're the one who's made it if you think I'm going to stand back and let you get away with not paying me.'

'I'll write you another cheque,' Janey promised him, adding frantically when she saw the look on his face, 'A personal one this time.' She had no idea why the cheque hadn't been honoured, and she wished desperately that Cindy was here to sort everything out.

'And wot's to stop that one being a dud, an' all? No, thanks. Jed, them's ours as well, over there in the corner.'

Janey gasped as one of the young men lumbered past her. She couldn't let them take the dresses, there'd be no stock left.

'Look, I'll pay you in cash, all right? I'll go to the bank

straight away and withdraw it, only please leave those dresses where they are.' She was nearly in tears, fighting panic as well as shock now.

For a few seconds it looked as though he was going to refuse, but then grudgingly he agreed, 'All right, but I'm coming with you, and these two are staying put, and so are them frocks.'

All too conscious of the whispers she could hear all around her, Janey somehow managed to walk out into the street although her legs had turned to jelly.

Her bank wasn't very far away, although it was busy with young King's Roaders drawing out money for the weekend, chattering happily about the fun they planned to have.

By the time it was her turn to go up to the window, Janey's hands felt clammy.

'I'll pay you the amount of the returned cheque,' she told the supplier, trying to sound as businesslike as she could, 'but if there is any more money outstanding I shall need to see an invoice. There's obviously been a mix-up somewhere along the line.'

She spoke to the waiting cashier, asking to see both the shop and her own personal statement. Her own account, she knew, would have a decent amount of cash in it as she had recently received a payment from her trust fund, but when she saw the shop statement her eyes widened in dismay. The account was overdrawn by nearly five hundred pounds! How on earth had that happened? Her knees had gone all shaky, she didn't trust herself to ask any questions or demand any explanations. Instead she went to one of the cashiers and drew out enough money from her own account to pay the supplier.

There was no point in her trying to telephone Cindy – she would have to wait until Monday to learn what was going on. It should have been impossible for the shop's account to be overdrawn, but Cindy was bound to have an explanation, Janey comforted herself as she set out for the pub to meet Charlie.

Rose's hands were sticky with perspiration as she clung to the steering wheel of the Mini, driving as though she had all the furies of hell chasing after her, taking corners at a speed she would never normally have contemplated in her frantic need to escape – not so much from Pete, as from the horrible reality of what she had done.

Her heart was jumping – from panic and remorse, or from the drug she had taken? Rose didn't know which, nor did it really matter. The effect was the same, whatever the cause: a relentless, frighteningly heavy racing heartbeat, combined with a sweaty sickly feeling, and a pounding headache.

How could she have behaved like that? The drug might have lowered her resistance, removed her inhibitions, but surely it couldn't have made her do what she had done, not unless there had been a part of her that had wanted to behave like that, not if somewhere deep down inside her there wasn't something that meant that she was – what? A whore like her mother?

Rose gasped as she took a corner too fast, and then

braked, sending the Mini skidding across the thankfully otherwise empty road, to come to a halt inches short of a deep ditch.

She stalled the car but was shaking so much that she couldn't restart it for several minutes, and then when she did, she felt so sick with nerves and despair that she could only drive it slowly to a small lay-by and pull in whilst she tried to calm down.

She was not her mother, she was herself. But what was herself? What if the drug had revealed her true self? What if in the past that true self had simply been kept under control? What if now, like a genie released from a bottle, there was no way she could force that true self back into captivity again?

Rose longed for the comfort of Josh's reassuring presence. He would have understood. He would probably have laughed and teased her and made her feel that what had happened wasn't really so bad after all. But Josh wasn't here, and if he had been then last night wouldn't have happened in the first place because she would have been safe with him.

She was shaking, sick inside with fear and panic. She wiped her hand over her cheeks to remove her tears. She couldn't stay here like this. She must forget what had happened. She must forget it and tell herself that she wasn't her mother.

Rose turned the key in the ignition. It took three attempts before the Mini's engine fired. Carefully and slowly she pulled back on the road. She must look forward, not back, but with her driving mirror there to remind her of what lay behind her, Rose dreaded looking in it and seeing the spectre of her inheritance staring mocking back at her.

Janey looked at her watch – again. She'd been sitting here in the pub for over half an hour waiting for Charlie. She scanned the crowded bar area again but there was no sign of him.

It was silly feeling let down and disappointed because Charlie wasn't here for her to pour out her troubles to, she acknowledged. *She* was the one who gave *him* a supporting shoulder to lean on, not the other way around. Right now, though, she felt it would be very comforting to be looked after. She had a small pang of longing for Denham, with the comfort of the calm sureness of her father and the loving kindness of her stepmother to turn to.

Janey reached for her cigarettes and lit one, the nicotine helping to soothe her. She was being awfully silly getting herself into such a state over something that was just a mix-up and that Cindy would soon sort out once she was back.

Thinking of her friend and partner helped to calm her. Cindy had told her to leave the financial side of the business to her, Janey reminded herself. Cindy would sort everything out. She had been silly to panic. Cindy would laugh at her when she told her how worried she had been, and remind her, no doubt, that she had no head for money.

She was home now. Safe. Rose's hand shook slightly as she poured herself a cup of tea, and then held it between her hands as she sat in the kitchen.

It had been an unexpected bonus to arrive back and find that she had the house to herself. The first thing she'd done was run herself a bath and then scrub her skin clean, anxiously checking for any remaining paint.

She'd heard enough descriptions of people tripping out to know that what she'd experienced was not unusual, but that didn't stop her feeling horrified. The whole episode was something she desperately wanted to forget.

She heard the front door opening and then Janey calling her name.

'I'm in here,' she called back. She must just behave as though the whole thing had never happened. She must tell herself that it *hadn't* happened . . .

Chapter Forty-One

By Monday morning Rose had managed to convince herself that whilst she felt like curling up into a small ball every time she thought about Saturday night, there was no point in mentally beating herself up for it. Unless she chose to tell someone, which she most certainly was not going to do, it was unlikely that anyone was ever going to know about it.

She doubted that to Pete the episode was anything out of the ordinary and news worthy of sharing, even if he was fully able to remember it – or her. Doubtless there had been a procession of willing bedmates through his life, amongst whom she was hardly likely to merit even the vaguest memory.

Thus armoured against her own guilt-ridden conscience she was able to report to David Mlinaric very firmly and determinedly that although she was grateful to him, the project needed an architect and not her.

That done, she settled down to work on the storyboard she was creating for the drawing room of a newly married couple who had moved in further down Cheyne Walk.

She'd been working on it for less than half an hour when the flowers arrived, an enormous and very artistic display of white petals and greenery from Pulbrook and Gould, which smelled and looked divine, and which Rose knew must have cost a small fortune.

The attached card said, 'Hi, groovy chick – you were the best ever. See you when I get back, Pete xx.'

Rose was still staring at it, appalled, when Josh walked into her office, doing a deliberate double take when he saw the display.

'Not missed your birthday, have I?'

Rose's reply was distracted. She was itching to conceal the card, but she couldn't without him noticing, so she tried to turn his attention to something else.

'Have you spoken to your solicitor yet about ending the partnership?'

'Yes, that's what I've come round about. So who are the flowers from then?'

'Oh, no one, really, just a client.'

He moved closer to the display and before she could stop him he grabbed the card.

'"Hi, groovy chick – you were the best ever." A client, you say?'

Thoroughly flustered, Rose retorted, 'You shouldn't read other people's personal mail.'

'You aren't other people, you're my best mate,' Josh told her. 'So come on, give. Who is he?'

Later Rose was forced to admit to herself that she had behaved very childishly indeed. Just because Josh had hurt her feelings by referring to her as a mate, that was no excuse for her practically boasting about having gone to bed with someone.

'He is a client,' she insisted, 'or at least that's how we first met. His name's Pete Sargent, and—'

She wasn't allowed to get any further.

'Peter Sargent? *The* Pete Sargent? The lead singer in Feelgood?'

'Yes, that's right.'

She shouldn't have said anything, and she didn't know why she had. Yes, you do, she corrected herself. You did it because you're jealous that Josh has fallen in love with someone else, so you wanted him to know you'd been to bed with Pete. That just shows how silly you are because why should Josh even care?

At this revelation Josh was prowling round her office, frowning.

'Look, Rose, I don't want to interfere—'

'Good.'

'But it's a bit like you are my kid sister, and no guy wants to see his kid sister getting herself involved with someone like Pete Sargent.'

'Why not?' What was she doing? She knew perfectly well why not. Pete was dangerous, bad news, and he had brought something out in her that had shocked and terrified her until she had managed to convince herself that it had been a one-off, something that could not and would not ever happen again.

'Because I don't want you to get hurt, that's why not. The guy's a rock singer; he's got to have girls crawling all over him, he's—'

Was that envy she could hear in Josh's voice?

'Sexy?' she asked him briskly.

Josh was looking at her as though he couldn't believe what he was hearing.

'Yes, and, you know . . .'

'I know what? That I can't have a sexy boyfriend, is that it?'

'Rose, what's got into you? Don't be silly. That isn't at all what I meant and you know it. I'm concerned about you, that's all.'

She almost relented and told him there was nothing for him to worry about, but then she remembered that he was not concerned enough about her to stop his girl-friend from breaking up their partnership.

'Will Patsy approve of that? You being concerned about me. After all, she doesn't approve of our partnership, does she?' she heard herself asking him with unexpected enjoyment. What on earth had got into her? She had never imagined herself ever behaving like this, never mind enjoying it.

Josh was looking bewildered. Guilt overtook her earlier enjoyment.

'Look, it's nothing for you to worry about,' she tried to reassure him.

But he misunderstood her and retorted, 'You mean it's none of my business any more, is that it?'

She wanted so badly to reassure him, to hug him and hold him tight, but of course she couldn't.

'I've got to start learning to stand on my own two feet sometime, haven't I?' she told him, trying to ease the emotional tension. 'After all, you're going to America . . .'

'Yeah. You're right, I am. It's just . . . well, I guess I've been looking out for you for so long that it's become a habit. One I obviously need to break,' he said simply, closing the door behind him as he left.

Cindy was on the telephone when Janey arrived at the shop on Monday morning. She'd called round at Charlie's flat on her way to the shop to wish him luck for his afternoon casting, and that had delayed her. Some of the other young actors and models he knew had been there and so Janey had ended up agreeing to join them all on an anti-Vietnam War march on the American Embassy on Saturday afternoon.

'I'm so glad you're back. Something dreadful happened on Saturday,' she told Cindy once her partner had finished her phone call. Mondays and Tuesdays were always slow so Janey didn't have any girls working then, which meant that she and Cindy were on their own.

'What happened? Did you lose the petty cash again?' Cindy laughed.

Janey always found her partner awesomely efficient, and she was proud of her business skills, but sometimes, despite the fact that they were such good friends, when Janey was feeling particularly sensitive she felt that Cindy's manner towards her could be just a little hurtful and dismissive, as though she were a child who Cindy tolerated with amused contempt but no respect. She may not be good with the practical side of running the business but she *was* a good designer. Their skills were different but surely equal.

'No, the petty cash is fine, but we do seem to have

lost some money,' she told her, explaining what had happened with the supplier, and finishing worriedly, 'I was expecting there to be plenty of money in the account. Sales have been good, I know that.'

The small pause before Cindy responded increased Janey's anxiety, as did the faintly exasperated look her partner gave her before saying calmly, 'Well, yes, they have, but there has been quite a lot going out, you know, wages and so forth, and the outlay for the new season's clothes. The rent has gone up – I did tell you but you were going through a design crisis at the time and weren't really listening. These things can mount up more than you think. I can show you the figures and go over them with you again, if you like?' Cindy's smile was kind and made Janey feel dim.

'No. There's no need for that.' She could see that it was the answer Cindy had been expecting. 'It's just that I hate the thought of not paying our suppliers on time and having our cheques bounced.'

Cindy laughed. 'You are silly. That's the way business is conducted these days.'

'But if we don't pay on time we'll end up with a bad credit record and no one will supply us.'

'That's even sillier. You'll always be able to get fabric from your mother.'

For some reason Cindy's comment hurt. Janey did buy silk from Denby Mill, it was true, but she was scrupulous about paying the market price for it and not asking for or accepting any favours from her stepmother.

'I didn't get the chance to tell you on Friday,' Cindy was saying now, 'but I think I've managed to set up a meeting with a buyer from Saks. She's coming over in September and she wants to have a look at the new lines.'

'But that's before the new season show,' Janey protested.

'Well, that's OK, isn't it? Look, I thought we agreed that we want to make a success of this business?' Cindy was struggling to be patient, Janey could tell.

'Yes, of course,' she agreed obediently.

'I mean, I've put a hell of a lot into everything I've done here since we became partners and I'd hate to see a terrific opportunity I've really worked for slip away from us because of some superstition you've got about people seeing your designs before you show them in public.'

Janey felt guilty and uncomfortable. She *was* superstitious about not letting anyone see her designs until she was ready to show them, and she knew that it aggravated Cindy, who found her hard to understand at times. Janey sighed. Clearly she had a lot to learn about business. Thank God she had Cindy.

Chapter Forty-Two

Emerald's heels tapped angrily along the pavement. It was a week now since Max had walked out on her and he still hadn't been in touch with her to apologise.

She just hoped that he had rung her whilst she'd been out. He was bound to have got over his bad temper by now, and naturally would want to make up with her. She thrilled at the thought of the way in which he would want to do this, and started to walk faster.

The daily Emerald had bribed into staying on whilst she was out was waiting with her coat on and her forehead creased in an anxious frown, complaining that her husband would be wanting his tea and that Emerald had said she would be back at three and that now it was half-past four.

'Have there been any telephone calls?' Emerald asked her, ignoring her complaints.

'Oh, yes, there was one.'

Emerald relaxed, the easing of her tension followed by a surge of triumph. She had known Max would telephone all along. How could he resist her?

'It was your mum, and Her Ladyship said as how

she wanted to know if young Robbie had had all his inoculations.'

'Are you sure that was the only call?' Emerald demanded. 'You didn't go out, did you, after I told you that I wanted you to stay here?'

Mrs Wright drew herself up to her full height and told Emerald indignantly, 'No I didn't, and there was no more calls,' before marching past Emerald with her head held high. Her mother didn't know how fortunate she was to have loyal hardworking staff, Emerald thought crossly after she had closed the door behind her daily. Mrs Wright was her third daily in as many years, whilst her mother still had the same cleaner coming in to clean the Walton Street shop and the Cheyne Walk house that she had had for as long as Emerald could remember.

So Max *hadn't* telephoned. Well, that meant nothing other than that he was in one of his moods. He was bound to be at Annabel's tonight. After all, it was Jeannie de la Salles' birthday and they'd both accepted her invitation to join the small group of close friends with whom she and her husband were having dinner. Emerald intended to make sure that when Max saw her he'd want her so much that he'd regret the way he'd behaved and come running. Now, what was she going to wear? It would have to be something very special . . .

Janey was trying to concentrate on the pattern she was cutting for one of her new designs, but she simply couldn't. She hadn't seen Charlie for days, and she was missing him. She'd tried to telephone and leave a message via the call box telephone shared by everyone who lived in the house where he rented his bedsit, but no one had replied.

She'd mentioned her longing to see him to Cindy, but for once Cindy hadn't been as sympathetic as Janey had expected, telling her rather sharply that Charlie couldn't be expected to hang around his bedsit waiting for Janey to call when he had his own career to think of.

Remembering that conversation now, Janey put down the chalk with which she had been marking out the pattern on the fabric spread all around her on her bedroom floor. She preferred to work like this on the first rough make-ups of her designs, cutting them out the way she had once cut out her dolls' clothes and then sewing them on the small hand Singer sewing machine she had been given for her thirteenth birthday. Normally this private first stage of a new creation was one of the ones she enjoyed the most – seeing the fabric take shape as she worked on it, until it took on its own life form and excited and enchanted her with its possibilities. However, right now her heart wasn't in it, because she was yearning for Charlie.

Emerald had deliberately timed her arrival at Annabel's to ensure that Max would have had plenty of opportunity to worry that she wasn't coming. She was wearing a new dress, one she'd bought in New York earlier in the year, a gold quilted Cellophane evening dress, sleeveless, with an embellished gilt collar. It was very short and had been inspired by sci-fi movies. Lee Radziwill, Jackie Kennedy's sister, had apparently bought the same dress. Jeannie's birthday gift – her favourite scent, Guerlain's

Shalimar – was wrapped in gold foil paper that matched Emerald's dress.

Emerald's arrival at Annabel's caused exactly the reaction she had wanted: other women studying her with silent envy whilst their male escorts simply stared at her like little boys gawping at a forbidden treat as she was escorted to the table. One quick glance had assured her that Max was there, looking deliciously handsome and dangerous in his dinner suit. Ignoring him, Emerald went to Jeannie, kissing her friend's cheek as she handed her her gift.

'Oh, how lovely!' Jeannie thanked her, adding mischievously, 'You look positively gift-wrapped yourself. Now who, I wonder, do you intend such a luscious present for?'

Everyone laughed, including Emerald, who retaliated by giving Jeannie's husband a deliberately provocative smile, saying, 'Well, let me see. It's Peter's birthday soon, isn't it?'

Jeannie laughed and tapped her wrist. 'Naughty. As if I'd let you anywhere near by dear husband, especially looking like that. That dress is simply gorgeous, Emerald,' she added as Emerald sat down next to Max, still ignoring him.

'Do *you* like my dress, Max?' she asked him once the conversation had moved on and she was able to talk privately to him. Adding provocatively, 'You'd have thought at the price I had to pay for it that they'd have thrown in a matching pair of knickers. As it was, I've had to go without.'

'That's you all over, isn't it, Emerald? Expensive

wrapping round something cheap. Where I come from the only kind of girls who don't wear knickers are those on the game. They can earn more, see, when they don't have to waste time getting them off.'

Emerald stared at him. This wasn't the response she had expected at all. She knew she looked her best; the attention she had already attracted had proved that. By rights Max ought to be grovelling to her, telling her how sorry he was and how empty and long the last week had been for him without her.

She had to wait until the waiters had served the first course of asparagus with hollandaise sauce before she could lean towards him and warn him, 'I don't much like what you're implying, Max.'

The look he gave was unapologetic and cold. 'Is that so? Well, I don't much care,' he told her, mimicking her own manner.

The meal was almost over, coffee and brandy had been served, the men were smoking their cigars, and Max, who hadn't spoken to Emerald since their exchange during the first course, was leaning back in his chair intently watching a pretty brunette at another table.

Emerald could see the curiosity and amusement in the eyes of some of the other people around the table, especially the women, as they too observed Max's very obvious interest in the brunette. Emerald knew that she wasn't exactly popular amongst her own sex and that there would be plenty of women watching what was happening now and secretly enjoying the prospect of seeing her humiliated.

A surge of righteous anger, mixed with a sense of injustice, filled her.

She had come here tonight with one purpose in mind and that had been to make up with Max, she told herself, conveniently forgetting that she had sworn that she would demand a grovelling apology from him first; she had dressed for him, concentrated her time and her attention on him, she had let the world, *her* world, those who were regulars here – the well born and the wealthy – know by her behaviour that she had given Max special privileges and this was how he repaid her.

Infuriated by his behaviour Emerald demanded sharply, 'Someone you know?'

When Max turned to her, her heart missed a beat. There was a look in his eyes she had never seen before, cold and implacably hard . . . and . . . somehow actually threatening.

'No one questions me,' he told her acidly, 'but most especially not a woman.'

'It was the way you were looking at her,' she protested, putting her hand on his arm, her eyes widening in humiliated shock when he roughly threw her arm away. She knew it would leave it bruised.

Had anyone else seen what had happened? Emerald's pride wouldn't allow her to be made a fool of in front of other people.

'You're supposed to be here with me,' she reminded him in a hissed whisper, but he was still looking at the brunette. 'Max?' she protested unsteadily, but he was ignoring her, pushing back his chair and getting up, walking away from her – again.

Ignoring Jeannie's curious entreaty, Emerald shook her head and, pausing only to grab her handbag, hurried after him, following him out into the street, in a growing mood of anger.

Outside, after the smoky semi-darkness of the club, the milky light of the long summer evening made her blink. Max was heading towards his E type car, which she could see parked several yards down the street. Emerald hurried after him, grabbing hold of his arm as she reached him and tugging furiously on the sleeve of his jacket as she demanded, 'What do you think you're doing walking out like that? How dare you behave like that to me? How dare you?'

'Get out of my way.'

'No. Not until you apologise to me for—'

'For what?' Max stopped her, demanding cruelly, 'For giving you what you asked for, what you were begging for? You know what you are, don't you?' he said before Emerald could catch her breath to reply. 'You're a whore, a stupid dumb whore ready to open her legs to any man who asks.'

Something – not just shock or anger, but something deeper and far more hurtful – pierced through the armour of Emerald's self-confidence. Like a trap door opening on some hidden inner secret, it was there in front of her, the ogre, the ghoul, the fear she kept locked inside herself. He was right. That's all she was, however she dressed it up. Just like her father, a man who slept with women for money.

'That's not true.' Panic shrilled her voice, her gasp of protest turning to an involuntary moan of pain when

442

Max hauled her between his own body and the car and pushed her back against it so hard that her back screamed in agony. For the first time the thought of his savage sexual possession wasn't exciting at all. In fact it was loathsome, loathsome and frightening.

Emerald began to struggle. The force of the blow when Max hit her across the face had her head snapping back and tears of pain stinging her eyes.

Holding her shoulder with one hand, he gripped her hair with the other, forcing her head back so that she had to suffer the contemptuous look he was giving her.

'You think you're so much better than anyone else, but you aren't. The only difference between you and the tarts out on the streets on the game is that they are clever enough to get paid for it. You might fool your fancy friends but you don't fool me. Let me tell you something about yourself. Without that fancy accent of yours and the fancy title that goes with it, you'd be down in the gutter where you really belong, because you're nothing. *Nothing.* And you and I both know it.'

'No, that's not true!'

'Now you're lying as well, and this is what you get for that.'

There wasn't time for her to defend herself or even to scream out in protest as his fists thudded into her body over and over again, driving the breath from her lungs, leaving her gasping.

Frantically she pleaded with him to stop. 'No, Max, please don't, please stop . . .'

She could hear him laughing as he taunted her.

'Why? You're enjoying it really, aren't you? Women

like you always do. It's what you deserve.' Each word was accompanied by another blow.

As little as she wanted what was happening to her to be witnessed by anyone else, Emerald looked desperately towards the club, hoping that someone would come to her rescue, but the street remained resolutely empty.

'You won't get away with this, Max,' she warned him. 'I shall report you to the police.'

Too late Emerald realised her mistake.

'Oh, you will, will you?' His voice was soft and yet so very sinister, lifting the hairs at the nape of her neck.

'No . . . I won't say anything, Max. Just let me go and we'll forget the whole thing.'

'Let you go? It will be my pleasure.'

Relief flooded through her. But instead of releasing her as she had expected, he punched her again. Harder this time, the force of the blow making her head snap back in an automatic recoil action that allowed Max to grab hold of her hair and bang her head back against the lamppost. Just in time Emerald managed to angle her neck so that the blow only caught the side of her head. The force of it had made her bite her own tongue and she could taste the blood. Her nose was bleeding as well, the blood dripping onto the pavement. Every bit of her body was screaming its agony of red-hot pain.

'Max,' she protested pleadingly.

'You and I are going for a little ride together,' he told her, ignoring her plea, kicking her savagely in the groin so that she collapsed against him.

He opened the car's passenger door, and manhandled her into the seat. Emerald tried to push him away, but he shook her violently, and then punched her so hard that she thought he must have broken her ribs. Her body contorted, leaving her gasping for air and filled with pain. She had to get away from him, but she could hardly breathe, never mind move. Still, though, she tried to break free, but Max wouldn't let her go. Instead, his hand gripped her throat, exerting a bruising pressure on her windpipe. Choking and gasping, Emerald clawed at his arm, only to collapse when he hit the side of her face so hard with the flat of his hand, not once but twice, that the force of the blows knocked her out.

When she came round a few seconds later, Max was already driving them away from the club. She could taste fresh blood in her mouth, pain knifing through her face.

Now she really was afraid. Everyone knew about the efficiency with which the East End's underworld gangs got rid of those they didn't want around any more.

Max was driving down Sloane Street now. She had to get away from him. Where were the police when you needed them? Her head was aching, thumping horribly, the pain and dizziness making her feel sick. What was he going to do to her?

Rose got up from her desk. She'd worked later than she'd planned but now the light was fading and she was hungry. She'd kept the décor of her studio plain and simple, furnishing it with pieces from the newly opened Terence Conan store, Habitat, on Fulham Road.

She had just finished closing the windows when she saw the E type roaring down the King's Road from Sloane Square. She gave an idle glance and then frowned as she recognised Emerald sitting in the passenger seat, her disinterest changing to concern as someone stepped out to cross the road in front of the car, forcing the driver to stop with a squeal of brakes.

Having reassured herself that the pedestrian had made it safely to the other side of the road, Rose was about to turn away when she saw the passenger door being thrust open as the car started up again, and Emerald falling from the car onto the road. The E type pulled slightly into the kerb, and then started to reverse towards Emerald's prone unmoving body. For several seconds Rose was too disbelieving, too horrified to do anything. Emerald would be killed if he reversed over her, surely he wasn't actually going to, but then to her relief she saw that the car was moving forward again, and picking up speed, the driver obviously not intending to stop.

Rose rubbed her eyes. Had she merely imagined what she'd seen?

There was only one way to find out. Grabbing her keys, she raced for the door, locking it behind her, and then ran down the stairs to the main exit to the building.

It was almost dusk, that odd twilight time when the sky remains light whilst closer to earth the air is heavier, somehow, and darker. The street was empty – too late for people to be going out and too early for them to be going home. Rose heard the distant growl of the E type's engine.

Something moved in the gutter, a shimmer of gold fabric fluttering in the wind.

She ran to the roadside and crouched down, her heart thumping as she looked at Emerald's still body. As her anxious gaze adjusted to the growing darkness Rose could see that the gold dress Emerald was wearing was ripped, exposing her creamy flesh. Hastily she removed her own jacket and placed it over her.

Chapter Forty-Three

The dark head moved and Emerald gave a low moan.

She was alive. Rose released a shaky breath, only now willing to admit how much she had feared the worst.

Emerald opened her eyes and then blinked before saying flatly, 'Oh, it's you.'

'Don't move,' Rose warned her. 'Just stay where you are whilst I go and get help.'

'No.'

Rose could hear fear as well as arrogance in her voice as Emerald looked down the road. Fearing that the E type and its driver might come back?

Rose's lips compressed. She could guess who the driver was. Everyone knew about Emerald's affair with the supposedly reformed East End gangster.

'I'm all right,' Emerald told Rose as she tried to struggle to her feet and had to stop, collapsing back on her knees when nausea from the pain overwhelmed her.

'Emerald,' Rose protested, automatically going to her aid and putting her arms round her to support her.

'Just get me a taxi, will you, so that I can get home. I'll be all right once I'm there.'

'You need to see a doctor. You could have broken something . . .'

Emerald shook her head. 'I'm fine. It was nothing. Just a bit of a . . . misunderstanding. Help me up,' she commanded, clinging to Rose's arm as she gave in and helped her to her feet.

Rose was relieved in a way that Emerald could be so demanding and, well, so very Emerald. For a moment, seeing her there lying in the gutter, she'd been really afraid.

Now, though, that Emerald was on her feet, clutching Rose's jacket around her ripped dress, Rose was appalled to see her split lip and the cut on the side of her face. And for all that Emerald might say she was all right and had managed to stand up she was still doubled over, the only colour in her face coming from the bloodstains on her skin.

Rose came to a swift decision. 'I'll take you,' she told her. 'I've got the Mini round the corner.'

She was still supporting Emerald, and she could feel the sag of relief from her body, far more telling than any words.

Once they were in the car, Emerald leaned back in the passenger seat, her eyes closed, her breathing shallow, quite obviously in no state to make conversation, ask questions or give orders.

Rose didn't care what Emerald said, her cousin needed urgent medical attention, and that was exactly what she was going to get. She set off west as fast as she dared.

It was only when she heard the screech of an ambulance siren that Emerald opened her eyes, but by then it was too late. Rose had parked the Mini right outside the entrance to the casualty department.

A uniformed hospital porter was bearing down on them.

'You can't park here,' he began as Rose wound down the window.

'It's my cousin. She's . . . she's had an accident – a – a fall – and I'm dreadfully worried about her.'

The porter looked at Emerald and then grunted. 'Stay there. I'll bring you a wheelchair.'

'I told you to take me home,' Emerald hissed furiously to Rose once he had gone.

'And I told you that you needed medical attention,' Rose fired back, amazed to realise how easy she was finding it to hold her own with Emerald after all this time.

The porter had returned with a wheelchair and a medical orderly, the two of them expertly getting Emerald out of the car and into the wheelchair, ignoring her protests.

As soon as she had seen them safely wheeling Emerald into the hospital, Rose restarted the Mini. There was nothing for her to stay for now was there? Emerald was perfectly capable of sorting herself out and wasn't going to want or need her around. And besides, why should she put herself out even more for someone who had always treated her so badly?

The orderly wheeled Emerald into casualty. Lighting up a cigarette, he told her off-handedly, 'You're going to have a long wait with it being a Saturday. Place is full of them mods and rockers wot was having a bit of a ruckus on the Edgware Road earlier. Your old man had a go at you, 'as he? Given you a fair old pastin', by the looks of it.'

Emerald's mouth compressed. How typical of Rose to have brought her somewhere like this. No doubt it had amused her to abandon her here. Emerald's vision suddenly blurred.

'Here, you've dropped this,' the orderly told her, handing her Rose's jacket.

The denim felt unfamiliar beneath her touch. Emerald wouldn't dream of wearing something like that. She started to release it – to reject it – and then for some reason instead she tightened her hold on it and gripped it, lifting it towards her face. It smelled of Rose herself and the light floral scent she always wore. There was a tight painful ache at the back of Emerald's throat, that brought more tears into her eyes.

Crying? Her? For Rose, whom she loathed and despised?

Rose had almost reached Cheyne Walk when she stopped and turned round, mentally deriding herself for every yard she drove back to the hospital, as she listed all the reasons why there was no need or point in her doing what she was now doing.

The first thing Rose saw when she reached the casualty department door was Emerald, sitting in a wheelchair, tears in her eyes and clutching Rose's own denim jacket like a child holding a comforter.

Emerald hadn't seen her and instinctively Rose stepped back into the shadows. Her heart was pounding heavily

451

and unsteadily. She wanted to turn and leave – run away from what she had seen and the demands having seen it imposed on her. She had every reason still to dislike and resent Emerald. There was a tight ball of unwanted emotion squeezing her throat.

Damn, damn, damn, she swore under her breath but she still stepped forward, swinging inside with enough noise to make sure Emerald saw her and could compose herself.

Rose had come back? Emerald's fingers tightened around the denim, whilst the orderly greeted Rose's return with obvious relief, announcing, 'I'll leave 'er wiv yer now 'cos it's time I went off duty.'

He'd gone before either of them could object.

'I suppose you've come back for this,' Emerald told Rose, throwing the denim jacket towards her with contemptuous disdain.

'No,' Rose told her equably, scooping up the jacket, 'that isn't why I came back. Has anyone seen you yet?' she asked without giving Emerald the chance to launch another salvo.

'No. And I don't need to see anyone. I'm perfectly all right.'

Rose arched an eyebrow and opened the plain black leather Hermès Kelly bag she had treated herself to with her first commission cheque because she had loved it and because it was large enough to hold her writing pad, pens and pencils, and a tape measure. Riffling in it, she found her compact, which she handed to Emerald without a word.

Emerald opened it and looked at her own reflection,

aghast. Her lip was swollen and crusted with dried blood. Her cheekbone was swollen and shiny, and there was matted blood in her hair from the cut on the side of her face.

'Well, I feel all right,' she told Rose, but shakily.

To Rose's relief a nurse came bustling up. She sized them both up with what was obviously an experienced eye, looking from Emerald to Rose, and then asking Rose, 'Name?'

Rose knew exactly what was meant by Emerald's indrawn breath. Emerald was a well-known socialite whose name would be recognised even if right now her face couldn't be.

Stepping forward, Rose said firmly, 'It's Em-Emma. Emma Pickford.'

The dark gaze studied Rose again. Because of the way she looked? Because of the way she spoke? Probably the combination of both, Rose thought.

'Address?'

Quietly, Rose gave the nurse the address of the Cheyne Walk house.

'Friends, are you?' the nurse asked.

'We're cousins,' Rose told her, earning herself another swiftly assessing look. She knew what she was thinking – how would they be related?

'So I'll put you down as next of kin then, shall I?'

This time it was Emerald who answered her saying, quickly, 'Yes, please.'

'*Your* name then?' the nurse asked Rose.

'Rose. Rose Pickford.'

'So what happened then?'

They looked at one another, and then quickly, before she could change her mind, Rose fibbed, 'We were at a party. We went with some friends – I can't really remember where it was. There were lots of people there, and as we were leaving Em-Emma . . . I fell down the stairs.'

'And landed on her?' The nurse turned to Emerald. 'I suppose you're going to stick to the same story, are you?'

Emerald nodded.

'Mmm. Right. Well, you can stay here,' the nurse told Rose, going to the back of the wheelchair.

'No. I want her to come with me,' Emerald said.

For a moment Rose thought the nurse was going to refuse but then a commotion by the door as some new patients arrived distracted her and as she left Emerald she called, 'Third cubicle on your left.'

The young doctor was thorough and patient, finally pronouncing that Emerald was very lucky that she had got off as lightly as she had, with badly bruised ribs and what would probably end up as a black eye.

'We'll get you cleaned up and bandaged, and then you can go home. You'll be in pain for a few days, so I'll give you a prescription for sleeping pills and painkillers. If you aren't starting to feel better within the week then you'll need to go and see your own GP. You'll need to have someone with you for tonight. I don't think there's any risk of concussion but just in case, I can only release you if you can assure me that you won't be on your own.'

'Perhaps you ought to stay here in the hospital—' Rose began in alarm. But Emerald told the doctor, 'She'll be with me. She's my cousin.'

It was just gone two o'clock in the morning when they finally got back into the Mini.

Rose started the engine. She felt completely drained of energy, exhausted and shivery with the aftermath of shock.

As she reached for the handbrake, Emerald, who hadn't spoken to her since they had left casualty, looked straight ahead through the windscreen and said quietly, 'Thanks.'

Rose wasn't sure which of them was the more astonished, her or Emerald herself, who was now looking away from her and demanding fretfully, 'For goodness' sake, are you going to drive this thing or are we going to sit here all night?'

Chapter Forty-Four

New York. Sunshine. Pretty girls. This was the life, Ollie acknowledged, or at least it would have been if he hadn't been having to work with Princess Frigid Knickers today.

He'd been in *Vogue*'s general office the previous week, waiting to see the fashion editor when he'd overheard some of the girls talking about Ella, marvelling about the fact that she was keeping some guy or other dangling. He was quite a catch, according to what Ollie had overheard, and they were bemused by Ella's attitude to him. Well, he wasn't. He'd seen in London how she'd worked that ice princess stuff of hers. He felt sorry for any poor sod who got the hots for her. They'd have to take a blowtorch to the ice. Personally he liked his women hot and willing. Luckily for him there was no shortage of his kind of girl, either in London or here in New York.

He was fortunate that *Vogue* had offered him the use of an apartment belonging to a fellow photographer – a photojournalist who was working overseas for a year. The apartment came with everything Ollie needed, and a view over Central Park. The photojournalist was well connected and had family money. Oliver too had family money now, of course, thanks to his real father. Funny how he'd not been able to stop wondering and wishing about the man who had fathered him: wondering what he'd really been like and wishing that he had spent more time with him. That's what happened when life held too many unanswered questions and a kid didn't get to know who his dad was until it was too late.

This had to be the longest interview and photo shoot she'd ever been involved with, Ella thought tiredly.

She'd been sick in the night – something she'd eaten, she suspected – and although she was fine now, the combination of lost sleep, a demanding interviewee, an even more demanding photographer, and the fact that the post had brought her the most intoxicating letter from Brad, telling her that he was wishing the summer away so that he could be with her, had resulted in her feeling both wrung out and somehow also weirdly elated.

The interview had gone well, and she'd got some wonderful quotes, not because of her interview technique so much as Oliver's ability to use his well-documented sexual chemistry on any and every woman – except, of course, her.

Maisie Fischerbaum, the eighty-year-old philanthropist whose art collection was on loan to the Guggenheim and promised to it after her death, had been a wealth of anecdotes – some so potentially scandalous that they were unprintable. She and her late husband had, it seemed, known and met everyone, including President Kennedy, whose death, even now, was so raw and unbelievable, and whilst Oliver flirted with her and photographed her,

Ella had kept on asking questions and taking down the answers in shorthand.

The afternoon had been punctuated by the frequent appearances of Maisie's maid, bringing in Martinis, Maisie's favourite cocktail, and Ella had been amazed to see just how much the old lady could drink without it affecting her, other than to make her increasingly flirtatious with Oliver, and even more garrulous.

Embarrassingly, at one point she had asked Ella if she was sleeping with Oliver. After Ella had shaken her head and said tersely that their relationship was very much a professional one, Maisie had pursed her lips and given Oliver a sidelong look.

'Professional, is it?' she said to Ella. 'In my day there was only one kind of professional activity a girl would have wanted to share with a good-looking man like him.'

To Ella's surprise, Oliver had come to her rescue, telling Maisie, 'She's already got some handsome New Yorker chasing after her.'

Of course, Maisie had wanted to know who the handsome New Yorker was, and Ella had inwardly cursed Oliver for somehow or other knowing about Brad.

'He's another journalist,' was all she allowed herself to say.

Now Ella and Oliver were standing back outside in the baking heat of the late afternoon. It was five o'clock, and even the trees in Central Park looked heat weary, their leaves drooping, as she too drooped, unaware that Oliver was studying her.

She had a very different body from the models he

photographed, Oliver recognised, much curvier, with full breasts and a narrow waist rather than the more androgynous look that was currently so fashionable; a woman now, not the soft-fleshed young girl she'd been when he'd first seen her, nor the too-thin hyped-up person she'd become when she'd been taking those wretched diet pills. She looked far better than when he had last seen her – far, far better, he acknowledged. Her hair was tied up, restrained in a sleek chignon, her blouse and skirt combination as crisp-looking as it had been when they had left the *Vogue* office earlier, except for the fact that he could see a small bead of sweat lying in the hollow at the base of her throat, trembling as it prepared to roll down between her breasts. What would she do if he reached out and captured it, licking it off his fingertip like a boy licking an ice cream? He was tempted to try it just to find out.

Maisie's comment and Ella's response, confirming the existence of her New Yorker boyfriend, had brought out his hunting instinct. Oliver never had been able to resist seducing a woman away from another man – just as his father had seduced his mother away from her husband? He gave a dismissive mental shrug. So what if he had? She'd obviously been willing, and he was obviously his true father's son.

The hot breeze did nothing to cool the air. Oliver could see the Pierre up ahead of them.

'Fancy a drink?' His invitation surprised him just as much as it did Ella, who was looking at him with that haughty expression of hers.

Ella was just about to refuse – after all, neither another

drink nor Oliver's company held any appeal for her whatsoever – but when she opened her mouth to do so, a light came on inside her head. The key to unlocking her self-made prison and being Brad's lover was standing in front of her. That knowledge made her feel dizzy and shaky, as though she'd suddenly stepped from dry land onto somewhere far more unsteady – unsteady, but also unexpectedly exhilarating.

Her agreement wasn't the response Oliver had expected. He nodded, not sure why he had asked her in the first place, but aware that he had assumed she would refuse, and that that would have given him the opportunity to bait her and see how she reacted.

She had no idea why she hadn't thought of this solution before, Ella acknowledged, sitting in the bar of the Pierre Hotel minutes later whilst she drank her second Martini. She'd drunk her first quickly, like someone taking medicine, which in a sense was exactly what she had been doing, using the alcohol to create a comforting barrier between her and the reality of what she was planning to do.

Oliver had slept with dozens of girls, everyone knew that. All she had to do was let him do whatever it was he did to make him so popular with her sex, and that way rid herself of not just her virginity but, just as importantly, her lack of experience. Somehow it didn't matter at all that Oliver would know about her inexperience, but then she had no wish to impress him, had she?

Things weren't going quite as she'd expected, though, she admitted, sitting on the plush velour banquette whilst

Oliver sat opposite her, the table between them. She was on her third Martini now, and beginning to feel a bit desperate. Everyone knew that Oliver pounced on all his models; she may not be a model but, without being vain, she knew that she was reasonably attractive now, even if she hadn't been when Oliver had known her in London – and Venice, where he *had* kissed her. So far, though, Oliver hadn't made any move on her at all. Was it because of something that she wasn't doing? If so, what? She looked around for inspiration.

A couple came in, the man leading the woman over to the banquette. Once she was seated, she patted the space next to herself invitingly, encouraging the man to sit next to her.

Of course!

Ella turned to Oliver, suddenly frozen.

She had to. It was now or never. Just think about what's at stake, she urged herself. You want to be with Brad, don't you? You're already in love with him, and he wants you – or rather, he wants the woman he thinks you are, the woman you're never going to be if you lose your nerve now.

She tried to smile and wondered if the result looked as forced and unnatural as it felt. She had to clear her throat before she could speak, her voice sounding stiff to her own ears as she asked Oliver, 'Why don't you sit here next to me?'

Oliver almost spilled his drink. Ella, the ice queen, was coming on to him? Impossible. He must be imagining it.

He looked at her. No, he wasn't imagining it. He wasn't that desperate for a shag either, he told himself. Mind, by the looks of them she had got good tits. And besides, what else was he going to do with his evening?

'I've got a better idea,' he told her, inching his chair closer to her, on familiar territory now. 'Why don't you finish your drink and then we'll go back to my place?'

Relief and panic surged through her in dizzying spurts. She felt distinctly wobbly but at the same time triumphant.

Oliver's apartment was on the Upper East Side, the smart side of the park, their cab depositing them outside it with what felt like breathtaking speed. During the ride Ella had sat with her back ramrod straight, staring ahead, whilst Oliver had lounged easily at her side, playing with her fingers and humming under his breath. She had looked at him – once – only to look quickly away again when she'd realised that his lounging position had dragged the fabric of his jeans tightly across his groin, rather explicitly revealing what their journey was all about.

That was enough to have her heart hammering and make her mouth go dry.

A uniformed concierge opened the outer door to the apartment building for them. This was the more the kind of place she had imagined Brad living in than Oliver, with his carefully scruffy appearance and his overlong hair. It was certainly far smarter and more expensive than her brownstone apartment, she thought, as Oliver ushered her into the elevator, and pressed the button.

'Alone at last,' he told her with a mock leer.

What on earth was she supposed to do? How did other

women behave when they were in this situation with a man like Oliver? Presumably they were highly delighted, whilst all she felt was highly apprehensive. The lift started to move, jolting her off balance, so that she fell against Oliver, who immediately caught her in his arms.

She had been here before and, extraordinarily, her body seemed to know it, her senses reading and recognising him.

How disturbing to think that for all these years her own flesh had stored a memory of a mere handful of seconds in his arms.

'That's how I like my women,' Oliver teased her, 'throwing themselves at me.'

Arrogant pig. Just in time she bit back the retort.

He kept his arm around her as he guided her down the corridor to his apartment, massaging the back of her neck with his free hand as he unlocked the door.

'Want a drink?' he asked.

Ella was about to shake her head, but then nodded instead. Dutch courage? Well, why not? She was going to need it.

'G & T?'

Ella nodded again.

The apartment had an enormous living room with an off-white deep-pile carpet and a huge black leather sofa. A long rosewood sideboard sat against the wall opposite the fireplace, whilst the fireplace wall itself was painted a deep purple. Several paintings hung on the walls, all of them female nudes, as was the bronze on the coffee table.

It was very much a man's room, sexual and somehow predatory, just like the Rolling Stones music Oliver had put on. Since there was nowhere else to sit Ella had sat on the sofa, feeling the cool slipperiness of the leather heat up under her bare legs, so that she was sticking to it as she clung to one corner of the sofa. Her hand shook slightly when she took the gin and tonic Oliver brought her. She took a sip and then gasped. It was strong, much stronger than she was used to.

'Good?' he asked her suggestively as she took another gulp of her drink.

He was sitting down beside her, resting his arm behind her. She was trembling even more. Hastily she put her drink down on the coffee table before she spilled it. As she straightened up Oliver drew her into his arms.

It felt rather disturbing, not because she felt uncomfortable there but because it was much too pleasant.

Ella allowed herself to relax slightly.

'So,' Oliver asked with a grin, 'when did you first start fancying me?'

Ella was outraged, her outrage turning to apprehension when Oliver traced with his fingertip the bare flesh just inside the open but modest V neck of her blouse, and then leaned forward to kiss her.

His mouth felt warm and firm, knowledgeable. He kissed well, Ella was forced to acknowledge as he teased her lips with small kisses, using the pressure of his tongue tip to coax them apart but not then sticking his tongue down her throat, as she had dreaded he might. She had other things to worry about than his tongue, though. He might have one hand in her hair, removing its pins, but the other one was deftly flicking open the tiny buttons of her blouse.

464

She had wanted this, Ella reminded herself, and for a very good reason. Brad.

'Great tits,' Oliver whispered against her mouth. 'Shame to keep them in captivity, though.'

Somehow her shirt was half off and he was unfastening her bra.

Ella sucked in her breath. Pretty little beesting, barely there breasts were the fashion, with many women going braless, but Ella was a 34D, her breasts firm and rounded.

Oliver was thoroughly absorbed in the discovery of just how sexy two handsful of soft dark-nippled breasts actually were, and was enjoying himself too much to notice Ella's tension.

'There are tits and there are tits,' he breathed ecstatically, 'and these are . . . these are making me feel soo horny.' He lowered his head and started playing with her nipples with his tongue and then his teeth.

Wild fires shocked through Ella's body. Brad had caressed her breasts, discreetly and over her clothes, in the backs of cabs when he had been kissing her. His touch had made her ache and feel eager for more, but it hadn't prepared her for the clamouring that now had her back arching and her breath escaping in what sounded like a high moan of arousal.

Had he really called her an ice maiden? Man, had he been wrong, Oliver acknowledged, as he reached for the zip on Ella's skirt.

This was it, she thought. Soon it was going to happen.

'Come on.' Oliver got to his feet and took hold of her hand.

Uncertainly Ella looked at him.

'We can't fuck in here,' Oliver told her. 'One of us will end up stuck to the ruddy leather, and besides, the bed's much more comfortable.'

The bedroom was as masculine as the living room, with a huge bed with black silk sheets, which made Ella want to laugh hysterically.

'Can't say they're my cup of tea either,' Oliver acknowledged, 'but there you go.'

He was removing his shirt as he spoke and then reached for the belt of his jeans. His white T-shirt stretched tightly over his chest, revealing his toned body as he tugged it off. Ella's stomach muscles clenched as he dropped his jeans and his underwear and then stepped out of them.

Ella's breath caught and locked in her throat. His erection reared up firmly and eagerly from its bed of thick dark hair. Some of it was going to be inside her, and then . . .

But what was *she* supposed to be doing? Surely not just standing here staring at him, feeling awkward and uncertain, and clutching her blouse around herself whilst her skirt half hung off? Somehow she couldn't see Brad being impressed by that.

Quickly she removed her blouse, her bra coming off with it, and then her skirt.

Oliver's eyes widened slightly.

She was keen. Normally girls waited for him to undress them. He liked it, though, that she was so eager. He reached for her, pulling her tight against his body, his cock rubbing against her bare flesh as he kissed her, holding her head steady as he did so.

Soon they were on the bed, getting there via more kisses, and Oliver's hand sliding between her legs, he approving that she was very wet.

It was surprising to discover how disappointed she felt when Oliver stopped playing with her nipples, and how intense the urgent aching and pulsing inside her grew when Oliver touched her there.

She tried experimenting a bit by touching him, stroking her hands over his shoulders and his upper arms, even kissing his throat, as well as grappling with the rigid phallus, of which he was so proud. That had been a slightly unnerving experience, especially when Oliver had thrown back his head and groaned. But now he was positioning himself between her legs. Once she was no longer a virgin then she could get down to the business of becoming an experienced and a good lover, Ella comforted herself.

'God, I love these,' Oliver announced, fondling Ella's breasts and then kissing her firmly as he thrust into her, and then stopped when she tensed and he felt the unexpected barrier of her tight muscles. 'What the hell . . . ?'

Oliver had gone still and was looking at her with disbelief.

'You're a virgin.'

'No. Yes. Don't stop now,' Ella almost wailed. 'I have to do it. I must.'

She was panicking, beside herself with anxiety and dismay. He couldn't *not* do it. Not after all this.

Oliver looked at her. She was trembling violently, like someone who had screwed up their courage to breaking

467

point. His mind reacted bitterly to his choice of words. He eased himself away from her and got off the bed, standing up and going to stare out of the window with his back to her.

What the hell was going on? A bloody virgin. Whatever it was that was motivating her, it certainly wasn't as, he had initially congratulated himself, her desire for him. He should have been furious, but surprisingly he discovered that he was actually intrigued and curious.

He turned round. Ella was still lying on the bed, but now she had pulled the sheet over herself.

'OK,' he said, 'let's start at the beginning. What are you doing here? And don't bother saying because you've been lusting after me ever since we first met because I won't believe you. What is this all about? Making the New York boyfriend jealous?' he guessed.

Ella was so horrified that she sat up, saying fiercely, 'No. He must never know about this.'

'OK, so let's see . . . You're missing him and thought that having a quick fuck with me would tide you over until you see him? Oh, I forgot, you haven't ever had a fuck, have you?' Oliver's voice dripped with sarcasm.

Ella clamped her lips together. This wasn't turning out as she'd expected at all.

'I would have done if you hadn't stopped,' she told him.

Oliver paced the floor and then stopped in front of her.

'Why choose me?' His whole manner made it plain that he was not at all thrilled that she had.

'Because I thought you'd be good at it.'

Oliver digested her words in silence.

'Why now? If you've saved it for this long you must have had a reason.'

'Yes.' There was no point in denying it.

'Like what?'

'Look, I don't want to talk about it. I just want to get rid of it, all right?'

'Nope. No explanation – no shag,' Oliver responded promptly.

He was half expecting her to refuse to tell him, but he realised that he had underestimated her need to rid herself of her virginity when she exhaled and told him, 'I need a cigarette.'

He produced two and lit them both, passing one to her. Only then did he see how much her hands were trembling. He drew deeply on his own cigarette before removing it from his lips to put to her own and then taking the one he was still holding for himself.

She obviously wasn't a habitual smoker; her movements were awkward, the cigarette like the sex she had wanted: something that had to be endured as a means to an end rather than enjoyed for itself.

As soon as she felt strong enough, Ella stubbed out her cigarette and told Oliver, 'Well, you see, it's like this . . .'

It took him almost an hour and several cigarettes to get the whole story out of her: the nutty mother, her fear that if she fell pregnant and had a kid she'd end up the same, the unfairness of the pill not being available when she was younger, and then, last of all, her longing to impress and please Brad. Brad, for whom Oliver had suddenly developed a very strong surge of jealousy, for no reason that he could logically understand.

He stubbed out his final cigarette. 'So basically you want me to teach you how to be good in bed?'

'Yes,' Ella agreed.

'Bloody hell.'

What did that mean, Ella wondered apprehensively. She had made a total fool of herself and for that she could blame too many Martinis. She was now stone-cold sober, though, and beginning to feel sick.

There was no way he was going to do what she wanted, Oliver decided. Hell, the women he took to bed wanted *him*, not someone else. He had a sudden surge of need to have the satisfaction of making her want him.

'You're sure?' he checked.

Ella nodded. He was going to do it? That feeling invading her belly had to be relief, she decided, and not a sudden desire to change her mind.

'OK then, let's get started.'

Chapter Forty-Five

Rose opened her eyes cautiously, reluctant to wake up but not knowing why until she remembered the events of the previous evening. She was in Cadogan Square, in Emerald's house and Emerald's guest bedroom.

Emerald had quite obviously expected her to disappear, having driven her home, but Rose, mindful of what the doctor had said, had refused, pointing out that she had given him her word that she would stay.

'Look, I am not going to have concussion,' Emerald had told her.

'You don't know that,' Rose had retorted, refusing to give in.

She looked at the bedside clock, groaning when she saw that it was almost ten o'clock in the morning. It was just as well she didn't have any client appointments today, she admitted as she pushed back the bedclothes and pulled on the satin robe that Emerald had given her last night, along with what had looked like a brand-new set of expensive underwear – a satin half-cup bra ornamented with lace and a pair of matching French knickers – not her sort of thing at all.

Something in her expression must have given her away because Emerald had taunted her, saying, 'They won't corrupt you, or turn you into a sex maniac, you know. My God, that would be the day that anything or anyone could do that to Auntie Amber's little darling.'

Emerald at her best – and her worse.

Rose sat down on the bed. Last night had, in its way, been almost as crazy as the night Pete had spiked her coffee. If anyone had told her that she would ever be in a situation with Emerald that would make her feel protective towards her, worried about her, she would have told them categorically that they were mad. And yet last night . . . Inside her head she still had an image of Emerald clutching her jacket, with tears in her eyes. Not acting or manipulating, but really crying because she felt afraid and alone.

Half an hour later, showered and dressed, Rose knocked on Emerald's bedroom door. When there was no answer she turned the handle quietly and opened it anyway.

She had expected Emerald to be asleep, but instead she was awake, sitting up, looking fretful.

'I'm going down to make myself a cup of tea,' Rose told her. 'Do you want one?'

'No . . . yes . . . Rose, don't go yet. There's something I want to say.'

Was she going to thank her again, Rose wondered ruefully. That would make it another day to be highlighted in her diary.

'I want you to promise me that you won't ever say anything about last night to anyone, but especially to

Mummy. I know you're her favourite, Rose, and that that was why you did what you did last night.'

Rose frowned. She wasn't going to argue with Emerald about who Amber's favourite was or wasn't – there wasn't any point – but she was going to put her right on one thing.

'I didn't do it for Aunt Amber.'

'Then who did you do it for? Not for me.'

'I did it for myself,' Rose told her, and as she said the words she knew suddenly that they were true. A wonderful sense of strength and power and rightness flowed through her. She had done what she believed to be right, not out of fear or to earn herself favour but because it had been right.

She turned back towards the door,

'Rose,' Emerald stopped her, 'you haven't promised yet.'

Rose looked at her, on the point of telling her that she had never had any intention of telling anyone, and then thought quickly.

'I'll only give you my promise, Emerald, if you promise me that from now on you won't have anything whatsoever to do with Max Preston.'

Emerald shuddered. 'Are you mad? Do you actually think that I'd want to after last night?'

'That isn't the answer I want,' Rose told her firmly.

Emerald badly wanted to laugh but her ribs and her face were too sore. Did Rose actually really think that she would take Max back after this? Emerald never wanted to see him again. The words he had hurled at her, as much as the blows he had inflicted on her, had touched something raw and painful inside her; the vulnerability that came from knowing who had really fathered her, and what she might so easily have been without all that her adoptive father had given her.

No, she never wanted to see Max again because she couldn't bear the pain of her own vulnerability.

'I promise,' she told Rose.

'Then I promise as well,' Rose smiled.

As she struggled to stand upright in the churning mêlée, Janey wondered if coming on the anti-Vietnam War march had been a good idea after all. She fully supported the marchers' cause, but Charlie, whose idea it had been in the first place, hadn't turned up at their designated meeting place. Then she hadn't been able to back out of the commitment to go and get him out of bed, where she knew he was probably likely to be, because his friends were insisting that it was time to leave for the march. Now she was in danger of getting caught up in what was taking on the appearance of a very nasty fight indeed between some of the marchers and the police.

The original cause of the friction had been some of the more hot-headed marchers throwing bottles at the police cordon outside the American Embassy. Scuffles had broken out when the police had moved to stop them, and now Janey, carried along by the movement of the crowd, found that she was much closer to the violence than was comfortable. A missile of some sort, thrown from behind her, whizzed past her, just missing the side of her head, aimed for one of the policemen a few yards away. Some protestors were already lying on the ground and being dragged away. Janey had lost sight of Charlie's friends. The noise was deafening, especially when the police started using loud-hailers to order everyone to disperse.

A fight broke out in front of her between two of the protestors, and quickly escalated. Janey wasn't the sort to panic easily, but the violence now sweeping through the marchers around her made her want to run. She could see a street opening a few yards away and began to make for it, struggling against the press of the crowd.

Somehow she managed to make it to the edge of the crowd. She could see the faces of the onlookers now, their expressions disapproving.

Suddenly the police moved forward determinedly, forcing the marchers back, causing some of them to turn round and plunge back into their own ranks. Janey could feel herself being swept back, away from the side street. Another few seconds and she would be dragged into the vortex of thrashing bodies that was the beginning of a dangerous stampede. If she lost her balance now she would be trodden underfoot. Panic filled her.

Someone grabbed hold of her arm. She tried to shake them off.

'Janey . . . This way . . .'

The voice in her ear was familiar. She turned her head in its direction as she was pulled towards the safety of the pavement, falling heavily against her rescuer as he finally dragged her clear of the panicking marchers and into the relative peace of a nearby doorway.

'John, what on earth are you doing here?' she demanded

once she had got her breath back and had pushed herself free of her childhood friend.

'I had some estate business to attend to,' he told her, 'so I thought I may as well spend the weekend in town. I was thinking of calling in at Cheyne Walk; your mother gave me your telephone number.'

'Oh, yes, you must,' Janey told him warmly. She was still leaning on him. He felt so nice and solid and safe, somehow, that she was reluctant to move away.

The sound of the confrontation was beginning to die away as both marchers and police moved down the road, leaving the two of them virtually alone.

'You're a true knight in shining armour, John,' she told him affectionately. 'I was beginning to get frightened. I wouldn't have joined the march if I'd known it was going to turn violent. Charlie, my boyfriend, should have been with me, but he obviously overslept. I'd better go round to his flat now and wake him up. He's got an audition this afternoon. He's an actor.'

'I'll go with you,' John told her, heading off her objection with, 'I insist. It's what your father would expect me to do.'

How Charlie would laugh when she told him about John's old-fashioned protective gallantry. She would have laughed herself, Janey suspected, if she hadn't been feeling so shaky and somehow so relieved to have his support and his familiar comforting presence at her side.

'You won't tell the parents about this, will you?' Janey begged him. 'They'd worry and I'd hate that.'

'Only if you promise me that you won't put yourself in that kind of danger again.'

Janey looked at him in astonishment. 'That's not fair.'

'Risking your life isn't fair either. I was worried that you might lose your balance before I could get to you,' John told her firmly.

Janey's heart melted. He had been worried about her. How sweet. Charlie never worried about her. She was the one who worried about him. This made an unexpectedly welcome change.

Charlie's one-room, and the share of a communal bathroom, flat – for which Janey had her own key, since she was the one who paid the rent, and because Charlie was prone to locking himself out – was in a tall narrow terrace of Victorian houses off the Edgware Road, the majority of the other flats in the house also let to young students.

Charlie had the ground-floor flat and, just as Janey had expected, the curtains were still closed.

'It looks as though Charlie is still in bed,' she told John, feeling guilty on her boyfriend's behalf when she saw the disapproval in John's honest hazel eyes. Quickly she came to her Charlie's defence. 'Charlie is a night owl. He simply can't sleep if he goes to bed too early.'

It was the truth. Even when they weren't out somewhere partying with his friends, he preferred to stay up late playing his records until the early hours of the morning. He would then sleep well into the day, sometimes missing important casting auditions because he hadn't woken up, and then complaining when, as he saw it, other far less talented actors than he got work whilst he didn't.

'He's very talented,' Janey felt compelled to add, even

though John hadn't made any further comments. 'He does a lot of modelling, but what he really wants is to get into acting, especially in modern plays. Charlie wants to focus on modern drama. He says that it's immoral to keep on doing plays by someone who's been dead for four hundred years and that theatres should be producing works by young playwrights.'

John nodded. Privately he thought there was nothing more rousing than a bit of Shakespeare. At least a chap could understand what was happening, and feel his heart swell when he heard the familiar lines. Not like the modern stuff. What was it they were called? Kitchen sink dramas? He hadn't met Janey's boyfriend but he had heard Jay talking about him, and although Jay hadn't said so in so many words, John had gained the impression that he wasn't too impressed. It hadn't been said outright, but John had also gained the impression that Janey was dipping into her own money to help fund her boyfriend. John couldn't imagine a situation in which it would ever be acceptable for a chap to expect to be financed by a young woman, especially a decent young woman like Janey. A very nice young woman. He'd always liked her. Liked her a lot, in fact.

Janey noticed the young musician from the flat above Charlie's looking in derision at John as they crossed the narrow hallway. With his long hair, jeans and floral shirt, the musician was the epitome of the King's Road scene, whilst John, who was wearing grey slacks, a navy-blue blazer, and a white shirt with a modestly spotted tie, his hair cut short back and sides, looked more like someone of Janey's father's generation.

She removed her key to Charlie's room from her handbag and opened the door.

Charlie's bedsit had a small section curtained off to provide a kitchen, the rest of the space taken up by a bed settee, which was more or less always left in the 'bed' position, a camping table, a couple of bentwood dining chairs and a huge old wardrobe with a broken door that that to be wedged closed with a piece of cardboard and had one foot missing. A television was perched precariously on a too-small stand, whilst the bookshelves either side of the ancient gas fire groaned under the combined weight of, amongst other things, an old Dansette record player, some books, a guitar, which Charlie had insisted he wanted and then had never played, and over a year's worth of dust.

The heavy velvet curtains that hung at the window had come via the Walton Street shop, having been thrown out by a client for whom the shop was making new ones.

Janey knew the interior of the flat so well, right down to the threadbare place in the ancient Turkey carpet covering the lino, and which had to be avoided when one was wearing heels, and so didn't need to hesitate as John did in the gloom.

The room smelled of pot, and as usual Charlie's clothes were heaped on top of one of the bentwood chairs, but not just Charlie's clothes. Janey could see the bright colours of a girl's dress poking out from the legs of Charlie's jeans. It was one of her own designs, she recognised absently, as her brain and her heart raced to analyse what the fact that the dress was there meant. She looked towards the bed where, through the gloom, she could now see that there were two heads sharing the pillow. Her heart won, thudding into her ribs with a mixture of shock, betrayal and pain. John, who had come into the room behind Janey, looked from Janey's white face towards the bed, and realised immediately what was happening. Instinctively he stepped between Janey and the bed's occupants, but it was too late. Disturbed by their entrance, the girl had woken and was now sitting up, dragging the coverlet around her as she did so.

'Cindy!' Janey knew that her lips had formed her partner's name; she could hear the sound of it exploding inside her head.

Charlie was awake now as well, the pair of them huddling together in the untidy bed, Charlie scowling and looking defiant in the way that he always did when he had done something wrong and wasn't going to admit it. Cindy, meanwhile, was looking almost amused. Neither of them, it seemed, was the least bit repentant.

'Come on, Janey, let me take you home.'

She had almost forgotten that John was there, but now it was a wonderful relief to be able to turn to him and let him take charge, ushering her solicitously back out into the early afternoon sunshine, whilst patting her hand tenderly.

She knew that he had flagged down a taxi and was helping her into it, but it was as though she was distanced from it, as though a part of her wasn't really there and had been left behind in the Edgware Road flat. Images flashed through her head. Charlie had been sleeping with his arm round Cindy, and facing her, something he had never ever done with her. In fact, she had never actually spent a whole night with him. Cindy had looked so beautiful, with the subdued light giving her skin a soft lustrous gleam. She'd had that heavy-eyed look of a woman who had enjoyed good sex. Pain speared Janey as keenly as any knife as she realised just how long it was since she and Charlie had actually had sex.

When they arrived back at Cheyne Walk, to Janey's relief John took charge of everything, putting on the kettle and making them both a cup of tea.

'Would you like me to telephone your parents?'

'Oh, no,' Janey said immediately. 'There's no point in worrying them.'

'You should have someone with you.'

Janey managed a small smile. John really was so sweetly old-fashioned and chivalrous.

'I'm not on my own,' she pointed out. 'You're here with me – not that I want to delay you. You've done so much already. Besides, Rose will be back later, I expect.'

'I'm not leaving you here on your own,' John told her firmly.

'Oh, John . . .' Somehow this evidence of his kindness brought her closer to tears than Charlie's betrayal had. 'I can't let you do that. You must have things to do.'

'Nothing that can't wait. Now, you drink that tea whilst it's still hot.'

'You sound just like my father,' Janey told her with a shaky smile.

'He's a fine man.'

'Yes.' A tear rolled down her face.

'Don't, Janey. He's not worth it.'

John took the cup of tea from her and folded her into

481

his arms, comfortingly patting her back, much as though she was still the same little girl she had been when they had all played together, Janey recognised. It felt like the safest place on earth.

Chapter Forty-Six

Ella lay in Oliver's bed watching the early morning sunshine paint shadow patterns on the ceiling. Her body felt soft and relaxed, different somehow. A sharp thrill of knowledge flared through her. It *was* different. Last night she had had her first proper orgasm. Just thinking about it sent an aftershock through her, making her clitoris ache reminiscently.

It was nearly a week since she had first gone to bed with him, but last night had been the first time she had stayed all night.

She rolled over onto her side so that she could look at him. He was still asleep, his overnight growth of stubble darkening his jaw. Who could have thought that sex could give so many different pleasures, so many different sensations? She could look back now on the Ella she had been a week ago with both superiority and amusement. How naïve and foolish she had been, and yet at the same time how wise. Knowing what she did now, feeling what she had felt now, Ella knew that it would never have done for her to have gone to Brad as she had been. In her naïvety she had definitely made the right choice.

Things were working out remarkably well. Tomorrow Oliver was leaving New York for five weeks with the fashion team to do an important shoot out in the desert. His absence would bring a natural end to her tutelage She was grateful to him for everything that he had taught her, but of course it would be wrong for her to continue having sex with him now.

It would be the end of the summer before Brad returned to New York, by which time Oliver would be on his way back to London. No wonder she was feeling so relieved and so happy.

Last night had been skin-shiveringly wonderful. Her toes curled in on themselves in remembered delight as she replayed the things Oliver had done. There was no need for them to share this intimacy any more; by rights she should get up and leave now, whilst Oliver was still asleep. She had achieved what she had set out to, after all, and it was unnecessary for her to be here now in his bed, breathing in the scent of him, her body luxuriating in its memory of the feel of him against it and within it.

She could have sworn that she hadn't made a sound, but nevertheless Oliver was awake now, turning his head to look at her, giving her that triumphant, arrogant look she had come to recognise.

'Come here.'

The smile he gave her as he lifted his arm so that she could move closer to him told her all she needed to know about what he had in mind.

She could ignore his invitation. She could turn away. She should certainly do both, but she didn't, and now it was beginning all over again, the delicious anticipatory build-up that would soon become an insatiable demanding ache, that would then . . . Aaahh, it was too late to go on thinking now. Too late to do anything other than feel and want and need for just one more time. Just one more time wouldn't hurt anyone.

For the third night running Emerald couldn't sleep. In fact, she hadn't slept properly since she had last seen Max, which was a week ago now, and she knew why, even though she resented admitting it. There was an emptiness inside her, an ache, a need that infuriated her just as much as it ate into her, and it wasn't for Max, the very thought of whom now made her shudder with distaste.

No, the cause of her inability to sleep was much closer to home. In fact, it might be said that it was 'home', she acknowledged irritably. It was Rose's fault, with her ridiculous self-sacrificing behaviour, her . . . her very Roseness and the way it had made Emerald somehow so aware of her own isolation. The way it had made her recognise for the first time in her life what she had given up when she had set her own face so determinedly against being part of a loving family. That was because she would have had to share her mother's love with others, and why should she? The smell of Rose's denim jacket had touched a nerve inside her so painfully that even now just thinking of how she had felt in the hospital was like touching a raw wound.

If Rose had really had the concern for her she had pretended to, then she would be here with her instead of leaving her on her own.

But as hard as Emerald tried to reach for the comfort of the old tried-and-tested familiar contempt and animosity she had previously felt for Rose and the rest of her family, that new ache prevented her from doing so. The house felt so empty, even Robbie's room immaculately tidy without him here.

Robbie. Her son. *Her* son. Emerald looked at her alarm clock. Half-past three in the morning; too late to telephone her mother, but in the morning . . . She lay back against her pillows and closed her eyes.

Janey couldn't sleep. She desperately needed someone to listen whilst she talked through the problems she felt she was having with one of the new designs. She dare not think of anything but work. The merest thought of Charlie had her eyes welling with tears. She'd been so excited when she'd visualised the finished outfit inside her head. A simple little shift dress from the front, with a daringly low cut-out of a figure eight at the back, the fresh green and white patterned cotton she wanted to use trimmed with plain white braid. Then over the dress there was to be a summer coat, in the exact green of the patterned floral fabric, and lined with it. It would have three-quarter sleeves cuffed in the patterned cotton, huge buttons covered in it and a swing pleat at the back infilled with it. The whole idea really excited her. She'd even thought of adapting it for the Christmas season, in rich velvet, in dark colours, with the keyhole covered in cotton lace dyed the same colour.

The trouble was that no one was wearing green. Some people even thought the colour unlucky. Charlie had a gorgeous green floral shirt . . . No, mustn't think about Charlie. Must keep working. At least that never let her down.

Janey needed to talk to someone who would understand. She was desperate. It was four o'clock in the morning, that meant that it would be around ten o'clock in New York. As quickly as she thought of solving her problem by speaking with her sister, the idea was smothered by reality: the cost of the telephone call – if she could get through – the length of time it would take to explain things to Ella, who would, she knew, demand exact and, to Janey, unnecessary detail.

Rose would sympathise, of course, but Rose was so practical, so purposeful, sooo organised and good at everything she did that Janey hesitated to reveal her own insecurities to her.

She had no one. There was no one for her to turn to, Janey thought miserably. Her eyes were beginning to sting again, and she reached for a rather damp handkerchief. And then she remembered John telling her that she could always turn to him, in that serious oh-so-reliable John voice of his. A small giggle broke through her despair at the thought of her explaining the finer points of dress design to dear lovely but unfashionable John. And he *was* a dear. So very kind and reliable. Just thinking about him made her feel much calmer. Janey started to yawn. Perhaps she would be able to sleep after all. Dear, dear John . . .

'Yes, Mummy, that's right,' Emerald confirmed, as she wound the white cord of the telephone round her finger.

'That's why I'm telephoning. I've decided it will be better for Robbie if he spends some of the summer in London, so I'm coming down to Macclesfield for him today. We'll stay overnight and then travel back tomorrow. Of course I'm sure. I am his mother, after all.'

Chapter Forty-Seven

'I just thought I'd come and see you and give you a little warning. I know that you're in love with Josh so there's no point in you denying it.' Patsy leaned across Rose's work table to stub out her cigarette in Rose's ashtray, making it plain as she had done since she'd walked in unannounced minutes earlier that she was the one who was in control of the situation. 'And there's no point either in you playing this silly game of dragging out the winding-up of the partnership.'

'I am not dragging out anything.' Somehow Rose managed to keep her voice steady, even though inside she felt as though she was dying with shame and humiliation. Knowing that Patsy knew that she loved Josh was like having the skin ripped off an unhealed wound. It made Rose feel exposed and vulnerable. But that didn't mean that she was going to let Patsy make accusations against her that just weren't true.

Patsy gave her a contemptuous look. 'Josh loves me, not you, and he can't wait for us to go to New York. But thanks to you he's stuck here until this business of the partnership that you foisted on him is resolved.'

Rose could feel her face starting to burn.

'Oh, I don't blame you for wanting to keep him. In fact it was rather clever of you to tie him to you with the partnership, but you must see that he doesn't want it, or you, any more.'

'Josh knows that I am perfectly willing to end the partnership,' Rose told her. 'The delays are not being caused by me. It's Josh who has insisted on waiting until the lease expires before formally ending things.'

'Because he feels sorry for you,' Patsy answered. 'We both do.'

Rose winced, hating the thought of the two of them discussing her.

'Josh can leave for America any time he likes, as far as I'm concerned,' Rose defended herself fiercely.

'Then why don't you tell your solicitor to get the partnership ended? Like I said, Josh is only hanging on here because he feels he owes you something.'

Patsy stood up, her hair swinging immaculately onto her shoulders, her mini revealing the long length of her slim legs. Her whole bearing was one of triumph as she walked out of the room, leaving Rose too upset to focus on the work she had been doing.

She'd been thinking of calling round to see Emerald later. Ridiculously, she'd been worrying about her cousin – not that she had expected Emerald to welcome a visit from her – but now she felt too vulnerable to see anyone, never mind Emerald.

An hour later, when she was still unable to concentrate on her work, Rose decided that there was no point in continuing to sit at her desk doing nothing other than think about Josh and her own misery. She had always found that walking was a good cure for her occasional creative blocks, and right now she needed to escape from her workroom, where the air still smelled of Patsy's scent, even though Rose had opened the windows to dispel it.

She was wearing a silk shift with a pop art design on it in tangerine and black against a white background, the striking combination perfect for her colouring, several fine thin gold bangles circling her wrist. As she caught sight of herself in the mirror, she noticed that her hair needed trimming. She had stuck to the same shiny bob for several years now; Josh claimed that it was the perfect style for her. But soon there would be no Josh to cut her hair for her, no Josh to hold secretly in her thoughts and her heart late at night when she couldn't sleep, no Josh to talk to about her work. No Josh, full stop.

Her hand was reaching for the door handle when it turned, and the door opened inwards to reveal Pete Sargent.

His greeting was accompanied by a long curling smile, which unexpectedly set off a fizz of reaction inside Rose's stomach.

'Pete, you're back.' What an inane comment to make, Rose derided herself. Obviously he was back; he was standing there.

'Got back yesterday.'

He looked lean and tanned, his jeans clinging to his thighs, the top buttons of his shirt unfastened, his hair curling into his collar. He looked rough and untidy and very sexy.

'So I thought I'd call by and see if you were free for lunch.'

Of course she should say 'no'. After all, they had nothing in common, she assured herself hastily, not wanting to remember exactly what they did have in common. In fact, she was opening her mouth to turn him down when she had a sudden image of Patsy's smug expression when she'd spoken to her earlier.

'I was just going for a walk,' Rose told him instead.

'Great. I'll come with you. We can walk in the park and have a picnic.'

'We can't do that,' she protested, although in reality the prospect was very tempting.

'Why not?'

'Because you are Pete Sargent. You'll be mobbed by fans, hordes of screaming girls.'

'I'll wear a disguise, and if that doesn't work then you'll just have to protect me from them.'

It was no use, Rose realised, he was not going to give in, and besides, he had just made her laugh, for the first time in a very long time indeed.

Reaching for her hand, he added, 'Of course, if you really wanted to protect me you could always marry me.'

Rose laughed again.

'Don't laugh,' he told her. 'I mean it.'

'But, Mummy, I don't want to go back to London'.

Emerald had arrived at Denham just over an hour ago to find that her mother had already told Robbie that she intended to take him back to London with her, and now her son was looking reproachfully at her. His dark hair

492

was flopping over his forehead. Emerald raised her hand to push it out of his eyes, about to comment that he needed a haircut, and then stopped.

'Apart from anything else you need a haircut.' A hazy memory stored many years previously came into sudden sharp focus of another boy with the same dark hair and the same stance. Luc, of course. Funny how the memory could store such things – things the brain should have been too immature perhaps to register because she could only have been a two-year-old at most, at the time. Luc would have been older than Robbie, but not much.

Robbie, who had been on the point of scowling, suddenly broke into a wide smile, announcing enthusiastically, 'Uncle Drogo's here,' before setting off at a run across the lawn towards the two men coming out of the house.

Without looking at her mother, Emerald said, 'He looks like Luc.'

'Yes,' Amber agreed.

Still keeping her face averted from her mother, Emerald continued, 'They resemble him then, do they? The painter?'

Amber exhaled, flinching from the raw bitterness of the way Emerald pronounced the words.

'Not really. Luc actually looked very like Robert, probably because he had Robert's mannerisms. Jean-Philippe's hair was dark but so were his eyes; Luc, like Robbie, had blue eyes. Luc adored Robert and copied everything he did.'

Emerald, who was watching Robbie coming towards her, flanked on one side by Jay, on the other by Drogo, tensed abruptly as she saw that Robbie was walking with exactly the same stride as Drogo.

A surge of conflicting emotions rushed through her.

'Mummy, do I have to go back to London?' Robbie demanded as the three of them reached the spot where Amber and Emerald stood. 'Only Uncle Drogo is going to do lots of exciting things, like going for walks and looking for fossils and things.'

'We can still do that in London, old chap,' Drogo assured Robbie. 'We could go to the Natural History Museum, if you like—'

'Yes. And can we go to Madame Tussauds as well?'

Emerald was about to point out to Drogo that he had no right to make arrangements that included her son without asking her permission first, but before she could do so Drogo was turning to her and asking, 'Did you drive down from London or come on the train?'

'The train,' she answered him in a sharp voice.

'Then how about going back with me in the car? I was planning to drive back tomorrow anyway.'

Robbie's excited, 'You mean in your new Bentley?' warned Emerald that there was no point in her trying to refuse. And besides, it was ridiculous of her to feel somehow that being transported back to London in the comfort of Drogo's Bentley was something to be avoided.

Chapter Forty-Eight

'Oh, c'mon, Janey, it was nothing really.'

It was ten o'clock on Monday morning and they were in Janey's office. Janey had barely slept or eaten since she had found Cindy and Charlie in bed together, despite John's kind efforts to persuade her to do so. Her head still ached from all the crying she had done, but Cindy, in contrast, looked not just relaxed about the whole thing but almost amused.

'Nothing?' Janey retorted, her voice rising. 'How can you call being in bed with my boyfriend nothing?'

'Because it was. OK, so Charlie and I bumped into one another on Friday night, and I ended up going back to his place with him, and the one thing led to another and we went to bed together, but so what? I don't know what you're getting so uptight about. That handsome guy you were with on Saturday is a friend of yours, right, and I'll bet the two of you have shared a bed when the mood's taken you.'

'No, we haven't,' Janey denied. John was good-looking and kind, but somehow she had never thought of him in *that* way before. He had always just been John.

'More fool you then,' Cindy told her. She shrugged. 'Why don't we just forget Saturday, Janey? Personally I think you're making a fuss about nothing, and making a bit of a fool of yourself as well, if you don't mind me saying so.'

'I can agree to that,' Janey snapped at her. 'I certainly made a fool of myself over Charlie.'

'You don't need to worry about me and Charlie. Charlie is yours. What happened meant nothing to either of us, and if you'd just calm down and stop acting like a provincial, and remember instead that this is London and—'

'Charlie is not mine and I don't want him to be. In fact, I don't ever want to see him again.'

Cindy lit herself a cigarette and drew slowly on it before exhaling and telling Janey dismissively, 'You're getting things totally out of proportion.'

'I find my partner in bed with my boyfriend and you say I'm getting things out of proportion? You'd obviously . . . had sex.'

'Yeah, well, people do. So what? It didn't mean anything.'

'Maybe it didn't mean anything to you but it certainly meant something to me,' Janey told her.

Cindy gave a small contemptuous laugh. 'I hadn't realised that you were so behind the times, Janey. No one bothers about a bit of sex between friends. Everyone does it. Poor Charlie, you've really upset him.'

Cindy was enjoying making fun of her, Janey suspected. The partner she had admired had become someone she didn't very much like.

'I don't want to talk about it any more,' Janey told her.

'That's fine by me,' Cindy responded. 'Let's just forget it.'

'I can't do that,' Janey was forced to tell her. 'I'm sorry, Cindy, but I want to end the partnership.'

'Because Charlie fucked me? Did you really think that someone like Charlie wouldn't fuck anyone else just because he was going out with you?'

Janey's heart was thudding in heavy sledgehammer blows. 'It's a matter of trust, Cindy. If I can't trust you then I can't work with you, and I think we both know anyway that it would be impossible for us to continue as partners now.' It was the truth, and Janey was relieved to have managed to vocalise what she thought.

'I know we put a clause in our contract that said we had to give one another two months' notice if we decided to end the partnership. I'll speak to my solicitor and arrange for him to send you an official letter. In the meantime, whilst we work out the two months we have to stay in business together, I'd be grateful if we only discuss business matters and not personal ones.' Janey held her breath. She hated rows.

But to her relief Cindy merely shrugged and said laconically, 'Suit yourself.'

Chapter Forty-Nine

'I can find my own way back to my shop, you know,' Janey teased John.

He was up in London on business – something he had been doing frequently just recently – and had taken her out for lunch – something else he was doing frequently, and not just for lunch but to dinner as well. He was coming up to London at least twice a week and staying all weekend most weekends. She had got so used to his company now that she missed him dreadfully when he went back to Macclesfield.

He was being a wonderful friend to her, a real shoulder to lean on, during these recent difficult weeks whilst she and Cindy worked through the notice period.

'I know you can, but it's a gentleman's responsibility to ensure that a lady returns home or, in your case, to her shop, safely.'

John might sound serious but he was smiling at her, and Janey couldn't help but smile back.

She was feeling astonishingly happy these days, given what had happened, and hadn't missed Charlie one little bit. That was all down to John, Janey knew. He was relaxing to be with, and so very kind, spoiling her, treating her with an old-fashioned courtesy that was incredibly sweet.

Today she'd had a rather self-indulgent lunch hour, Janey admitted, with them making plans to take a boat trip to Richmond on Sunday if the weather stayed warm. John had come round to the shop to meet her at just gone twelve, and now it was gone half-past two. She was smiling as she walked into the shop after she had said goodbye to him.

Fiona, the most senior of her salesgirls, was waiting for her.

'There's something I need to talk to you about,' she announced.

Janey agreed absently. John wasn't returning to Cheshire until late on Sunday and he had insisted on picking her up later so that they could have a drink together, a drink that would lead to them sharing dinner, Janey suspected.

'Cindy never paid us our wages yesterday, and she hasn't been in at all today,' Fiona complained.

Janey's heart sank. She was naturally finding it difficult to work with Cindy at the moment, and wished that they'd agreed on a month's mutual notice, not two. For the last week Cindy had been working from her flat, and Janey had been relieved by her absence. There were only another three weeks to go now before the partnership was finally ended.

'I'm sorry,' Janey said to Fiona. There'd obviously been a mistake of some kind. After all, Cindy wouldn't deliberately not pay the shop assistants. 'I'll go to the bank now and draw out some money for the wages.' She looked at her watch. 'I'll have to go now before they close, and you'll have to find out how much everyone is owed.'

Fifteen minutes later, Janey was sitting in a chair in her bank manager's office, and trying desperately not to act like a baby and burst into tears as she listened to the manager explaining to her that she could not draw any money out of the shop's account because there was no money in it.

There had been a mistake. But it wasn't Cindy who had made it. It was her.

'But there must be some,' she protested. And not just some but surely rather a lot, because only ten days ago, at Cindy's urging, she had transferred a huge amount of money from her own personal account into the business in order that they would be able to pay for the manufacture of the new season's orders. Cindy had told her that she'd been able to negotiate an extra discount from their supplier if they paid early.

As she told Mr Beard all this he looked increasingly grave. A clerk was sent for, and an instruction given. Mr Beard's secretary produced a cup of tea, half of which Janey spilled into the saucer of her delicate china cup in her anxiety, as she waited for Mr Beard to study the papers and the cheques he had had brought to him.

'Well . . .' he said, steepling his fingertips together, his elbows on his desk, his stance the reason, she guessed absently, for the shiny patches on his suit. 'I think we have an explanation. It seems that your partner has drawn cheques made out to herself on the account.'

'Not . . . not for all the money, surely?' Janey protested, still unable to comprehend what was happening.

'I'm afraid so,' the bank manager confirmed.

'But . . . but she can't do that.'

'I'm afraid that legally she could,' Mr Beard told her, 'since there is nothing in the bank account mandate to prevent her from doing so or to limit the amount of money she was allowed to draw.'

'Then I can't get the money back?'

'Not unless she is willing to return it,' Mr Beard agreed.

From the way he was looking at her Janey suspected that Mr Beard shared her own belief that there was no way that Janey's money was going to be returned. No one emptied a bank account in the way that Cindy had done and then simply agreed to pay it back.

Nevertheless, on the way back to the shop Janey tried to convince herself that it *could* be a mistake; that despite their quarrel over Charlie, Cindy couldn't have actually taken the money, and that there would be a perfectly reasonable explanation for its absence.

But as Janey quickly discovered, the money wasn't the only thing that had gone missing: Cindy herself was missing as well. The girl who eventually answered Janey's anxious telephone call to her flat announced that Cindy had left and that she had told her she was going back to America.

'They were both going,' she informed Janey, 'Cindy and that boyfriend of hers, the one that's the model.'

Boyfriend?

'You mean Charlie?' Janey asked. Her stomach felt hollowed out with panic and the longing for this not to be happening.

'Yes, that's the one.'

So much for Cindy telling her that she and Charlie

were just friends, Janey thought dizzily, reeling from the blow she had just been dealt. Had they planned to rob her all along, or had Cindy merely acted spontaneously out of spite?

What difference did it make? She had let them make a fool of her and she didn't want to see either of them ever again.

Thanking the other girl for her help, Janey replaced the telephone receiver and leaned back against the wall. This couldn't be happening. But it was, it was. She had been such a idiot, believing them both, never suspecting, whilst they'd been stealing from her, stealing her trust, her belief in them, her love and her money.

Oh God . . . God . . . What was she going to do? She needed help, and she needed it quickly and desperately, Janey knew. There was only one person she could think of whom she could trust to give her that help, only one person she wanted to turn to.

She knew that John had intended to return to his club so she rang him there, her fingers tightening round the telephone receiver as she waited for him to be informed that she wished to speak with him.

'Janey?'

Just the sound of his voice was immediately comforting.

'John, something terrible has happened. Could you come round to the shop now?'

'Of course.'

He would think her a complete fool all over again, and of course she was.

* * *

To her relief John arrived at the shop within half an hour, listening in silence whilst she told him what had happened.

'I have to pay the girls, John, and I just didn't dare ask the bank to lend me any money.'

'Are you saying that you want me to lend it to you?'

Janey's heart sank. He wasn't being anything like as sympathetic as she had believed he would be. Had she made yet another mistake, and another misjudgement? Was he not after all the true white knight she had secretly been thinking him in her heart?

'It just seemed natural to . . . to turn to you for help.' She was feeling really uncomfortable now, and wishing that she had not telephoned him and spoiled her silly romantic fantasy that he was something – someone – very special. 'I'm sorry if I've put you in an embarrassing position. I didn't mean to. I know my parents will help me and, of course, I've got my trust fund.'

If anything John looked even more grave – and disapproving.

'I'm sorry.' He was shaking his head. 'But I have to warn you that I can't help you.' Janey felt as though the bottom had dropped out of her world – not because he was refusing her but because she had been so wrong about him. She had believed that he was a true knight in shining armour, gallant and dependable and wonderful, but when had her judgement ever been any good? She only had to think of Charlie and Cindy to know that it wasn't.

'Not unless, that is . . .'

Janey, who had been looking down at the floor and

biting her lip, looked up at him. His face had gone a bit pink.

'Not unless what?'

'Not unless you say that you will let me propose to you.'

Propose to her?

Feeling giddy and thrilled, and as though by magic all her earlier anxiety and misery had disappeared, Janey said breathlessly, 'You mean you want to ask me to marry you?'

'Yes.'

'Oh, John!'

In a near delirium of relief, Janey flung her arms around his neck and lifted her face towards his.

Oh, but this was heaven, after all that she had just been through: to be held so was tightly and lovingly, so protectively by darling John, Janey thought as she returned his kiss with excited enthusiasm.

Being married to someone like John, who would look after her, would be wonderful. Being in his arms felt so right, as though they had always been meant to hold her, Janey thought.

Held in John's arms, it came to Janey that with John she would never need to worry about trying to make things right and trying to make him happy, trying to win his approval, because he loved her, truly loved her.

Tears filled her eyes.

'He isn't worth your tears,' John told her.

'I'm not crying for him,' Janey told him truthfully. 'I'm crying because knowing you love me makes me feel so happy.'

* * *

'I was going to wait until Christmas to ask you,' John told her later, when they were sitting drinking the champagne he had ordered, 'but I was worried that some other chap might come along and bag you before I got the chance, so . . .'

'So when I had to ask you for help you decided to make me listen to your proposal now,' Janey finished for him happily. 'Oh, John, it's almost like fate meant us to be together, isn't it? What with you rescuing me from the march and then me finding out about Charlie, and now this; just like all the time fate's been showing me how perfect you are. Not that I needed to be shown, not since you were so kind over Charlie. I thought then how wonderful you were and how lucky the girl you eventually married would be.'

John gave her a passionate look and squeezed her hand.

'There'll be some compromises to be made, I know,' he told her. 'My place is in Cheshire, running the estate, and you've got your shop here in London. I dare say we'll work something out, though. Your parents did, after all. Jay runs the estate and Amber has her business here in London.'

Janey's heart overflowed with gratitude. Darling, darling John, who was so traditional and old-fashioned, loved her enough to want her to be happy so much that he was prepared to make the kind of compromises that none of her previous boyfriends had ever considered making.

'My designing is important to me,' she agreed, 'but I can do that just as easily at Fitton Hall as I can here in

London. I want to be with you,' she told him fiercely, 'not separated from you. Oh, John, I never knew that love could be like this. I think it was worth losing all that money because it's made me so happy. You've made me so happy.'

'Good. Because making you happy matters more to me than anything else,' John told her truthfully.

He'd fallen in love with her the night of her twenty-first birthday party, but had never thought he'd stand a chance – him, a dull fellow, a countryman – not when she was here in London surrounded by far more dashing and attractive chaps. But fate had stepped in and now she was his.

Chapter Fifty

'Feeling a bit better now, old chap?'

Emerald glared at both her son and Drogo.

'Oh, do stop fussing over him, will you, Drogo? There's nothing wrong with him. He's simply being difficult because he doesn't want to have lunch at the Savoy.'

They were in Hyde Park, where Drogo had taken Robbie riding earlier in the morning, something he had been doing virtually every morning since they had returned to London. But now, to Emerald's irritation, Robbie was complaining that he had a headache and didn't feel well.

She knew what was wrong really. Given the chance, Robbie would have spent every hour he could in Drogo's company – he positively worshipped him – and was sulking because she was taking him away from his hero, to go home and get changed for her lunch engagement with Jeannie de la Salles at the Savoy.

When Jeannie had telephoned she had told her that she had some important news for her, but then refused to divulge it over the telephone, so naturally Emerald wanted to find out what it was.

And now here was Drogo, typically trying to undermine her authority and encourage Robbie to be difficult. Emerald gave them each another glare. They were standing side by side, and whilst she had been speaking Robbie had moved closer to Drogo and was now almost leaning against him, Drogo's hand resting protectively on the little boy's shoulder. Protectively? What was he supposed to be protecting Robbie from? She was his mother.

'He does look a bit pale,' Drogo told her.

'There's nothing wrong with him,' Emerald snapped. 'I dare say if I were to give in and tell him he could stay with you, his headache would disappear within seconds.'

Too late Emerald realised that she might have betrayed herself. It came too close to the way she had felt as a child, this feeling she got when she saw Robbie with Drogo and was forced to recognise the closeness they shared, the relationship from which she was excluded, for her to ignore it.

Unwanted tears stung the back of her throat as she turned away from Drogo and Robbie. She scarcely knew herself sometimes. The intensity of her emotions made her feel so vulnerable: the fear that Max had beaten into her – not of his return, but of what the fact that she had ever wanted him in the first place said about her; the panic that came when she told herself that it was surely unthinkable that without her adoptive father she could ever have become one of those women Max had compared her with; the resentment, the jealousy she felt when Robbie aligned himself to Drogo, rejecting her; the fear and rejection she felt whenever she remembered how she had felt in the hospital, holding Rose's jacket.

She tensed as she felt Drogo's hand on her arm.

'Why don't I take Robbie back to Lenchester House with me? Then you can go to your lunch without having to worry about him.'

'No. Don't you think I know that is exactly what he's hoping for and why he's claiming to have a headache? No, he's coming with me.'

The look in Drogo's eyes, a mixture of anger and pity, whipped up her own temper.

Grabbing hold of Robbie's arm, Emerald told her son curtly, 'You can stop all this right now, Robbie, because it won't work. Come along, it's time to go home and get changed for lunch.'

'Oh, you decided not to bring Robbie with you then?' Jeannie asked Emerald as they embraced.

'No.'

Emerald was still seething about Robbie, who, when she had told him to go and sit downstairs and wait for her to finished getting ready, had told her that he felt nauseous and then had promptly been sick. Deliberately induced sickness, of course. She could remember doing much the same thing herself as a child. It had always worked with Nanny, but she was made of sterner stuff and she had sent Robbie to get undressed and have a bath, telling him that since he had made it impossible for her to take him out with her he would have to stay at home on his own – in bed. He had, no doubt, been hoping that she would give in and send him round to

Lenchester House and Drogo rather than leave him in on his own. In fact she wouldn't have put it past Drogo to have put him up to the whole thing, just to get the better of her. Well, they would both have to learn that Robbie had to do what she said.

'It's probably just as well. Just look how busy this place is. I'd thought that with everyone away for the summer it would be virtually empty. I'd forgotten about the American tourists.'

Emerald had to wait until they were seated at their table, the light salads they'd both ordered in front of them, before she was able to demand, 'So tell me then, what is this important news?'

'It's about Max.' Jeannie leaned closer to her, her voice dropping to a hushed whisper as she continued, 'He hasn't been around for the last few weeks. I thought that was because you and he had split up but now apparently he's in the most dreadful trouble. He's been arrested, apparently, something to do with that dreadful East End murder. You know, the one where the victim was battered to death? It was in all the papers.'

'You mean that gangland—'

'Shush . . .' Jeannie warned her. 'Peter says that we shouldn't talk about him in case the police start asking us questions, but I've heard that Max owed someone important from the East End an awful lot of money. He did always like to gamble heavily.' Jeannie gave a small shiver but Emerald could see that she looked more excited than afraid.

'You're not still seeing him, I take it?'

Emerald's mouth compressed. So Jeannie didn't just

want to impart information; she was hoping she might get some juicy titbits back from her.

'No, I'm not,' she answered her truthfully. 'It was only ever a very casual sort of thing,' she added, giving a small dismissive shrug for emphasis. 'And in fact if you hadn't introduced him to me I would never have given him a second look.'

'Well, we had no idea that he was still involved with . . . with the underworld. He always gave the impression that he had put all that kind of thing behind him.'

'As we should put him behind us,' Emerald told Jeannie pointedly.

Because of the busyness of the restaurant, it was later than Emerald had expected when she and Jeannie finally said their goodbyes.

As she made her way back to Cadogan Place she told herself that it would have done Robbie good to realise that he couldn't behave in the way that he had. He was growing up fast. He would be going back to school soon, and that meant taking him to Harrods to replace those items of his uniform he had grown out of.

Robbie was a good scholar and had won the praise of his headmaster. Perhaps she ought to have a professional photograph done of him to send to Alessandro and his mother.

Alessandro and his royal bride had still not produced any children. The thought of how galling it would be to Alessandro's mother to see Robbie's photograph lifted Emerald's spirits and put her in a much better mood.

*   *   *

Drogo stood in the library of Lenchester House and looked up at the portrait of his predecessor, demanding ruefully, 'Well, Duke Robert, what do you think? Do I find myself a wife and beget myself an heir, or do I keep on hanging around and hope that one day Emerald is going to fall for me?

'No, you're right, it doesn't look very much as though she will do, but at least it looks like that no-good bloke she was running around with is out of the picture.

'It's that poor little kid I feel the most sorry for. A boy needs a father, right? And the honest truth is that I love him already like he was my own.'

He looked away and then back up at the portrait.

'So what do you say we give it another few months – just until Christmas? You agree? That's good, because I appreciate your advice, man to man, duke to duke, you having been there before me, so to speak.'

Emerald felt sick and faint with panic. She was in Robbie's bedroom and her son, far from being ready to apologise for his earlier transgressions and admit that he had been pretending to be unwell, was patently very unwell indeed.

She sat down on the edge of Robbie's bed. He was barely conscious, his face flushed and his skin burning.

Emerald called his name, reaching for his hand, willing him to respond rationally, but instead he simply shivered and moaned, patently oblivious to her presence.

He really was ill, and needed a doctor quickly.

Her heart pounding, Emerald hurried into her own bedroom, picked up the receiver of the white telephone beside the bed and dialled the number of her private doctor in Harley Street.

It was several minutes before the ringing telephone was answered at the other end.

'I want Dr Ruthers to come round immediately. My son isn't at all well,' Emerald told the receptionist.

'That won't be possible, I'm afraid.' The receptionist's voice was crisp. 'Dr Ruthers is in Scotland, shooting, at the moment.'

'But there must be someone,' Emerald protested.

'Dr Ruthers' locum has had to go to a family funeral. He'll be back tomorrow. If you're really worried you could take your son to Great Ormond Street, the children's hospital, you know.'

Emerald replaced the receiver and hurried back to Robbie's room. She was probably worrying unnecessarily. Children did seem dreadfully poorly when they were sick. Now she would probably find him sitting up in bed and demanding orange juice and biscuits.

Only she didn't. If anything he looked even worse. Was it her imagination or had he someone shrunk and become smaller, frailer in the few minutes she had gone? Fresh panic seized her, a different panic this time. She wanted to pick him up and hold him, anything to stop him getting worse, to keep him with her, to . . .

The hospital, the receptionist had said. Emerald hesitated. She needed help, someone . . .

She went back to her bedroom and looked at the telephone and then taking a deep breath she picked up the receiver.

Drogo was attempting to finish *The Times* crossword when the phone rang, and he was glad of the excuse to stop. The butler hadn't been too pleased initially when Drogo had announced that he was going to have his calls put straight through to him rather than having the butler answer them, but Drogo had insisted.

'Drogo, it's me, Emerald. Drogo – it's Robbie. He's sick and our doctor is away. The girl said to take him to Great Ormond Street, but . . .'

He could hear the fear and panic in her voice, and his stomach muscles clenched against what she was telling him as he answered, 'I'm coming round. I'll be with you in ten minutes.'

'It's all right, darling, Mummy's here,' Emerald whispered to her son, holding the small hot hand tightly in her own, and when he made no response, adding almost pleadingly, 'Uncle Drogo's coming.' But there was still no response, as Robbie lay huddled on his side, facing away from the window with his eyes closed and his breathing strained and ragged.

Where was Drogo? He should have been here by now. She got up and went to stand in front of the bedroom window, looking anxiously down into the square.

He'd said ten minutes and that had been over fifteen minutes ago.

A Rolls-Royce, stately and shiny, turned into Cadogan Place, momentarily obscuring her view of the pavement. As Emerald waited impatiently for it to pass she realised that it was slowing as it approached her house, and then she saw Drogo striding swiftly down the street towards them, and everything bar her relief vanished as she almost flew down the stairs to let him in.

Only when she opened the door, he was standing on the pavement in deep discussion with a much older man who had got out of the Rolls-Royce.

Frantic with anxiety, Emerald was just about to demand his attention when he turned towards her and told her, 'I took the liberty of telephoning Dr Salthouse and asking him if he could come straight here, Emerald.'

A doctor! Emerald could almost have cried with gratitude.

'He's upstairs,' she told them both.

It seemed to take an age for the doctor to complete his examination of Robbie. Emerald answered his questions as best she could.

'I thought he was just pretending when he said he had a headache and felt sick. It was something I used to do myself at his age when I didn't want to do something.'

It was her fault that Robbie was so ill. Her fault. Her heart felt as though it was being gripped by giant pincers and torn apart. How, why had she not known until now how very precious to her her son was, how infinitely more important than anything else in her life?

'It's my fault that he's so poorly. I should never have left him.'

The words were torn from her as she gazed helplessly at her sick son.

'You mustn't blame yourself.' Drogo's voice was calm

and firm, his clasp of her hand unexpectedly comforting. She wanted to cling to it, Emerald realised.

The doctor had folded back the bedclothes and unfastened Robbie's pyjama jacket. On her son's torso Emerald could see a rash of spots.

'What is it?' she asked the doctor anxiously. 'He's had chicken pox and measles and—'

'I think the best thing for your son right now, Lady Emerald, would be for us to get him into hospital,' Dr Salthouse told her, without answering her question.

'Hospital?' Her worried gaze lifted to Drogo's face not the doctor's. 'Then it's . . . it's serious?'

Dr Salthouse looked at them both and then said slowly, 'I can't say for certain just yet but I think that Robbie may have meningitis. There's been a small outbreak in the city over the summer, and of course it is contagious.'

Emerald stared at him.

'Meningitis? But that's . . . that's very dangerous, isn't it? Children die from it. I . . .' One look at Drogo's face told her that she was right and that he shared her fear.

'We mustn't look on the black side, Lady Emerald. We don't know yet that Robbie does have meningitis and if he does, then we have penicillin.'

'But I read in the newspapers last week that three children have already died recently.'

'If I may use your telephone, Lady Emerald, I will arrange for Robbie to be admitted to Ormond Street. They'll send an ambulance.'

'I want to go with him.'

The doctor frowned.

'Lady Emerald and I will follow the ambulance in my car, Doctor,' Drogo suggested, taking charge.

The unthinkable, and unbearable, was true. Robbie had meningitis, and he was a very sick little boy.

He had been given aspirin to help break the fever, and penicillin to fight against the infection.

'And if it doesn't work?' Emerald had asked the paediatrician at the hospital.

The look he had given her had confirmed what she already knew.

'He's going to die, isn't he?' she had demanded hysterically. 'My baby is going to die and it's my fault.'

'We don't know that,' the paediatrician had told her. 'Meningitis is a very serious disease, yes, but in some children it can disappear almost overnight, leaving them untouched. Others survive the infection but go on to have problems later in life. Yes, there are those who sadly do die, but it is too early to say yet what will happen with Robbie. All I can say is that he is in the very best place now to be helped, and the penicillin gives us a fighting chance of overcoming the infection.'

Emerald had been close to collapse when the doctor had left them. Only the fact that Drogo was there to witness both the effect of her neglect of Robbie and her own weakness as she realised what she had done, kept her from doing so. This was a thousand times worse than the fear she had experienced when she had been the one in hospital.

Sister came bustling into Robbie's private room in a rustle of starched cotton, her shoes squeaking on the shiny clean linoleum, bringing into the room with her a fresh wave of disinfectant-laden air.

'Now, Lady Emerald, why don't you go home and try to rest? We will telephone you in the morning. Visiting hours are—'

'No. I'm not going anywhere. I want to stay here with Robbie,' Emerald stopped her immediately.

Sister's expression firmed. 'I'm afraid that isn't possible.'

'I can't leave him. What if he . . . ?' Emerald blinked away agonised tears, unable to stop herself looking desperately at Drogo.

'Sister, you won't be aware of this, of course, but several weeks ago Lady Emerald approached me to ask if I would co-chair with her a committee she is planning to set up to raise money for this hospital in the name of her late father, my predecessor. Lady Emerald has a particular interest in sick children. Sadly her own brother lost his life at a very young age. I'm sure in the circumstances, as a particular friend to the hospital, it might be possible to allow Lady Emerald to stay here in Robbie's room with him?'

Emerald had to admit that Drogo's appeal had been masterly.

Whilst she held her breath in desperate hope, Sister gave Drogo a look of cool irony, before saying, 'I believe the premature baby unit is desperately in need of incubators, which will cost around a hundred thousand pounds. Do you suppose that Lady Emerald's committee will be able to raise that amount, Your Grace?'

'I can guarantee it,' Drogo answered her promptly.

Sister looked at Emerald and then turned back to Drogo.

'Well, well, then but I must stipulate that Lady Emerald can only stay provided she does not disrupt or add to the work of my nurses.'

'I won't,' Emerald assured her fervently.

Sister had gone, leaving the room in a swish of starch that somehow or other she managed to make sound very disapproving. And Emerald and Drogo were alone in the room with Robbie.

She had to thank him, she couldn't not do, but just like all those other times when she had desperately wanted to deny and defy the Emerald that so seemed to delight in being unpleasant and difficult, Emerald was for some reason afraid to do so.

'I've got to go now,' Drogo was saying to her. 'You'll want me to let your mother know—'

'No. No, there's no point in worrying her. She can't do anything.'

'She could be with you.'

Emerald shook her head. 'No, I don't want her here.'

It was a lie. She desperately wanted not to be alone with her fear that Robbie might die. But it wasn't her mother she wanted with her, she realised with a small stab of surprise, it was Drogo.

Chapter Fifty-One

Unable to bear looking at it, Ella stuffed the doctor's appointment card into her handbag, her fingers stiff and clumsy. The smell of anaesthetic and other darker things was still in her nostrils. Was it clinging betrayingly to her; to her skin and her hair and her clothes?

She felt as though, if she wasn't careful, she was going to burst into tears and she mustn't do that. Ella took a deep breath as she approached the entrance to *Vogue's* offices.

She had hardly recognised herself these last seven weeks. She was normally so calm, and on those occasions when she wasn't, she was extremely good at concealing it, but just lately, it had been as though her emotions had gone totally out of control and quite spectacularly so. She wasn't sleeping properly, she had a breakout of spots on her face for the first time in her life, and most telling of all, she was being sick in the morning and she had missed her period – twice.

As she had wept in the office of the gynaecologist whose name she had managed to obtain only under the promise of shared secrecy from one of the other girls at work, it should have been impossible for her to get pregnant. She was on the pill, after all, and the pill stopped you getting pregnant, but the combination of the lack of her period and the all-too-evident morning sickness couldn't be ignored.

The knowledge that she was pregnant had filled her with horror and fear.

She still felt that way now, even though this morning she had been to see the gynaecologist to get the results of the pregnancy test he had done for her a week ago, and which had confirmed that she was indeed carrying Oliver's child.

She was relieved, of course, that the doctor had agreed to terminate her pregnancy for her, but she was still sick with shock and fear, still unable to understand why the pill had failed, and unable to allow herself to relax until it was all over.

The termination of a pregnancy was illegal, but there were doctors who performed such a procedure – if one was desperate enough, or rich enough. Ella felt that she had been lucky. One of the other girls at *Vogue* had guessed her condition and under pressure from Ella had given her the name of a doctor who she had 'heard' carried out safe terminations in properly sterile conditions – for a price and only on word-of-mouth recommendation from someone else in the know.

'You are perfectly healthy,' he had told her this morning after he had said that her test had indeed confirmed that she was pregnant. 'There is no reason why you should not give birth to a healthy child.'

'But I can't have a baby,' Ella had wept. White-faced, she had then told him about her mother, whilst he had listened, nodded and then told her to see his nurse to make an appointment to come in in another week's time for a D and C.

It might now be fall, with the leaves on the trees in Central Park turning the most glorious shades of crimson and gold, but the sun was still warm, too warm for her autumn coat over her new plaid autumn miniskirt and its toning deep plum cable-knit jumper, which she was wearing with a pair of suede boots from Biba, which Janey had sent to her, and which had been sighed enviously over by the whole of her office.

Fall. In less than a month now Brad would be back in New York. He had written to her the previous week to say that he was in the process of finishing his book, and making arrangements to return to the city and that he was very much looking forward 'to seeing you again and taking up from where we left off to go somewhere very special'.

Once those words would have thrilled her and filled her heart with excitement and joy. Once. For a very brief window of time between going to bed with Oliver and realising the nature of the unwanted consequences of having done so.

Oliver himself was preparing to return to London. She had seen him briefly the previous day when he had come into the office to discuss with the fashion editor the photographs he had taken on the desert shoot. From what Ella had heard, *Vogue*'s legendary chief editor, Diana Vreeland, had declared them absolute masterpieces.

Ella knew that he had seen her because he had looked at her, but to her relief he hadn't made any attempt to speak to her. That was exactly the way she wanted things. They had nothing to say to one another, after all. She would be relieved when he had gone back to London. Once, the fact that he was here would have been enough to have her worrying and anxious, but now the deeper and more pressing fear of her pregnancy had pushed all the other feelings she might ordinarily have experienced to one side. Dr Goldberg had warned her to buy herself some painkillers. He had written down what she must get. She had put the piece of paper away safely, hadn't she? Anxiously Ella opened her handbag to check.

Oliver was just leaving the *Vogue* building when he saw Ella coming down the street towards it, a slender attractive figure in her plum and black coat and her suede boots, the sun shining on her hair. Something unfamiliar and unsought stirred unexpectedly inside him. A desire, a need to go up to her and . . . and what? Claim her? He might have had shagging rights with her for a handful of days, but that was over. She didn't look particularly happy, he noticed. In fact she looked downright unhappy, her face paler and thinner than he remembered it. What was the cause of that? A fall-out with the boyfriend?

Instead of going in the opposite direction as he had

intended to do, he turned, his loping stride taking him towards her.

She was still fussing around with her handbag. Typical of a woman, Oliver thought as he reached her and said her name, putting his hand on her arm as he did so.

Oliver! Ella's open handbag slipped from her suddenly numb fingers, disgorging its contents onto the sidewalk.

Immediately she was bending down, ignoring the dizziness caused by her sudden descent, frantically trying to collect her belongings, but Oliver had squatted down in front of her and his hands were quicker than hers, and bigger, enabling him to gather things up with more speed than she could.

She really was incredibly sexy now, Oliver decided smugly, thanks to him. Already he could feel his body responding to her proximity. Mentally he weighed up the chances of persuading her to share a farewell fuck with him, his mouth curling into the smile he would use to begin coaxing her. He had her purse in his hand, and her lipstick, along with some pieces of paper, one of which had a business card stapled to it. Idly he turned them over, and scanned what was written on it. He had always been a nosy sod, according to his mother.

The words, once read and understood, became a physical force that swung the world off its axis, before it shuddered jarringly back again. He looked from the pregnancy test result he was still holding, to Ella's white face.

'You're pregnant.'

There was no point denying it. Not with him holding the evidence in his hand.

'Yes,' Ella agreed, as they both stood up. 'It was an accident. I don't know how it happened.'

When Oliver gave her a disbelieving look, she insisted, 'I was on the pill. It shouldn't have happened. Anyway, you don't have to worry about it. I'm having a . . . a termination. It's all arranged.'

'You're getting rid of it?'

His forthright words made her flinch, and want to cover her still flat stomach protectively with her hand, but she managed to resist doing so as she confirmed, 'Yes.'

'And this is the doctor who's doing it?' Oliver demanded.

'Yes. Not that it's any concern of yours.'

She was beginning to feel shaky and close to tears. She couldn't let him see her crying, as though . . . as though what had happened between them meant something when it hadn't meant anything at all.

Not trusting herself to say any more, Ella sidestepped him and then almost ran the rest of the way to the *Vogue* building, not daring to look back, and only relaxing once she had reached the comparative safety of her office. It was only then that she realised that she had left her pregnancy confirmation and D and C appointment card with Oliver. Not that it mattered. She was hardly likely to forget the date and time, was she?

How could she have been so reckless and rash? Rose's hand shook as she touched her newly cut hair. Its shortness still felt strange after wearing Josh's long bob for so long. It was too late to regret what she had done now. What had been done could not be undone. There was bound to be comment – and criticism – questions asked, and feelings hurt because of her secrecy, but right up until the last minute she had not been convinced that it would actually happen and that she would go through with it. But then Josh had rung to say that he needed to see her urgently about something that Patsy had told him, and that had tipped her over the edge – or rather, her pride had seized her by the hand and dragged her over it – and she had made her decision. Maybe she would regret it but at least it would protect her from the humiliation of being told by Josh that he was really sorry that she loved him but that he loved Patsy.

The palms of her hands felt damp. He would be here any minute.

Would he come alone or would Patsy be with him? Would he – they – accuse her again of clinging to him out of pitiful unrequited love? If so, she had her answer ready.

Josh arrived five minutes later, taking the stairs to her workroom two at a time. Mercifully, he was alone. She could tell it was two at a time because of the sound of his feet on the stairs and because that was the way he always took them. Like an early warning system, it gave her time to prepare, time to compose her face into a smile that was friendly but not loving, warm but not tender, welcoming but not needy.

She stood up as he came into the room, watching him as he came to a halt several yards away from her.

'I've got something important to tell you.'

He hadn't noticed her hair.

'If it's about the partnership—'

'Fuck the partnership,' he interrupted her.

Her heart was racing, which wasn't good, and neither was the familiar ache of sweetness and vulnerability flowering inside her in all its helpless, insidious treachery.

'I'm not going to America.'

The shock was almost a physical blow, sending her reeling back from what it might mean. She tried to sound normal.

'Patsy won't be very pleased about that.'

'Fuck Patsy as well,' Josh stated. 'Don't you want to know why I've changed my mind?'

'If you want to tell me.'

'I'm not going because of you.'

Her chest tightened against her inhaled breath.

'I can't leave you behind.'

He was shaking his head as though he found the admission bemusing.

'The truth is that I don't want to leave you behind.' His voice was softer now, and warmer. He was coming towards her. He reached for her hand and smiled at her. 'I've been a fool, Rose. What I really wanted has been there in front of me all the time, but it was only when I was about to walk away from you that I recognised what I'd be losing.'

She could feel herself trembling.

'I'm staying here and we're going to get married and—'

Rose shook her head. 'I can't marry you.'

'Why not?'

'I'm already married. Pete and I were married a week ago.'

Chapter Fifty-Two

'*What?* Why? Why have you married him when you love me? And don't try to deny it because I know that you do, even if it took Patsy to show me what I should have seen for myself years ago.'

'He asked me. And . . . it seemed the right thing to do.'

They looked at one another, and then Josh turned and strode out of the room, leaving her alone in its aching silence.

He still hadn't noticed her hair.

Ella had arrived in plenty of time for her appointment. The receptionist had smiled at her and ticked her name off a list on her desk, and the nurse who had then arrived to escort her to her room had been brisk and professional.

Now she was dressed in a hospital robe, waiting . . . waiting for the doctor to come and take away what was growing inside her so that she could go on with her life, waiting for it to be removed so that she need not fear the madness its birth might bring her.

It wouldn't be long now. The nurse had said that she was first on the list. Soon someone would be along with a pre-med, then they'd sedate her and then . . .

Ollie scuffed the leaves that had fallen in the park. They made a crisp dry sound, releasing their scent into the air. During his childhood, the sights and sounds of autumn had been restricted to East End fogs and the harsh rattling coughs of the elderly. The first time he could remember seeing fallen autumn leaves had been when he'd been off school with a bad chest. His mother had taken him to work with her, telling him to stay out of sight and keep quiet, as she'd taken off her hat and coat and pulled on her pinafore in the kitchen of the house she was cleaning. His father's house, he knew now.

He'd sneaked out into the garden whilst her back had been turned, scuffing the dried leaves much as he was doing now and thoroughly enjoying himself until right in front of him he'd seen a pair of highly polished black shoes. He'd looked upwards over the immaculately pressed, knife-edge-creased trousers and then the overcoat, until finally he'd reached the sternly harsh face of the man looking back at him.

He'd panicked then, remembering his mother's warning, and he'd turned to flee, only to catch his foot in something and take a tumble.

He'd been terrified at first when the man had picked him up, fearing all manner of unwanted consequences, like his mother's hand against the back of his bare legs or, even worse, his dad's belt, but the man hadn't said anything, simply held him firmly so that their eyes were

530

on the same level and looking at him in silence, his hands suddenly tightening on his arms, before he finally put him back down on the ground.

That memory was all he had of his father – everything and nothing. He had never been able to ask anything of the man who'd given him life, but he had been given that life, unlike his own child. Today its life was going to be extinguished, taken before it had properly started.

He'd reached the exit to the park before he'd even realised that he'd started to move, hailing a cab and giving the driver the address that he hadn't known until now he'd memorised.

The receptionist listened to him, purse-lipped and frosty-eyed.

'I'm sorry—' she began.

'No you're not,' Oliver stopped her, 'but you bloody well will be if you don't tell me where she is, and fast.'

A nurse gaped at him as he ran down the corridor, trying to step out in front of him, protesting, 'You can't go in there.'

Ella could hear the altercation taking place in the corridor through the numbing fog of her pre-med. Then the door to her room was thrust open and Oliver burst in.

'She can't leave now. She's had her pre-med.' That was the nurse, standing between her and Oliver.

'Fine,' Oliver told her. 'Then I'll stay with her until she can leave, but there's no way my kid is going to be aborted. Got that?'

His words shocked through Ella's pre-med, kicking her slow heartbeat into thudding anxiety.

'I'm going to go and find the doctor. He won't put up with this,' the nurse was threatening.

'You go and find him, and tell him when you do that I'll be suing him for trying to abort my kid.'

The nurse had gone but Oliver was still there, leaning over the bed, his hands on Ella's arms, as he insisted, 'Come on, we're getting out of here.'

The pre-med seemed to have taken away her willpower to do anything other than simply go along with the almost dreamlike things that were happening to her.

One minute she was lying in bed and the next, or so it seemed, she was in Oliver's arms and then in a taxi, then a lift and then finally in another bed, where finally she was allowed to sleep.

Oliver looked down at Ella's sleeping body, torn between elation and disbelief. What the hell had he done? The last thing he wanted was a kid. Just as his dad couldn't have wanted him. But he had allowed him life, he had watched over him as best he could, he had provided for him and for his mother. The mark of a man. And Oliver simply didn't have it in him to be less of a man than his father had been.

Ella woke up slowly and reluctantly. Her hand was lying on top of the bedclothes, against her flat belly. Tears trickled from between her closed eyelids. She had to do what she had done, but there was still grief and guilt to be borne. Her child would never be born now, but better that than to have a mother who later tried to kill it in her madness.

Someone was standing beside the bed.

'Christ knows what was in that ruddy pre-med. You've been out for nearly two hours.'

Oliver. What was he doing here?

Ella's body jerked beneath the bedclothes as she struggled to sit up, realising as she did so that 'here' wasn't a hospital bed, but instead the bedroom in the flat Oliver was renting.

Vague memories stirred, disembodied and out of focus.

'The kid's still there,' Oliver told her abruptly.

Still there? She looked at him uncomprehendingly.

'I couldn't let you do it.'

He couldn't?

Finally Ella found her voice. 'That decision wasn't yours to make.'

Oliver shrugged her argument aside. 'The kid's mine. And another thing: no kid of mine is going to grow up not knowing who its dad is, or not having my name.' Like he'd had to do. 'That means that we're going to have to get married.'

Married? Her and Oliver?

'No,' Ella refused immediately.

'Yes,' Oliver insisted, adding unkindly, 'You haven't got any choice now. I can't see that posh family of yours putting an announcement in *The Times* to tell the world that you've had a little bastard.'

Ella flinched.

'You can't mean it. I told you what happened to my mother,' she reminded him desperately.

Oliver wasn't going to be swayed. 'I do mean it. We've created the kid between us and there's no way that he's

533

going to grow up like I did, not knowing who his proper dad is. Once he's been born, you can do what the hell you like – walk out, divorce me, do whatever you like, but the kid's going to be mine and he stays with me.'

Chapter Fifty-Three

Four days, four days, nearly five, nearly a week, and Robbie had grown weaker with each hour of every one of them. He looked frighteningly small and fragile beneath the hospital bedclothes, his eyes huge in their hollowed sockets above his sunken, waxen cheeks.

'Uncle Drogo?' His voice, so thin and frail, the effort of speech so obviously draining what little strength he had, tore at Emerald's heart. She loved him so much Why had it taken her so long to realise what a truly precious gift he was?

'He'll be here soon,' she answered him.

She mustn't let it hurt that Robbie seemed so much brighter whenever Drogo was here.

When Drogo did arrive a few minutes later, what she saw in his face, the exhaustion, the tension, the fear and the longing to cling on to hope, were, she knew, all mirrored in her own.

Since Sister had a rule that only one of them was allowed to be with Robbie, Emerald bent down to kiss her son's forehead and then turned towards the door.

She couldn't remember the last time she had eaten

but the very thought of food made her nauseous. Stepping out of the hospital into the September sunshine was as disorientating as seeing people going about their normal day-to-day business, oblivious to her pain, to Robbie and the twin powers of life and death that fought over him.

She had barely left the hospital since Robbie had been admitted, relying on Drogo to bring her clean clothes and other necessities. Up ahead of her she saw a small church. Without intending to, she walked towards it. The doors were open, the scent of incense heavy and sweet on the air. A head-scarfed women emerged from its dark interior.

On impulse Emerald stepped inside and then halted. She was an intruder here, someone who had no place and no right to be here. The only time she went to church was if she was attending a wedding – or a funeral. A shudder ripped through her.

Her eyes were accustomed to the gloom of the interior now. She watched as a woman walked past her, crossing herself and then lighting one of the waiting candles, sheltering the frail flame from the cold draughts of the church.

Robbie's life was like that candle, flickering helplessly at the mercy of his illness. Like the candle he too needed someone to protect him and guard the flame that was his life.

Emerald walked unsteadily toward the candles, her hands trembling as she reached for one.

'I'm sorry, God,' she whispered as she tried to light it, 'but I haven't got a headscarf.' Would it count against her, against Robbie that she was in God's house with her head uncovered? Would he inflict a terrible punishment on her for her lack of respect?

'Will it be someone special ye've come to pray for, then?'

It took Emerald several seconds to interpret the Irish accent of the woman now standing next to her. Small and elderly, her eyes were sharp and curious.

A drop of wax from the wavering candle spilled onto the table as Emerald tried to hold it steady, followed by the slash of a tear.

'My son. He's very ill. It's my fault.'

'Sure, and there isn't a mother in the land who doesn't think that when her little ones ail. Even the Blessed Mary, I dare say.'

As she spoke the old woman nodded in the direction of the statue of the Madonna several yards away.

''Tis to her ye should make your prayers, for she well understands the tears of mother.'

'I haven't got a headscarf,' Emerald whispered. 'I don't—'

''Tis what's in your heart ye have always wanted to hide, but there's no place for that in here. A mother's heart is always open to her child, no matter that that child be blinded by its own foolishness. All ye need is to cast aside pride and have faith.' The old woman's hand curved round the flickering candle flame, allowing it to steady and grow. 'Go to her now and open your heart to her, and she will hear you.'

Emerald turned to look at the Madonna and then turned back to the old woman but she had gone.

Praying to a statue? Heavens above, how her set would laugh.

Emerald took a deep breath and picked up the candle. As she knelt in front of the statue the air around her seemed to sigh and settle.

How did one pray to her? The only prayers Emerald knew was the kind that came from the Book of Common Prayer.

Open your heart, the old woman had said.

'I'm sorry about not having a headscarf. So silly, as I have such pretty and smart ones at home, but of course Drogo wouldn't think to bring me one.

'It's my son, Robbie. Robert. He's dreadfully ill and it's all my fault. I don't deserve to have him spared for my own sake but please spare him for his. I'll do anything, be anything, give anything, if only Robbie doesn't die. I'll be the best mother in the world, if you let him live. I'll do everything I can – anything – to make him happy in future. Please, please don't let Robbie die.'

Candle wax sizzled in the drip of her tears as she leaned towards the Madonna from her kneeling position, pleading for her son's life.

It was a long time before she finally got up and made her way back out of the church and into the sunshine.

'Emerald.'

'Mummy.' At the entrance to the hospital Emerald gazed at her mother.

'Drogo telephoned yesterday to tell us. I came as quickly as I could. He said that you'd probably gone out for some fresh air.'

'I told Drogo not to tell you. There's no point in you being here. Robbie really only wants Drogo, and the doctor says that he must be kept quiet and not have too many visitors.'

Her mother's hand was on her arm and somehow Emerald didn't have the energy to shake it off.

'I didn't come here for Robbie, Emerald, much as I love him. I came for you, and for myself.'

'What?'

'You want to be with Robbie, don't you, because he's in pain? Because he's your child. Well, you are my child, and being a mother doesn't stop when your child becomes an adult, you know.'

'It's my fault that Robbie is so ill.'

'Mothers always blame themselves when their children suffer. I blamed myself terribly when I thought I might lose you before you were born, and then when you were born safely and you rejected me I told myself it was my own fault because I'd been so afraid when I first knew I was carrying you.'

'You wanted to get rid of me, I suppose?' Emerald suggested tiredly.

'No, never that, never for a minute, but I was afraid of what your birth would mean for all of us, for you, born illegitimate and with no father, for Luc who adored Robert and who believed Robert was his father, for myself, and for Robert, who already had so many hurts of his own to deal with and who I believed would want to bring our marriage to an end. I went home to Denham—'

'To see Rose, I expect. You always loved her more than you did me.'

'Not more, Emerald, just differently, because you see I believed that Rose and I were very similar. We'd both been rejected and hurt by those who should have loved us. We were both outsiders, unwanted and unloved. I saw in her so much that I'd felt myself. Rose wanted me to love her, whereas you, it seemed to me, did not.

'I felt you hardly needed my love, you had so much from Robert, who adored you from the minute you were born, and from my grandmother, who saw in you a great deal of herself.'

'It made me angry when you always fussed over Rose instead of me. I wanted you to put me first.'

'All of you come first, Emerald, each and every one of you. When you have more children of your own you will understand what I mean.'

'More children? I don't want more children. I just want Robbie to live—'

Emerald broke off as she saw Drogo come hurrying out of the hospital, calling her name when he saw her, demanding urgently, 'Come quickly, both of you.'

Emerald's race to Robbie's room was greeted with disapproving looks from all those who saw it, but she didn't care.

She hadn't wasted time asking Drogo what had happened. Every second lost in getting to Robbie's side took an extra breath of life from him. If he was to die then she must be with him, to hold him and warm him and keep him in her arms until he had been fully taken from her.

The first thing she heard as she pushed open the door to Robbie's room was a young nurse exclaiming cheerfully, 'And you've really eaten all that ice cream by yourself, have you? Are you sure?'

And then Robbie's unmistakable voice – a mere whisper, it was true, but still Robbie's voice – confirming, 'Yes. I have.'

Emerald put her hand to her lips, afraid to say his name, afraid to do anything other than simply stare in disbelief at her son, who was propped up against his pillows, with a tray, a spoon and an empty tub in front of him.

Chapter Fifty-Four

It was just over a month since Robbie had left hospital, but Emerald was still going into his bedroom several times a night, just for the relief of knowing that he was there safe and alive.

Any minute now he and Drogo would be returning from their walk around the neighbourhood to see how other people's bonfires were growing compared to their own in the back garden of Lenchester House.

The bond between the two of them had, if anything, strengthened. Robbie worshipped Drogo and would spend every minute with him if he could.

From the drawing-room window Emerald watched as they walked towards the house together. Robbie was even beginning to sound like him.

When Robbie had been lying desperately ill in hospital, and she had thought she would lose him, she had made a promise. Now Emerald decided it was time for her to fulfil it.

She had to wait until Robbie was safely out of the way, which meant that she had had to get Drogo's support in sending Robbie upstairs to make a list of the fireworks he most wanted.

As soon as he had gone Emerald closed the drawing-room door and leaned against it, blocking Drogo's exit as well as Robbie's unwanted return.

'There's something I want to discuss with you,' she told Drogo.

'About Robbie?'

'About Robbie,' she agreed. 'Robbie practically worships you, Drogo.' It was a hard admission for her to make but it had to be done. 'In fact, I believe he would rather spend his life with you than with me.'

She moved away from the door, unable to bear the steady intensity of Drogo's concentration on her.

She'd wanted to lead up to things slowly and carefully, hoping that Drogo might guess what was coming and do the asking for her, but now suddenly she was too impatient to wait, too anxious on Robbie's behalf to delay.

'Once upon a time you asked me to marry you,' she began as lightly as she could.

Drogo inclined his head. 'And you told me that I was the last person you'd want as your husband. Definitely not your choice of Prince Charming.'

Emerald exhaled a breath of mingled impatience and irritation. 'I was just a girl then, Drogo. Now I'm a mother, Robbie's mother. And the fact is, well, if you still want to, then now I will marry you.'

'For Robbie's sake?'

'He adores you. He talks about you night and day. He's a boy, Drogo, and he needs a man in his life, a father, and the father he would want is you. I know that.

543

'You need to marry,' she pointed out when he said nothing. 'The dukedom needs an heir, and I've already proved I can produce a son. I know what being your duchess will entail.'

She looked at him. What was he thinking? It was impossible to know from his face. Watching him, it came home to her how much he had grown from the awkward young Australian she had baited so cruelly. He was a man now, confident, at ease with himself. Something happened low down in the pit of her stomach, a keening ache that caught her off guard and stung colour into her face.

'So if I say yes, then I get Robbie, I get an heir and I get you. But what do you get, Emerald?'

'Me?' She was honestly confused by his question. 'I get Robbie's happiness. He loves you, Drogo. He needs you and so do I, on his behalf.'

He still wasn't saying anything.

'I know you may find it hard to believe that I genuinely want to put him first, but something's changed for me. I've changed. When it thought I was going to lose him I realised how much I loved him. I made a promise, a vow that if only he lived, then I would do everything I could to make him happy and keep him safe. Can't you see, Drogo? If you don't marry me then one day you will marry someone else, one day soon perhaps, and then Robbie will lose you.

'I know that I'm not really Robert's daughter, but—'

'That doesn't come into it,' Drogo stopped her, real emotion now in his voice. 'It was you I wanted to marry, Emerald, not your genealogy.'

'But now you don't want to marry me any more?'

'What would you do if that was the case?'

A small frown pleated Emerald's forehead. 'You are Robbie's godfather. It wouldn't be ideal but I'd ask for your word that you'd always make a place for him in your life, that you'd spend time with him.' Her voice thickened, her eyelids dropping to cover her expression from him as she told him. 'That you'd love him.'

It seemed an age before Drogo spoke again.

'If we do marry there'll be a condition.'

'Anything,' Emerald told him recklessly.

'No more Max Preston. In fact, no more men of any kind.'

'Is that all? I loathe the very thought of Max, and as for other men . . . I made a bargain – Robbie's life for my promise to always put his best interests first. Don't you see, Drogo, *that* Emerald, the old Emerald who thought only of herself and her own pleasure, has gone. Our marriage won't be about me having a good time or . . . or enjoying sex. Drogo, what are you laughing for?' she demanded, feeling affronted when he burst into laughter.

'You've got an odd idea of what it takes to persuade a man into marriage,' he told her, reaching out to catch hold of her hand and then gently tugging her towards him. 'Of course I still want to marry you. I've never stopped wanting to, nor stopped hoping that one day you will. Much as I do love Robbie, it isn't just for his sake that I practically camp out on your doorstep, you know.'

His voice was amused, tender, the timbre of it close

to her ear affecting her in the most unexpected and extraordinary way.

'I'll make a bargain with you, Emerald. Yes, I'll marry you, provided the only man in your bed from now on is me, and provided you agree that we should at least try for good sex. I mean, we do have an heir to get, after all, Maybe an heir and a spare, and a couple of girls as well. May as well found a dynasty; there's all that money to find a home for.'

'Drogo,' Emerald started to protest, and then stopped, had to stop in fact, because Drogo was kissing her, and suddenly it seemed the most natural thing in the world to throw her arms around his neck and hold him close so that she could kiss him back.

His hand had just burrowed under her sweater, his touch on her bare breast and her nipple pleasingly sure and skilled, when Robbie pushed open the door, coming to an abrupt halt.

'Uggh! You're not kissing? That's for cissies,' he said with disgust.

'And would-be mummies and daddies,' Drogo whispered in Emerald's ear as he discreetly straightened her sweater and told her, 'I think we should resume this affirmation of our agreement to provide Robbie with a father, my heir-to-be with a mother, Osterby with a mistress and my bed with the only woman I've ever really wanted to hold in my arms there, a little later on, don't you?'

His hand was still cupping the side of her breast, aching tormentingly now for more of his touch whilst her lower body pulsed with the need he had aroused.

But she had made a promise to put Robbie first, she reminded herself, as she pulled away from Drogo and told her son, 'Robbie, darling, guess what. Uncle Drogo and I are going to be married.'

'You mean that we're all going to be living together?'

'Yes.'

'Good.'

Emerald looked at Drogo.

'Very good,' he agreed. 'In fact very, very good indeed.'

Part Three

Chapter Fifty-Five

February 1977

Amber was the only person in the hospital waiting room. Outside it was still dark. There had been snow on the road from the heavy fall earlier in the day and she had been terrified that the ambulance wouldn't be able to get through.

How was it possible that Jay, who was so fit, could have had a heart attack? Amber shivered and squeezed her eyes tightly shut in prayer.

'Please don't take him from me,' she begged silently. 'Please let him live.'

They'd wanted her to go home. They'd said there was nothing she could do, but she wanted to be here; she wanted to be with Jay.

The family would have to be told, of course. Amber tried to concentrate on the practical issues that would involve. Janey and John and their two children, both boys, were close at hand at Fitton Hall. Robbie, who loved his grandfather so much, was away skiing with friends, taking a year out before going up to Oxford, whilst Emerald and Drogo and their two girls would be at Osterby. Emerald, who was so desperate to give Drogo a son, and so angry because she had not done so.

Ella and Oliver were in New York with their daughter, and Rose would be in West Sussex. As always when she thought of Rose, Amber's heart ached over the distance her niece had put between them, withdrawing from the close relationship they had once shared.

In the early years of her marriage Rose and Pete had always spent Christmas at Denham with the rest of the family, but more recently the problems with Pete's health, caused by his drinking, meant that he was not well enough to go anywhere and as Rose virtually refused to leave his side, neither did she. Rose had put up a wall between them – between herself and all her family, in fact – fending off all Amber's attempts to find out why, and Amber could only suppose sadly that it was because of her marriage, and out of some kind of loyalty to Pete, perhaps thinking that her family might be critical of him in an attempt to be protective of her. Rose was a very proud and a very private person, but Amber feared that she was also a very lonely person and her maternal heart ached for the niece she loved so much and still thought of as a daughter. And finally, of course, the twins. Polly would have to come from Venice, where she lived with her husband, Rocco Angelli, and their twin sons, whilst Cathy was living in St Ives with her artist partner and her two daughters from other relationships.

Jay loved their shared progeny so much, as they did him.

They couldn't lose him. They mustn't. How could such

a healthy man have a heart attack? Amber's body shook violently.

It had been a perfectly normal February day. In the morning Jay had driven over to see one of their tenant farmers, and Amber had had a charity committee meeting. Then in the afternoon they'd gone together to the mill for their regular monthly meeting with its manager.

When they'd got home Jay had complained about an ache in his arm, she remembered. He'd thought he must have got it from chopping wood for the fire. They'd laughed about the aches and pains of getting older – Jay was in his early seventies now, and she was sixty-four – not old at all really.

Over dinner they'd talked as they always did about their family, especially their grandchildren. They'd been in bed before midnight.

It had been just gone two o'clock when she'd woken up to find Jay sitting up in bed, clutching his chest, his face pale grey and beaded with sweat in the light of the bedside lamp she switched on.

She known immediately then, of course, panic coursing through her to set her own heart beating heavily and too fast, as she'd rung 999, whilst Jay protested that there was nothing wrong with him, and that she wasn't to fuss.

He'd still been protesting when the ambulance had arrived.

The door to the waiting room opened, the sight of the consultant, summoned from his own bed, sending Amber a surge of mingled hope and fear, the sensation reminding her of a long-ago visit to Disneyland and the ride she had gone on there with her grandchildren. Then her terror had been limited to the duration of the ride and the knowledge that it would soon be over.

'How is he?'

She had, Amber discovered, risen from her chair and was now clutching the back of it for support. How many times must the consultant have heard those anxiety- and dread-filled words and seen fear and grief in a relative's face?

'His condition is stable.'

The calm tone, the soothing smile meant nothing really.

'Is he going to . . . will he live?'

Such simple words but ones so heavily weighted with her love and her fear.

The consultant's smile was professional and meant to soothe but Amber could see behind it to the pity and the reality it tried to mask.

'He has had a major heart attack, which he has survived. His condition, as I have already said, is now stable. The next forty-eight hours are crucially import-ant. That is when patients are most vulnerable to further attacks.'

Further and *fatal* attacks was what the consultant meant, Amber knew. Her hand tightened on the back of the chair, her knuckles showing white through her skin.

'I want to be with him.' Somehow she managed to make her voice steady and calm.

The consultant was frowning. 'Your husband is in intensive care.'

Amber knew all about the hospital's intensive care ward. After all, she and Jay had done a great deal to help to raise the money to ensure that the hospital had such a facility.

'I shan't be a nuisance. Jay would want me to be with him. He would expect it.'

Now her voice was firm with conviction. Jay would want her to be there, and if they were not to be lucky and he was to be taken from her, then she wanted to be the one who was there with him, to surround him with her love in those last moments between life and death.

'Very well,' the consultant agreed. 'Sister will arrange for you to be gowned up, but first I expect you'll want to get in touch with your family.'

She should do that, of course, but Amber was more anxious to get to Jay. If these were to be Jay's last hours on earth then selfishly she wanted them for herself; she wanted the luxury of concentrating on him alone, of communing with him in the silence of the dark hours; she wanted, she acknowledged, to be only Jay's instead of having to be a mother and a grandmother, instead of having to juggle the complex needs of their family when all she wanted was to hold to her these precious last hours with the man she loved. But as always her duty to others commanded her. They too loved Jay and would never forgive her if a delay on her part meant that they were denied the opportunity to share his last hours.

She dipped her head in acquiescence, her 'Very well' reminding her of the youthful Amber she had once been, obeying the grandmother she had half feared. Jay would have recognised that tone and that dipped head because

Jay had shared those years with her. Now her fear had a stranglehold on her emotions and her thoughts, panic – a child's panic, almost – of losing all her emotional security clawing at her. Jay was her life, her whole reason for being; she couldn't lose him. She was trembling as she followed the nurse to the small room from where she could telephone the news.

Chapter Fifty-Six

Janey couldn't sleep and she knew, although he was lying silently beside her in their big comfortable marital bed, that John wasn't sleeping either. How could they after what had happened? Her heart started to race with a familiar mixture of fear, panic and disbelief.

In the ten years they had been married Janey had never once given any thought to their financial security. John was a careful and a prudent man, not the kind of man who would ever take any kind of financial risk, especially not with the estate that had been handed down to him which had passed through so many generations of his family and which he in turn would hand down to their own son.

He had believed his investment was safe, he had told her with tears in his eyes. He would never have made it if he had thought otherwise. Investing money with several other local landowners, people he had known all his life, had seemed, under the aegis of one of their number, such a good decision. And so it had been – at first – making enough profit to buy back some of the land that had been sold during his father's time, but then something had gone dreadfully wrong, and now all the money was lost. According to John they were virtually penniless.

John hadn't told Janey at first, not wanting to worry her, but then he had come to her white-faced, his voice low with shame and despair, to tell her what had happened.

They had done their best. It was too late now to regret the money spent on the purchase of more land; on the expensive cattle-breeding programme inspired by the success the Duke of Westminster was having with his own prize herd; on the new roof for Fitton Hall – so very costly because the whole building was listed; on the modernisation inside. But like so many landowners they were land rich and cash poor. The estate barely covered its own running costs, never mind paid them an income, which was why John had wanted to try to generate more money in the first place. Over the years they had had to dip into Janey's inheritance and now what was left was next to nothing, barely enough to pay the children's school fees. Fitton Hall itself was mortgaged, the money raised used to modernise the estate, which had been so badly neglected by John's father and his stepmother.

Lying awake in the darkness filled with fear and panic, Janey thought enviously of Emerald, whose own personal fortune ran into millions, never mind Drogo's vast wealth. Emerald would never need to lie awake in her bed at night with her heart pounding with sick fear because there was no money.

It was so unfair that this had happened to John, who had only wanted to do his best for them all and for

Fitton. Her own father would understand that, and he would want to help them, Janey comforted herself. He and John had always got on well. They could go to Denham and talk to him. She would have to manage things discreetly, of course, so as not to humiliate poor John. Her panic began to recede.

Yes, her father would know what to do . . .

She was just drifting off to sleep when she heard the telephone ring.

Emerald lay beneath the smooth weight of her expensive Egyptian cotton sheets, her body completely still as she looked up through the darkness. The London house's master bedroom had only just been refurbished using Designers Guild 'Geranium' fabric to create a luscious four-poster bed effect. Emerald had invited her mother round to see it, watching the faint shadow darken Amber's eyes as she studied the fabric that had become so very desirable and praised.

Her mother's Walton Street shop still retained its long-standing and loyal clients, but the younger, more modern buyers had moved on, leaving the shop and Denby Mill's fabrics distanced from the excitement garnered by their more 'with it' rivals. Her mother needed someone younger to take up the mantle of responsibility for the design side of the business but there was no one; Rose refused to leave Sussex, Polly was glued to her Italian husband and his family, and Cathy would no doubt scorn the mere designing of fabric patterns as unworthy of her creative muse.

February. How she hated English winters. By rights

they should have been at Courchavel skiing – Robbie was – but Dr Steptoe had warned her against taking any kind of risk, and besides, she needed to be within easy reach of the Lancashire hospital where he was based in order for the revolutionary treatment she was undergoing to take place.

Her heart gave a flurry of anxious thuds, the threat of nausea gathering in her stomach and clogging her throat. Beneath the protection of the bedclothes she put her hand on her flat stomach. She had already had one son, and then two daughters; why couldn't she produce for Drogo, for the dukedom, that all-important son? Just thinking about her failure to do so filled her eyes with angry tears. She had tried hard enough, in the early years expecting with every month that she would conceive, and becoming increasingly angry and frustrated when she did not. Emerald hated not achieving the goals she set herself. And then when, two years after they had married, she had finally become pregnant it had simply never occurred to her that she would not have a boy. The mere thought of daughters appalled her. But daughters were exactly what she had had. Two of them, delightful, clever girls, but what good were they since they could not continue the family line?

Their births, two years apart, had caused her to redouble her attempts to produce a son. Drogo had complained that sex had become more of a chore than an expression of their love for one another. Emerald had refuted that claim, telling him passionately that it was because she loved him so much that she wanted to give him a son. But she had not conceived again. Next year she would be forty. Time was running out for her. For her, but not for Drogo. Now the true cause of her fear was laid bare. Somehow during their marriage, she had succumbed to the vulnerability she had always sworn would never claim her and she had fallen in love – with her husband. Drogo might say that she mattered far more to him than having an heir, but one day he would mind, she was sure of it, and when that day came he would look past her and see that there were other younger women who could easily give him the son she could not.

She had been at her lowest ebb, filled with the bleakest despair and most bitter anger and resentment when she had heard about the Lancashire doctor who was involved in the development of so called 'test tube' babies.

She had driven up to the hospital where he was based, without saying anything to Drogo, and had demanded to see him, too impatient to waste time by writing and not wanting to risk being put off by telephoning. He had explained to her that his research was still in its infancy and that whilst he had been able to implant into women's wombs the embryos that had been developed outside them, none of those pregnancies had gone anything like full term or resulted in the birth of a living child. He had, though, admitted under pressure from Emerald that he was continuing with his research and that he was putting in place a programme he was hoping would lead to the successful birth of a living child. Emerald had then insisted that she wanted to join that programme as one of his potential mothers.

When she had told Drogo, though, he had been vehemently opposed to the whole thing.

'I want to give you a son,' Emerald had told him passionately. 'I want that more than anything else, Drogo.'

'We already have Robbie and our girls,' he had answered her.

'They cannot inherit the dukedom,' Emerald had pointed out, knowing what Drogo's reaction would be. It was an old worn issue between them, after all, and, true to form, Drogo had told her, 'You matter far more to me than having an heir, Emerald; you know that. This Steptoe chap says himself that he has not as yet had any real success and that there are risks attached to the procedure.'

She had refused to give in, though, and eventually and reluctantly he had given way. That night she had rewarded him – in bed – and had been surprised by how much she herself had enjoyed having sex with him again simply for the pleasure of having sex. It had been a long time since she had thought of sex as anything other than a means of conceiving a son.

That night had created a new sexual intimacy between them, but it would be short-lived. Once her treatment started that would be the whole focus of her attention. She didn't intend to allow anything to prejudice its outcome.

Later on this morning she would drive up to the northern hospital to begin the round of tests and procedures that would ultimately lead to the eggs that would be harvested from her resulting in live embryos, which could be transplanted into her womb to produce the son she so longed for. There was no way of guaranteeing that she would have a boy, of course, but if the procedure could result in a successful pregnancy then she would repeat it until she did produce a son, such was her determination.

Dr Steptoe had been reluctant at first to allow her on to his programme, insisting that he didn't want to interrupt it to accommodate her, but then another woman had dropped out and she had received a telephone call from him informing her that there was this window of opportunity if she was free to take it. If she was free . . . Nothing would have stopped her from making sure that she was free.

The sudden sharp unexpected ring of the telephone cut across her thoughts, making her nerves jump and jangle.

The ringing telephone had woken Drogo, who was switching on his bedside lamp and reaching out for the receiver. He slept naked – they both did – and his movement disturbed the covers, revealing the tanned flesh of his muscular back. He still had a good body, taut and masculine in a way that still aroused and excited her, and she moved closer to him whilst he answered the call.

Chapter Fifty-Seven

'John! Jay's had a heart attack?' Drogo's voice was strained with shocked disbelief.

Emerald stiffened. Her stepfather was a fit and healthy man – how could he have had a heart attack? She leaned closer to the telephone, one hand on Drogo's bare shoulder to balance herself as she tried to listen in to the conversation.

'He's in Macclesfield hospital and Amber is with him. Have you spoken to Amber herself? No. Are you and Janey on your way to the hospital now? Did they give any indication of the severity of the attack? I see, so they're waiting for the test results then. Yes, the first twenty-four hours are the most dangerous. We'll let Robbie and the others know, that way you can get off to the hospital without any more delay. Give Amber our love and tell her that we're thinking of her.'

As Drogo replaced the telephone receiver, Emerald demanded, 'Jay's had a heart attack?'

'Yes. According to what the Hospital have told John, it happened in the early hours and the Hospital either can't or won't say yet how serious it was. I've said that we'll let the others know.'

'Yes, I heard you. Janey will be going to the hospital?'

'Yes. John said that he'd ring us from there just as soon as he'd got any news.' He was swinging his legs out of their bed. 'The others' telephone numbers . . .'

'They're in the book in the top right-hand drawer of my desk. Drogo, you know it's today that I have to go and see Dr Steptoe?' Emerald reminded him.

'Yes.'

He was pulling on his robe. Outside the sky was still dark, as reluctant to cede its darkness to the morning as the citizens of the sleeping city would be to cede the comfort of their beds to the misery of the raw February weather. The central heating must have come on because she could hear the familiar gurgling of the system cranking up to warm the house.

'I suppose you think I should drop everything and rush to Macclesfield?' she accused him sharply.

'It isn't what I think, but what you feel,' Drogo answered her gently before heading for the bathroom.

She couldn't go. She *had* to keep her appointment with Dr Steptoe. If she didn't the opportunity to harvest her eggs would be lost and she would have to wait until he was ready to begin a new programme, which wouldn't be for many months. Drogo knew that. Jay wasn't her father and she wasn't the 'child' whose support her mother would most want. All the old familiar bitterness diluted by the intervening years suddenly resumed its full strength. Why should she sacrifice the chance to provide Drogo with an heir simply to be with her mother?

What had Amber ever done for her to deserve that kind of sacrifice? The old emotional wounds, which for years now had seemed healed, had begun to ache again beneath the scar tissue, inflamed by fear and panic.

Drogo was coming back out of the bathroom bringing with him the scent of clean skin and rubbing at his damp hair with a towel. She loved him so much, and she knew what he would want her to do.

Inside her head she had a mental image of the man she still truly thought of as her father – Robert – smiling lovingly at her. He had given her so much love, so much more than just his name and legitimacy. His moral code might seem old-fashioned by modern-day standards but Emerald knew full well what he would have expected of her, and somehow it was important that she didn't disappoint him or let him down, even whilst a part of her raged furiously that she could not lose this opportunity to begin her treatment. Jay was next to nothing to her, whilst the baby that could potentially become the future duke was everything. Surely Robert and Drogo could understand that?

But even as she opened her mouth to tell Drogo that she intended to keep her appointment she knew that she couldn't.

'I suppose I'd better go to Macclesfield.' Her voice was tight with the effort it took to control what she was really feeling. 'It isn't what I want to do, but I know that I have to.'

Drogo put down the towel.

'Yes,' he agreed, and although he didn't say it, Emerald knew that he had been hoping that she would make that choice. She could see his love for her in his eyes, and her own filled with tears.

'Why now, today of all days, Drogo?'

'I don't know, but I do know how much it will mean to your mother to have you there.'

'Jay isn't even my father.'

'No, and it's because of that that she will need *you*, Emerald, and not just Amber but everyone else will as well. They will need your strength and your support. And as for this business of a son, how many times do I have to tell you before you believe me that I have all that I want, in you and the children we have – Robbie and the girls? You alone would be more than enough—'

'No, Drogo. You say that but it isn't true. You are the Duke of Lenchester. You need a son of your own to pass the title to.'

'Emerald, I know how important that is to you but it never has been to me. Perhaps it's because of the way I grew up – as an Aussie not knowing about the dukedom – I don't know.'

'You say that now, but what if you change your mind? What if you stop loving me because I haven't given you a son?'

'That will never happen. I will never stop loving you.' He drew her close to him and wrapped her in his arms.

To everyone else who knew her Emerald was someone they thought of as formidable, but Drogo knew that hidden behind that outer defence was an Emerald who had grown up believing herself to be unloved and unwanted and who had reacted to that by being diffi-cult and demanding, even arrogant and sometimes actively unkind, rather than let others know how alone and afraid she really felt. He knew too how much it mattered to her that she provided the dukedom with an heir. Sometimes he feared that that mattered more to her than anything else, including her own happiness.

'I'd better go and ring the others,' he told her, releasing her.

Chapter Fifty-Eight

Rose wasn't in bed when the telephone rang. She rarely slept much beyond six o'clock, and she never slept deeply any more. Her senses were too attuned to the need to listen, a habit she had developed in the early years of her marriage, waiting anxiously for Pete to return from the pub, and then counting the stages as they passed safely.

First, the sound of the car coming up the drive, her breath held tightly in her chest until he had stopped the car and she knew that there hadn't been an accident. Then waiting for him to come in, knowing from the time it took him to get his key in the door how much he was likely to have had to drink. At first she had waited up for him, often falling asleep downstairs in a chair, having previously lost the battle to persuade him not to go out, not to drink and, if he did, not to drive, but then gradually – so gradually she hadn't even realised that the habit had crept up on her until it was established – she had taken to going to bed when midnight came and went and he still wasn't back. It was nothing for Pete to return at one or two in the morning and then to stay downstairs drinking even more.

Once he was safely home the other anxieties began: that he would drink more, that he would fall over and hurt himself, that he would fall asleep downstairs and then be sick in his sleep and choke to death. To protect him from those fates she had to be constantly on guard, on duty, to cajole and coax him upstairs to bed, half supporting his weight, half dragging him up the stairs, collapsing sometimes under his dead weight, her heart filled with a mixture of burning anger, shame and despair, streaked with pity, guilt and her instinctive need to try to love him despite everything.

Perhaps if they had had a child, children, things might have been different, but Rose had been too afraid to take the risk for that child. It would have been difficult enough for him or her to deal with the reality of Rose's own background and everything that meant, without further burdening the child with an alcoholic father. That had been the emotional reason she had stuck so determinedly to taking her contraceptive pill, but there had been practical reasons as well, once Pete's drinking and consequent dependence increased. How could she look after a baby when she already had a husband who needed looking after like a child?

That had been in the early years of his drinking. For the last six of them there had been no need for her to worry about using contraception, and no opportunity either for her to reconsider her decision not to have children, because Pete had lost both the interest in and the ability to have sex with her – another consequence of his alcoholism. Drink was his lover, his beloved, his friend, his tormentor – drink was his world and his everything

– and as Rose had learned once she had taken their doctor's advice and attended local Al Anon classes, there was nothing she could do to alter Pete's behaviour. Only Pete himself could do that. The only person whose behaviour she had any control over was herself. That had been dreadfully hard for her to accept. In the early days she had still believed that she had the power to stop him drinking and make him 'well' again.

Mixed up with her despair over Pete's drinking there was also guilt: did he drink because he regretted marrying her? Did he wish he had married someone else? Was she the cause of his drinking? She had even questioned whether her marriage to Pete was in some complex way an attempt on her part to rewrite her own past and her father's problems with alcohol. Had she, at some deep-rooted level, believed that if she could help 'cure' Pete then she would somehow have paid back her 'sin' of being born and being hated so much by her father that he himself had turned to drink to drown out his bitterness? Who knew what motivated anyone to do the things they did?

The truth was that she knew that she should be guilty – guilty of marrying him out of numb despair because she thought she had lost Josh. Guilty of wishing she had not married him when Josh had told her that he loved her. The weight of that guilt had made her feel like a thief, stealing from someone. She had married Pete because she had been afraid of being alone with what she was and what she had lost. She had used him to give her what she'd thought was a new identity that would protect her – not consciously, of course, but nevertheless that was what she had done. Never ever during their marriage had she let Pete know that she still loved Josh, never once had he indicated that he had guessed that she did, but always at the back of her mind was the guilt of knowing that she could not give him what marriage to her entitled him to, because she had already given it to Josh. She had tried to compensate for that, devoting herself to him, making him her whole life, but it was a life that had an emptiness at its heart. For that reason she couldn't blame Pete for his drinking. He had tried to give up in the early years of their marriage. Twice he had voluntarily gone into a private hospital to be dried out. The second time he had suffered such violent seizures that the staff had thought he was going to die.

But he hadn't.

He was, though, according to his doctors, killing himself. Destroying himself was a truer description in Rose's opinion, a slow painful relentless destruction of his own body and mind that left her feeling helpless and anguished.

After his first 'drying out' attempt they had gone to Hong Kong for a holiday that was supposed to mark the beginning of a fresh start. It had been Pete's suggestion. He had wanted to give her the chance to 'find' the Cantonese side of herself but the trip had left her feeling far more of an outsider in Hong Kong than she now did in England. In Hong Kong she had discovered that the unwritten rules separating not just the Caucasian from Oriental, but marking the many divisions that lay within each of those categories, were complex and fiercely adhered to and protected. There was no defined 'place' for someone like her, with her wealthy Western background and upbringing, and the blood in her veins from a mother who had been amongst the lowest of the low. She had been treated with a mixture of suspicion and disdain, and had found nothing of the mother she had lost as a baby.

Unlike her father, Pete was not a violent alcoholic. He simply withdrew into himself and into a place where, in his rare moments of sobriety, he swore he was comfortable, even though the process of getting there was destroying him.

The nerve endings in his hands and feet had become so damaged that he could barely walk or hold anything, his liver now all but destroyed. He lay upstairs in the room Rose had tried to make as comfortable as she could for him. It could be weeks or months; no one could say.

She couldn't leave him unattended, not even for a few hours, because when she did, despite his fragile state of health, he would try to go out – to drink and find the comfort and the company he craved. Sometimes Rose wondered if it wouldn't simply be kinder to let him go, but the fear of him dying alone and uncared for wouldn't let her.

The phone rang, startling her.

It wouldn't be Josh, of course. He wouldn't ring this early in the morning. He wouldn't ring at all any more now, she reminded herself, because she had told him not to.

It had been a shock when Josh had come back into her life last year, simply arriving at the door to announce that he had decided to give up his salons in New York and come home.

She hadn't intended to get involved with him. But somehow she had let her guard slip, and before too long she had been admitting to him what she had refused to admit to anyone else, which was that she should never have married Pete. From there it had been an easy if treacherous step to admitting that she loved him, had always loved him and would always love him.

'Leave Pete,' Josh had urged her.

'I can't. He needs me,' she had answered. 'He hasn't got anyone else.'

'What about your needs, Rose? And what about mine?' had been Josh's response. 'Don't we matter? It's not too late for us . . .'

Surreptitiously Ella eased her toes out of her shoes as soon as the elevator door had closed, concealing her in its shiny polished womb.

She had been attending a book launch that had gone on longer than expected and her feet were aching from standing all evening exchanging small talk. Her role as the editor-in-chief of *NY* magazine took her to many such events. *NY* was considered by those in the know to be the city's most prestigious and successful magazine, and Ella had been thrilled when she had been invited to head it up as its chief editor when it had first started up four years ago.

Its unique blend of a tough editorial stance on political issues combined with what was lauded as the best gossip column in town had brought in an audience that took their politics seriously, but was still fashionable enough to need their insider gossip fix.

Add in seriously good fashion pages, a section devoted to the arts, and a diary that knew all about who had been where, wearing what and with whom, and how much they had donated to their favourite charity, and it was easy to see why *NY* had become such an iconic read.

Long before the elevator had stopped on the lower floor of their two-floor Park Avenue apartment, Ella had her shoes back on and her back straight. Not that there would be anyone to see her: Maria, their housekeeper, would have gone to bed; Olivia too would be fast asleep in the bedroom that had only recently been redecorated, the walls of which she had immediately, to Ella's irritation, insisted on covering with the blown-up photographs she and Oliver had taken together: street scenes from New York, beach scenes from summers in the Hamptons, portraits of the city's extraordinary cavalcade of raw humanity.

Right from the moment of her birth, despite the fact that she had been a girl and not the boy he had been so confidently expecting, Oliver had adored his daughter. Where Ella had thought that Olivia's blue eyes and dark hair had come from her own father, Oliver had announced that they came from him; where Ella had felt that her strong nature had come from her great-grandfather, Oliver had claimed it came from his own strong-willed mother, and they had fought over the rights to own family input into Olivia just as they had fought over everything else.

What they had not fought over was how much they

both loved her. Far from suffering from post-natal depression, Ella had fallen immediately and passionately in love with her daughter.

She unlocked and then opened the door to the apartment, knowing already that Oliver wouldn't be there – but not knowing exactly where he would be working.

She could take a guess, though, she acknowledged cynically. Oliver was an acclaimed and much-in-demand fashion photographer, and Ella did not forget that it was as a fashion photographer before their marriage that he had regularly slept with his models. Theirs had never been a love match; she had no emotional claim on him, nor he on her. They had never discussed it, but she knew that Oliver had been aware of how assiduously Brad had courted her after Olivia's birth. It was true that she had been tempted – Brad was, after all, the kind of man who was far more to her taste than Oliver – but she had not been able to forget that it was because of Oliver, and thanks to Oliver, that her life now held the most precious thing it ever would hold – Olivia. It was Oliver who had, with her, created Olivia, and Oliver who had prevented her from aborting her. And it was Oliver too who had married her for the sake of Olivia.

Because of all those things, because she believed that a child needed the love of both parents and the security that those parents being together brought, she had stepped back from the opportunity to have the affair with Brad that might ultimately have led to the break-up of her marriage.

Oliver had never challenged her about Brad but then why should he have done so? He didn't love her, after all.

Somehow that hadn't mattered before. They weren't the only successful Manhattan couple whose marriage was based more on practicality than romance. But then Oliver had not loved someone else.

Ella could remember quite clearly the moment she had realised that Oliver wasn't just shagging the stunningly attractive young model he had been photographing for *Vogue*, but that he had actually fallen in love with her. It had been on Christmas morning when she had inadvertently interrupted his snatched telephone call to her. Oliver must love her to have rung her on Christmas Day, a day that since her birth had been sacred to Olivia. Not that Ella had challenged him about it. There wouldn't be any point. Their marriage was a civilised arrangement in which accusations about infidelity had no part. Now she was simply waiting for him to tell her that he wanted a divorce. She could, of course, beat him to it and tell him first that she wanted to divorce him, but she knew that Olivia would never forgive her and would blame her for the break-up of their family, and she didn't want that.

She went into the kitchen to make the cup of tea she always made for herself when she came in late. There was a note propped up against the kettle, written in Maria's hand. The first time she read it, Ella's brain refused to accept its message.

She reached for it, her hand trembling as she read it again. Her father had had a heart attack and was in hospital. No, it couldn't be possible. She had seen him in January when she had flown over to England for a meeting to discuss the possibility of launching a sister magazine to her own in the UK, taking Olivia with her, and he had been his normal fit, healthy self.

It had been Drogo who had rung, but when Ella rang back there was no reply, so she rang Fitton Hall instead, her heart jerking into her ribs when John confirmed that her father was seriously ill and in intensive care.

She ran a successful magazine so there was no reason why she should dissolve into panic just because she had to book herself a transatlantic flight, but her hands were trembling and so was her voice as she made the telephone arrangements that would get her home and to her father's bedside.

There was no point in waking Olivia, although Maria had to be told her plans, and given a message for Oliver, who was away on a magazine shoot and not due back for several days.

Her father sick, perhaps even dying. It seemed impossible, and ridiculous when she had lived her own life here in New York for going on for twenty years, that she should suddenly feel so vulnerable and bereft, so much a child in fear of being deserted. So very much alone.

Chapter Fifty-Nine

Janey started up from her chair in the waiting room as the door opened, relief flushing her face when she saw Emerald. They had never been close but she had been on her own here for what felt like hours since John had left to return to Fitton Hall, promising to come back as soon as he could, and the weight of her fears for both her father and for her and John's futures had grown heavier with every minute. She hesitated but then her emotions overwhelmed her. She and Emerald had grown up together, they had a shared family history, and right now that meant far more to Janey than any differences between them.

'Emerald.' Her feelings choked her voice as she hurried over to her stepsister, and then burst into tears.

Emerald didn't know which of them was the more astonished when she herself closed the distance between them and put her arms around Janey in an almost protective way, before insisting efficiently, 'Tell me what's happening.'

'Nothing,' Janey managed to sniff through her tears. Who would have thought that having Emerald of all people here would be so immediately reassuring? 'Nothing's happened. It's just that it's such a relief to see you,' she admitted. 'I've felt so alone.'

'Have you seen your father?' Emerald asked her, covering her own unexpected emotional reaction to Janey's admission with a practical response.

'No. Mama, your mother, is with him, and according to the nurses she simply won't leave him. She's been told I'm here and that you all know, but she still won't leave him. You know how devoted to one another they've always been.'

'Have the Hospital said anything?' Emerald asked her.

'There's nothing new they can tell us yet. These next few hours are critical. It must be so awful, mustn't it? I've tried to imagine how I would feel if it was John. I can't bear to think like that, though; it's too dreadful to contemplate.' The words were tumbling out now in her relief at no longer being alone, but whilst they might sound muddled to anyone else, Emerald knew exactly what Janey meant.

For the first time ever, Emerald found herself exchanging looks of shared understanding with her stepsister.

The nausea Emerald had felt earlier returned, but she fought it back. Now was not the time for her to acknowledge how fearful the prospect of being without Drogo made her feel.

'I've never imagined something like this happening. You don't, do you?' Janey asked her almost plaintively. 'Dad's always seemed so . . . so just there, and you don't stop to think that one day he might not be. I'm so afraid for him, Emerald. I don't want him to die.' She started to cry again.

'Then you mustn't start thinking that he might,' Emerald told her firmly. 'You must tell yourself that he's going to get better.'

Her words had more of an effect on Janey than she had expected. Her stepsister gave her a watery attempt at a smile and told her, 'I wish I was more like you, Emerald. You're always so . . . so in control of things. Nothing ever seems to go wrong for you. You and Drogo are so lucky.'

Lucky? Her? If only Janey knew!

'Janey, you have a husband who loves you, and two healthy sons,' Emerald pointed out firmly. Two sons, not just one, and certainly not none at all, she thought. Was Janey really so blind that she couldn't see that Emerald was the one who envied her and that she had something that Emerald wanted desperately? At her lowest moments she'd often envisaged her siblings, and especially Janey and Polly with their sons, exchanging conspiratorial looks as they discussed her inability to give Drogo an heir. But Janey seemed oblivious to the direction of Emerald's thoughts. Instead she was shaking her head and giving a bitter little attempt at laughter.

'Two healthy sons who any day now will be sent home because we can't pay their school fees any more – that is, if Fitton is still ours and they still have a home to come back to. I was going to ask Daddy if he could help us. Now I feel so selfish for even thinking of that.'

Janey had no idea what had made her admit so much to Emerald, but it was too late now to call back the words and in a strange sort of a way it was actually a relief to have said them. It must be something to do with the immediacy of the situation and the intimacy of the waiting room and all that both portended.

Emerald frowned. She had always assumed that John and Janey were comfortably off.

'What's happened?' she asked her bluntly. 'And don't tell me nothing because something must have.'

The role of sibling confidante was a new one for her and she was surprised at how easily she slipped into it, and even more surprised by how comfortable it felt, almost as though she was taking on something that she had secretly wanted and had felt incomplete without.

'John invested all our money with a . . . a friend, who then went and lost it all, is what's happened,' Janey told her equally forthrightly, for all the world as though she had been confiding in her all her life. 'He's worrying himself sick about it all. I don't know what I'm going to do, Emerald. If Dad survives this I can't possibly worry him by telling him and asking him for help.'

'How much have you lost?' Emerald asked.

Janey hesitated, looking over her shoulder even though they were the only two people in the waiting room, before admitting, 'Just over a million pounds – everything we had. You see, when the investment didn't make the profit they had been expecting they all put more money in on the advice of this so-called friend. Poor John. It's all so difficult for him. You see, he's always been so good with money, and so . . . so sensible and dependable. I've leaned on him all through our marriage, and now I feel – well, I feel guilty, Emerald. I should have taken more interest in our financial affairs. I shouldn't have just expected him to shoulder all the responsibility.'

Emerald thought quickly as she absorbed what Janey had told her. Drogo had said that the family would need her, but even Drogo could not have anticipated something like this.

'Look, why don't you let me help you?'

Janey's face went bright red. 'You? But . . . well, why should you?'

Why indeed?

'We are family,' was the only answer Emerald could give her, 'and my mother is bound to sense that something is wrong. You know what she's like.'

'Well, yes,' Janey agreed. 'But I couldn't take money from you, Emerald.' She sounded mortified. 'I didn't tell you because . . . of that, and besides, John would never agree. His pride would be dreadfully hurt.'

'Then don't tell him,' Emerald said practically.

Ignoring her, Janey said shakily, 'I can't let you give me a million, Emerald.'

She had always known how independently wealthy Emerald was, but to make such an offer . . . Janey was torn between the emotions of gratitude and disbelief, and the more practical awareness that John would not want her to accept.

'You mean you'd rather your boys were embarrassed by being asked to leave their school and that you lost Fitton?' Emerald's voice was deliberately scornful. 'I thought better of you than that, Janey.'

'I can't accept it,' Janey repeated, but Emerald sensed that her resolution was wavering.

'It's what Jay would do, if he could, and it's what my own father would want me to do. We're family, after all, Janey. Your boys are my nephews, and I'd like to think that if anything happened to me or to Drogo that my girls would be able to turn to someone—'

'Of course they could. You know that.' Immediately Janey's maternal instincts were aroused, just as Emerald had known they would be.

Secretly Janey would have loved a daughter and she adored Emerald's girls.

How strange, Emerald reflected, she hadn't realised or understood until now just how much and how easily she had always deep down inside herself taken it for granted that her daughters would, if necessary, be mothered by one of the siblings she had grown up resenting.

'I'm not doing this for you, Janey,' she continued determinedly, 'I'm doing it for all of us. You live closest to Denham, after all, and you won't be able to help my mother and your father properly if you are worrying about John's debts.'

What Emerald was saying was true, Janey acknowledged.

'We're a family,' Emerald repeated, 'and we've got a difficult situation ahead of us. You will be called upon to contribute your time, and it's only right that I should make my contribution, which in this case will be helping to enable you to play your part.'

'Well, since you put it that way . . .' Janey gave in. It would be such a relief not to have that dreadful worry hanging over them, and it would enable her to concentrate fully on doing everything she could to support Amber.

'I do,' Emerald told her. 'And I'm sure there's some way we can arrange for the trustees to discover that there is some money owing to you from your trust fund, so that John's pride doesn't have to be affected.'

Janey made a small sound that could have been a protest or a giving in.

'So that's settled, then,' Emerald said firmly, seizing on Janey's response as the latter. 'We'll get everything sorted out properly as soon as we can.'

Before Janey could come up with any more objections she changed the subject, filling her in on the practical arrangements Drogo had put in hand, and adding, 'Drogo should be back soon. He phoned Robbie after John telephoned us, and then Polly, and he's arranged to pick them both up from Manchester airport and bring them straight here. We've sent a car to collect Cathy.'

'Will Rose come, do you think, and Ella?'

'I don't know.'

Would Rose come, Emerald wondered. There had never been any discussion of the rift between her mother and the niece to whom she had always been so close, but they were all aware of it.

Initially Emerald had been pleased, even triumphant. Amber was her mother, after all, and it was only right and proper that she, not a usurper like Rose, should be her favourite. But then her triumph had somehow lost its savour. It was funny how one act could wipe out the whole history of a relationship and change it for ever, be it an act of great generosity or an act of great unkindness.

In the space of one evening, a handful of hours, Rose

had, through her own act of kindness, changed Emerald's own life completely. Neither of them ever spoke of that night on the rare occasions when they met, but it still lay between them, a secret that linked them and which for Emerald had provided a vital escape from perpetual envy.

Would Rose come? It surprised Emerald to discover just how much she hoped that she might.

Chapter Sixty

What was happening in Macclesfield? Rose looked at the telephone. She so desperately wanted to be there, she realised with a small surge of shock.

It had been so many years now since she had stepped back from the old special closeness of her relationship with her aunt, filled with the bitterness and pain of discovering that Aunt Amber had simply been using her and had never loved her as she had pretended to do.

She had seen less and less of 'the family' as Pete's health had deteriorated – not that there had been an open breaking-off of her relationship with them. She was actually godmother to one of Janey's sons, and the elder of Emerald's daughters, but she had not expected to feel this irrational driven need to be 'there'.

Why should she? Aunt Amber did not need her to be there. After all, she had three daughters and two stepdaughters who all meant far more to her than Rose did.

But *she* needed to be there, Rose recognised. She wanted to be there; she had to be there.

Quickly she crossed the kitchen floor and picked up

the telephone receiver, dialling the number she knew by heart.

The moment the ringing at the other end was silenced, she knew instantly it was Josh, just from his breathing.

'It's me,' she told him. 'Rose. I need your help.' She wasn't really giving in to her own desire or to her love for him, she wasn't doing this for her own sake, she was doing it for Amber, to whom she owed so very much.

In less than five minutes it was all arranged. Josh would come and keep watch over Pete, freeing her to go to Macclesfield. She had struggled so hard to keep Josh out of her life, to deny herself and him any opportunity to share their love for one another because she was married to Pete, but now fate had stepped in and she really had no choice.

'So what am I to say to Mr Oliver when he comes in?' Maria demanded.

Looking up from checking that she had her passport safely in her wallet, Ella said, 'Tell him that I have had to go home because my father has had a heart attack. I must go, Maria, the cab's waiting. Look after Olivia for me and give her lots of hugs from me, won't you?' She couldn't delay any longer, otherwise she would miss her flight and there wouldn't be another one until the morning. Please God, let her father still be alive when she got there. It was pointless now to wish that she had spent more time with him during that last visit in January.

Josh arrived exactly when he had promised he would. Just the sight of him was enough to fill Rose with all the emotions she knew she had no right to have. She had married Pete willingly; no one had made her. She could not simply walk away from him because she loved Josh.

She felt so dangerously close to giving way to what she felt, to being weak. It was heaven to be in Josh's arms and held safely there, in their familiar comfort and warmth.

'I shouldn't have telephoned you.'

'Of course you should.' Josh's thumb wiped an escaped tear from her cheek, as he added softly, 'I'd have been as jealous as hell if you'd asked someone else. I want you to feel that you can always turn to me, Rose, for whatever you need.'

'I know that I can, and . . . and I wanted you to be here, but it's so wrong of me to . . . to involve you.'

Josh smoothed her hair off her face and then cupped it in his hands so that he could look into her eyes.

'Nothing that happens between us or that we feel for one another could ever be anything other than perfect and right. What was wrong was my stupidity in not realising how much I loved you, and letting you go. No, don't say anything. I know you are married to Pete, I know you won't leave him, but that doesn't have to mean that you and I can't be friends, does it?'

'Friends?' Rose's voice broke over the word. 'Josh, I can't trust myself to be just friends with you.'

'Then trust me instead to protect you and the future we will one day have, because I promise you that you can. I know how you feel about the duty you believe you owe to Pete.'

'He needs twenty-four-hour care, Josh. He can never

be well – his drinking has done too much damage to his body – but he could live for years as an invalid. No matter how much I love you and want to be with you, I can't abandon him.'

'I wouldn't ask you to. Let me help you, Rose. Let me share your life with you, even if it is only as a friend.'

'I couldn't ask that of you.'

'You don't have to ask. I'm the one making the offer. I love you and without you my life has been unbearably empty. When I bumped into Ella on Fifth Avenue and she told me about Pete, I knew that I had to come back to be with you. Don't shut me out, Rose. I need you just as much as Pete does. One day we will be the same age as your aunt and uncle. I know more than anything else that when the time comes I want yours to be the last hand I hold and the last face I see. You may be Pete's wife but you are my love, and you always will be. Somehow we'll find a way to make it work, Rose, I promise you.'

And Josh always kept his promises, she knew that.

Chapter Sixty-One

'We've been here ages, Emerald. What do you think's happening? No one's told us anything.'

Emerald could hear the anxiety in Janey's voice.

'You stay here,' she told her. 'I'll go and see if I can find out anything.'

The hospital was busier now than it had been when she had first arrived. One of the two women on the reception desk for the intensive care ward looked sympathetic when Emerald pointed out that they hadn't seen anyone who was able to explain how Jay was, but the woman wasn't able to say exactly when they would see the consultant.

'I can organise some tea for you,' the receptionist offered, 'and I'll try to have a word with the ward sister.'

'If you would, please,' Emerald thanked her. 'My mother is still with my stepfather and naturally we're all concerned about her as well.'

'Did you manage to find out anything?' Janey asked as soon as Emerald returned to the waiting room.

'No, but they're going to send us some tea.' She looked at her watch. 'Drogo should be here soon.'

It irked her a little to have to acknowledge that Drogo was likely to have more success in obtaining information from the hospital staff than she was herself, but the years had developed in Emerald a certain pragmatism over some things, and she knew there was no point in getting angry about things she couldn't change. Not when there were matters that needed to be dealt with that she could organise.

'When the others get here we'll need to have a talk about the future,' she warned Janey. 'I know that the first priority for you and Ella and the twins will be your father, and what's happening now, but we have to be practical as well. There'll be things to discuss and arrangements to be made.'

In case her father died, Janey knew Emerald meant.

In the small ward Amber was oblivious to everything but Jay. At some stage she had started to talk to him, just a few words at first, more speaking her own thoughts out aloud than anything else, and then she had felt his fingers tremble against her own and she had known that he had heard her, so she had kept on talking, not about her fear of losing him now but of the past and the happiness they had shared, the love they had shared. She had laughed as well as cried as the memories flooded over her and with their release had come a sense of peace.

She was still holding his hand. She felt tired, her eyes dry from the heat, and her throat raw from talking. Love was such a wonderful gift when it was shared, transforming those who shared it, illuminating the dark side of life, transcending mortality.

* * *

'Drogo.'

Robbie was nineteen and considered himself an adult, but the minute he saw Drogo he felt his eyes sting with tears, his emotions reminding him of the way he had felt as a boy, knowing always that he had his stepfather to turn to for comfort and protection.

From the depths of Drogo's warm hug he asked uncertainly, 'How's Gramps?'

'The last time I spoke to the Hospital they said he was holding his own.'

'Will he . . . is he . . . is he going to die?'

'I don't know, Robbie,' Drogo answered honestly. 'He's had what sounds like a serious heart attack, but on the plus side, your grandfather is a very strong and determined man, and if anyone can survive something like this then it's him. We'll know more once the consultant has the results of the tests that have been done.'

'When I saw him at Christmas he was joking that he'd put me to shame if he came skiing with me.'

'I dare say he would have done, as well. We've got fifteen minutes yet before your aunt Polly's flight comes in from Venice, let's go and have a cup of coffee whilst we're waiting for her.'

Manchester; funny how it always smelled of rain, even on a dry day like today, Polly thought, as she stepped off the aircraft.

'Polly.'

She hadn't expected anyone to meet her at the airport, but it was a relief to hear Drogo call her name, although disappointingly he had no further news about her father.

'Will we be able to see Gramps, Drogo?' Robbie asked as soon as the three of them were in the car and Drogo was driving them south towards Macclesfield.

'That will depend on the consultant. I've already spoken with his secretary and she's confirmed that he will see us and bring us up to date with what's happening once he's seen Jay and checked over the tests they've already done.'

'He's alive, though, now, isn't he?' Robbie pressed his stepfather anxiously, asking the question Polly had not felt able to voice.

'Yes he is,' Drogo confirmed.

'Have you seen him?' Robbie asked.

Drogo shook his head.

A young nursing assistant came into the waiting room carrying a tray with two thick earthenware mugs of tea on it, some sachets of sugar and a couple of small packets of biscuits, which she put down on the melamine coffee table before exiting the room.

'I never thought I'd be so grateful for a mug of tea,' said Janey as she reached for one of the mugs.

Emerald looked at the remaining mug. The tea in it was dark and so strong that she could actually smell it. Reluctantly she reached out to pick up the mug and then stopped as her stomach recoiled from both the sight and the smell of it and heaved nauseously.

'What's wrong?' Janey asked.

'Nothing,' Emerald fibbed. It wouldn't do to have Janey

thinking she was so badly affected by Jay's heart attack that she felt sick; not when, as Drogo had said, she must be the strong one.

She couldn't face drinking the tea, though, and it was still there untouched when Drogo arrived ten minutes later.

'Where's Polly?' Emerald asked him after she had greeted Robbie with a hug.

'She'll be in a second. She wanted to ring Rocco to tell him that she'd arrived safely.'

Emerald nodded. 'Drogo, I'm thirsty, but the tea they brought is dreadfully strong. Could you sort out some water for me, do you think?'

'I'll see what I can do.' Drogo looked at his watch. 'But first I want to give the consultant's secretary another ring and find out exactly when he's going to be here.'

The arrival of the twins in the waiting room virtually at the same time as one another provoked a new round of sibling greetings and hugs followed by a fresh spate of anxious questions.

'Drogo has gone to telephone the consultant's secretary,' was all Emerald could tell them. 'We won't know anything more really until he has seen Jay.'

'Can we see Daddy, and where's Mummy?' Cathy, the elder of the pair, demanded.

'No, and she is with your father,' Emerald answered. When she saw that the twins were about to start protesting she reminded them both firmly, 'Don't forget that your father is in intensive care, and will probably be sedated.'

'Emerald's right,' Janey supported her, looking up as Drogo walked back into the waiting room.

'The consultant was delayed,' he told them, 'an emergency that required his immediate attention, but he should be here shortly. Amber is still with Jay and is refusing point-blank to leave, as one would expect.'

'Poor Mummy,' said Cathy. 'She and Daddy have always been so devoted to one another.' In her voice was the fear that none of them wished to put into words – that Jay might not survive.

Thanks to Drogo fresh tea and coffee had appeared, along with bottled water for Emerald, and some surprisingly good sandwiches, according to Robbie, who was the only one so far who had eaten any of them.

'There's no point in us coming all this way to be here if we aren't even going to be allowed to see Daddy,' Cathy fretted.

Emerald exhaled and then said coolly, 'Yes there is. It's an excellent opportunity for us to deal with certain important issues, although I'd have preferred to wait until Rose gets here.'

'You think she will come then?' Janey queried.

Emerald didn't know, but she did know that the problem she wanted to discuss could not be properly discussed or resolved without Rose.

'She certainly owes it to Mummy to be here.' Cathy's voice was sharp, and loud enough to carry past the slightly open door to where Rose was hesitating outside in the corridor. 'Especially when you think of all that Mummy did for her.'

'No more was done for Rose than for any of the rest

of us—' Emerald started to point out, coming to an abrupt halt as Rose pushed open the door and stepped into the waiting room.

'Except that you are all either her own or Jay's daughters – and in the twins' case both – whilst I am not,' she said quietly.

'Oh, Rose, Cathy didn't mean anything,' Janey was quick to say, and just as quick to get up and give Rose a fierce hug. 'We're all on edge because we're so worried.'

Cathy, who was now looking self-conscious and guilty, confirmed, 'Janey's right. I'm sorry, Rose, I didn't mean it the way it sounded.'

'No? Then what did you mean? Perhaps that since my father was disinherited by our mutual great-grandmother I should not, like everyone else, have had a trust fund? Or maybe perhaps that since I am what I so obviously am, that I should, as that same great-grandmother was so fond of saying, been sent back to the slums of Hong Kong and left to die there?'

Rose could see that she had shocked them all. That hadn't been her intention but the conversation she had overheard had somehow not just touched a nerve but pressed a spring that had released a jack-in-the-box of destructive self-defence.

'Now it's my turn to apologise.' She gave a tired shrug and pushed her hand through her hair.

'Behaving as though we're still in the nursery isn't going to help anyone,' Emerald told them all. 'Now that Rose is here I think we should talk about what will need to be done, whilst we have the chance. We've got a lot of things to sort out whilst we're here together,' Emerald reminded her siblings.

Janey paled and looked close to tears whilst Robbie tried to look grown up as he stood by her side.

'I don't think that this is an appropriate time to be talking about this kind of thing. Don't you think we should wait and see what the consultant has to say before we start making any plans?' Cathy challenged Emerald sharply. 'After all, the parents may have made their own arrangements for if anything should happen.'

'On the contrary,' Emerald told Cathy sturdily, 'I can't think of a more appropriate time. The discussion I want to have applies whatever the future might hold, and in my opinion is best discussed now whilst we have the time to do so. We need to talk about the business. We all know how much the business means to Mummy.'

When no one made any comment Emerald continued, 'You may all have been too busy with your own lives to notice what's been going on with the London end of things, and of course it's only natural that I should have seen more and been more aware of it because I live there.'

'What do you mean?' Polly demanded. 'The factory is doing very well. I know that Angelli puts a lot of business its way.'

'The factory may be doing well but I am talking about the Walton Street shop,' Emerald clarified. 'Mummy hasn't been coming down to London as often as she once did, and I rather expect that she won't want to come down at all in future, no matter what happens.'

'Well, the shop can be closed down, can't it?' Janey asked,

after a long pause whilst they all digested what Emerald was saying.

'It can, yes,' Emerald agreed.

They didn't share the kind of closeness with one another that would have enabled her to explain how she had felt when she had seen her mother's face when she had looked at Emerald's Designers Guild bedroom, even if she hadn't been the kind of person who loathed talking about her own feelings. To see such sadness and loss in her mother's expression had reminded Emerald of how important to her mother the interior design business was. At the time that hadn't really mattered, but now somehow it did.

'The property could be sold quite easily, I imagine,' Janey continued.

'Very easily,' Emerald agreed, 'but I don't think that's what we should do.'

'What do you mean?' That was Cathy, the rebel who had always taken delight in doing the opposite of what was expected of her.

'We all know how much silk means to Mummy, both via Denby Mill and the Walton Street shop, how passionately she has always felt about her own father's designs and the heritage that goes with all of that. More than anything else she wanted that heritage to be preserved and woven into a future.'

'Well, yes, we all know that, Emerald. That was why she sent me and Polly to Italy to train at Angelli's.'

'That was part of the reason,' Emerald agreed. 'The other part was surely that she hoped you would give back to Denby Mill and the Walton Street business something of what she had given you.'

There was a small tense silence, and then Polly objected, 'Oh, that's good coming from you, Emerald, trying to make us feel guilty about the shop, and make sacrifices because we trained at Angelli's, whilst you get off scot-free because all you ever did was be a deb and marry Drogo.'

'It wasn't my intention to make you feel guilty. I simply wanted us to discuss what we felt we could all do to help get the business back on its feet. And as for making sacrifices, well, there's only one of us who would have to do that.'

They all looked at her.

'Who?' Janey asked.

'Rose,' Emerald announced. 'It was Rose who Mummy always wanted to take over from her.'

'That was a long time ago, Emerald. I have Pete to think of now, and it's years since I worked professionally as an interior designer,' Rose protested.

'We all know how much the Walton Street shop and its business has meant to Mummy,' Emerald continued, ignoring Rose's outburst. 'After all, she wanted all of you to be involved in its future, and she planned for that.'

A shared uncomfortable and guilty silence met Emerald's unexpected comments.

'It's my belief that, more than anything else, whatever happens to Jay, what will give Mummy more comfort and hope than anything else will be the survival and renewed success of the Walton Street business. At the moment it's dying on its feet and it needs new life breathed into it.'

Emerald paused, but none of them had missed the significance of her choice of language.

'Its designs are old-fashioned, and so is the shop. The whole business needs revamping, and that is something we could all contribute to. It needs new designers for the fabrics. You two, Polly and Cathy, could take on the fabric design side of things.'

'No.'

'Impossible.'

The twins spoke together.

'I live in Italy now, Emerald, and even if I could make the time, it's been years since I last did any designing,' Polly told her.

'I'm an artist, Emerald,' Cathy protested crossly.

'I'm not suggesting that either of you design the fabrics yourself – as you've both said, neither of you is really qualified to do so any more – but you, Polly, are married to a man who provides what is regarded as the best training for young untested designers there is, and you, Cathy, have the skill to recognise the potential in the young graduates coming out of St Martins and the like. There is nothing to stop you selecting the best of the new designers straight from college, and nothing to stop you and Rocco, Polly, offering them a chance to spent six months with Angelli's, really learning their trade, with a view to them then giving at least a year each to the Walton Street shop designing new fabrics.'

Polly felt curiously light-headed. How extraordinary that it should be Emerald, of all people, who should have come up with such an innovative and exciting idea. What Emerald had suggested had so many possibilities, so many potential challenges, so much about it that was unexpectedly close to her heart.

'And before you say that you can't check out St Martins students from St Ives, Cathy, what is there to stop you and Sim spending some of your time in London, and opening a gallery there as well?'

'I don't want a London gallery.'

'Maybe you don't, but what about Sim?'

Emerald had touched on a nerve. Sim was a wonderfully creative sculptor; he deserved and needed a wider audience for his work, Cathy knew that.

'You could send both the girls to St Paul's – I'm sure they're clever enough – and you could even display some of your work in the Walton Street shop until we find the right place for a gallery, and as a family you could stay in the Chelsea house when you are in London.'

She had been outmartialled and outmanoeuvred by an expert, Cathy recognised. But she wasn't going to give in just like that; that wasn't her way.

'You're doing a lot of talking about what we should be doing, Emerald, but what exactly are you planning to do personally to help the business, apart from telling us what to do, of course?'

'I shall be using my address book to drum up new clients for the Walton Street business. As a starting point I shall offer two or three of London's top charity organisers an auction prize for their next charity ball of a room makeover by Walton Street.'

Cathy gave a protesting gasp. 'But that will cost thousands.'

'And as an investment will bring in a hundred times more than it costs,' Emerald blocked her protest crisply.

'Emerald's right,' Janey felt obliged to agree – and not

because of the money Emerald had promised her. Janey could remember the demand she herself had created for her clothes all those years ago when favoured friends had worn them. She gave a small sad sigh. 'It all sounds wonderfully exciting. I feel quite envious,' she admitted.

'You will have your role to play as well, Janey,' Emerald assured her. 'I'm hoping that Rose will agree to take on the role of interior designer, but she'll need help, and I think the two of you could work really well together.'

'I can't leave Pete,' Rose reiterated.

Emerald looked away from her and down at the floor, and Rose knew what she was thinking: that one day Pete was going to die and leave her.

'But how do you know that Mummy will want us to do any of this?' Polly asked. 'We could be taking something from her that she doesn't want to give up.'

This time it was Drogo who spoke up. 'For what it's worth, my guess is that Jay will pull through this but Amber won't want to leave him to travel up and down to London, Emerald is right about that. I believe, like Emerald, that Amber will be grateful to you all for taking over for her.'

'So it's down to you, Rose,' Emerald said challengingly. 'Will you do it?'

Rose wanted to refuse, she wanted to remind them of what Cathy had been saying about her only a short time ago, but most of all she wanted to let the bitterness and all the hurt of rejection and abandonment she had bottled up over the years spill out in front of them as she told them exactly why she was refusing.

Only somehow she couldn't. Somehow, instead, she

was nodding her head, giving in, as she had always given in, being weak as she had always been weak, and despising herself for it.

Amber felt the now familiar rush of air that meant that someone was approaching Jay's bed, but she didn't lift her gaze from her husband's face to see who it was. Every second was too precious for a single one of them to be wasted.

It took the sister's determined, 'Mr Stanhope wishes to speak to you,' to drag Amber's attention away from Jay to look at the consultant.

'I won't leave Jay,' she told him immediately.

A square-looking man in his fifties with a bald head and a steady gaze, dressed in a crisp white shirt, a bow tie and a pin-striped suit, he smiled at her.

'Your family are in the waiting room. I've promised to talk to them.'

'Have you got the results of the tests yet?' Amber asked him, ignoring his hint that it would be easier if he talked to them all at the same time.

'Yes.'

'And?' Amber pressed, adding determinedly, 'You'll have to tell me here because I won't leave Jay.'

The consultant looked at the sister, who pulled up a spare chair for him so that he could sit down.

Chapter Sixty-Two

'Drogo, do go and see if you can find out what's happening,' Emerald urged her husband. 'The consultant was supposed to be here ages ago.'

'Do you think that Daddy knew about his heart?' Janey couldn't stop herself from asking after Drogo had gone.

It was a question none of them could answer, but their growing tension was reflected in the way they all reacted when the waiting-room door opened several minutes later, heralding Drogo's return.

'The consultant's with Amber, and he'll be coming to speak to us in a few minutes.'

'He's with Mother?'

'Is that a good idea?'

'What if it's bad news?'

'She shouldn't be seeing him on her own.'

Before Drogo could answer them the door opened again and this time it was the consultant.

The introductions had been made and tea had been brought, Emerald once again forced to hold back her nausea the minute she smelled the strong brew, and now they were all sitting waiting to hear what the consultant had to say.

Janey was sitting on the edge of her chair with her hands underneath her so that she could resist her old childhood habit of nibbling at her nails, whilst Rose was sitting next to her, so white-faced with tension that she looked as though she was wearing rice powder. Polly and Cathy had drawn their chairs closer together, whilst Robbie was sitting between Emerald and Drogo, Emerald holding his hand and Drogo placing a supporting arm around the back of his chair.

'As you all know, Jay has had a heart attack.'

'But how serious is it?'

'Will he have another?'

'He is going to get better, isn't he?'

'How is Mummy?'

The consultant nodded in acknowledgement of all their questions.

'To answer your last question first, Amber is being incredibly brave and strong, and she is insisting on remaining here at the hospital with Jay. I have told her that I will only allow that if she agrees to take some rest herself. A private room will be put at her disposal for that purpose. It is the least we can do since your parents have been so generous in their fund-raising for the hospital.'

'And Jay himself?' Drogo asked.

The consultant frowned. 'The tests show that the attack was severe. However, we can be reasonably optimistic that as there hasn't been a second attack, his condition has now stabilised.'

'Does that mean that he's going to live?' Janey asked shakily.

'Hopefully, but from now on, as I have already told Amber, he will have to be careful not to do anything that might provoke a second attack.'

'But surely there are operations,' Cathy began. 'I've read about people having whole heart transplants.'

'Yes, that's true, but that kind of operation is not appropriate in your father's case. There are new treatments for his condition being undertaken in South Africa and America, but it is too soon as yet in my opinion to know how successful these are in the long term. However, with care and if he lives relatively quietly from now on, with modern drugs there is no reason to suppose that he will not live out his normal life span.'

The consultant could see their relief and, indeed, almost feel it in the air of buoyancy and delight that was filling the room.

'There is still some way to go before we can pronounce him fully out of danger,' he warned them, 'but I have every confidence in your mother's ability to ensure that everything that needs to be done to aid his recovery and his future health will be done.'

The consultant had gone, there had been tears and smiles, shared hugs and emotional laughter between the three who were Jay's daughters, whilst Rose and Emerald stood slightly to one side.

Janey had offered all those who wanted one a bed at Fitton, but Emerald had said that they should go back to Denham instead because there would be things to do there to prepare for her mother and Jay's eventual return.

The others, including Rose, had agreed that they would take on the responsibility for the Walton Street shop, and now Emerald acknowledged she felt very tired and was longing for a hot bath.

There was something, though, that she still had to do. Something important. A debt that had to be repaid and that belonged to the memory of a busy A&E department and the way she had felt when Rose had been there for her.

'The consultant told Drogo that Mummy asked if Rose was here.'

Rose could feel the colour burning up under her skin.

'I think that one of us should stay and that it should be you, Rose. You always were her favourite.'

'No. I wasn't, I—'

'Yes you were. She as good as admitted it to me years ago, when she told me that she felt that the two of you shared a special bond.'

There was nothing Rose could say or do now, other than simply give in.

'Do we know yet whether or not Ella is coming?' Janey asked.

Drogo shook his head.

Looking at her siblings, Emerald recognised that she no longer felt like an outsider amongst them. Without it being planned or worked for, finally she had what as a child she had longed for so fiercely and rejected even more fiercely – acceptance.

* * *

608

In the intensive care unit Amber smiled shakily through her tears of relief and gratitude.

'Thank you for not leaving me,' she whispered to Jay, and she was sure that the small twitch of his lips meant that he had heard her and that he was smiling at her.

Now with the crisis over she was able to think about its effect on their shared family. Sister had told her about their arrival and their anxiety. Was Rose here? Her heart jumped with pain. She had never stopped wondering what it was that had caused Rose to become so distant towards her, and never stopped grieving for the bond that had been lost, either.

She could still see Rose now as the tiny sick baby she had been when she had first seen her and had felt those unmistakable pangs of maternal protective love for her. That love had grown with Rose – the niece who, in her heart, Amber had always thought of as a daughter.

Drogo waited until no one else could overhear them to ask Emerald, on the way to the car, 'What was all that about the consultant saying that your mother had asked for Rose?'

'It's about mending fences, healing rifts and paying debts,' Emerald told him, grimacing as she added, 'I don't know what's the matter with me today, Drogo, but I've felt dreadfully sick every time I've looked at a cup of tea, and now all I want to do is go to sleep, when I should be too worried about what's going on to even think of sleeping. The last time I remember feeling like this was—' Abruptly Emerald stopped speaking at exactly the same moment as Drogo stopped walking and turned towards her.

'When you were first pregnant with Emma,' he finished for her.

'I can't be. I mean, we haven't even been trying, and . . . oh, Drogo!'

She was in his arms, trembling, as he held her close.

'I daren't even hope that I might be in case I'm not,' she admitted. 'I mean, if I was pregnant now, after all this time, it would almost be a miracle. Oh, Drogo . . .'

Ella was exhausted and frantic with anxiety and misery. Her flight had been diverted to Charles de Gaulle because of some problem with one of the engines, instead of landing at Heathrow, and then she had had to wait for a connecting flight to Manchester.

The plane had landed in the darkness of the early February evening in an icy wind laden with a wet sleet that was somehow far colder and wetter than even the worst of New York's winter snowfalls, and certainly far worse than the crisp stinging cold of the skiing season in Vermont.

Her antagonism towards weather that she felt was being deliberately inhospitable made her sharply aware of how Americanised she had become and how alien her own country now felt.

Manchester wasn't home any more; it was simply a cold damp place, the airport staffed by people whose accents, striking an unfamiliar note, jarred on her nerves.

She still had to get to the hospital. What would she find there? What if her father had had another attack? What if he wasn't . . . but no, she must not think like that.

She had travelled light, with a small case as hand luggage, so there was nothing to stop her going straight through Customs and heading for the arrivals area. The long line of people several deep, straining against the barrier, waiting for those coming off the newly landed planes took her by surprise, and then had her hopefully scanning their faces, hoping she might see one that was familiar. But when she did see two familiar faces she stopped dead in her tracks in disbelief.

Oliver and Olivia. How was it possible for them to be here?

She must have asked the question, she knew, but if he had heard it Oliver wasn't answering it. Instead he was taking her case from her, the warm gust of his breath against her face as he did so filled with the familiar smell of his favourite menthol chewing gum.

'Mummy, we beat you to it.'

That was Olivia, dancing up and down as she beamed at her.

'My plane was diverted.'

'Yes, I know.'

That was Oliver, his voice grim and his face shuttered.

Ella grabbed hold of his arm. 'What are you doing here and why have you brought Olivia?'

'Why do you think? I'm your husband and Jay is her grandfather. Where else should we be? I might not be able to stop you from shutting me out, Ella – after all, I learned years ago how ashamed of me you are, the working-class photographer husband you never really wanted to marry – but I'm damned if I'm going to let you shut out Olivia. She has a right to be here. She's just as much a part of your family as you are. The same blood runs in her veins as runs in yours – your sisters are her aunts, their kids are her cousins. You might not like that, you might prefer to pretend that she and I don't exist because you'd have rather had someone like Brad father your kids, but he didn't and I did, and I'm not having my daughter excluded from her family because her mother's a snob who can't bear her family knowing the man she married.' He gave her a bitter look. 'What exactly is it you think I'm going to do – eat peas off my knife? Or is the fact that I am what I am enough to make you ashamed of me, without me having to do anything to prove my unworthiness?'

They were almost alone in the arrivals hall now and, to Ella's relief, Olivia was fiddling with her transistor radio, which Ella had once bought her in London and which the little girl had brought with her, no doubt trying to tune it in to a pop music station, and hadn't, Ella hoped, been able to hear Oliver's fiercely angry speech.

His words had rained down on Ella like a fire storm, shocking her into immobility.

In fact, she was so taken aback, so stunned by what Oliver had said, that the only response she could manage was a shaken, 'I have never been ashamed of you.'

'Then why have you always refused to have your family over or let me meet them properly?'

Ella badly wanted to sit down but there was nowhere to sit apart from the bench where Olivia already was.

'That was for your sake,' she told Oliver truthfully. 'Because you are always so busy and because I didn't want you to feel that I expected you to behave like a proper husband just because you'd married me. It was for your sake, Oliver,' she repeated when she saw that he was simply looking at her, 'because I wanted you to have your freedom. And don't tell me that you didn't want it. That model you rang on Christmas Day . . .'

'Because she'd rung me earlier, out of her head on acid – she didn't know what century she was in, never mind what day. She thought we'd got a shoot.'

Ella could see that he was telling her the truth. 'You mean you aren't in love with her?'

'*What?* Are you crazy?' Oliver made a sweepingly dismissive and frustrated gesture with his hand. 'There was never anyone else after you – there couldn't be.'

Her legs were threatening to stop supporting her. She felt shaky and filled with a mixture of disbelief and – ridiculously – hope.

'You married me because of Olivia.'

'Yes,' Oliver agreed. 'And, like the working-class lad I'd grown up as, once married my loyalty was to you – my loyalty and then my love. That's how it is with us working-class boys. Our wives and the children they give us come first in our hearts and our lives, or at least that's how it was with this working-class boy.'

'You never said.'

'How could I when you were mooning around over your lost American hero?'

'I was doing no such thing.'

'You were mooning around over something or someone.'

'Didn't it ever strike you that you might not be the only person to discover that the creation of a child can

613

lead to you finding that you love the person you created that child with? Especially when you're a woman who knows all she does know about good sex because of the man who created that child with her.'

'Are you saying that you loved me?' Oliver's voice was both hoarse and uncharacteristically lacking in its normal self-assurance.

'No,' Ella told him crisply, suddenly finding her courage. She could see pain in his gaze before he hid it from her. 'I'm not saying that I loved you, Oliver, because my love for you isn't in the past, it's here now in the present, and it will be there in the future.'

It really was ridiculous for two people of their age, who were married to one another, and whose daughter was sitting within watching distance, to be kissing so passionately in public, and all the more so given the circumstances, but somehow the sweetness of the moment meant too much to be denied, and it was several long minutes before Ella could bring herself to let Oliver end the kiss.

Still held tight in his arms she reminded him, 'We need to get to the hospital. My father . . .'

'Is holding his own and doing very well,' Oliver assured her. 'I spoke to the Hospital when Olivia and I got through Customs. Emerald had left a message for you to say we're to go straight to Denham, because that's where the rest of the family are.'

The family. How easily and comfortably Oliver said those words, and how right they sounded coming from him. The family, her family, their family. She loved them, of course, but the reality was that the true family of her heart was this family: Oliver and Olivia and her.

Sister had come in to insist that since Jay was now out of danger, Amber was to go and eat the meal she'd ordered to be taken to the waiting room for her.

'There's no sense in you making yourself ill,' she had pointed out, 'especially not now that Mr Fulshawe is over the worst.'

Amber was still smiling over those words: 'Mr Fulshawe is over the worst' when she pushed open the door to the waiting room, her contented smile turning to one of disbelief and joy at what, or rather who, she saw waiting for her.

'Rose. Oh, Rose. My dearest dear girl.'

Overwhelmed by her emotions, Amber held nothing back, hugging Rose to her as tightly as she could, her tears spilling onto Rose's face.

The familiarity of her aunt's rose and almond scent, her warmth and, above all, the emotion she exuded instantly transported Rose back to a time when her world had held no greater joy than to be held in her aunt's arms. How naïve she had been then.

'The consultant said that Jay is going to get better,' was all she could manage to say when Amber had finally released her.

'Yes. Thank God. Oh, Rose, you don't know how much it means to me to have you here.'

'Emerald felt that one of us should stay, although I know you would probably have preferred it to be Emerald herself. After all, she is your daughter.'

Rose had meant the words to sound cool, unemotional, level; setting the demarcation line between the past she had once inhabited and the present where she now lived, but to her chagrin instead they sounded more like the jealous reproachful outburst of a small child.

Amber looked at her niece, her heart aching for the relationship they had had before Rose had retreated from her.

Amber abhorred emotional blackmail and yet she couldn't stop herself from saying truthfully, 'Yes, Emerald is my child, the daughter of my flesh, Rose, and I love her as I love all of you, but you are and always have been the daughter of my heart, and as such you are very special to me.'

It was more than Rose could bear.

'If that's the truth then why have you never told me that John might be my half-brother?'

Amber's heart was pounding so heavily, it felt like an unbearable weight. She sank into a chair, her hand against her chest. It all seemed so long ago now, that terrible time and its dreadful consequences. She never spoke of it, not even to Jay.

'Ella and Janey's aunt Cassandra told me, if you're wondering how I know,' Rose continued. 'She'd recognised that I had a bit of a crush on John and naturally she wanted to make sure that I didn't get any ideas above my station. Not that she needed to worry. I was quite content to hero-worship John from a distance. I knew that with my background I could never be anything to a Lord Fitton.'

'Oh, Rose . . .'

The pain and bitterness in Rose's voice pushed aside Amber's own anxiety, her heart returning to its normal steady beat, her one desire to reach out to her niece. This was Cassandra's revenge, of course, for what had happened so long ago. The destruction of a very precious bond, a lifetime of pain for an innocent victim, and for Cassandra herself the satisfaction of having delivered those blows.

'Cassandra told me how you'd all hoped that I wouldn't survive, how it would have been better for everyone if I had died.'

'Rose, that isn't true.'

'How my own father hated me and wished that I had never been born.'

Amber's throat closed on the lump of pity and love that had formed there.

'Come and sit down. Please,' she begged.

Rose gave in and sat down in one of the other chairs.

'The whole situation is so complicated, Rose. Your father, my cousin, was a charming, self-willed and spoiled young man, handsome, indulged by our grandmother, and loved by me. I thought him the best and the kindest of cousins. But Greg's outward charm concealed a great deal of inner weakness. He had an inability to accept the responsibility for . . . for his own mistakes and errors of judgement. There was an . . . an affair with Lord Fitton's wife.'

'John's mother?'

'Yes. But John had already been born when the scandal broke and our grandmother had to send Greg away to Hong Kong. There was to have been another child, but John's mother . . . well, there was an accident, and she drowned in one of the Fitton Hall pools. Cassandra found her.' Amber stopped and took a deep breath.

'Rose, I must ask that what I am going to tell you now remains always just between the two of us.'

'And if I can't agree to that?'

'Then I cannot tell you.'

They looked at one another.

'Very well then,' Rose agreed. 'You have my word that I will never speak of it to anyone else.'

Amber nodded. 'Greg wasn't the only person with whom John's mother was having a relationship outside her marriage.'

Rose tensed. This wasn't what she had been expecting to hear.

'There's no easy way to say this, Rose, but the fact of the matter is that Cassandra was very much involved with her, almost obsessively so.'

Rose stared at her aunt, the colour draining from her face, her mind a whirlwind of barely possible thoughts.

'You see, Rose, sometimes a secret isn't simple but instead is the result of a complex tangle of things past and done, meaning that the secret can't be brought out into the open without many innocent people being hurt. None of us can say that Greg could not have been John's father, but neither can we say that he was. It is my belief that Cassandra hoped to have a son of her own with John's father and that if she had done so she would have tried to have John disinherited. Without a son, when John's father died it was in her own interests for John to inherit. John grew up believing himself to be Lord

Fitton Legh's son. The estate is his whole world. Perhaps someone should have spoken out all those years ago.'

'No,' Rose said shakily. 'No. It would have been cruel and unnecessary.'

'I can see now that you should have been told once you were old enough to understand. Greg was your father, after all.'

'And I was the child that no one wanted; the half-Chinese embarrassment, that you all wished did not exist.'

'Rose, that isn't true. I loved you from the first minute I saw you. You touched my heart as no other child has ever done. Here in my heart you have always been loved, always been mine.'

Against her will Rose could feel the tug on her emotions, but she wasn't going to give in to it.

'If that's true, and you loved me so much, why did you leave me at Denham with a father who couldn't care less about me and a great-grandmother who would have happily seen me dead? It is true, isn't it, that Blanche ordered the doctor not to try to save me? And yes, before you ask, Cassandra did tell me. If you had really loved me you would never have left me there. You would have taken me with you.'

'Rose, I couldn't. There were reasons. Luc was already at school and you would have been alone in the nursery. Robert . . .' Amber's voice broke slightly as she remembered how hard those days had been. 'I had a duty to Robert that meant I wouldn't have been able to be with you.'

'So you abandoned me, hoping that I would die; that

I wouldn't grow up to ask the kind of awkward questions that might lead to the secrets that had to be protected being exposed. You didn't love me at all. Cassandra was right, you just pretended that you did. Didn't you ever stop to think about what you were doing? Wasn't it bad enough that you had stolen from me the right to know that I might have a half-brother, without taking my love as well in exchange for worthless lies?'

Rose started to get up. She had said far more than she had ever imagined herself saying – too much – and now she felt drained and exhausted, but somehow still not cleansed of all the old hurt or the pain that went with it. She had loved her aunt with a child's trusting love, and the hurt her aunt's betrayal had caused her would always be a part of her.

'Rose, please listen to me.' Amber had stood up now as well. 'I did leave you at Denham, yes, but you were never alone and unprotected just as you were never out of my thoughts. You see, Rose, I entrusted you to the one person I knew beyond any other I could rely on to look after you and be your guardian angel for me.'

Rose frowned. There was so much emotion in her aunt's voice that she was compelled to listen.

'What do you mean?'

'I entrusted you to Jay, Rose. He visited you every day, he wrote to me to tell me how you were. He took photographs of you for me; he was there for you all the time, when I could not be. He carried my love to you, and kept you safe.'

Rose bit her lip, trying to hold back her tears. Amber's words had put a totally different slant on everything, showing her a care and a commitment she had never known existed and which she knew as an adult could only have come from love.

'The minute I looked at you, I felt such a bond with you, Rose. For me that bond is still there.'

'I was so hurt by what Cassandra told me. I felt—'

'Exactly what Cassandra wanted you to feel.'

They looked at one another, exchanging unsteady smiles.

It was Amber who moved first, reaching out to touch Rose's hair and then her cheek, and then they were hugging one another, both of them crying and smiling.

There was no going back to the past and what had been lost there – that was impossible – but there was the future and the chance to rebuild their relationship together.

Epilogue

'To Emerald. Many, many happy returns.'

Everyone raised their champagne flutes in acknowledgement of Drogo's birthday toast, whilst Emerald herself looked ruefully at her own glass of lemonade. She was four and a half months pregnant now, and over the weeks of morning sickness, but the thought of alcohol still nauseated her.

Drogo and her mother had organised a family get-together at Denham to celebrate her birthday and, unexpectedly to Emerald, the whole family were there.

'That was a wonderful suggestion of Drogo's to John that we start holding an annual open-air rock festival at Fitton, Emerald,' Janey told her. 'John's thrilled to bits about it. Oh, there's Ella. I must go and have a word with her to congratulate her. How lovely that both of you are having babies this year.'

As Janey hurried over to her sister, Rose seized her opportunity to have Emerald to herself.

'There's something I want to know,' she announced.

'Mmm?'

'Why did you tell me that Mama had asked me to stay at the hospital with her when Jay had his heart attack?'

The old closeness between Amber and Rose had returned to such an extent that Rose was now back to calling Amber 'Mama' again.

'Oh, good heavens, Rose, that was months ago.'

'That's not good enough. You and I both know that she didn't ask for me, and that it's thanks to you that she and I are back to where we were.'

Emerald looked at her cousin. 'Very well. Do you remember the night you took me to A&E after Max had hurt me?'

'Yes,' Rose said.

'You left your jacket with me, it smelled of you and it made me feel . . . it made me feel that I wasn't alone. You made me feel that I wasn't alone, Rose, despite the awful way I had treated you when we were growing up together. I clung to that jacket like a baby, but then you know that, don't you?'

The question slipped in so unexpectedly had Rose's eyes widening.

'I saw you, you see,' Emerald told her. 'There was a mirror near to me and when I looked into it I saw you stop and then step back because you knew I wouldn't want you to see me crying like a baby clinging to a rag comforter. That's why I told you that Mummy had asked for you. I owed you. I had a debt to you I wanted to repay, and just as you'd seen my pain and misery, so I'd seen yours.'

'Oh, Emerald.'

'Oh, Rose.'

They looked at one another and then they both started to laugh.

'You OK?'

Rose nodded her head and smiled up at Josh. This was their first outing together since Pete's death six weeks earlier.

Rose still didn't know just what had woken her that night, what had caused her, impelled her, to go to Pete's bedroom, but as she had told Josh, she liked to think that it was love. Not the love she had for Josh – that was his alone – but a strong love nevertheless, a love that Pete had known she had for him and which he had called upon so that she would be there with him for that precious short time before his life slipped away. She had seen immediately that he had had some kind of seizure, or stroke, and had called out the emergency doctor, who had arrived within fifteen minutes. He had told her that he felt that Pete didn't have very long to live and had asked her if she wanted him to send for an ambulance to take him to hospital. Rose had looked at Pete and something in his eyes had given her her answer.

She had reached for his hand and held it tightly, keeping her gaze on him as she told the doctor, 'No, I think he would want to be here.'

Pete's fingers had moved within her clasp and Rose had known she had done the right thing.

The doctor had nodded his head, said that he would see himself out and that she was to call him if she felt she needed to. They had had two hours, not a long time in which to say all that Rose wanted to say, but somehow it had been enough. She had told him of her guilt, and her sorrow, she had asked for his forgiveness and given him her own, and once she had started to open her heart to him the words had flowed in a cleansing healing flood that washed away what wasn't needed.

She had talked of the first time they had met, the night they had spent together, and she had seen him smile at her with the side of his face that could still move.

She had seen that he was sinking, his skin becoming soft and waxen, and she had got up from the bed to go to the windows and open them wide. Wasn't it said that the soul needed to fly free?

It had taken her only seconds, but when she returned to the bed she could see that he had slipped further away from her.

She had held his hand, told him how special he was, and then kissed his forehead as he breathed his last breath.

They had never spoken of his death or his wishes, but somehow it had been as though they had and that she knew beyond any doubting what to do.

There had been a simple church service, and then a wake that was a magnificent celebration of his life to the sound of his music and the voices of those who remembered him best.

Life was such a precious gift. Rose smiled again at Josh.

They had agreed that she would sell the house and that they would be together without making any concrete plans. There wasn't any need. They knew their own hearts too well to need them. It was enough that they were together.

'I still feel I've let you down.'

'Well, you haven't,' Janey told John fiercely. 'Marrying you has brought me so much happiness, John.'

'When I damn near bankrupted us?'

'You've given me something far more important than money. You've given me love, John. You've loved me without asking anything of me other than that I love you back. We're so lucky, we've got each other and the boys, and Fitton.'

She would never, Janey promised herself, let him know just how frightened she had been or how much it had shocked her to discover that he could be vulnerable and weak, just as she could herself. More than ever now John needed to be her hero, her knight in shining armour – for his sake, not hers. She was the strong one now, the one on whom he depended, not the other way around. Swings and roundabouts, that was marriage, Janey thought to herself.

'Have you told Emerald yet that she isn't going to be the only one adding to the next generation?' Oliver murmured in Ella's ear.

'I think everyone knows, though I am only just three months,' Ella reminded him.

'Mmm. I think I can remember the exact night,' Oliver teased her.

Amber surveyed her family. So many years, so much love, she could almost feel it in the air, like the soft warm wind of the South of France, carrying with it the mental images and memories of all those now gone who had played their part in creating the children and grand-children who were here today, and carrying with it too their love.

Love didn't die. It was always there, a rainbow dance just out of sight like laughter on the wind.

'This would have made Robert so happy and proud.'

The sound of her husband's voice had her looking at him with love and gratitude.

'So you sense it too?' she asked him. 'You sense like me that Robert knows, that he and Luc know and share in this, in the family?'

Jay knew her so well; she never needed to explain things to him. She knew he would understand why she wanted to include her first husband and the son she had lost in today's joy.

It was Emerald who, seeing her mother and her step-father smiling at one another, went over to her own husband and whispered something to him, so that a few minutes later, with everyone's glass refilled, Drogo raised his own to say warmly, 'Another toast, this time to Amber, who is responsible for all of this, and all of us – in one way or another.' His hand swept in an amused gesture, followed by appreciative laughter.

'Amber.'

'Mama.'

'Grandma.'

Please let them all always have today's happiness, Amber thought protectively. Please let them all have love.

The 1950's Style Guide

Loved the glamour of Penny Jordan's *Sins*? Learn how to get the look with our ultimate 1950's style guide . . .

Teen

Think pedal pushers. Think leather jackets. Think *Grease!*

❤ Team your favourite **pedal pushers** with an off-both-shoulders **t-shirt** and finish with a **leather jacket**, wearing the collar up. Accessorise with a coloured **scarf** around the neck and hair pulled back into a **ponytail**.

Let's Twist Again . . .

Off to a dance with your new beau, but still searching for that perfect outfit?

❤ Grab your **poodle skirt**, team it with a short-sleeved **blouse** and sling a **cashmere sweater** across your shoulders. Wear hair half-up half-down and tie with a **ribbon**. Don't forget your dancing shoes!

Desperate Housewife

Stuck at home doing the housework all day? Be the glamest girl on your street with the following combination . . .

❤ For this look you'll need a **full-skirt dress**, preferably with a **polka dot** print. **Belt** it around the middle to pinch in your waist, accessorise with **pearls** and pull your hair in a **French pleat**. Protect your clothes with an **apron**.

Golden Girl Glamour

If the timeless glamour of Marilyn is your thing, then this is the look for you.

❤ Team a white, chiffon, **halter-neck dress** with high-heeled **sandals**. The dress should have a full, pleated skirt, which is cinched at the waist, giving you a fantastic hourglass figure. Finish with **diamante** earrings and necklace and **curl** your hair, leaving it loose.

Working Girl

Even when you're on the job from nine 'til five, you still want to look your best. Let us show you how, 1950s style . . .

❤ Dig out your **pencil skirt** and **stockings**, and team them with a double or single breasted short **jacket** with a nipped-in waist. Finish with high **heels**, short **gloves**, and backcomb your hair into a **beehive**. As an alternative to the beehive, this look can be worn with a **pillbox hat**.

SILK

Penny Jordan

Dangerous liaisons . . .

Skeletons in closets . . .

A scandalous web of lies and deceit . . .

The Pickfords are just your average family.

Cheshire, the 1920s, a time of great glamour and decadence, high living and loose morality, a time where anything goes – and does.

Amber Vrontsky is the heiress to the Pickford dynasty, presided over by the formidable Blanche.

Obsessed with social climbing, Blanche wants nothing more for her granddaughter than a titled husband – something which, despite her immense wealth, she failed to secure.

But Amber is a free spirit, intent on forging her own artistic career with the silk she loves so much. Unable to disobey Blanche, however, she moves to society London to become a debutante – and enters a world of illicit affairs, drug-taking, gambling, lavender marriages . . .

From the lavish decadence of society London to the opium dens of the Far East, the chic boutiques of Paris to the Nazi-controlled streets of Berlin, *Silk* spans the depravity and the glamour of this tumultuous time.

Spoil yourself with this dazzling, decadent treat by international multi-million-copy selling Penny Jordan – the ultimate guilty pleasure for fans of Danielle Steel and Penny Vincenzi.

ISBN: 978-1-84756-073-5

Out now.

What's next?

Tell us the name of an author you love

| Penny Jordan | Go ▶ |

and we'll find your next great book.